The Stuff That Never Happened

The Stuff That Never Happened

Happened

A Novel

Maddie Dawson

Shaye Areheart Books
New York

Copyright © 2010 by Maddie Dawson

Published in the United States by Shaye Areheart Books, an imprint of the Crown Publishing Group, a division of Random House, Inc., New York.
www.crownpublishing.com

Shaye Areheart Books with colophon is a registered trademark of Random House, Inc.

Library of Congress Cataloging-in-Publication Data
Dawson, Maddie.
    The stuff that never happened : a novel / Maddie Dawson.—1st ed.
        p.   cm.
    1. Married people—Fiction. 2. Triangles (Interpersonal relations)—
    Fiction. 3. Cuckolds—Fiction. 4. Domestic fiction. I. Title.
    PS3604.A9795S78   2010
    813'.6—dc22   2009035945

ISBN 978-0-307-39367-8

Printed in the United States of America

DESIGN BY BARBARA STURMAN

10 9 8 7 6 5 4 3 2 1

First Edition

TO JIM,

for everything

The Stuff That Never Happened

[one]

I started crying at Crisenti's yesterday, over by the frozen foods. This was not cinematic, attractive weeping either; it was full-frontal, nose-running, eyes-streaming near-blubbering. I had to pull my cart over to the side of the meat case while I searched through the lint in my coat pocket for a tissue.

I could not begin to tell you why this happened now, except to say that it's February in New Hampshire, which if you ask me might be reason enough to break down. It's been six months since Nicky went off to college and Sophie got married, and somehow on an ordinary Monday afternoon at the supermarket, it all caught up with me. I'd made it through Christmas all right, and the first anniversary of my mother's death, and then through the season's first eighteen snow-storms—and suddenly I was crying about all of it: how life is never going to be the same as it was when the children were home, and how Grant has never forgiven me for stuff that happened twenty-six years ago, and how I have somehow gotten to be almost fifty years old and all I have to show for it is a bunch of picture books.

Picture books! That makes them sound dignified, like art perhaps. But I'm talking board books—the kind with animals dressed up like people. Pigs in dresses! An aardvark who wears plaid scarves! I've just finished illustrating a book about a mama squirrel trying to get her babies to go to bed. And you know the weird part, the thing that Grant would never believe? I *love* this mother squirrel. I love the fact that I painted her wearing a yellow workout suit and that when she was nestled on her little couch reading to her babies, she looked radiantly happy in a very non-rodent way.

Remembering that, I had to put my hand over my mouth so the sobs wouldn't escape.

"Mrs. McKay?" said the boy behind the meat counter. Not a boy—he's a man, really. He was one of Sophie's friends. He had been at our house dozens of times over the years, one of the hordes of young people who were always there playing basketball in the driveway, skating on the pond, eating dinner, even sleeping over. He had the lead in the school play the year Sophie was a sophomore. Brad, that's his name. Brad Simeon.

And because young people should not have to see the older generation falling apart and guess what's in store for themselves, I straightened myself up out of the collapsed-crazy-lady position.

He smiled, wanted to know if I was okay. Perhaps the pork chops weren't to my satisfaction?

I looked down at the package of two thin, gray pork chops I was holding in my hand and actually laughed. Do they see a lot of that in grocery stores—people breaking down in tears of disappointment over the meat products? I said they were just fine, perfectly wonderful, and then he asked how Sophie was getting along, and regaining my footing, I launched automatically into my proud motherly spiel: Oh, she's just fine! Married, yes, and living in New York, and pregnant now, actually. Did he know? *Yes*, I'm going to be a grandmother. Why, thank you—no, I don't *feel* old enough to be a grandmother, but in our family, we reproduce young, ha-ha.

And Nicky?

Mother spiel number two: Oh, *so* happy at the university! Doing winter hiking just now, and yes, still playing hockey—can barely get that boy to open a book, he's so busy with the other things (I don't say we suspect girls, drinking, and drugs) but he'll learn. Just hope he doesn't get kicked out before he figures out he's there to get an education! I gave a good imitation of my whattaya-gonna-do laugh.

Just then, thank goodness, Brad's boss called him back to the ground beef machine, and he shrugged and smiled and slipped back into that little brightly lit, glassed-in room they have for the meat guys. "Tell Professor McKay hello," he said as he left, but by then he was turned the other way, so when my eyes filled up with tears again, he didn't have to see.

SO I tell my therapist about it, pork chops and all. (Therapists like to be notified of any public breakdowns, you know.) Ava Reiss is her name. I've been seeing her for just over a year, ever since my mother died, and we sit together once a week examining all the mundane and not-so-mundane incidents of my life, like two ladies sorting through mismatched socks. I am always just about to tell her that I'm not coming anymore, that this isn't really working, but then I keep on.

"You cried in the grocery store?" she says. "And what were you feeling?"

"Well, for starters, it was embarrassing."

"No, I mean why did you start crying then, do you think? What did the pork chops represent?" She is about forty-five and has straight brown hair, and she wears cashmere sweaters and long skirts with tights that always match her sweaters. I think that says something about her personality. You have to be a very conscientious shopper to get sweaters and tights that match, don't you think? Once I told her that it makes me uncomfortable that she won't ever let herself laugh at any of my jokes, and she said that I use humor to deflect real feelings, and I said, "So? What do you suggest I use?" which she didn't appreciate.

"The pork chops . . . the pork chops, I think, represented, ah . . . dinner?" I say, and she purses her lips as though I'm deflecting again, so I explain that dinner is a topic fraught with complicated feelings for me. Dinner, you see, was the time I always loved the best. We were the family in the neighborhood with the house where all the kids congregated. Every community has a house like that; who knows how it happens, how kids discover they can go there and have a social center, and maybe a second home, but they just do. For years that was our place. I felt so privileged, so honored to be there orchestrating it. I loved the noise and the music and even all the complications. We had—actually, we *have*—a long oak dining room table, scarred and beat-up but beautiful because of those scars, and it was always heaped up with homework and art projects and science labs, costume-making projects, wonderful jumbles of clutter and chaos . . . and I'd be there in the middle of it all, listening to the kids talking and gossiping and teasing each other while I worked on my book illustrations and cooked, and then I'd push everything aside and bring out a pot of chili or big platters of eggplant Parmesan, blue bowls of chicken soup, spaghetti, pots of my spicy beef stew, homemade bread and rolls. There was something bustling and safe about the big kitchen, the light and the noise, the table and the laughter.

I try to explain to her how this—being the neighborhood house— had been new to me, like nothing I'd experienced growing up. I was born and raised in Southern California, in endless acres of a subdivision consisting of stucco four-bedroom houses, all built just yesterday and all with sliding glass doors and swimming pools and kids drag racing down the streets and never congregating anywhere. This whole small-town New Hampshire quaintness was something I thought existed only in the movies. But Grant grew up here, in the very house we now live in, playing hockey, sledding, and skiing, and for him, this is just what normal means: a mom and a dad, two kids, a clapboard house, ice skates hanging in the mudroom, a woodstove, rocking chairs on the porch.

Meant. What normal *meant.* We are now finished with that phase of normal, and, if he has anything to say about it, I fully expect we are going to turn into his parents any day now. Now *we're* the older couple who lives in the old McKay house—the farmhouse with the curvy road, the apple orchard, the pond, the barn and the gate that never closes right because the hinge is perpetually and heartrendingly broken, a symbol of all that never will be fixed.

Everything is different now, I say to Ava Reiss. I don't recognize my life anymore. We sit there in the silence of her office, listening to the sleet clicking against the gray windowpane.

"Look, I know what you're thinking," I tell her. "You think I'm just feeling sorry for myself, when that's not it at all. I read the women's magazines. I know that people who are about to turn fifty can do anything they want to do. Apparently women today are supposed to stop menstruating and use all that extra time we no longer need for changing tampons to go and cure cancer or something. Grant says I now have time to do my *art*, like I should just stop doing children's books and, I don't know, start doing Picassos or something. Like he thinks this is something I've just been waiting to get around to but couldn't because I had to cook dinner every night."

She taps her pen against a pad of paper she has on her lap. "You know, Annabelle, people sometimes use this time to reconnect with their husbands. After all, isn't he actually going through the same experience you are?"

And bingo, there we are: staring right smack at the problem. It's not the stupid pork chops, it's not the stupid book illustrations; it's that I'm lonely. Grant—my so-called partner and fellow survivor of the parenting years—is *not* going through the same thing at all, or at least you'd never know it. He has taken this time to throw himself into writing a book, and by "throw himself," I mean that he has no time for me or for anything else. He's living and breathing the history of a factory from the turn of the last century. I think if you took an MRI of my husband's brain right now, all you would see would be factory ledgers and chapter headings and pages and pages of footnotes having to do with the wording on picket signs.

I wake in the mornings to hear him already typing away in his study, and then he stays up until the middle of the night reading over his day's work and grimacing while he clears his throat and makes little dissatisfied grunting noises. You'd think it was physically painful for him to read his own sentences.

Even dinner, once the time of connection and togetherness and— okay, I'm trying not to use the word *communion* here, but I see I have to—even dinner has lost its sense of communion and has gone silent and cold. There we are, looking like refugees, huddled over our plates, wordlessly picking at our food. It's not surprising that the thought of dinner would make a person weep over the pork chops in the grocery store. I've had to take to playing Miles Davis CDs just to keep the sound of our silverware from clinking me into a full-blown depression.

Last night, after I'd timed the silence at twelve whole minutes, I said to him, "So, do you have any memory at all of our previous life? You know, raising children and all that?"

He swam up from Factory World, blinking like somebody returning from very far away, and looked at me in surprise. He reached for a roll and said drily, "I remember that one of them—a girl, right?—had a name that started with an *S*, is that correct?" He furrowed his brow and cleared his throat. "And wait. Wasn't there also a boy?"

I was so pleased to see something of his old sense of humor that I smiled. "Why, yes," I said. "The girl is Sophie, and the boy is Nick. He used to sit right where you're sitting. Often spilled his milk. *Quite* often, actually."

"Ohhh, yes. And what's become of them, do you suppose?" he said, and we had a decent, even playful conversation for a couple of minutes, during which I pretended to remind him that Sophie is now twenty-three and got married last summer in our backyard ("Remember the pretty lanterns?") and that Nicky is a freshman at the University of New Hampshire, off spilling his milk in a college cafeteria now, surrounded by jocks of every description and possibly lots of admiring girls, too.

"And Sophie is going to have a baby in the spring!" I said, and he actually laughed and said, "No kidding! But how is that possible, when she's still a baby herself?"

"I know." I really was caught up in the playacting then, and I added, perhaps unwisely: "But—well, and this is a little bit sad—she's living alone in New York just now." It's true: Whit, her husband, is in Brazil working on a documentary film he'd signed up to do before she got pregnant—something they had been planning to do together. When the pregnancy was confirmed it was too late for him to back out, and so he went ahead, with her permission.

From the way Grant's face flushed, I knew right away this had been a mistake, taking the conversation back down this road, with all its dangerous twists and turns. It occurred to me that maybe I had done it on purpose, to get at least *some* reaction from him. He said, "What brain chip has to be missing for that idiot not to know that when your wife is carrying a *child* you don't take off across the world?"

So I said my usual thing, which is that Sophie and Whit will be fine, and he'll be back in time for the birth, and that it's all none of our business.

But by then he was finished with his dinner, and I could see the curtain coming down in his eyes. He'd said his allotted number of words for the whole month, probably, and so he went mute again, pecked me on the cheek with his skinny, dry lips, and headed back upstairs to wrestle with chapter four. I cleaned up the kitchen, turned off the lights, and then went up to my study in the attic, where I sat down at the computer and messaged with both kids, hearing about Sophie's nausea and backache and about Nicky's excited plan to hike in the snow next weekend.

"Are you being careful?" I typed to him, and he responded: ☺. That's supposed to be an answer.

When I joined Grant a couple of hours later with our tea, he was still pecking away and humming. He stopped for a moment and sighed, and then he took off his glasses and rubbed his eyes before reaching up to accept the china cup I was holding out.

"How's it coming?" I said, and he shrugged and read me the last paragraph, something about the speech the foreman made during the strike of 1908.

"It's good," I said.

"No, it isn't. It doesn't *sing*."

"It's the history of *labor relations*, honey. That wouldn't sing even if you goosed it with a stick."

"I have goosed it with sticks."

"Well, there you go. It won't sing." I started giving him a shoulder massage, which he tolerated silently, still squinting at the page. "How does this feel?" I said. "Is this where the knot is?"

He was silent.

"No, I feel it now. It's more over here, isn't it? *This* is where your neck gets so tight when you're writing." I kneaded with my thumbs until he moaned, tilted his head back a little, and closed his eyes.

"You know what I just realized?" I said. "I figured out the thing I really miss about not having the children here."

"Mmmmph."

"When you have kids around, you have to do things that you maybe don't want to do, but they turn out to be fun. Like sledding. Nobody goes sledding unless they have a kid with them. But that's stupid. We could go sledding ourselves. You know that? We're not so old, and we have the sleds. Some weekend afternoon, we should take some time off from all this . . . *stuff*, and just go outside and sled down the hill a few times. Like we used to do."

"Sledding? Are you kidding me?" This, from the man who would drag us outside during even the coldest winter days to make sure we got the maximum potential out of every snowfall.

"Yeah. Wouldn't it be fun?"

"Why don't you just go sledding by yourself?"

I kneaded the neck muscle a bit harder than necessary. "Now there's a depressing thought. Sledding alone. It's worse than bowling alone, and a guy wrote a book about how pathetic that is."

He pulled away with a grimace. "Annabelle, perhaps you haven't really noticed, but *I* have a book to write. Do you not see these stacks of papers and this calendar up here with the pages flipping past? I'm hardly a person who's looking for other things to do right now. And I have to get back to it, if you don't mind."

"No, of course I don't mind. It's just that I think we need to have fun sometimes, too."

"This *is* the new fun," he said. He snorted and returned to his typing—he uses the hunt-and-peck method, which causes him to look slightly alarmed as he writes, as though he suspects the letters might have moved since he last looked—and I stood there next to him, sipping my tea and watching our reflection in the window. It was one of those picturesque scenes, with snow clumped charmingly along the panes like in a movie about winter, and we seemed so gleaming there in the safe, yellow lamplight of his study, standing together like in a portrait, as if we were just slightly better than ourselves, safe and peaceful. Well—except that Grant was scowling, and his shoulders were holding his anger like a tensed coil, and you couldn't quite see the big hole in my heart.

BEFORE I left Ava Reiss's office that afternoon, I told her I had realized that I'd never have the fun of sledding with the children again, or of doing a million things in that married, companionable way. My life had changed in large, almost indescribable ways.

She got up and turned on a lamp, and then she said, "It is a big change, Annabelle. But what do you think it all means?"

"I think maybe it means I don't want to be married anymore," I said slowly.

There was a silence, and then she sighed and said kindly, "Wow. Well, Annabelle, this is something we're definitely going to have to examine. I'm afraid our time is up for today, but we'll take this up next week."

JUST IN case you're growing concerned that you have stumbled into a story about a bored, displaced, middle-aged woman whose husband

has gone all distant on her and whose only hope is to persevere, trying to grope her way through life while she seeks meaning through
causes and self-examination and blah blah blah, let me ease your
mind. This is not the way this is going. Believe me, I wouldn't put you
through that, not when there are so many other things you could be
doing.

The truth is much more complicated. The truth is that I'm actually
in love with another man.

His name is Jeremiah, and I haven't bothered to tell Ava Reiss
about him, because, frankly, Jeremiah and I haven't talked to each
other in some twenty-six years, and I know what she would say about
that. She would ask how I could even think of this as real. She would
think I have carried on without any real, you know, *payoff*. I'm aware
from other remarks she's made that love for her is something that is
supposed to pay dividends that you can draw on, more like social security than a dazzling, mysterious force that shakes you out of your
complacence and makes you ask questions and laugh at the mystery
even as you're cursing it and wishing for it to solve itself and knowing
that it can't be solved.

I would have to tell her that this is *that* kind of love. This, I would
say cheerfully, is love that, by her definition, does absolutely nobody
any good, and never has and probably never will. Yes, yes, I'd say with
a big smile, it's utterly useless. Ava Reiss would never get the soul-
enhancing part of it, or understand that Jeremiah is here with me,
that he's taken up residence in my head, staked out some territory for
his very own, and that he is as present to me as Grant is these days.

Maybe this is common. Perhaps the whole human race goes
around with an ache like this. Maybe we're all dreaming of a person
from the tantalizing past who sits there, uninvited, watching from the
edge of our consciousness, somebody you find packing up and moving out of your head just as you're waking up in the morning, and
whose essence clings to you all day as though you have spent the
night with him, wandering off together somewhere among the stars,

making out on strangers' couches and in train stations and football stadiums, laughing over things that make no sense at all.

Oh, crap—so now you see why I don't speak of him. I do it so badly. It comes out all wrong, goopy and sentimental. Only my best friend, Magda, even knows the whole extent of things, and she only dimly understands the trade-offs I have made; she knows the pact I made with Grant, she knows that the heart of love is good no matter where it lives inside you, and I suspect she also knows that months go by in which I am sustained by the firm, warm hand of Jeremiah reaching out to me while I sleep, even while I am snuggled close to Grant, who is snoring softly beside me, most likely dreaming of people marching in lines, carrying picket signs that say, ON STRIKE.

1977

I met Grant McKay in California when I was twenty, before I knew that falling in love was actually a liability of mine and not a talent. Back then, I was always smitten with one person or another. I could be sitting in my Renaissance English class and fall in love with the professor for the way he explained a John Donne poem, and then be hung up on him for the rest of the semester even if he never did another inspirational thing. I was always just about wiped out by love for the guys I sang with in my own little rock band, the Oil Spills, although my chief boyfriend was the bass player, Jay. And I had recovered from another, even more official boyfriend left over from high school back home in Northridge, but he'd joined the army and disappeared to Germany, so all I had of him was his picture on my bulletin board. I walked around on the alert for love. I was an appreciator of people's best moments.

Grant showed up at a party my friends were giving, looking ridiculously out of place. He resembled a six-foot-tall orphan, an abandoned overgrown baby-man, with his blond hair and his pasty pale skin— and I first spotted him standing by himself in a corner of the kitchen, leaning against a counter with his arms folded across his chest. He was watching everything going on through big black Buddy Holly– type glasses with lenses like Coke bottles and trying to be invisible. His hair was cut exactly wrong, and he was dressed like he'd just come from a job interview, in pressed khaki pants and a navy blue V-neck sweater. I heard somebody whispering, "Who's the narc?" and somebody else said, "He's all right. He came with Simon."

I was a junior at the University of California at Santa Barbara at the time, and the party—billed as the Total Armageddon Party—was taking place in the off-campus apartment, in Isla Vista, of some of my more raucous friends, Janelle and Rennie. It was actually a party to celebrate that they'd been kicked out of their apartment for being, as the landlord had written in a letter on a piece of lined notebook paper that hung on the fridge, "too loud, too rood, steeling other peoples parking spases and causing lewdness and noise that if everyone did them would result in a total Armie Geddon." At a spec-ified time we were all going to set off cherry bombs in the living room, Armageddon-style. Janelle had gone around earlier handing them out.

I was supposedly there with Jay, but he was seeing another girl, too, so I used parties as a time to make sure I could surround myself with enough other guys to make him jealous. The world was crazy that way in 1977—nobody ever said anything they really meant; it was all for fun anyway—and Jay was up on the roof smoking weed with three other guys and that other girl he was seeing. Her name was Flaxen or Foxie or something like that, and she was always flicking her red ringletty hair, and when she laughed she made a sound like a nervous horse, and I was not going to go up there to watch him make a fool of himself over her.

The trouble was, there wasn't much to do in the apartment without Jay there to observe me. I was wearing a tight short skirt, my long blond hair was perfectly parted in the middle and completely straight, thanks to Magda's steam iron, and I had on just the right amount of eyeliner and eye shadow. Feminism was important, but if you were in a rock band as I was, you still paid attention to how you put on your makeup.

The apartment was crowded and smoky. We'd all—except Grant, of course—been to parties here tons of times. In the back bedroom there were the usual shenanigans: someone Rennie knew had brought a brass hash pipe and some Turkish hash, and you could hear screams of laughter. In another room, with the door closed, people were most likely having sex, or getting ready to. People were always having sex at these parties; you'd have to be nuts to put your coat down on a bed. It would get fornicated upon. A wrestling match blared from the television set in the living room, and there was the usual crowd of spectators—guys mostly, and the girls who were trying to impress them—shouting at the TV.

Grant was standing next to the fridge, squinting at the Armageddon letter, and I wanted him to move.

I said, "Excuse me, do you mind if I see if there are any beers left?"

He turned and looked at me with that blinking, gray-eyed stare of his. It was even more pronounced back then. His hair, which was fuller in those days, and therefore more in his way, fell across his eyes, and he brushed it away. He stepped away from the refrigerator. I saw him looking at my very, very short white leather skirt.

I said, "Do you want a beer?" and he said heavily, as though he were in great pain, "Not really, but I might as well."

I handed him a Bud. "That's funny, isn't it?" I said. "That letter from the landlord."

"Do you think so?" he said.

"Well, yeah. I mean, the landlords are just idiots."

"I don't know," he said. "Except for a few spelling and grammatical errors, I think they're making a good point. They're probably sick of the place getting trashed all the time. Can't blame them for that, I guess."

"Yeah, well, I gather from Rennie that they're not the nicest people . . ."

"Most likely I wouldn't be nice either if people treated my property like a trash can." He said this perfectly pleasantly. Then he said, "Besides which, they're probably immigrants trying to make good, and English is a second language for them, and they're confused by—"

"Okay, okay," I said. "You made your point."

He smiled, and I took a sip of my beer and felt my face grow a little warm, knowing I'd been caught trying to be tougher than I really was. I was trying to be hard and cool in those days, but I was finding out what a softie I really was. My mother had called me the week before to say that she and my father were separating, and since then I always felt like I was about to burst into tears. I'd sensed all along that they weren't ecstatically happy, but whose parents were? In the suburban Southern California neighborhood where we lived, everything *looked* normal, but nearly every house had some hideous secret: divorce, affairs, fights, abortions, bankruptcy, wife-swapping, drug overdoses. My family had just kept plugging along, and I guess I thought my parents knew something other people didn't know about how to hold it together.

My mother worked as a receptionist in a dentist's office and cooked dinner (a protein, a starch, and a vegetable, with fruit for dessert) every night. She took care of my father and my brother and me, always smiling except for those rare times when she went into what my father called her "black moods." Then there was no pleasing her. She'd clean the house and slam doors, screaming at us like a maniac—but then it would pass and she would go back to normal, sweet as pie.

When she called to tell me about the separation, her voice was oddly cold and flat. She was normally warm and brimming with an embarrassing surplus of emotion—she was the kind of person who was always getting into long, intimate conversations with strangers in the line at the grocery store, much to my mortification—but now it was as though she were reading from a script written and handed out by the Association for Conversations with Adolescents About Divorce, and she was checking off their recommended tips as she went along. She said the separation was a decision that had been made, she wasn't asking for my advice or input, it wasn't my or my brother's fault, she and my father both loved us and wanted us to be happy, but the fact was that she and he had *differences* and they were *embarking on a trial separation that might or might not lead to divorce.*

She didn't expect me to be happy about it, but she expected my understanding.

"SO WHEN is this Armageddon going to begin, do you think?" Grant said, clearing his throat, the first of many such nervous tic throat-clearings I would be hearing for the rest of my life.

"Don't ask me. This feels like an ordinary party to me," I said. I looked at him more closely. "Haven't you ever been here before?"

He said no. That's when he told me his name and that he had borrowed a friend's car, and when he went to return it, the friend had dragged him along to the party, promising him that they wouldn't stay long. The friend was with the people watching wrestling.

"So you're a student?" I said.

He smiled a tight little smile and cleared his throat. He'd been a math major as an undergraduate, but now he was getting his PhD in history, with a concentration on labor relations, and he was finishing up work on his thesis, about the children of migrant workers who came to California during the Depression. He shouldn't even be here. He still had some work to do on the introduction.

"Wow, that sounds like a sad subject," I said. "Kids and migrant workers . . ."

"Yeah, I'm not in it for the cheerfulness," he said. "But when you get into it, into the people's stories, you find out all kinds of stuff."

"Like what?"

"Oh, you don't want to know."

"I do. I really do."

He studied my face for a moment, as if he were trying to figure out if I was just making fun of him. He didn't seem to be the most confident guy in the world. "Well, the children had their culture, their games and their songs, and so even while they were being moved from place to place, it was the children who were responsible, really, for assimilating the new culture in with the old-timers' versions. That's all."

"Oh. So it's stories," I said. "You're really telling stories."

"No. It's analysis. Charts and graphs and all that. But then there's this undertone. That's what historians are looking for. Come on, you don't want to hear about this."

I narrowed my eyes at him. "Why do you keep telling me what I do and don't want to hear about?"

"Because nobody wants to hear about it. Even my *mother* doesn't want to hear about it."

"Look, we're making polite party conversation," I told him. "One of the rules is that when a person asks you a question, you're not supposed to insult them by saying they don't care about what they're asking about. You're supposed to answer, and if you see their eyes glaze over, *then* you know to stop talking."

He looked at me, and then he smiled a little. "Well. It's good to have the rules explained once and for all. And what are you studying?"

I said I was majoring in art education because I liked to paint, and he raised his eyebrows.

"Well, why don't you major in painting, then, instead of education?"

"Because I can't make a living as an artist, so what I'm probably going to end up doing is teaching elementary school," I said.

"But is that what you really want to do?"

"Oh, I have no idea," I said. "My father told me education would give me something to fall back on. And anyway, who in this world gets to do exactly what they want to do?"

"See, I just don't get people who think like you. Why give up before you even try? And I don't think elementary school kids need more teachers who don't really want to be there. Why don't you just have the courage to strike out on your own and be a real artist, and not settle for teaching before you even try?"

"Excuse me, but do you know *anything* whatsoever about how to make polite party conversation?"

"I think I'd rather have a real conversation."

"But I've only known you for five minutes, and already you're sitting in judgment about what I want to do with my life."

He looked pained.

I took another sip of beer and smiled at him. "Now the way this is *supposed* to go is, you would say, 'Oh, you're studying art education. That's fascinating. And what paintings do you like?' and then I'd say, 'Oh, actually, I'm studying the abstract expressionists right now,' and *you*, being you, might say, 'Oh, I find that to be a load of crap most of the time—all those jumbled-up colors—why, a five-year-old could do better than that,' and then *I* might explain what I have learned about abstract expressionism and why it's valid, and then you'd say something else about how labor history is the greatest thing ever, who knew, and then we'd finish our beers and go our separate ways and that would be that."

"What would be polite about my calling abstract expressionism a load of crap?"

"Well, that falls under a technicality, actually. While it's not exactly polite to say something is a load of crap, it's acceptable in this case because, number one, it's representative of your honest feelings, and, number two, it's not directly related to a personal choice that *I've* made and that you're insulting. After all, I just said I was studying it; I didn't say I was the premier abstract expressionist in the United States or something."

He was staring at me, but I could see a little grin starting to curl its way around his mouth. "Oh, I see. And how does making false assumptions about somebody's taste in art figure in? Is that considered polite?"

"Well, it depends."

"Ah. This is where the rules get weird. I guess this is why I don't come to parties so much. But the truth, in case you're interested, is that I happen to like art a lot, and I do know something about abstract expressionism, and I think it's fascinating and has a lot to tell us about our inner lives."

I stared at him. "You read that in a book."

"No. I happen to believe it." He straightened his glasses. "And I also

happen to believe that some people are put on this earth to do art—
to record their inner experience, as it were—and that other people
should dabble around trying to explain the universe through number
theory, and that other people should chart data about migrant workers in Central California, and that all of those things are fine."

"That's very democratic of you."

He flushed. "And, while we're at it, I don't think people should rent
apartments and then trash them with cherry bombs."

Well, I didn't either, not really, but amazingly enough, I hadn't
given it much thought until right then.

Janelle came over to get a beer out of the fridge, and she said,
"Ooh, Annabelle, who's your friend?" She was laughing and rolling her
eyes because he was clearly *not our sort.* I saw Grant notice that, and
he looked down at his shoes, and I couldn't help it, I might have actually started to fall a little in love with him right then.

"Has Jay met this guy?" she said, laughing at the ridiculousness of
that, and then she left, screaming to the crowd at large that it was almost the end-of-the-world moment.

Grant looked at me. "Well, I think that's my cue to leave. It's been
nice talking to you."

"Wait," I said, but just then Jay came down from the roof to get
me, bursting through the back door with his dilated eyes and the
smell of smoke clinging to him like a tail. And then—well, this was
bad—I moved closer to Grant and grabbed his arm so that Jay would
notice and maybe would be even the slightest bit jealous. But it
didn't matter anyway, because Jay and his friends were all wasted and
laughing at nothing, swooping into the kitchen, yelling about something between their bouts of hysterics, and it turned out they'd seen
the cops turning onto the street with their red lights on, and we'd all
better get out because we were probably all going to get arrested for
possession.

Somebody laughed and yelled, "Holy *shit*! Evacuate!"

"Set off the cherry bombs!" somebody else called out.

"No, firecrackers! I've got firecrackers!"

"Where are the matches? Get the matches!"

Jay wasn't even looking in my direction. He was caught up in the swarm of people all busy laughing and grabbing more beers to take with them when they ran. A guy took out a book of matches and started to light a firecracker right near me, and then Grant took hold of my elbow and steered me out of there, like it was just the most natural thing in the world. We went outside through the back door and were already on the sidewalk, walking fast with our heads down, by the time the first firecracker went off. Behind us, we could see the red and blue lights flashing from the squad cars, and hear a cop on a megaphone saying, "COME OUT OF THE BUILDING NOW."

Outside, the night was chilly and smelled a little like gunpowder, but as Grant and I walked, it started to smell instead like the ocean, which was only two blocks away. We slipped into a companionable walk, happy to be out of there without getting arrested. Sometimes when the wind was blowing in just the right direction, it felt as though you were inhaling salt and minerals and everything that would lead to good health, I told him. He laughed at that, and I asked him how old he was and he said he was twenty-five. And then he didn't say anything else, just sort of cleared his throat a few times. He was very tall, and I had to take an extra step to keep up with him, but then he noticed that and slowed down a little bit. He chuckled and said he wasn't used to walking with anyone so short.

"Hey, I didn't get to set off my cherry bombs," I said.

"Thank goodness," he said.

"I have two of them in my pocket," I said, and showed him.

"I'm surprised anything can fit in the pocket of that skirt," he said. "If it wasn't also short, you probably couldn't even move your legs in it, much less walk. It would be mathematically impossible."

"Hmm. There's actually math for skirts?" I said.

"Well. No. Not really. But I suppose there could be a formula. It would be geometry. Or trig. Could be a new practical use for math."

"Anyway, it's really just my costume skirt," I said. "I wear it when I sing in a band."

"Oh. So you were planning to perform at the party, then?"

"No."

He laughed. "Tell me this. Do you ever make any sense?"

"What doesn't make sense about that?"

"Why would you claim the skirt is short because it's a costume that you wear when you're performing, yet then admit that you were wearing it on an occasion when you weren't going to perform? You twist logic all around."

I took a deep breath. "Well. If you want to know the truth, I wore it because I'm in a band with my boyfriend. He's that guy who came running down from the roof. He'd been up there with another girl all evening, and I wore the skirt because . . . well, I just wore it because he likes it when I wear it, and I thought he'd pay more attention to me than to her if I had on this skirt. It was stupid, really." I couldn't believe I was telling him this stuff.

"Ah. And what was he doing up on the roof with some other girl if he's your boyfriend?"

"Yeah, well, he's not what you'd call monogamous."

"Oh, he's *not*? Well, that's interesting of him."

I laughed. "Yeah, he's pretty interesting."

"A real find. Makes you wonder how guys get the deals they get."

"Do you have a girlfriend?"

He laughed. "Do I seem like the type of guy women are interested in? Did you notice women flocking over to talk to me at the party?"

"I talked to you."

"You only talked to me because your boyfriend was hanging out with somebody else, and you wanted a beer from the fridge I happened to be standing in front of."

"No. I talked to you because you were sort of nice. About art and all." I smiled at him. I was thinking he might ask me to go somewhere else with him, maybe walk down to the beach or into town or

something, but he didn't. We got to his friend's Datsun, which was unlocked, but Grant didn't have the key to drive it. I was thinking that
most guys would have assumed we were going to at least sit in the car
and make out for a while, but Grant didn't seem to have the confi-
dence required to suggest something like that. We just stood there,
leaning against it, him with his hands jammed in his pockets. I already
felt like I needed to take care of him somehow.

"Are you from California?" I asked him after a long silence.

"No. I grew up in rural New Hampshire, in a place you've never
heard of." He told me that he actually had a family *homestead*, where
generations of McKays had lived among a bunch of antiques and
cows. Snow, ice, presidential primaries, mountains, skiing, all that. I
liked his voice, the way he seemed so sure that home and parents
weren't totally bad things.

I said, just trying out how it sounded: "My parents are getting
divorced."

He blinked. "That's a bummer."

"Well," I said. I shivered and wrapped my arms around myself. "I
guess they think they stuck it out long enough. And now that my
brother and I are nearly grown, they don't see why they have to live together anymore. It's really no big problem. I mean, I *am* grown up. I
can handle this."

"Still," said Grant. He looked at me closely. "You probably didn't
think this would ever happen."

"Yeah." I looked off into the distance. A car was coming toward us
down the street, and its headlights swept the road, where a crab was
running across the yellow line.

"Probably makes it easier that you're at school. You have other
stuff to concentrate on."

"That's for sure," I said. "I have loads of things to think about."

"You do?"

"Yeah. I do."

"Is one of those things why you hang out with a guy who's not monogamous, and why you go to parties where people throw cherry bombs?" He was laughing.

"Would you just listen to yourself? At least I *go* to parties. At least I don't tell people they shouldn't major in what they're majoring in."

He threw back his head and laughed harder. "Ah, a feisty one!" He ducked, as if he expected I might want to hit him. So of course I pretended to, thinking he'd grab my hands and we'd play-wrestle and then he'd kiss me, and we'd go down to the beach and make out and maybe I could start being in love with him for real.

But none of that happened. He didn't seem to know what the possibilities were, and after a while, I couldn't find a place for him in my overactive love imagination, so I got bored and said goodnight and walked myself home. I threw the cherry bombs in the garbage, and they made a *pop-pop-pop* sound that almost stopped my heart.

2005

Grant and I make love on Wednesday mornings at seven o'clock.

What? You don't have a schedule for something like that? Perhaps you think that sex should arise spontaneously, whenever both people are so inclined. Maybe you are one of those silly, conventional people who think that passion shouldn't be regulated.

Believe me, this scheduling thing was all Grant's idea. And because I like sex and also because I had decided to try to stop arguing with him over minor things, I agreed to it. He'd read a study that said middle-aged people often get so tired or so busy that they just let sex slip out of their routine. He said it was such an irony, how couples spend all those years trying to do it quietly so the kids won't wake up, or being so hungry for it between times that they ignore all safety precautions and attempt it in the shower (very dangerous), or else they fall on each other during their ten minutes of alone time during the Saturday morning cartoons (unsatisfying)—and then suddenly, middle age hits, the kids move out, and *bam*! Nobody's in the mood, and evenings are spent retreating to their separate corners of the house, and then, and then...

"And then what happens to them?" I asked when Grant first brought up the topic. This was before his book had swallowed him up, but perhaps he already knew it was sneaking up behind him, ready to devour him, and he was trying to arrange all the loose ends and appointment calendars before he succumbed. It was the week after Nicky had gone off to school. We still had not mapped out the shape of our grief, and we were standing in the kitchen with the late-afternoon September sun slanting through the kitchen window, suggesting possibilities.

"What?" he said, and his eyes twinkled. "What happens to them? Oh. Well, I suppose their penises fall silent, their marriages fail, and then civilization as we know it slides into a deplorable decline. And I, for one, don't think we want to be responsible for that."

So Grant and Annabelle McKay are doing their part for the free world. We make love each and every Wednesday morning, barring flu, final exams, or faculty meetings. Standing there at the calendar that day, Grant said it had to be Wednesday because it's the morning that he has late classes so he doesn't need to rush off. And it couldn't be the weekend because he likes the NPR shows too much—and why rush through lovemaking just for the sake of *Car Talk*? And it couldn't be at night when we've gone to bed because he likes to take a shower after sex, and since he would have already taken a shower in the morning, that would mean he'd need to shower twice in one day, and that would be a waste of water, as well as a waste of time, and when a man is writing a book, there is no sense in wasting even one second.

See? I'm doing it again—telling things all wrong. I'm making him sound like an automaton, when the truth is that I like making love with Grant; he's enthusiastic and good and efficient at it, and it's kind of sexy knowing that on Wednesday morning I am going to get his full attention for at least twenty minutes. Just the other day I got together with some of the faculty wives for lunch, and we got to talking about husbands and sex, as occasionally we've done through the years, standing together at faculty parties and on the sidelines at our children's soccer games. This time we had a shocking agenda item: the history department chairman, Grant's boss, had upped and left his wife of thirty years and married a grad student—a *student*—with no warning whatsoever. Naturally we had to have an impromptu meeting about that, hear all the stories, point fingers at the wronging parties, discuss what we would do if that were ever *us*.

Everybody else was stunned and disapproving—you could see it in their faces—but I was a little, well, fascinated. So we got to talking about sex, and it turned out that Grant may be right about the middle-aged thing: lots of couples just aren't doing it anymore, and for no other reason, it seems, than that they fell out of the habit. There were complaints and justifications around the table: husbands who stay up too late watching sexy movies on cable rather than come to a flesh-and-blood wife, and ones who have let themselves get run down, and then encourage their middle-aged wives to have boob lifts and start wearing black lacy things. Some husbands have become boring old farts. They can't talk without lecturing; they read their wives edifying articles from the *New York Times*. We laughed and shouted and spilled things and banged on the table with our fists. Julie McNamara, who insisted we all order a bottle of wine if we were going to talk like this, suddenly turned to me and said, "Oh, Annabelle, don't you dare complain. You're so lucky to have somebody like Grant. At least he hasn't gained so much weight that he has to wear one of those breathing machines just so he won't die in the night."

This is the gold standard for judging husbands—that he doesn't have to breathe into a machine to keep from dying? Everybody laughed about how Grant never does anything wrong, and then Joanna Caprio, whose husband, Mark, made a pass at me at a party ten years ago, said that the best thing about Grant is that he's got a reputation for being totally immune to any kind of extramarital funny business. At parties, year after year, she pointed out, you can count on him to stand off to the side and chat about labor statistics all night long, and not once get drunk and go off dancing with any of the other women. And nobody has ever heard of a student trying to entice him into giving her a better grade by offering to sleep with him. The whole idea is *unthinkable,* said Joanna, and I could see everybody picturing my staid and upstanding husband trying to score with some student—a thought that made them laugh and shake their heads.

I joined in a little uncomfortably, glad they couldn't see the way I was shredding my napkin in my lap. *Yes,* I wanted to say to them. *Yes, that is all true, but he is coiled up like a spring. You complain about your husbands boring you by reading you articles from the newspaper, or pontificating about the nightly news, but my husband doesn't speak. It's as if I'm not there at all.*

And if something takes place that Grant doesn't like—well, then it's as though it never happened.

ANYWAY, SO Wednesday morning arrives, and sure enough, I wake up to the radio coming on at precisely seven o'clock. I can hear Grant tapping away at his laptop in his study. Jeremiah is once again just flitting out of my head, after a dream in which we were on a train that doubled as an outdoor café where you could buy croissants.

From down the hall, Grant clears his throat with that "ahem" sound he makes. And then he calls, "Annabelle? I'll be there in just a minute, okay?"

"Okay," I say.

"Don't start without me."

"Then you'd better get in here. You know how impatient I am."

He laughs, and I hear him typing furiously. Finally he appears in the doorway, blinking and rubbing his hands through his hair, looking like he just pulled himself out of a trance. Which I suppose is what he did. At least half of him is still in 1908.

I smile at him. At fifty-three, he looks exactly like what he is: a patient, enduring labor historian, professorial and calm. He was never what Sophie and her friends would call a hottie, but I have to say he's held up well. He still has most of his formerly full head of blond hair, faded now but flopping over his forehead in the front and sprouting a fence of cowlicks in the back. Unlike me, he also still has the same flat stomach he had twenty-eight years ago, and his knees and elbows are so pointy that he can do serious damage to me when he turns over in bed. Even his monogamous penis—I probably shouldn't be talking about his penis, but what the hell—even his penis is gangly, like he is, yet professorial and dignified.

He doesn't say anything, simply starts taking off his yoga pants and T-shirt, folding them up in a neat pile, frowning.

"How are you?" I say, pulling the down comforter and quilt aside to welcome him back to bed. I catch only a brief glance of his flat, pale butt, his professorial penis—and then he gets in and presses his freezing-cold skin against me. I yelp. "Good God! You've turned to ice!"

"It's February, Annabelle." He pronounces the first *r* in *February* very precisely. I always say FebYOOary, which drives him nuts. "It's even snowing outside."

"It's *always* snowing outside here, and that is why God invented fleece bathrobes for people who get up early. Here, never mind. Put your hands here, and I'll warm you up." I put his frozen hands under my sweatshirt, at great personal sacrifice, and press my face against his. He blinks at me; he is always blinking his watery gray eyes. He probably needs lubricating eye drops, and I should talk him into going to see Sam, the eye doctor. I'll have to remember to make him an appointment. Maybe he'll even keep it. "I think you may be technically halfway to being cryogenically frozen. How long have you been up?"

"Since four. I didn't sleep well," he says heavily, then clears his throat. Quite unattractively, actually. "I was tossing and turning all night so I finally just got up and went in to write the new section."

"Oh, that's too bad. Did you get a lot done, at least?"

"Some. Not really. I don't want to talk about it. It's time for our other concerns now." He sighs and closes his eyes and concentrates, which means we are entering sex mode now. I kiss him on his cold lips and he smooches me back, but I know him well enough to know that he's not thinking about me or sex; he's still locked in his book, and his body is not going to consent to anything else right now.

"Uh-oh. Factory World seems to have followed you back to bed," I say lightly.

He's silent for a moment, and then he says, "It's awful. This morning I realized that I've got to interview more descendants. I don't have enough. Not nearly enough."

"It'll be okay," I say. "You've gotten five survivors, and the pictures of the kids inside the mill, and the daughter of the foreman—"

"It's not enough, Annabelle," he says, a tad sharply. "And now I've got to stop for days and grade exams. I have dozens of essays to read. Dozens! And on top of that I'm not sleeping."

I stroke his hair. "Well, if you're tired, maybe you should go back to sleep for an hour or so. We certainly don't have to—"

"Wait," he says. He sits up, round-eyed with alarm. "Do you have any paper in the nightstand?"

"Stationery, yes."

"Can you get it?"

I roll over and get the box of fine powder-blue Crane stationery, which came from my mother's condo when we cleaned it out after she died, and I find a ballpoint pen and roll back and hand the box and the pen to him. I have a momentary pang of sadness—this stationery, my mother. "This will just take a sec," he says. "Then we'll go on with our schedule."

"Fine. Don't worry about it. I have all day."

He frowns while he writes, and the tip of his tongue sticks out. I lie propped on one elbow and watch him, notice how gray his whiskers have recently become. But I am thinking that this moment could be funny, you know. We could both laugh about how lovely it is to know somebody so well that you're relaxed enough to stop making love and, oh, say, take some precoital notes on a labor relations problem. Instead—and maybe this is just because of Jeremiah floating tauntingly around the room—I feel a growing wad of irritation just under my breastbone. I know this feeling: it's a cousin of the mood that made me cry among the pork chops.

"I certainly hope this is going to be one of those breakthrough moments for the book," I say. "Are we postponing our orgasms for some good reason at least?"

He waves me off. He doesn't like the word orgasm; he once told me it's an ugly word, and that it makes the sex act sound like something clinical.

"Listen," I say after a moment, as he turns the paper over and writes on the back. "What do you say we just pretend that this is Tuesday instead of Wednesday, shall we?"

"Wait." He keeps writing for a few seconds more, and then he stops and stares at me as though he can't quite remember what I just said. He clears his throat. "What? Tuesday? You want it to be Tuesday?"

"Yes. This is ridiculous. Let's shake hands and meet here again tomorrow morning. Or—what the hell—even *next* Wednesday. Or better yet, in the spring."

"All right, all right. It's now officially Tuesday," he says, missing the point entirely, and you can't tell me it's not on purpose. And then the book, victorious, decides that was quite enough human conversation, thank you, and reaches up a long, slippery, octopus arm and pulls him back into the smoky unfairness of Factory World. When I get out of bed a few minutes later and head to the shower, he's writing furiously.

Which is fine. Perfectly understandable. We've been married practically forever, as I may have mentioned. You can have an off year, especially a year when you're writing a book—but you have to talk about it. That's all I'm saying. And it's fine to skip making love, even after you've made a big deal about setting up a schedule—but don't you have to acknowledge that it meant something to you, that it was a loss, no matter how tiny?

I pull on my terry-cloth bathrobe—I, at least, don't run around naked when it's so cold in our bedroom that you can see your breath—and head to the bathroom. I pee and brush my teeth and then, just before I get in the shower, I find myself staring in the mirror. My forty-nine-year-old face looks back at me, and even with all its morning creases and puffiness, it's a face I've at last come to accept. I used to think my skin wasn't smooth enough, but now I don't care. It looks as if somebody has drawn pencil lines around my hazel eyes, which were always my best feature, and my wild mass of curly dark blond hair that I spent years trying to tame into sleekness is now cut to shoulder length with highlights to cover the gray strands, thanks to L'Oréal. But it's okay, good enough. So much that used to seem so important—abolishing crow's-feet and occasional gray hairs—really doesn't matter at all.

I lean forward into the mirror. *Jeremiah, I am going to be a grand-mother! Can you believe it? Me—the one you said was the youngest person you ever slept with? I am almost fifty years old now, Jeremiah, so I don't even want to think of how old you are. But I'm okay. I mean, I could stand to lose ten pounds, but I refuse to be one of those women who thinks about that all the time. I have things on my body now that a man can hang on to: real hips and boobs. Possibly even some back fat, I'm not sure. I won't let myself look.*

This is very bad, talking to Jeremiah in the mirror. It's bad enough when my mind goes off on its own and constructs a whole scenario about him while I'm sleeping, but his presence absolutely must be chased out of my waking thoughts. I poke out my stomach and pat it. Oh, this ten pounds could so easily turn to fifteen. The truth is, despite my brave talk about not caring about my appearance so much, I know that soon I'll either need to think about losing some weight or start buying underwear that's made of industrial materials. I won't be able to stand myself.

When I get out of the shower and walk back across the hall to get dressed, Grant is still sitting up in bed, scrawling on my mother's stationery. He puts down the paper and takes off his glasses and rubs his eyes hard. "This book is *killing* me," he says.

"You and me both," I tell him. I put on my bra, snapping it in the front and then sliding it around and up over my breasts, once known around here as the Girls. I have to lean forward to tuck them in, which makes me feel a little self-conscious. But when I turn, I see that Grant is not even watching me. Instead, he's picked up his piece of paper again and is reading it while he talks.

"You know something?" he says. "Tonight, don't even wait for me for dinner. I think I'll stay in my office and grade those freshman essays. And then I can work on chapter five without being interrupted. That's what's killing me here—these constant interruptions."

"Actually," I say, and feel a shameful flicker of satisfaction—really, this is one of my worst qualities, smugness—"as you *may* remember, tonight we're having dinner with the Winstanleys. At the Villager." Clark Winstanley is the head of the history department; he's the one newly married to the grad student. Rumor has it that he's arranged a series of dinners to reassure the faculty and their spouses that he's still in his right mind. Either that or he's showing off his total splendiferousness in being able to land such a young chick. The faculty wives are mixed on their verdicts.

Grant's face is filled with dismay. "Are you kidding me? That's tonight?"

"Yep."

"But I've got to work!"

"Yeah, well, some would say this *is* your work."

"Gah! Doesn't he have anything better to do than parade around showing off his stupidity? He might as well just pull out his dick and challenge everybody to a pissing match. Why do *I* have to suffer because some bastard decides to have a midlife crisis?"

"Because this particular bastard is your chairman, maybe?"

"For Christ's sake. I do not want to have to think about his sex life!"

I laugh. "This isn't going to be a dinner to think about Clark's sex life. This is a dinner so that Clark can try to make everything seem *normal*. All you have to do is talk about the usual topics and behave yourself. Trust me."

"What's her name again?"

"Padgett."

"Padgett. Right. I would've guessed Brittany or Tiffany, something of that ilk."

He runs his hands through his hair and looks longingly—some would say even with lust—at the piece of paper he's been furiously scribbling on. He purses and unpurses his lips, sighs, throws his arms up to heaven, beseeches the fates through clenched teeth, and finally stomps off to the shower.

Oddly enough, I feel happy for the first time this morning. At least we're going out. And Grant has to go along.

"SO DID you know that Clark Winstanley was dumping his wife before he went and did it?" I say to Grant on the way to the restaurant. "Do men talk about these things?"

I have to say, I'm a little bit obsessed right now with people who chuck their old lives out the window. There's something sick about this, I know, but I've never felt better about stuffy old Clark Winstanley.

"What?" he says. "What things?"

"Did you know that Clark was divorcing Mary Lou? Because I've been wondering what men say to other men when they're thinking about something big like this."

Grant peers out into the snowy darkness, probably doing a calculation about how many flakes per minute are falling, and whether in a moment he might have to turn on the windshield wipers. He hates to use the wipers; you would think it actually cost extra money to run them. It drives me crazy, this miserliness with windshield wipers. I can't see the road when he's driving, I tell him, and he replies that I don't *have* to see the road. I can sit there and be relaxed, knowing he's never had so much as a fender bender.

"So did he say anything to you specifically? Did you sense anything?"

"God, Annabelle." He laughs harshly. "I have no idea."

"It seems you'd remember something like a guy saying, 'I'm break-ing up with my wife.' Or maybe you'd even see the new woman hang-ing around. Did she ever come to department meetings?"

"Why are you doing this?"

"What?"

"Thinking about these people this way, when it's none of your business."

"It has nothing to do with whose business it is," I say to him. "It's the human condition, Grant. Women care about these things. We talk about marriage. Did you even know that? Women are hungry to talk about these things with men. I want to know what you think!"

"Sometimes . . ." he says with a sigh.

"Sometimes what?"

"Nothing. Sometimes I just wish you weren't so silly."

My mouth actually drops open, and I have to concentrate on clos-ing it again. I look out the window and do not speak to him until well after we've arrived at the restaurant, which is quite elegant, with thick carpets and a massive fireplace and honey-colored hurricane lamps on the tables, the kind of place with huge padded booths and plaques on the wall. Clark and the grad student are already sitting at a table, side by side, only she's turned away from him and is looking down at something in her lap while he sits and watches her and sips a drink. He drinks manhattans, straight up, as I recall from twenty-three years of faculty parties.

Silly! What a word. I can't get over Grant calling me that.

Clark jumps to his feet and kisses me on both cheeks, and then he introduces us to La Wife, even though of course I already know all about her via the grapevine. I know that she's getting her master's in environmental science and that her full name is Padgett Halverson-Winstanley, which sounds to me like three last names, and the word is that she's not the traditional type of trophy wife, which is code for the fact that she's not particularly beautiful or sexy. She's the new breed of young wife, meaning she's opinionated and brainy and scrappy and wears funky clothes, in the way that Mary Lou Winstanley, with her station wagon filled with her five kids and a whole bunch of soccer equipment, could never pull off. Clark met Padgett at a conference he organized. Soon after they met, she transferred to the college here, and then—voilà!—six months later he got a divorce from Mary Lou, who kept the house and the cars. I was never close friends with Mary Lou, who was a little bit cold to people she considered "outsiders" like me, but everyone said it was just awful for her to get dumped like that, like an old cloth coat. Still, when I see her in the grocery store these days, she looks just the same as ever, wearing jeans and sweatshirts with the college name on them, her short hair feathered out in wings. Somebody told me she got a great divorce settlement.

Clark shakes Grant's hand and then nudges Padgett, who remains seated, and I see that the reason she's looking down is that she's texting somebody on her cell phone. She looks up and gives us both a vacant smile and holds up one hand, but her other hand never stops its lightning-quick dance over the buttons of her phone, her thumb flashing two giant silver rings.

"She's arranging a meet-up for the environmental students," Clark says by way of explanation, and I feel sorry for him, having to use words like *meet-up* when he means *meeting,* and also for the fact that you can just see in his face that he wishes she would sit up straight and talk to us. *Don't worry,* I want to telegraph him. *I know she's not going to be the old kind of faculty wife, and it's just fine with me.*

"Well!" he says. "It's so lovely to see you, Annabelle. May I say that you're looking quite . . . relaxed."

This is puzzling, and since I am anything but relaxed, I figure it is code for something. Relaxed, meaning tired? Relaxed, meaning that I'm letting myself go?

"You look awfully relaxed, too, Clark," I say, and Grant sits down, growling about how he's not relaxed in the slightest.

"You need a drink, then," Clark says, summoning the waiter.

"What I *need* are days that last thirty-six hours instead of twenty-four so I can get my work done," Grant says. I kick him lightly under the table, which has always been our deal: I'm to remind him to be social if he seems to be acting like the curmudgeon he can be. He purses his lips but then mumbles something about a drink being a good idea, and Clark starts talking about the last time he and Padgett were here, which he remembers as being exceptionally good, and he nudges Padgett into agreeing with him. And then the conversation comes to the first of its many halts of the evening. Padgett's phone lets out a little bleat, and she snatches it up and reads the screen. Clark takes another sip of his manhattan and the waiter takes our drink orders and slips away.

I lean over and compliment Padgett on the exquisite silk scarf she's wearing, and she tells me a little stiffly that it was made in Indonesia from silk produced by worms that are fed an organic diet of blah blah blah, and these are evidently happier silkworms than have ever been found in the history of the world. I say, "These are the silkworms who no doubt have health coverage and day care and profit sharing," and she actually laughs. I feel Grant rolling his eyes—after all these years, I can feel his eye-rolling even if I'm not looking at him—but, screw him, I don't care. After that, it's easy to get Padgett to give all her many opinions, on everything from the melting polar ice caps to the *vital* importance of wearing organic cotton and eating vegan food.

"So," she says, definitely warming to me, "do you work, or do you just stay home and raise kids?"

Clark, who looks as though he might slit his own throat, quickly leans over and tells her that I am actually a very fine, *accomplished, award-winning* book illustrator with lots and lots of books to my credit.

"Oh, yes," Grant says. "She's just finished the illustrations on a fascinating treatise about a squirrel's evening called *Bobo and His Blankie Go to Bed*." He sees my face and quickly adds, "It's a silly story, but Annabelle's drawings are very lovely."

"I'm sure it's wonderful," says Clark.

"Thank you, Clark. Grant thinks that now that the children are grown, I could be painting more serious things. He can't face the fact that I *like* doing children's books."

Grant makes some kind of protesting noise, but the waiter shows up just then and the subject fortunately gets dropped. Later, Padgett starts making fun of Clark for not knowing what tempeh was when she first met him; and then, when the wine, the food, and my smiling questions have all made her excruciatingly comfortable, she tells a funny, slightly off-color story about their wedding, involving a non-English-speaking hotel employee thinking Clark was really Padgett's father! Imagine that. And this employee was sure that—ha-ha—the bride's father was inappropriately trying to gain entrance to their bridal suite during what the clerk was sure was an intimate moment. So there was poor Clark, jiggling his card key in the lock while the employee is meanwhile trying to head him off and get rid of him while the youngsters seal the deal.

When she's finished, I laugh, but the two men sit there in silence. Grant grabs his drink, so he can hide his eyes behind the glass, I'm sure.

Padgett looks around at their blank, even faces. "Like this guy had never seen an old guy marrying a young woman before?" she says, laughing. "And meanwhile, all you wanted was to get in your own hotel room, didn't you, snoopy?"

Snoopy?

I'm surprised that Clark hasn't tried to somehow stop her from telling this story. Instead, he lets out a high-pitched giggle and dives into the remains of his manhattan. I can't help it, I start laughing, and then Padgett laughs, too, and Clark seizes her hand and says, "Well, on that note, shall we tell them our news, sweetheart?"

Oh God, I think. *They're having a kid.*

I sit up straighter in my chair and am glad that I haven't already drunk too much wine so I can sense the very fun nuances that I'm sure are coming my way. I can feel Grant tense up beside me, ready to ward off all discussions that might reveal anything that would cause any further thought about their sex life. He's suffered enough.

Padgett just shrugs and looks down at her lap, which probably means she's reading her cell phone. I swear, this woman has had about a billion messages flashing back and forth through dinner—and I am enjoying an image of her in the delivery room texting away while she's pushing the baby out, and also enjoying the idea that I am the first person to get this news and wondering how people will take it.

Clark clears his throat, and says in his momentous, department-chairman voice, "Wellll—you sure you don't want to tell them, darling?" When she shakes her head, he says, "No? Well, then I will." He takes a deep breath. "We're taking a leave of absence and we're going to travel the world!"

Grant stares straight ahead.

Now they're kissing. Planting little tiny kisses all over each other's faces. Clark pulls away, and his face is sweaty and he's grinning, gums showing like mad, like he's a fool for love, he's so pleased with himself, and he says, "Padgett here hasn't seen much of the world, so *I* have the pleasure of taking her to all my favorite places. And of course, we're hoping to find a few of our own." He puts his big bald forehead onto her smooth, unlined one, like a mind meld you'd see on *Star Trek*, and then they clink glasses, and, tardily, Grant and I toast them, too.

And then Clark leans forward and says in a low voice to Grant, "I'm going to recommend that you take my place as acting chair."

I can feel the waves of dismay coming off Grant, as he tallies up all the time that little mission will take, in addition to his *book* and his three courses, and the essays he needs to grade. He clears his throat and says this is something he'll have to think about.

"It's a career move that I think you're ready for," says Clark, which I know Grant will find to be the most condescending remark ever, given that he is two years older than Clark and was trained at Columbia and is definitely slumming it by teaching here at this tiny little college, and everybody knows it. "It won't be until the fall semester, which will give you time to finish that book of yours, and who knows but by then you may want to goose up your résumé and maybe get some extra attention from all the important awards committees, eh?"

Then he and Padgett go all kissy again, and her phone starts clamoring for her attention, and by the time the four of us have walked out to the parking lot, shivering in the cold, Clark has pretty much made it clear that Grant has to take the acting chairmanship—for God, for country, and for love, and I know this husband of mine: in some corner of his mind, he's actually flattered, if still a bit stiff about the whole thing. He doesn't like to be told how to feel about anything.

We drive home in silence for the first five miles, and then Grant says, "Well, I guess it could be a good thing, being chair, you know."

"Yes."

"I mean, I never would have sought it."

"No, of course not."

"But if it's not until the fall . . . I'm on track to finish this book by then, and I could have an easier schedule, not teach so much, who knows, even maybe do some more research."

"I like the sound of an easier schedule," I say, and he actually reaches over and squeezes my hand and smiles at me. I think maybe he's going to apologize for being such a jerk and say that once this book is done, another thing that's going to get some of his time and attention is our marriage. Instead he says, "God almighty in heaven, shoot me if I ever get like Clark Winstanley!"

"With pleasure."

"No, really. Get a gun and take me out to the woods if I ever go off the deep end like that. He's gone stark raving mad for that woman! And is she just the rudest . . . ?" He shakes his head, words having failed him.

I do an imitation of Padgett texting like mad, and when that makes him laugh, I do a monologue in her voice where she's dissing Clark for liking The Beatles, a group I pretend she's never heard of.

He pats my shoulder. "Sorry I called you silly."

"Just don't ever do it again, buster. Because I'll *show* you silly. And I would also appreciate it if you could manage *not* to insult my work when we're in public."

"Did I insult your work?"

"You always do. You think it's stupid for me to illustrate children's books—"

"Annabelle. How many times do we have to go over this? This is a compliment to you. I think your illustrations are very sweet, but I just know you're capable of so much more than drawing a squirrel named Bobo, no matter how significant he might be."

I look out the window.

"I'm sorry," he says. "I shouldn't have said anything. I'm proud of your work. Really."

"All right," I say grudgingly. "Apology accepted. I guess."

"Can I make it up to you? What if we stop and get some politically incorrect dessert? I'm starving after eating that rabbit food. Do you want to?"

"You know I do."

"Yeah, I know you do." He turns into a Friendly's, and we have sundaes piled high with whipped cream and nuts, and on the way home, we have to unfasten the top button of our pants so that we can continue to breathe. This is the good side of being married so long. It is so nice to be married, to let my stomach poke out.

"She's wicked, making fun of Clark," he says.

"She's just young. Do you realize she's only a little older than Sophie?"

He laughs a little. "I wouldn't be a bit surprised if she becomes another one of your waifs and strays. You just watch. A few months from now, I'm going to come home and you'll be telling me that Padgett is running away from a terrible childhood and that she's starting some environmental-slash-children's book illustrators' group, and you and she are going to cochair a conference where you make hummus to-gether out of organic chickpeas that you grow in the backyard."

"No, you forget she's going to travel the world."

"Well, otherwise, she's a perfect candidate for the Annabelle McKay Waif and Stray Project." I have this reputation in the family—unearned, I think—for always trying to fix people's lives, to put them in touch with the people they need to know, to get them to dress bet-ter, or stand up straighter. It's really that I'm the only one in the fam-ily who likes listening to other people.

"You wouldn't ever do that, would you?" I say, teasing.

"Do what?"

"You know, leave me for some student who wears only politically correct clothes and thinks she knows everything."

I am not serious; I would just like him to turn and look at me, to join me in playing at being smugly married for just one tiny moment before we walk back into the house. Don't I have a right to that, at least? For him to hold my hand as we go in through the garage, and perhaps give me even the pretense of suspense that maybe we're going to get inside and start up some kissing ourselves, maybe unwrap some of the layers we're bundled in, and—what the hell?—take a Wednesday *night* sex romp.

But he says in a low voice, "Don't be ridiculous. You know you never have to worry about that. We have our pact."

"I'm sure Mary Lou thought she and Clark had a pact, too. Isn't that what wedding vows are?" I say, and I move closer to him and in-terlace his fingers with mine.

"I don't mean *that* pact. I mean our *other* pact," he says, which is as close as he ever comes to mentioning the unmentionable. He doesn't look at me; he opens his car door and gets out slowly, and then I get out, too, and he walks in front of me through the kitchen door. It's dark and cold inside the house, which is exactly how I'm feeling inside. He snaps on the light over the sink, and I feel that old awful tugging inside me, that familiar dragging down of my mood. I have more to say. My throat is clogged with the wanting. But what? *What do you want to say to him, Annabelle?* I can hear Ava Reiss asking me that. Could I tell him, "It's the craziest thing, but lately I keep having these weird dreams, and you won't believe who's in them. . . . Oh, and here's a strange thing about me: yesterday I just started crying in the grocery store! What can that have been about?" Isn't there anything we could say to each other? Maybe there's some stuff there we forgot to examine a long time ago, and couldn't we just say it? Just *say* it?

I hold my breath and then say softly, ashamed at how scared I am, "Would you like to, you know, skip work tonight and just come to bed?"

He looks at his watch and sighs. "I've wasted too much time already. I've really got to knock out the rest of chapter five tonight. Seriously."

"Nice to be referred to as a waste of time."

"Oh, stop it. You know what I mean," he growls.

I know what I'd like to say. Now I know. When I asked him if he would ever do what Clark Winstanley did, I wasn't really asking about him. I *know* he wouldn't leave me for a younger woman, even if he could find one who wouldn't mind his constant ahems.

It's me.

I'm the one whose leaving I'm scared about.

[f o u r]

1977

*I*t was my brother, David, who broke the news to me that Edie and Howard, as we called our parents, were in no trial separation. The unthinkable had happened: our mom—our fully domesticated, chicken-roasting, housecleaning, dental receptionist mom—had met someone, and that was the real reason she was moving out.

"What do you mean, *met someone*?" I said. I was on the pay phone at the student center. If I looked out, I could see the campus lagoon sparkling in the sunlight. I almost couldn't breathe. I stuck my index finger in and out of the rotary dial, hitting every number in rapid succession, a kind of finger hopscotch.

"Yeah. A young guy. A stud artist guy, I don't know."

I laughed. Now this part couldn't be true. "A *stud*? Our mother is with a stud?"

There was a silence. David was a freshman, but he lived at home and went to the local junior college. He'd always been kind of a stoner guy, shy and gangly, with one girlfriend he'd had since seventh grade. They'd probably been quietly and earnestly doing it since they were thirteen. Once I'd found a condom in his room. After a moment he said, "Yeah. You won't believe this, Annie. He drives a VW bus with writing all over it, and he teaches art at some adult-ed class she went to. She's gone off the deep end, doing this whole weird feminist thing."

"Feminist thing? This is the same woman who cries if Howard is even two minutes late getting home."

"Yeah. I told you. She's gone off the deep end or something."

"Jesus," I said. "Are they fighting and yelling and screaming?"

"No," he said. "Howard's drinking again, but all he'll say is that Edie is just taking a little vacation from being a grown-up. She's not really here very much anymore. She's with that guy."

Two weeks later, my dad called me to say he'd been demoted at the bank because the bastards there didn't appreciate true service. I couldn't remember ever talking to him on the phone for longer than it took him to pass the receiver to my mother. Now he was slurring his words. A man works at a place for twenty goddamn years, rises up to district manager, and then he has some goddamn personal problems and he has to take some goddamn time off to sort them out and to *rest* while he figures out what he's going to do, and they just take away his responsibilities and bust him back to reading loan applications. He kept letting out little hacking coughs that I could tell he was trying to hide from me. Probably in addition to drinking, he'd also started smoking again.

"So, unless I win big at poker, you can forget about me paying your rent for the rest of the semester," he said. "And I certainly can't pay for college next fall. You might as well know all this right now so you can make your plans. Them's the breaks, kid. Life isn't fair, and it just got a lot more unfair."

I swallowed hard and tried to speak in a very adult voice. "Is this because you're so upset about Mom?"

"Listen, I won't have you talking bad about your mom," he said way too loudly. "You can't go through life blaming other people. That's the trouble around here, is all the goddamn blame for every goddamn thing."

"I'm *not* blaming her—but what the hell, Daddy?"

"Stop it! And I won't have you cussing, either. Your mother doesn't know what she's doing, and she deserves our sympathy. She's with a man who could be her son. She's going to need lots of luck in her second childhood."

"Do you—do you want me to come home?"

"Do what you want. Nobody's going to pay your tuition or your rent, so you figure it out. I didn't raise an idiot."

There was a muffled noise as he dropped the phone. When he spoke again, his voice sounded far away. "I don't know what to tell you. Maybe your mother's boy toy will pay your rent and tuition for you. Try that," he said, and after about thirty seconds of fumbling, he managed finally to hang up the phone.

BECAUSE TROUBLE has always come for me in clusters, three days later the guy in the apartment above mine fell asleep while his bathtub was filling, and water came through the ceiling—and then the ceiling itself came down in big wet chunks. The landlord said he couldn't get to it for another few weeks, and that we shouldn't use our tub in the meantime. He suggested we wash in the bathroom sink, which made us howl with laughter.

Luckily for Magda, she had a married sister who lived in Santa Barbara who agreed to take her in, but there was no room for me there, too. As it was, she was going to have to share a room with her five-year-old nephew.

And then the club where I performed once a week with the Oil Spills decided we weren't pulling in the big crowds anymore and they wanted to try out other bands.

"Before the universe sends the locusts and frogs, I think I have to go home," I told Magda. "I am obviously meant to take this quarter off and put my family back together."

Magda was a prime believer in signs from the universe. We both agreed that we'd find a way to room together again in the fall, one way or another.

That day I walked across campus to the admin building to see what you had to do to withdraw from classes, and whom should I see but Grant, riding his bike toward me. He blinked and slowed the bike, almost heading off the path and derailing two other riders behind him, who slid into the dirt.

"You!" he said. His bike skidded, and he jumped off. The two guys behind him flipped him the bird.

"Oh," I said. "Hi. Just so you know, you nearly killed those people back there."

"Sorry." He gave them a little wave and turned back to me. "How are you doing?" His cheeks were bright pink, and he was sweating.

"I'm fine, I suppose. Leaving school tomorrow. Going back home."

He cleared his throat. "Why would you do that?"

"I have to," I said. "I have so many good reasons you wouldn't believe it. Bad luck is raining down on me. You're actually taking a big chance even standing here talking to me. An airplane could fall out of the sky on us."

"Maybe I like to live dangerously. Give me the first three reasons."

So I told him about the ceiling falling down in my apartment, and my band getting laid off from its usual gig—but when I started telling him about my family's troubles, I could feel a lump in my throat.

"Everybody's falling apart at home, and my father has gotten demoted at his job, all because my mother has left him for a guy who's some kind of artist stud and drives a VW bus with writing on it. And I've run out of money, so I figure I'll just go try to help my family," I said.

"But why don't you just wait until the end of the quarter? Haven't you already paid for the whole quarter?"

"I haven't paid the rent for the quarter, and my dad can't help me—"

"Wait," he said. "There are only five more weeks left. You can find a way to support yourself for that long, can't you?"

I shook my head.

He looked down at the ground and cleared his throat, and then he looked up at the sky and squinted off in the distance and shifted his weight to his other foot. He said, "I think you should stay. You're an idiot if you give up your whole life just to try to save your parents. Why don't you stay with a friend for a while? Or get a part-time job as a waitress. You could make enough money to eat."

"Maybe, but my mom is obviously having some kind of crisis. And my dad might even be a serious alcoholic by now. Who's going to help them if I don't?"

Just then Jay came up behind me, as he liked to do, always scaring the hell out of me by running up and grabbing me. I saw Grant flinch as I was tackled and nearly lost my balance on my platform shoes. I yelled, "Jay! Will you *stop it*?" but he was laughing as he wrapped his arms around me and rocked us back and forth.

"Jay, this is my friend Grant," I said, struggling to duck out of his grasp, "so behave yourself, will you? We're having a *conversation*."

"Hi, man," said Jay. "Babe, I got us a gig at the Bluebird tonight."

"Really? The Bluebird?" I said. We'd always wanted to play there. It was a real townie place, not just for students. "Are they paying us?"

"Twenty-five. And free drinks."

"See?" said Grant. "Work is already coming to find you."

Jay looked more closely at Grant, with a quizzical who-the-hell-are-you smile. I could tell that he was going to try to stake out his territory in front of Grant. Like the way a dog has to pee on something to show he owns the place. And sure enough, there went his hands, snaking their way around to the front of my shirt, heading over to my boobs.

Grant said something about suddenly remembering that he had someplace he had to be. "Good luck to you," he said to me. "Hope you get back to painting."

"Stop it," I said to Jay, and slapped his hands away. He pretended to slap me back, and we got into a tussle, slapping at each other in a stupid, playful way, and when I looked around, Grant was pedaling off. His butt wasn't even resting on the seat; he was standing up as he rode, swaying back and forth, with those hopeless, job-interview khaki pants bound around his ankles with a rubber band.

"Who was *that* guy?" said Jay, and I said, "Oh, he's just some guy who enjoys telling me how stupid I am for going back home. He thinks I can just crash someplace until the end of the quarter."

This was a sore subject. Jay lived with three other guys, but he had his own room, and anybody but Jay would have invited me to come and live there with him. Two could fit in that single bed just fine. But he and I both knew that this would violate something very basic in our relationship that I was just beginning to understand: he was never going to be willing to help me with anything.

The next day, with my portion of the twenty-five dollars from our gig, I packed everything I owned in my beat-up blue VW. I kept losing heart for leaving, though, and when I finally went out to the car with the last of my stuff, I decided to give the universe one more chance to reverse its signs. If the radio was playing a happy love song, I'd call up Jay and tell him he had to let me live with him, and if it was depressing, I'd go home to my parents.

The next song was "No More Tears" with Barbra Streisand and Donna Summer, which was a problem. Are women happy or sad when they're singing, "Enough is enough" with their fists pumping in the air? I couldn't tell, so I had to wait for another sign. I drove around Isla Vista, passing the apartment I'd lived in freshman year and the bar that Magda and I walked to the night her mother died, and then I rolled past the building where I'd met a guy named Jack and all those guys who turned out to be surfers from La Jolla. I parked and walked on the beach—sometimes at night you could see the waves lit up by microscopic sea animals that provided their own light, like magic. Nothing seemed to be a sign.

It wasn't until I pulled into a gas station to fill the tank that I saw my sign: Grant, pumping air into the tires of his bike. He came over to my car and leaned in, looking at all my stuff packed up on the roof.

"You can't save them, you know." His voice was very quiet. "Don't throw away your life just to save them. It's not a fair trade, your life for theirs. And also, just so you know, that non-monogamous jerk you're seeing is an idiot." He gazed off in the distance, maybe over at the mountains, and then he leaned back into the car. "Look," he said, and sighed. "If you want, you can stay at my place for the rest of the quarter. I'm mostly awake all the time anyway, working on my thesis, but I'll sleep on the sofa."

I WENT home at the end of the quarter and immediately discovered that my father didn't know the first thing about getting my mother back. He was hopeless. All you had to do was walk in the front door to see that. For one thing, the house smelled like raw onions, and I had to pick my way through dirty clothes to get to the kitchen, where the overflowing garbage can was stuffed with empty TV-dinner trays. And the curtains were closed. My father hadn't even bothered to open them. How did he think he could get her back, if he wasn't even going to do that much? Edie was a firm believer in such amenities as air fresheners and light. She was a minty-smelling dental receptionist, after all; her values involved brushing and flossing twice a day, keeping your room clean, eating fruit, doing homework, performing good deeds for other people. This was the woman whose singsongy "Good *morning,* Dr. *Bland*on's office" was a deep comfort to dental patients all over the Valley. The truth was, my mother was a prize housewife, never once appearing bored with cooking and baking and cleaning and making little craft projects. She could do anything.

For my whole childhood, my father went away every morning to work in a bank, and he came home tired and crabby. He had but one job around the house, and that was to clean the swimming pool and manage the required chemicals. He'd go outside in the afternoons after work, still wearing his suit pants and his undershirt, and first he'd put a sample of pool water into test tubes, glaring at the results. I loved watching him do that, although it scared me, too. He hated being watched. If he caught you, he'd say something like, "What are you staring at?" So I always had to pretend I was out there doing something else. Then, after he'd gotten the pH corrected and the disease-causing strains of whatever was in our pool eliminated, he'd stand there like somebody who was hypnotized, skimming the oleander leaves out of the deep end. I'd play hopscotch on the patio while he worked because I liked to keep an eye on him. You never knew when he was going to say something funny. He was mostly quiet and mad-looking, off in his own world, but sometimes he'd do something like make a mustache out of tree bark and do a whole Groucho Marx act, from out of nowhere. You had to watch him. Sometimes I could coax him into coming into the pool with me, but he didn't really like to do things people asked him to do. He'd say he was too busy, but then when you weren't asking, he'd suddenly fly out of the door in his swim trunks and jump in, flailing around like a crazy man, and spend the next hour letting you climb on his shoulders.

My mother was always trying to get him to do things with us, like play board games, but he wasn't having any of it. She was somebody who could play Monopoly and lose everything and never get mad, no matter how many of her hotels you took. But my father would play like it was life or death. If he wasn't winning, you could see him getting grimmer and grimmer as the game went on, and one time when my mother had monopolies on Boardwalk and Park Place *and* had all the railroads, he got to his feet and pushed the entire board over and stalked out of the room, swearing at all of us. My brother and I sat there in stunned silence, trying to figure out whether or not we were going to cry. But my mother laughed and told us not to worry; it was just because he was a *real* banker, and he knew that life wasn't as simple as the game made it seem. She got up and went into the kitchen and made him a banana daiquiri, and then she went out to the backyard, where he was skimming leaves out of the pool in the dark. She turned on the pool light, and the backyard lit up in an eerie aqua glow, and I saw her touching his arm and then pretending to withhold his daiquiri from him. Pretty soon they were laughing, and he was reaching around her, trying to get the drink she was holding back from him. This was, I told my brother, the way you knew people were very much in love. That kind of thing was fun for them.

My mother and I talked about love and men all the time. "You see?" she said to me. "The way you handle men is you just have to *palaver* over them, make them think they're the most important thing in your life. They're so easy, really."

About boys, she said, "They don't really know what the hell is going on, or how anybody feels—and so we have to help them along with that. We women," she said, "are the ones responsible for how people feel."

When I told her that it seemed unfair we had to do all that, she laughed and said, "No, no, no! Oh no, honey. *We* got the best deal of all. Do you know how boring life is without feelings?" I must have been twelve then, and we were standing in the kitchen, and my father and brother were outside by the pool, staring silently in opposite directions. "Look at those poor saps. Wouldn't know what to say to each other if the house was on fire! What do you suppose they're thinking about?"

"Well," I said. "Daddy's thinking about how many leaves are in the pool now compared to how many were there yesterday, and David is thinking about soccer."

She erupted in laughter. "Exactly!" she said. "See? Isn't it fun? You can do it, too. You just have to read their minds, and then you can do anything you want with them."

She and my father went out every Saturday night to a club. But they put on a little show before leaving each time: my father grumpily knotting his tie and pretending he'd rather watch the basketball championships or the TV movie of the week, and my mother laughing and calling him a stick-in-the-mud—years and years of Saturday nights like this, with her pushing him out the front door, all for the amusement of David and me, who were lying on the floor watching TV. She'd always turn and wink at me as they left and make that little circle thumb-and-index finger sign that meant "okay."

Then, when I was thirteen years old, all the ladies in the neighborhood started up a consciousness-raising group, meeting every Thursday night just to talk. At first it seemed harmless, like more of the same visiting they'd done with each other around the swimming pools while we kids wore floaties and jumped into the deep end and they watched us. But as the years went on, the group seemed to get sort of strange. My father pointed out one time with an angry laugh that there had been three divorces in that group, and one woman had just left town without her family and didn't even bother to get a divorce or write to them or anything.

I asked my mother what the group was for. "What do you do there?" I said.

They talked, she said.

"But what do you talk about?" I was lying on her bed on my stomach with my knees bent, swinging my legs back and forth like a metronome underneath the ceiling fan.

"Well," she said, "we talk about our power. Something you're going to have to think about in your own life."

"You mean . . . how women know about all the feelings?"

She laughed. "Uh, *no*. We're all a little bit sick of having to be the ones who are responsible for taking care of all the feelings," she said. I sat up on the bed, suddenly interested. Hadn't I been the one to point out that this was too great a burden for women to bear? And hadn't she been the one to declare that we were the lucky ones?

She came and sat down beside me. "Women have been responsible for all the wrong things for too long," she said. "By the way, do you know everything you need to know about sex?"

I put my head underneath her pillow, and she laughed.

"Forget it, I'm not going to embarrass you," she said. "It's just that women have to take back their sexuality. We've let men dictate the terms for way too long. Look, did you ever wonder why I'm always telling you that boys are out for *only one thing*, and that you mustn't give in to them, because they just want to use you?"

"Yeah," I said in a small voice, thinking, *Oh, God, not this again.*

"Now I want to tell you something else: *you* are a sexual being yourself, and you, as a woman, have a need for sexual expression, too, and *you* have a right to experience that. Sex is just creative energy. It's beautiful, and it's there for all of us, not just men! And you know something? Your generation is the one that's going to have it all. The work and the respect and the feelings and all that, too." She gathered me up in a hug. "I am so lucky to have a daughter like you, so I can watch this all happen. You'll go to college and get a degree in something you really care about—something you can support yourself with so you won't have to depend on some *man* to see you through life. And don't you come to me telling me that you met a *really nice guy* and he's going to be the one to go to work and you're just going to drop out of school and stay home and make lots and lots of babies and keep him happy. Okay?" She was holding me and staring into my eyes. *"Okay?"*

"Okay," I said.

"And if you want orgasms, multiple ones even, you shall have them."

"Stop it," I said, and wriggled away from her. "I'm begging you."

MY MOTHER was living by herself in a tiny studio apartment furnished with stuff she bought in thrift shops, objects my straitlaced father would never have put up with: huge, overstuffed pillows, scarves, scented candles, and purple filmy curtains with stars on them. Most surprising of all was a water bed with a black velour bedspread.

"Come on!" she said. "This is the best bed in the world! You've got to feel it! Come on, touch it. Run your hand over this cover. Isn't that something?"

I went over and sat down gingerly on the edge of the bed and looked around. From there I could see the corner of the room that served as a kitchen, with its coffeepot and two-burner stove and dorm-sized refrigerator. And right in the middle of everything was a card table spread with all her arts and crafts. My father had always referred to her projects as "arts and craps," but now they clearly had top billing.

I looked down and felt inexplicably dizzy. *The Joy of Sex* was lying on the floor, and there was a man's leather sandal right by my foot. So the stud wore sandals. My toes curled up in embarrassment.

"You love it here, don't you?" my mother was saying. "I knew you would. It's our kind of place. A *woman's* place." I swallowed hard and nodded. She went to the tiny refrigerator and took out two Cokes and handed me one. She was smiling with all her teeth showing. "I knew you'd get it. I mean, I know it's small, but do you realize this is the first place in my life that has been just mine, all mine?"

I sighed. This wasn't going to be so easy, getting her to go back home to my father, not if she was willing to live *here*. She didn't even look the same as she used to. Her dark hair was longer, and she wasn't wearing it in a chignon anymore. It was down around her shoulders, loose and curly in a perm, and parted in the middle. She had on lots of eyeliner and blush. And she was wearing tight blue jeans and a hot pink shirt that didn't button up as far as it might have. She looked mind-blowingly young, even though, by my quick calculation, she was forty-two, and therefore ancient.

She saw me looking at her and did a little twirl. "Do you like my hair?"

"Sure," I said.

"It's long," she said. "I've always loved it long, but your father wanted me to wear it short or else in a bun, because that's how *his* mother wore her hair." She rolled her eyes. "All my life with this trying to measure up to his sainted mother." She bounced on the bed again and grinned at me. "But Dmitri likes it long."

She launched into a whole story about Dmitri the art teacher, and how he was handsome and free-spirited and beloved by all the women in the class—but it was my mother whom he'd identified with the most. He was *empowering* her to truly express her deep feelings, she said. Who could believe that there were men in the world who truly respected women and wanted the best for them, who didn't think of them strictly as sex objects, and yet because of that were the best lovers?

"Oh, Mom," I said.

She reached over and ruffled my hair a little. "Aw, I suppose it seems strange to you. You're seeing me in a whole new way, aren't you?"

I shrugged, not knowing what to say. Tears sprang to my eyes, and she hugged me. "Oh, my sweet, sweet angel girl," she said. "You've always been the one who understood me the best. Even when you were a baby, I could tell by those big hazel eyes of yours that followed me around the room that you truly *saw* me."

I burst into tears. She came and held me, and I had a thought that everything would turn out all right after all.

"Come on, come on, stop crying." She dabbed at my cheeks. "Look at me. I'm *happy*! I'm doing paintings again, and making jewelry. I'm finding parts of myself that I didn't even know existed."

I cried harder.

"Why, who knows what's still lurking around in this crazy brain of mine?" she said, smiling real big. "Maybe I'll turn out to be a doctor, or an *architect*. Or maybe some kind of sex therapist!"

Oh, God, I thought. *Don't start talking to me about sex. Could we please be like normal mothers and daughters, who don't talk about such things?*

She reached over and tucked some of my crazier curls behind my ear. "How's your father, speaking of sex therapists? That, by the way, is a joke."

"He says he's fine."

"Well, then he probably is fine. In his worldview, at least," she said.

The phone rang then, and she went over to answer it. Obviously it was Dmitri; I could tell from the way she curled her entire body around the phone receiver, holding it up to her face as if it were a beloved object. I stared down at the sandal on the floor as if it were a snake.

When she got off the phone, we went to a diner that we'd gone to a million times with my father and brother, a place where we'd often had breakfast on weekend mornings.

She leaned forward on her elbows and smiled brightly at me. "For starters, tell me all about the men in your life."

"Well," I said slowly, "I broke up with Jay three times and got back together with him only twice, which is for the best."

"Jay . . . Jay," she said, frowning. "He's the guy in your band? The sexy one?"

I couldn't remember ever describing him to her as sexy, but I said, "Yeah." Then, for the sake of accuracy, I added, "Well, he's good-looking. But he's not really that good for me."

"You know, even the not-so-good ones have something to teach us," she said.

I fiddled with the enormous maroon menu. Nothing in it sounded very good. My mother winked and said she was having a hamburger, to keep her strength up. I finally ordered a bowl of chicken noodle soup.

"I'm actually seeing someone else," I said, meaning Grant. He and I had been talking on the telephone at night now that I was here— long, drifty conversations about the meaning of life and how we both felt we were living our lives right now in reaction to other people. He was waiting to hear about teaching jobs, and I was waiting to see what was going to happen with my family. We both felt powerless. That's what we whispered to each other over the phone line, like it was a secret linking us together.

My mother beamed at me for realizing that I needed to break up with Jay. "You see? That's great," she said. "One isn't right, and so you move on. Pause, reflect, and get a new lover."

I wondered what she would have said if she'd really known. Before I came to LA, I'd been living at Grant's apartment for five weeks, and he didn't make a move on me until three days before I left. He'd given me his single bed while he slept on the floor on an egg crate foam mattress, first in the living room and then, because it was too cluttered in there with all the furniture, he'd moved chastely to the bedroom floor. We didn't even kiss. He was polite and respectful, what my mother—my *old* mother, at least—would have called "the perfect gentleman." Then one night he had simply come into the bedroom and sat down on the egg crate thingie and cleared his throat and said, "You know, I'm kind of *that way* about you."

That way. It thrilled me, that understatement. I'd watched as his Adam's apple went up and down and up and down, powered by nervousness, and I was already a little in love with him just from the way he snored softly at night and how, when my artwork was on display at the student center, he showed up there in a tie and stood for a long, long time looking at my paintings, and then took me out for coffee and told me that he wanted to understand every single squiggle on those canvases. I loved the cheerful tone of voice he had when he said "Good morning" to me each day, and also how he made sure to take all the hairs out of the shower drain and the way he tiptoed if I was studying for a test. He was the nicest guy I'd ever known.

He said quietly, "You don't have to have feelings for me. That's not what I'm asking for . . ." and I got up and went over and kissed him on the lips and pulled him down on the bed. We made love, and maybe because of all the restraint we'd shown up until then, or maybe because we were already in love with each other, or maybe because, underneath everything, Grant really does have a very high opinion of loving—well, it was just fine. Way better than with Jay. And then after three days of repeat performances, the quarter was over, summer had come, and I packed up my car and moved back to LA, because I had promised myself I would, and also because I had to save my family.

Which is why I was there, sitting across from my mother. I licked my lips. "So I have to ask you something," I said.

"Anything," she said. "Ask me anything at all!" She took out a pack of cigarettes and held one out to me with a questioning look. I shook my head, and she shrugged and lit it up and took a long, glamorous drag on it. I couldn't believe she was *smoking.* "In fact," she said, "I have all kinds of things I'm dying to discuss with *you*, too. Things that I would have *died* before ever talking about with *my* mother. But first let me just ask you this. Have you ever seen your own vagina?"

She said this in a conversational voice, didn't even lean forward and whisper. I choked on a sip of coffee.

"Lift your arms," she said. "It clears your airways. And if you haven't already, you should look at it, because it's utterly fascinating. Who knew? At this new women's group I go to, we took out mirrors and— well, we looked. No, stop laughing. Sit up. Don't be embarrassed. It is *mesmerizing*, I tell you."

"Mom!" I said, and she stopped, her fingers still fluttering, after outlining a vagina in midair with her cigarette. People were looking in our direction.

"What?" she said.

"Mom, please. I can't talk about this here," I whispered.

She laughed. "Oh, but it's fine to talk about these things," she said. "In fact, we have to! And by the way, just so you know, it's not really the *vagina* that you're seeing, it's the *vulva*. And that's a word you'll never hear!"

"I think I need to change the subject," I said, and she laughed.

"Okay. We'll talk about what you want to talk about," she said. "Shoot."

I stared into my cup of coffee for a moment, hoping a moment of silence would signify a suitable transition. Finally I said, "I need to know something. Do you ever see yourself going back to Daddy? I mean, when you're done with . . . all this?"

"All *this*? What exactly is *all this*? My life, you mean?" she said. She exhaled a plume of smoke and folded her arms. "Just tell me this. Did your father tell you to ask me that?"

"No. But look at him. He's a mess. He's been demoted at work, he—"

"I am not responsible for that, Annabelle."

"No, no, of course not. I just didn't know if you even knew about it—"

"I can't care about that right now!"

"But you lived with him for twenty-something years. And now he really needs you. And he really, really loves you."

"Okay, I'm going to explain this to you only because I love you and we can talk about anything. The truth is that I was not put on this earth to care for this one frail man, this man who doesn't want to feel things, who runs away from life and not toward it. How about *me*? Am I just supposed to give up *everything* just so that *one man* can think life is all rosy and beautiful for all time? One man, Annabelle! So that he doesn't *ever* have to face the fact that he has some responsibility to make other people happy, or to make them feel good or needed or *anything*? Is that all my life is worth? Is it?"

"But you know he loves you," I said weakly. "And he wants you to be happy."

"Oh, what the fuck does that even *mean*?" she said, and I blanched. This was another surprise, that my mother even *knew* the F-word. "I am going to tell you something. It may not be a big deal to you, but for the first time—*the first time ever in my life*—I am on my own. And I am sleeping with a man who cares about what that experience is like for me." She leaned forward and bared her teeth. "And you know what else? I am having *orgasms*!"

I put my head down on the table, dimly aware that my hair was in my soup. "Jesus, Mother."

An older man and his wife two tables away got up and asked to be moved to a different table.

My mother burst out laughing, but when I looked at her, she also had tears streaming down her face, streaking her makeup. "Don't look at me. Don't look. I'm a mess," she said, and wiped at her face with her napkin. "I'm sorry. No, I'm *not* sorry. I'm going to stop apologizing for every damn thing. And now I'm going to the ladies' room."

She got up and tottered away on her platform flip-flops, and I sat there, sipping my coffee and looking out the huge plate-glass diner window and thinking about sex.

Outside, some high school students sauntered past, the boys slouchy and scared and the girls wearing spiky boots and low-cut blouses and scary makeup like whores, and they were laughing and hitting each other and trying to push one of the guys out into the middle of traffic so he could be killed and ruin their lives for all time.

Look at them, I thought. I supposed it was sex that made them act that way. They were just trying to pass the time until one of them figured out how they could all get laid. They thought that would be the thing that would make them happy.

It seemed like the saddest thing in the world.

And yet, here we were: all of us doomed passengers in steerage on this huge ship of sex. Prisoners, even. I looked down at my fingers, which were twisting my napkin all around, turning it into a noose. And my poor mother was the most pitiful prisoner of all, reading *The Joy of Sex* and sleeping with an artist guy who couldn't even keep his sandals together in a pair. Where *was* that other sandal?

A MONTH later, to my astonishment, Grant showed up at my father's house. I had just finished mopping the kitchen floor, and I was eating a falling-apart taco and reading a magazine out by the pool when I heard the doorbell ring. I wiped my greasy hands on the back of my shorts and went to answer the door.

And there he was, tall and pale and blinking so fast it was as though *he* were the one shocked to see *me* there, as though I'd showed up in the last possible place on earth he would expect. We stood there, both of us speechless for a moment, and then he pulled me to him and kissed me over and over again. He'd rented a car and driven down from Santa Barbara that morning, he said, asking for directions along the way.

He was blushing. He looked so adorably awkward and amazed at himself, so utterly and unpretentiously charming I couldn't get over it. He reached into his shirt pocket and took out a piece of paper, all folded neatly into a square. It was a letter offering him a teaching position at Columbia University. "So I'm here to tell you that I'm going to New York," he said, breathless from all the kissing. "It's a job. I got the one I wanted."

"You're going to New York?" I said. "Wow."

I led him into the kitchen, and I poured us Cokes, and he told me about the job, and how it was closer to his family in New Hampshire, and how besides that, it was a wonderful opportunity, and he'd get to work with a guy he'd always wanted to work with. He'd been following this guy, some labor historian, for years, reading everything the guy had ever written, and now he'd be in the same department. The whole time he talked he was looking at me with such intensity I had to keep looking away. It was as though his eyes were lit from behind in a way I'd never seen before.

I was leaning against the kitchen counter and I kept dropping things; it was disconcerting, the way he was looking at me. Later he asked if we could go for a swim in the pool—he'd even brought his swim trunks along. Everything seemed surreal, like a slow-motion movie with the colors too bright. We couldn't stop laughing. I showed him that we had a waterfall that could be turned on, and he kept coming up to me and enveloping me in hugs, giving me little kisses all over my face.

"Have you ever made love in a pool?" I said to him, and he closed his eyes, pained.

"Don't talk like that! I don't ever want to think again about anybody you've ever made love with," he said in a whisper. "From now on. Ever again."

"No?" I said. "Okay, then."

He fumbled with the trunks for a moment, and I thought he'd

taken my question as some kind of invitation and was about to undress right then and there, when really pool sex was so much more
appropriate at night. But then I was astonished to see him pull something shiny out from the billows of blue cloth. Did men's trunks have
pockets? That was the main question rising up in my mind when he
took my left hand and held it out in front of us, like a specimen of a
hand floating on top of the pool water.

"I guess you've seen this coming," he said in a shaky voice. "But I
want you to marry me and come with me to New York." He was doing
something to my hand, trying to slip a ring on it, I realized too late,
after I'd pulled my hand away.

"Oh!" I said.

"Listen. I don't know how to do this right, but I really, really love
you," he said, and cleared his throat. He licked his lips and started
talking fast. "I think you're the sweetest, most beautiful girl in the
world, and I've been living for our telephone conversations. It's the
only thing that gets me through these days, knowing that I get to talk
to you every night. Keeping the secret about this job was the hardest
thing for me to do, but I wanted to tell you in person. And ever since
I knew I was going to come here and ask you this, I couldn't eat or
drink anything. And I know I'm different from you, and I'm probably
never going to be cool, but I love your paintings, I love that you do
art, I *get it*, and I won't ever tell you that you should do paintings that
match somebody's couch. I will keep you in paint and canvases for
the rest of your life, and if you really want to teach elementary
school, then I think you'll be the best teacher there ever was. And I
love that you dress so cute, and I love the way you smell and the way
you sing in the shower. I used to camp out on the floor outside the
door when you were showering just so I could hear you, and the first
time we made love was the best thing that ever happened to me, and
I was so afraid you were going to say it couldn't happen again. I just
want to spend all my time looking at you and telling you things, and
even though I'm just some nerd who thinks about strikes and con-

tracts all the time, I want you to know that I'm financially solvent right now, I have some investments, and I'll always do anything I can to make you happy. Your happiness is going to be the main thing for me. From now on. Forever. I mean that."

I laughed. Tears were springing up in my eyes. "I—"

He held up his hand, the one that was still holding the ring he'd tried to put on my finger. "I know what you might say—that we don't know each other well enough and that we should wait—but I feel like I can love you no matter what else I find out about you. And you know everything there is to know about me. You lived with me in my bedroom for five weeks, and I'm afraid that now you know me as well as I know myself."

I stared down at our legs and feet, which looked white and wavery through the blue, ripply pool water. Life was so much more complicated than he knew. Who gets *married* anymore, was what I was thinking. Nobody! This would be seriously shocking to people. I looked out at the old swing set at the other end of the yard, the one that David and I had spent hours swinging on as kids and which we now sat on every night when we smoked dope together. The truth was—I'd glimpsed it sliding around in the corners of my mind, but now it was blazing bright, front and center—that I was turning into my mother, my former mother, here in this house, dusting the furniture and opening the drapes and waiting for her to get over her little love affair and come back and take on this role again. But she wasn't coming back, and now my father was seeing someone new, a woman from across the street who had started sneaking casseroles over and inviting him to hot-tub parties. The truth was that my parents were out living their lives and they were all right. It had been pretentious of me, after all, to think I could save them, to think I could make one iota of difference. Grant had been right about that, and maybe he was sensible and smart and would be right about all the rest of the things that came up in life, too.

I looked up at him, and he'd gone blurry on me. I felt my knees buckle then, and he held me up and kissed me, and when we were done, I said yes.

He was so overcome he dropped the ring, and I had to dive down to the bottom of the pool and feel around until I found it and brought it back up to give to him so he could give it back to me.

[five]

I'm in my studio, drinking coffee and putting the final touches on the drawing of Bobo's mom, a bushy-tailed squirrel relaxing in her yellow workout outfit (with a suitable hole in the back for her tail), kicking back in her living room after she's finally gotten Bobo put to bed, when Sophie calls me. I see her number on the caller ID and get myself set for one of our typical conversations—how lonely she is with her husband away, how hard it is to work at a magazine with catty women, how worried she is about whether the baby will be normal— but when I pick up the phone, she is screaming. At first I can't even make out the words, but then I hear "blood" and "baby" and "help me," and I just want to climb right into the phone, and I want her to tell me what the hell is happening, but I can't get her to. She's mostly just shrieking, making hysterical, gulping sounds that don't add up to words.

"Sophie, please just stop screaming and tell me what's happening so I can help you," I say, trying not to shout.

And then she manages to tell me enough that I can fill in the details. She's at work, and she's in the ladies' room, and she felt something wet, and she looked down and there was blood everywhere. Everywhere. I close my eyes. She is calling me from the stall, and that's where she still is now—alone in the office restroom in New York City, with blood filling her shoes. I go completely, icily calm while I think of what we should do. I'm on automatic pilot, and then whatever is running my brain tells her that I'll click over and call her boss and then the boss can call 911, and somehow we'll get her an ambulance to take her to the hospital, and she agrees to this, even calms down enough to remember the extension number of the phone on the boss's desk. And we do all this, and the boss goes in and gets Sophie out of there, and an ambulance comes, and they take her to the hospital, I presume. And after all those wild, impossible phone calls—I am on the line hearing the boss talking to her, comforting her, hearing Sophie crying, hearing the paramedics arrive and come for her, putting her on the stretcher, the men's competent, gentle voices saying, "Can you lift up here? There, you're okay, that's fine"—after all that is done and it is time for just the waiting, I sit in my study in the sudden crash of quiet, and I look out at the pure white snowfall and think that she is probably losing the baby, and possibly losing her life as well, and I'm so stunned I can't even cry. Can't do anything. Can't lift my arms or breathe right.

Once I can move again, I call Grant, and he listens to the story, and at first I can feel him calculating what needs to be subtracted from this tale because it's me telling it. You might as well know that I have a reputation for exaggerating, and with medical stories particularly, I am not to be trusted. But then he understands—with my last breath of energy, I finally make him understand—and he says in a heavy voice that he has a class just beginning, but he'll assign them some reading, then he'll try to come home.

"Okay. No, you should stay at school."

"What do you mean? I thought this was what you wanted."

"I have to get to New York," I say. I feel so prickly and frightened that I can't bear the thought of anyone near me. It's as though my skin hurts, like when you're coming down with a fever. There are bargains I need to negotiate with the powers, places I need to travel all alone in my head. "It's fine. Really. Just wait there, and I'll call you when I know more."

He hesitates. "Should I call Sophie, do you think?"

"Grant, she's in the hospital. They're *doing things* to her."

"That's true," he says. "But why can't they tell us something now?"

"Because they're fixing her. And we have no choice but to let them take care of her for us," I tell him. "I love you," I say before I hang up. He says he loves me, too, and to let him know as soon as I know anything. Anything at all.

And then I hang up and of course I wish I had told him to come home. There is no pleasing me. I want him and then I don't want him. I pace around the house, and find myself doing odd things like turning on lights and turning them off again, dusting the furniture using the palm of my hand instead of a dust cloth, and standing in the doorways of the children's bedrooms. Nick's room was pretty much cleaned out when he left for college: he took all his sports equipment and trophies along with him. He barely lived in that room anyway. He was always outside, shooting hoops or climbing mountains or skiing, and if he was home, he was usually in a "boy nest" in the den, with his pillows, his smelly pile of fleece blankets, and his computer. All that's left are his posters of Star Wars characters, curled up at the edges. He wouldn't ever let me put them in frames.

But Sophie's room is now a shrine to her high school years. The bookshelves are still crammed with her field hockey and lacrosse trophies, old Baby-sitters Club novels, ancient *People* magazines, yearbooks, prom pictures. In the corner are her field hockey stick, her baby pillow, and her ice skates. She painted this room fuchsia when she was in ninth grade—Grant said it was the color of one of his headaches—and then she insisted on a huge polka-dot round rug in lime green, a maroon plaid bedspread, and burlap brown curtains. We'd gone along with the madness, joking that these colors showed latent avant-garde tendencies that meant she'd grow up to be some kind of true artist, but it turned out to be just a whim. Recently she told me the room never felt right, but she'd been too embarrassed to ask that we paint it white and hang up pink or yellow curtains, like everybody else had. Oh, she had my number, all right. I wanted to indulge her every creative impulse and create the perfect safe, artistic world for her from the very moment she slid out of me and I discovered myself in possession of a daughter—and she always thought she needed to be extraordinary to please me.

I do what I always do when I'm distraught: I call Magda in Atlanta. As soon as she answers the phone, I tell her what's going on, and even though she doesn't know one thing about pregnancy, she says that she's heard stories about bleeding, stories that didn't turn out to mean the end of the baby or the mother.

"It will be all right," she says.

"Are you just trying to make me feel better?" I ask her, and she says of course not because nothing can make a mother feel better when her daughter is in another city, bleeding. Magda doesn't have kids, so Sophie and Nicky have been her honorary children, and I have often sat in the middle of the night on the floor of my mudroom, whispering into the phone to her about some monumental child-related problem that I needed advice on. She finds it hilarious that I rely on her for counsel, when back in college she was a druggie of the highest order, and she's made it something of a lifelong policy to always be involved with bad, heartbreaking, or otherwise unmarriageable men. The nice ones bore her, she says. But she is wise and funny, and besides my mother, she's the one person who really knows me. And now that my mother is dead, Magda is the only one left.

My mind has been taken over by fire ants, I tell her, so she goes on the Internet and looks up pregnancy bleeding, and then reads me what I am sure are only the least upsetting parts. Oh, it could be placenta previa, she says, as if this is good news. That's when the placenta is just in the wrong place but not so, so dangerous. She says she will wish for that, and reminds me that she's a very effective wisher; that's how she's gotten all her lovers, her jobs, her apartments, and her red Saab convertible. And sure enough, the phone rings an hour and twenty-two minutes later, and it's Sophie at the hospital saying in a brave, controlled voice that she and the baby are both okay. The bleeding has stopped, and an ultrasound has shown that she has placenta previa but everything looks okay for now.

The doctor gets on the phone and explains that placenta previa looks far more upsetting than it is. "Mrs. McKay," she says, "I'm sure you were scared to death, but everything's really just fine. Sophie's doing very well now, and the baby's okay, like nothing happened."

"But there was so much blood . . ."

"I know. It's a very scary thing, but chances are, with proper precautions, things are going to go well for the rest of the pregnancy. Sophie is going to have to go on bed rest until delivery, because we can't take any chances that the placenta will separate from the uterine wall. Now, I understand that her husband isn't in the country—"

"Tell her I can come," I say quickly. "I'm on my way."

The doctor laughs. "That's just what I was going to ask you," she says. "Okay, I'm going to give the phone back to Sophie now. We'll be doing weekly monitoring ultrasounds from now on, but otherwise, I want her to stay in bed except to go to the bathroom."

"Oh, darling," I say when Sophie takes the phone. "Oh, honey! What a thing to have happen! Are you just exhausted with relief?"

"Yes," she says in a tiny voice. "You really don't mind coming to take care of me?"

"Oh, no! No! Of course I will. I'll wait on you hand and foot." I walk with the phone into my room and start pulling suitcases from underneath the bed.

"I know you're busy, and this is not okay, but I don't think Whit can leave—he won't leave the project now, but maybe in a few weeks he can get away, so it won't be for very long . . ."

She thinks I'm busy? Has she missed out on the news that I'm currently greatly underutilized? "I'll stay as long as you need me. Don't worry about that." I can bring the Bobo illustrations along with me and finish them there. I tell Sophie I'll pack up and get on the road as soon as possible. I look at my watch. It's about a five-hour drive to New York, and it's already noon. Let's see, I have to talk to Grant, and I should fig-ure out something for him about meals and all. He doesn't cook any-thing but eggs and grilled cheese, and his cholesterol is already high. I'll call my editor from New York, maybe even find a time to go see her while I'm in the city. I can hand-deliver the illustrations. But then my brain gets all caught up with what I need to do at the moment: where is the main suitcase, the one I always use? Is it in the attic?

"Are you going to be all right until I get there?" I ask her. "Can someone come and stay with you?"

"My friend Lori is off on Thursdays, so maybe she can come," she says. Her voice catches.

"Are you really, really okay?" I say to her.

"I guess so. I . . . will be. I don't know. I'm scared, Mommy." It's this *Mommy* that just about kills me. Makes me want to call for a LifeStar helicopter to come and whisk me there in minutes. She never should have stayed in New York alone and pregnant. I should have insisted that she come here while Whit was away, where I could watch her and help her.

"Shhh, shhh," I say. "Don't think about it all right now. One thing at a time. We're going to take this one step-by-step. The thing to do now is to have the hospital call a cab and get yourself home, and then call Lori to come and look after you, and I'll be there just as soon as I can."

"Okay," she says.

In the background, I hear voices indicating that they're moving her out of the examination room—or wherever she is—and readying her to go home in a cab.

"Can't I just stay here until my mom comes?" I hear her say, and I close my eyes.

Someone says something in an overly cheerful voice, and then Sophie says to me, "Okay, Mom, I'll see you at my apartment when you get here." And the phone clicks shut.

I call Grant with the intention of crying and being comforted, but all he says is that he'll assign a writing project to his late class and come on home, and that we can figure out whatever needs to be figured out. This is code for: I am not going to use any words that might let my office mate know what is really going on.

God forbid anyone should know our business.

When he gets home, he does not run over and take me in his arms the way a normal husband would. Instead, he stands there in the bedroom with his hands in his pockets, and does three typical Grant things in a row: clears his throat, blinks rapidly, and paces. Then he says, "Well, it's good you're going," and puts his briefcase down on our bed and picks it up again and sighs while he watches me pack. "I guess that's the right thing to do. I mean, I know it is. It's the answer." His Adam's apple bobs up and down.

"You're upset, I know," I say, and he says quickly, "No, I'm not. I trust the doctors. And Sophie's young. She'll be just fine. It's good you're going."

"Yes," I say. "It is. She can't manage by herself, and she's not sure when Whit can come home and take care of her. Not for a while, at least."

"*That's* the part that gets me. Damn it. Why did that idiot marry her in the first place if he had no intention of being a real husband?" he says. "Who goes to an orphanage in Brazil when he's got his own kid to think of?"

"I know, I know," I say. "He should come home. And for all we know, he's working it out right now."

"There's no working it out to be done," says Grant. "The way you *work it out* is you go get on the fucking plane. Or—oh, I know—you don't go in the first place when you find out your wife is pregnant. How would *that* be?"

Grant has been livid about this from the beginning, but I have surprised myself by actually seeing Whit's point, or glimpses of it at least: this film will be crucial to his career in a field crowded with talented journalists; besides which, he'll be home in time for the birth itself, and, with Sophie insisting loudly and often that she was not bothered by his going, why *wouldn't* he go?

What I had secretly *hoped*, though, was that Sophie would come and spend her pregnancy with us, back at home where we could watch over her. I had it all planned out in my mind, how we'd buy baby things together and talk about pregnancy and motherhood, how it would be a wonderful, joyous, womanly time that we'd always look back on fondly. I'd be there for every little kick and Braxton Hicks, and even more important, I'd get to know her better as the adult woman she is, and she could see me without all that adolescent angst hazing her mind. But no. She decided to remain in the city working through the pregnancy, and I had to hide my disappointment. Grant didn't seem fazed in the least by that part. "Why would she want to come here?" he said. "Her husband is the person she wants right now, not her *parents*."

You see? There is no point on which we agree lately. It's like yelling to somebody across a big divide.

"So how long do you think you'll stay?" he says. "Assuming that husband of hers decides that orphans are his top priority and I have to go kill him."

"Well, who knows? The baby is due in three months, and the doctor told me she had to stay in bed until delivery . . ."

He blinks behind his glasses. "Three months? You're going to be gone three months?"

"*Yes*. Three months."

"Jesus. And we didn't have Wednesday today, did we?"

"No, and we didn't even have it yesterday, when it really was Wednesday. Either in the morning or at night, when you passed up a fabulous opportunity."

He makes a face at me. "I like to keep to a schedule. We should have kept to our schedule."

"Well," I say. "You certainly have a romantic way of putting things."

"That's always been my specialty. And I gotta say, it's worked for me so far. It won me your heart, after all."

"Yeah, well. Luckily you had other charms." I pour my underwear drawer into my suitcase. "Also, you need to be careful with what you eat while I'm gone, okay? You can't just live on grilled cheese sandwiches and potato chips, you know."

He rubs his eyes and says, in a weary, put-upon voice, "I can make other things besides grilled cheese. Eggs, for instance."

"Eggs are also filled with cholesterol. You might have to eat those frozen healthy dinners. Lean Cuisine or something like that. Or— what am I even worried about? I suppose people will invite you over to eat with them once they hear you're all alone."

"Please. Would you stop this? Just stop. I'm not going to go eat at anybody else's house," he says. "God, what a nightmare that would be. Why would you even think I'd do that?"

"No, I suppose you wouldn't. You might be expected to talk, heaven forbid. But you know they're going to invite you."

"I've got to finish my book," he says. "I'm not likely to go looking for company when it's been bad enough with *you* always needing—"

I stop putting things in the suitcase and stare at him.

"No, forget it. I didn't mean that," he says, and laughs. "Oh my God, did I say that aloud?"

"Yes. As a matter of fact, you did. Quite aloud, as a matter of fact."

"Look, Annabelle." He pretends to be beseeching me. "Honey, darling wife. I *need* this time. I'll miss you, but I'm not going to lie to you and say that it's an unmitigated disaster that you're going. It will give me a chance to get this book done, and I won't have to worry constantly that you've gotten your feelings hurt because I'm not noticing that you are the unhappiest person in the whole world or that you're not doing the art you want to be doing, so you're miserable."

"Fuck you, Grant," I say, brushing past him into the bathroom to collect my toiletries.

When I come out, he's back in his office with the door closed. He does not fight. It would violate some sense of propriety that is vital to whatever the hell is at the core of that man. Long-suffering endurance, that's his gig. Waiting things out while the crazy-ass people around him go through their little scenes and dramas.

When I've packed everything I can think of, shoving things into suitcases and slamming drawers, I go to his office door and say, "I'm leaving. You might as well come out and see me off."

He comes out and takes my hands and looks guilty. "We shouldn't be mad when we say good-bye," he says.

I just want to be out of there. I look down at my shoes.

"Come on," he says. "Let's put all this aside and let our last few minutes be pleasant. Do you need me to say I'm sorry? Because I am sorry."

I sigh.

"Maybe you need me to get down on my knees and beg you for forgiveness. Is that what it's going to take?" He sees my expression and gets down on his knees on the carpet and takes my hands and closes his eyes. "Oh, please baby please, please baby please, don't go away mad."

"Just get up," I say. "You're not taking anything seriously."

"I am. I swear I am. Just tell me my crimes. I'm guilty as hell. I'll sign anything you got. It was a terrible thing to say. I don't want you to go. I really and truly don't." He takes me into his arms, mashing my face against his sweater. Then he laughs and squeezes me tighter. "I just want to write my book. Oh God, I just want to write this book. So much I want to write this book."

"Fine," I say. "Will you help me take my suitcases out to the car?"

"Anything! Just stop giving me the stink eye."

I go upstairs and get the illustrations out of my study to take along. Then I gather my coat and scarf and gloves while he hauls the suitcases out of the bedroom. When we get down to the car, the wind kicks up, and we don't seem to be able to think of how to say good-bye.

"So," he says. "I guess this is it for a while. Drive carefully, and call me when—"

"Grant, stop it. Look at me. Just look. Don't you even know that everything is wrong?"

He rolls his eyes. "What? *Why*, Annabelle? Why does everything have to be wrong?"

"Because you don't really even see me anymore, and it makes me sad. You just don't."

Now with the loud sigh. "For God's sake, Annabelle. How can you say that? I see you. I love you."

"But you don't love me passionately."

He gives another sigh, even more weary, this one meant as a warning. "Why do you need to do this right now? Of course I love you. What do you want? We've been married for twenty-eight years. Wait. Is this because we didn't have our usual Wednesday? It is, isn't it?"

"No!" I hit him in the arm. "God damn it, how can you think that? That *usual* Wednesday is all part of the problem!"

He looks blank.

"Nobody has to schedule passion!" I fold my arms. "Did you even know that? Nobody but you would even think of that. You're so bound up, so tied to your work that you don't even see me! You don't care about my feelings!"

He closes his eyes. "Why are you doing this? Why can't you let things sort themselves out before you make all these sweeping statements? Why do you have to see things so globally? That's the trouble here. You—"

"What evidence is there that you love me passionately, Grant McKay?" I say. I can't stop myself. "Come on. What *evidence* is there? And don't you dare say our Wednesday morning *appointment* for sex. Don't you dare."

"Good God. What is this? What's with you?"

"Tell me one other piece of evidence. Before I go away for three months, tell me one other piece of evidence."

"What? Are you sixteen or something? This is ridiculous."

I just keep staring at him. I adjust my purse to my other arm, signaling that I'm here for the long haul. He has to think of something.

"Well, I want you to drive carefully," he says after a while. He smiles at me. "And also I won't eat butter while you're gone."

"Great. You don't want me to die. And you don't want to die of a stroke. That's good. That's real evidence. Thank you so much for that."

"Look, Annabelle. I do love you, and you know it," he says. "But I don't like to be pushed this way. This isn't ever a good way, you know that. We know each other too well for this."

He gives me one of his ominous, meaningful looks over the top of his glasses, and suddenly I have an almost uncontrollable urge to just fling Jeremiah's name into the air. I can picture how it would happen, this unthinkable thing. I would lean toward him. "Jeremiah," I would say in a whisper, feeling the name roll around on my tongue, filling my mouth. "Jeremiah." I might say it again, for effect. Then how would I stop myself? *Jeremiah, Jeremiah, Jeremiah, Jeremiah.* I'd fill up the whole winter afternoon with it. The whole world would reverberate with the sound of it.

But *then* what would happen? I have this moment to weigh it carefully. Would Grant turn pale, tighten his mouth, and then swallow whatever anger he felt—or would he blow up at me, hurling all the suppressed anger of twenty-eight years? And would that really be it, the end of everything, the way he once said it would be? The day we agreed. *We won't speak of him. It didn't happen.*

We stand there, looking at each other. I am trembling with the feeling of the name rising up in the back of my throat. It's almost like nausea, this name . . . but then, what the hell am I thinking, even contemplating setting this fire when I am going away for three months? I finally say, "I have to go."

"Well," he says, and he licks his lips and looks right at me, and there's a glimmer of the old Grant behind his eyes. He puts his hands in his pockets. "Listen. Drive carefully," he says. "You've got to get on the road, and nothing is going to get solved between us today. I'll call you later."

And that's it. He just turns away and goes back into the house without looking back. Without looking back! How can you not look back when your wife has just accused you of not loving her enough? I get into our old Volvo station wagon—the symbol of our family life and everything that's gone—and slam the door as hard as I can, and then I can't resist burning a little rubber on my way out of the driveway, which is not so easy to do when there's a little bit of snow on the ground. You have to really work at it, but I'm up for the challenge.

[six]

1977

The first good thing about getting engaged was that I discovered I still had the power to shock my mother, who seemed to be making it her life's goal to go around shocking everybody else. We were back in the Orgasm Diner when I told her, and at first she just stared at me, and then she started fanning herself with the large maroon menu and laughing and clutching her chest and rolling her eyes. I waited. Then she leaned forward, narrowed her eyes, and said, "So tell me: are you just trying to act out some latent teenage rebellion against me? Why would you ever do this to yourself?"

"I happen to be in love," I told her.

She stirred her coffee without looking at me. Then she said, "May I offer an alternative plan for your consideration?"

I sighed and scratched at a scab on my elbow, which she took to mean, "Oh yes, Mother, please tell me an alternative plan to getting married to the man I love."

She said, "I think you should live with me for a while and work until we can both earn enough money to send you back to college. I see that I've made a mistake not having you live with me instead of being chief cook and bottle-washer for your father and brother. That would be enough to make anyone rush into a premature marriage."

"That is not it at all."

"You and I could join forces, you know. We'll both work and do art together. I'll make jewelry and you can help, and we'll go around to swap meets and crafts shows. And when we have enough money, we won't have to depend upon some man to—"

"How could that ever work? You live in one room, and you have a guy who comes to sleep over. How can you even think that I should live there, too? It would be awful."

She laughed. "Well, we'd have to find a bigger place, of course. But we could do that."

The waitress came over to the table. "I'll have a chef's salad," I said. My mother ordered a hamburger and fries, and then as soon as the waitress left, she started talking about empowerment again, and a meeting she'd gone to where the women had all vowed to support the sisterhood. And that led to her telling me about a woman who had a crush on Dmitri and how hard this was for my mother, who was, of course, his girlfriend. How could my *mother* be any guy's *girlfriend*?

She didn't seem to notice that I'd gone catatonic as a way of discouraging her from speaking. She kept drawing little circles in the puddle left by her water glass, and staring down at the table. "You know, it's *good*, really, to explore all of society's expectations about relationships. I mean, I was certainly not put on this earth to make Dmitri happy, nor he to make me happy. So if we find something good between us, then it doesn't make any sense to insist that we *always* have to do it. You see, that's what kills love—those expectations."

She looked at me, and I was obviously supposed to say something, so I nodded.

"You know what Dmitri told me? He said love is like a butterfly—"

"I know. And if you try to hold on to it, then you squash it," I said in my most bored tone of voice.

She looked surprised. "Yes! That's what he said. You already knew that. It's so . . . interesting to see things that way, isn't it? Really opens your eyes."

I nodded and waited a few beats. Then I said, "So. Just to recap, I'm in love, I'm getting married, and I'm moving to New York."

She looked at me. "Now *who* is this boy again?" she said. "Is this that Jay somebody? The sexy one?"

I gave her the rundown on the facts: he was *not* Jay, he was *Grant McKay,* and he was twenty-five and a labor historian, born and raised in New Hampshire, *normal* parents (here I gave her a pointed look), a farmer's kid, responsible, genuine, met him at school, new job at Columbia, loves me, I love him. What else?

"Is he a Republican at least?" she said.

"No, and neither am I."

"Well, that's too bad. That means he won't be making any money. Democrats don't care about money."

"Mom, Daddy's the only real Republican in the family. You're basically a Democrat, too, and you know it. You just don't want to admit it. You're even in favor of legalizing drugs."

She fixed one of her stares on me. "What I want to know is why you can't just sleep with him for a while until you get him out of your system. I don't see why you think you have to get married. You're not nearly old enough. Hell, *I'm* not old enough."

"Because I want to get married to him. And he asked me. He wants to get married before he moves to New York."

"Well, sure *he* does. But what is the possible advantage to you? Do you know that statistically, when a couple divorces, except for the financial problems women typically experience, a woman *thrives* emotionally and moves on with her life, while men just crumble up into a mess? Do you know what that says?"

"I'm not going to get divorced from him."

"Oh, hell. How do you know that? You can't know that. Fifty percent of marriages end in divorce. Look at me!"

"But I'm not you." I looked at her coolly. "And anyway, you and Dad are both doing fine now. You both got over this whole breakup thing in record time."

She laughed. "Yeah, because he found some other woman who'll completely submerge her life in his."

"This has nothing to do with me."

"Well, it should. If you love Grant, don't get oppressed by him. Just enjoy him for who he is, and then when you've had enough, you can walk away."

"I don't want to walk away," I told her. "Just because you made a big mistake doesn't mean I'm making one, too. This is it for me."

"Think of it. The rest of your life," she said. "Married to this guy."

"Mom, it's going to be fine."

"Is he good in bed, at least?"

"He's fine."

"Do *not* settle for fine."

"What do you want me to say? Okay, he's stupendous. He's a physical gymnast, he was the secret ghostwriter of *The Joy of Sex,* and women everywhere are jealous of me for landing such a stud muffin and sex machine."

She laughed. At least she had the grace to laugh. But then she looked off into the distance and bit her lip. "Oh, you poor, poor deluded baby."

DESPITE HER protests about my getting married, my mother still insisted on putting together a wedding with as much fanfare as a person could gather in a month's time. It was as though in her mind the *wedding* was something separate from the act of marriage, and she was programmed to do it up just right, in a certain way. A church, a bouquet, a white dress, something old and new and borrowed and blue, the whole bit. I drew the line at bridesmaids and ushers and also at the idea that I was to wear her Empire-waisted wedding dress, which she'd kept under her bed all these many years, but I was powerless against the Edie Bennett machine once it was rolling and insisting on a rented hall, pleated pink napkins, and white doves released during the ceremony. Oh, and shrimp-wrapped-in-bacon appetizers, served to the guests by young women carrying trays and wearing flowered sundresses. I invited Magda to be the best woman—I refused to call her the maid of honor—and even though she was blown away by the idea of my getting married when we were both far too young, as she put it, she agreed to come as long as she didn't have to wear a dress with a back bow and matching shoes.

I heard my mother telling her friends on the phone that it was hilarious that while most people's kids *refused* to get married anymore—they were all shacking up with each other—*she*, discovering in herself all the elements of new radicalism, instead had to contend with a daughter who *insisted* on getting married.

Despite this, she told my father that we had to work on family togetherness. This was a time to come together for my sake. All three of my surviving grandparents were coming from across the country, and they were to remain secure in their belief that my parents were still living together. Why hurt the innocent, after all?

"This seems to come from a primitive place in her brain," I explained to Grant. I was standing on his feet, and we were swaying together. "The tribal wedding lobe, up there near the frontal lobe, I think. She actually wants to invite all the uncles and aunts and all her friends and everybody I went to high school with. And she wants ice swans."

He wrinkled his nose and leaned down to kiss me. "Can't we just elope? No fanfare."

"Apparently that would be unforgivable."

He grimaced. "Well, then count me in. I don't want to do anything unforgivable right off the bat."

I wasn't completely sure he was going to be able to stand up to the whole Southern California social experience. He might as well have come from another planet. Even my parents were charmed by him in a sociological kind of way—a genuine New Englander flailing around in our brutal celebrity sun culture, the land of swimming pools, adultery, and divorce. It was as if a Puritan had fallen out of the smoggy sky and landed there, charming them with his quaint ways. My father flung his arm around Grant's shoulder and took him to meet his

bookie and all the guys at the convenience store, sort of a baffling introduction to what men needed to know to thrive in our world. My
mother, who was hanging around the house more and more, introduced him to homemade tacos and burritos and then sat up late,
soulfully discussing his parents' staid and faithful marriage with him
far into the night, and ended up weeping over the fact that she had
never had the opportunity to be supported by such a steady, church-
going, God-fearing community.

"Do you know what a difference that would have made? To have
had that kind of centeredness?" she said, and, watching her dab
her eyes with a tissue as Grant melted, I had to get up and exit the
discussion.

Then, two weeks before the wedding, without any warning at all,
she moved back home. At first she told me it was only because all the
grandparents were coming, as well as Grant's married and stable parents, and she needed to make our lives look a little less haphazard.
She needed to create a united front, make a good impression, she
said.

I was relieved. I didn't want us to come off looking as unraveled as
we were. I didn't know Grant's parents since there hadn't been time
for us to go to New Hampshire to introduce me, but it was unthinkable that his mother had ever gone to meetings to publicly look at her
lady parts. My mother moved into my bedroom and declared we were
like girlfriends having sleepovers. At night, in the dark, she told me
she was disappointed with Dmitri after all, and that her theory was
that a person's wedding set the tone for the entire marriage, and
maybe that's why she and my father hadn't been as happy as they'd
deserved to be: their wedding had been a quick ceremony at the jus-
tice of the peace because nobody had enough money to make a big
wedding. What did I think of that theory, hmm? That's why she was
personally making sure that *my* wedding would not be to blame if my
marriage didn't make it. This was practically a scientific experiment,
to see if a perfect wedding would lead to a perfect marriage.

Truthfully, all this prenuptial stuff was beginning to feel a little show-offy and over the top. Much to David's and my amusement, Edie had turned the dining room into a wedding headquarters, managing the nuptials like a business enterprise, shuffling piles of folders and papers, invitations, placards, and RSVP lists. She barked orders into the phone, yelling at florists and photographers and people who rented folding tables. The wedding presents arrived daily by mail, and were opened, catalogued, and then piled along the walls and under the table, awaiting their thank-you notes.

Living at home was really all for show, she had said gaily when she moved back in, but then we all noticed that it wasn't. She and my father, who had been chilly to each other at first, began spending more and more time together. Soon she was cooking dinner as she always had, and bringing my father drinks while he was skimming the leaves out of the pool. The woman across the street stopped issuing hot-tub invitations. There was no word from the mysterious Dmitri. After a few days, my mother said it was too cramped living with me in my bedroom, and she complained that I came to bed too late and then made noises in my sleep and got up to use the bathroom too much, so she might as well just move back into the master bedroom. Just to make things simple, she said. Besides, she didn't want *her* mother to be suspicious when everybody came to town.

By the time all the grandparents arrived for the nuptials, along with Mr. and Mrs. McKay from New Hampshire, my parents could have gotten an Academy Award in the category of Impersonating a Happily Married Couple. David and I were fascinated.

"Edie and Howard have now reached the limit, the absolute limit. This is *it*. The limit has been reached," I said to him one evening.

"And then some," he agreed, and we both started laughing. We were indulging in what we were calling the "Last Brother and Sister Reefer Smoke Fest" out by the pool. David had been pressed into service as the best man since Grant's friends from home couldn't make the trip, and so the two of them had spent a certain amount of time together. Being measured for the tuxes, for instance. David called Grant the nicest guy he'd ever met in his whole life and then he said, "But do you think he even has one fraction of a clue?" and we laughed.

"I'll bet you can get him to turn his life around and start smoking dope with you," he said.

"Oh, no, no, I'm quitting," I said. "This is it for me."

"Get out! You are not."

"No, I am. I don't really care about this."

"You're crazy. You won't be able to quit."

"Watch me. Last inhale. Here goes."

He shook his head. "Okay. If you say so."

"You could stand to cut back, too, you know."

"To each his own."

"David," I said.

"What?"

I told him I loved him. What I meant to tell him was that those nights out by the pool with him had been the best. And that Grant and I would always love to have him come to New York to visit. "Just because I'm getting married doesn't mean you and I can't keep in touch," I said.

And so, on the hot and gusty evening of August 7, with the Santa Ana winds blowing the palm trees all around and kicking up little dust eddies in the street, the wedding took place in a small stone church on Reseda Boulevard. The bougainvillea and oleander were in riotous bloom outside the church. I marched down the aisle, holding on to my father's arm, and in front of everybody, a clergyman said to Grant, "Do you take this woman . . . ?" and my brain just went on the fritz right then. Woman? Was he possibly referring to *me*? I almost couldn't remember anything else about the ceremony, except that I promised a whole bunch of things, and Grant stood there blinking and blinking and promised a whole bunch of things back, and people threw rice at us, and then we released two doves, which flew in opposite directions.

Later we danced and got drunk and Magda and my brother made toasts to us.

The next day we left to drive the three thousand miles to New York City, to begin our new life as married, upstanding, fully functional adults, inspired by the example of our four seemingly happily married parents, who stood in the street jumping up and down and flapping their arms and waving us off, screaming, "Good-bye! Good luck!"

When my mother hugged me good-bye, she whispered, "I'm sorry about all the mistakes I've made, and I just want to say that I think Grant is a wonderful guy. But promise me that you'll stay true to yourself, even though you're married. It's not easy to do, but you have to try. Promise?"

I was getting pretty good at making promises that day, so I said yes to this one, too, and then felt my throat constrict and my eyes turn to liquid. My mother's eyes filled up, and she shook her head and placed her fingers on my lips. "No, no, no, don't cry now. You're going to be okay," she whispered. "I know you will. Just take care of *you*. Take care of Annabelle."

By the time I joined Grant in the U-Haul truck, my throat hurt so much from unshed tears that I felt as though I'd swallowed glass, and I already missed my mother so much that I couldn't breathe.

[seven]

*Y*ou forget how small a New York apartment can be. Sophie and Whit—well, not Whit so much these days, but *Sophie* lives in an apartment on Twenty-second Street, a beautiful place owned by Whit's father, who is so wealthy and generous that he charges them nothing to live there. It has trees outside and an exposed brick wall inside, a black wrought-iron fence, a hedge (which now is merely sticks, of course), and an elevator that can make you remember all the upsetting things you ever learned about the law of gravity as it lurches and moans while hauling you up to the fourth floor.

But once you get there, you have a newfound gratitude for life, as Sophie once pointed out. You step out of the wire cage and you feel like kissing the carpet.

I get to New York City at about ten that night, and amazingly enough, find a parking spot right on her street, which, unlike New Hampshire roads these days, is not filled with snow. In fact, the air feels almost balmy in comparison. I step out of the car and for a moment feel I've been transported back in time. We didn't live specifically here, Grant and I, not in this neighborhood, but there's a way in which all of New York is alike when compared with, say, New Hampshire.

Sophie's friend from downstairs, Lori, buzzes me in, but Sophie comes running out from her bedroom and we stand there in the hall even though she should be in bed every single minute. I can't stop hugging her. I had told myself I wouldn't cry, but when I see her huge gray eyes filling with tears at the sight of me, I feel my eyes tearing up, too. We both dissolve into blubbering pitiable wrecks.

"Oh my God, today was so hard—I'm so glad to be here!" I say into her shoulder, and she clutches me and says, "Oh, Mom, I'm so glad you're here. Thank you, *thank you* for coming to me."

Is there anything more heart-wrenching than having your child weeping and thanking you for doing the very thing that you *should* do and want to be doing?

Lori smiles at us and pats us both, tells us to call her if we need anything, and then she slips out in the hallway with us both hollering thank-you's after her. We are giddy with thank-you's.

I stand back and get a good look at Sophie. Frankly, she looks as pale as I've ever seen a human being look, and besides that, she looks like a waif. This is perhaps because she's wearing a big sweatshirt of Whit's ("for luck, and so the baby will know him by osmosis, maybe") and flowered pajama pants and big fluffy bunny slippers, and her blond hair is tied back in a ponytail. She's such a combination of Grant and me; she's tall and willowy the way he is, and she has my round face and big eyes but his coloring.

"Hey, let's get you back in that bed," I say. "Aren't you supposed to be there full-time?"

"I know, I know. But I can't stay in bed every single minute, and I just want to make sure you're comfortable. Come on, let's get your coat off. The closet is too full of stuff, so I've been storing coats on the kitchen chair. But if that's too full, you can—"

"I'll figure it out. You go get in your bed," I say, and I take her by the shoulders and steer her back to her room, where her bed is all rumpled and the television set is on. I fluff her pillows and tuck her in, pulling the lavender sheets and comforter up. She looks up and smiles at me, and—I don't know—her eyes are so sad behind her smile that I have to fight the impulse to crawl right in next to her and just hold her for the rest of her pregnancy. Instead I say, "Oh, my! Just *look* at that nice mound of baby you have there. Wow! You've gotten so much bigger since Christmas. You look like a *real* pregnant person now."

"Yeah, try telling my body that."

"What are you talking about? Your body knows that. Your body is doing exactly what it's supposed to do."

"Mom, I know you're trying to make me feel better, and that's very nice of you. It's in your job description as mom. But it's very obvious that my body has no freaking idea what it's supposed to be doing, or otherwise it wouldn't be trying to kick this baby out of me."

"Kick the baby out of you? That is not what is going on. The placenta, which does not have a brain after all, just lost its sense of direction and got started in the wrong place. You're going to be fine."

"Only with medical miracles."

"Well . . . ," I say, and falter. She's looking at me with her chin tilted up just so, and I know she can read the worry on my face. "You have all the help you need. We're going to make sure that if it takes medical miracles, then you shall have them."

I tell her that I'll make us some tea. I'd actually stopped at a health food store in New Hampshire and bought some pregnancy tea, filled with herbs that will help any baby get a good start, I say brightly.

"Even a baby that's getting evicted," she says. "Good luck to it."

I smile and pat her belly and then escape to what passes for a kitchen in this tiny apartment. The kitchen is really just one wall of the living room, which is two steps past the postage stamp–size bathroom and approximately ten steps of hallway from Sophie and Whit's room. It's an ingenious use of space, actually; everything necessary to life is arranged on various shelves that line the exposed brick wall. The bowls are stacked on top of the dinner plates; the flatware drawer is designed to be a cutting board, too; the twenty-four-inch kitchen table is also Sophie's desk, and holds her laptop and a couple of file folders. Cookbooks, photo albums, towels, bed linens, unopened bars of soap—all these are luxury items that have had to be stored in decorative crates around and under the shelves and tables. It's like a

Chinese puzzle, Grant said: each thing has to nest into something else, or serve at least two purposes. Even the couch can become a double bed, which Grant and I slept in the last time we were here—when we brought Sophie back after Christmas—and as I recall, one has to be careful to keep one's toes out of the fireplace. I sigh, looking around the living room, marveling. How is it possible to downsize a life to the point where bringing home an additional box of tea bags can tip the kitchen into chaos? And yet I had lived this way myself for years in New York. So what was I thinking, bringing two suitcases? Where can I possibly put my things? And where in the world do they intend to put the baby's stuff, the diapers and paraphernalia—in the fireplace? We'll have to get to that.

While I'm waiting for the water to boil, I go into the bathroom, pee and splash water on my face. I can hear Sophie's cell phone ringing, and I stop and listen to her talking. It's obviously Grant. She's telling him I just got in, I'm in the bathroom, would he like to speak to me? No? Okay. Yeah, everything seems fine. Yeah, she's going to take it easy. Yes, she talked to Whit. He's upset. No, he probably can't come home just yet. Waiting and seeing. Okay, love you lots. Good-bye.

After I'm sure she's done with him, I open the door, and she calls to me. "That was Daddy on the phone. He said to tell you that you can call him back if you have anything you want to say. Otherwise, he's going to bed soon."

"No, I don't have anything in particular," I call back to her, in as even a tone as I can manage. This, of course, is an act of war from Grant, calling her cell phone instead of mine. Well, fine. If he wants to play the silent game, I'm all for it. It's much easier to deal with a marital standoff from five hours away. *Bring it on, baby.*

I make us tea and toast, and when I come back to the bedroom, chattering about how raspberry-leaf tea is supposed to be just the thing for pregnant women, Sophie is sitting on the bed looking big-eyed and frightened. She looks exactly like she did on her first day of kindergarten when she got mixed up and missed the school bus home, and she was sure they were going to kick her out of school for being too much of a baby to follow directions. By the time I had gotten to the school to pick her up, she'd been holding herself rigidly together for so long that at the sight of me, she burst into loud sobs, much to the mystification of the kindly principal, who had been standing there telling me how brave Sophie was.

"What? What is it?" I say. I put down the cookie sheet that's doubling as a tray for the tea.

For a moment she can't even speak. I sit down and rock her against me and make soothing noises, just the way I did back then, and finally she says, "Ohhh, Mo-ommm, I-I'm so scared."

"It's okay, it's going to be okay."

She can barely get words out she's crying so hard. I hold her and pat her back like I did when she was a little girl. "I didn't feel this scared until, until you came—bu-but now that you're really here, I know a really, really bad thing must be happening for you to come all this way."

"No, no. It's not so bad. You're going to be fine. I'm here just to keep you company while you stay in bed."

"*Mom.* You know it's not fine. The *baby* might not be fine."

"The baby is going to be perfect. You'll see. Now, come on, why don't you take a sip of this pregnancy tea I brought you? Raspberry leaves are—"

"How can you *say* that? What if everything goes wrong? What if my body doesn't know how to do this?" She blows her nose and throws a Kleenex on a huge pile of used ones.

"Listen," I say. "Your body knows how to do this. It's nature. And this happens sometimes, with the placenta. But the baby is fine. The doctors wouldn't have let you come home if they thought that baby was in any danger at all." I stroke her hair.

She sniffles and looks at me with her big eyes. *Go on.*

So I think of more stuff to say. "I think that this time, now, is the very worst of it, because of the uncertainty. But you know what?

Here's something my mother used to tell me when I would worry, and it really helped me. She'd say that no matter what happened—no matter how scared I got—we'd always be okay because we'd face it together. You won't have to be by yourself. Ever."

She buries her head. "This has been the most terrible time!"

"I know it has."

"No, not just this. Everything. The whole pregnancy. Ever since Christmas . . . when I came back . . . all I do is just cry and cry. And—and sometimes when I'm going to work or when I'm coming home, I think I can't breathe. The other day on the subway I had to sit down and put my head between my knees because I thought my heart was beating so hard that I was going to pass out."

"Oh, baby. That's an anxiety attack. You should have let me know."

"And at work, all the women in the office go out for drinks at night and have di-dinner together, but I never go. I *can't*. And I just don't know people who are like me. I've always had, like, a million friends, and now nobody even talks to me! Nobody my age is having a kid, just really older people are pregnant, even at the OB appointments, they're all in their *thirties,* and they all have husbands and nannies and . . . all I do is just come home every day all by myself. And Whit is so far away, and he doesn't get it." She throws herself down on the pillows, really wailing now. "I have *nobody,* and he doesn't even care!"

"He just doesn't understand," I say. "He cares, I'm sure, but he doesn't know what it's like. Even I didn't know you were having such a hard time. You hide it so well, darling. You seem so competent all the time."

"But I'm *not* competent! Maybe I used to be competent, but now I'm a stupid crybaby—and I'm all alone and my husband doesn't even love me enough to know he's supposed to be here with me!"

"He *does* love you—you told him that it was fine with you for him to stay away," I say, and she practically screams, *"I'm supposed to have to tell him I need him? He doesn't just know that? I'm carrying his child!"*

I can't think of anything to say, anything that would help. I love her, I adore her, but she's so different from the way I was at her age. What do you say to someone who's never really been disappointed by life before, who has always gotten all she wanted so easily?

She was at the center of everything back in high school: captain and top scorer of the field hockey team, the lead in the school plays; she ran the student government and made the honor roll every single semester. Even more important, she was always surrounded by people who wanted to be around her. She was almost never alone. It strikes me now that she didn't know how to be.

After high school, she didn't want to stay local and go to college near home, which surprised me a little. I suppose I shouldn't have been shocked. She was a college professor's daughter, after all, and Grant had been talking to her about the need to get as far as she could in her career. She picked Brown University, majored in communications, and despite my misgivings, did perfectly well away from home. I remember Grant shaking his head and chuckling as he said to me, "Of *course* she had to leave—to spread that Sophie magic around the region. New Hampshire had its turn with her for eighteen years, so it was only fair to give Rhode Island its chance."

We were the helplessly proud but humble parents, beaming when, alone in our bedroom at night, the pillow talk turned to our children's accomplishments. Sure, there were Sophie's successes, but also Nicky was showing himself to be quite a sportsman, if not the scholar she was—and I remember how it would sometimes feel like we were so lucky that our DNA, mingled together, had done more than either of us could have done separately.

And then, during her senior year, Sophie met Whit. He was from a wealthy family in New York, a film student and photojournalist, the kind of fast-talking, all-balls-in-the-air kind of guy who had so many plans and dreams and ideas it was as though he couldn't hold them all in his head. Grant, with his more plodding, deliberate way of going about life, disliked him almost immediately, but I knew my daughter, and I could tell that Sophie was determined to get this guy, that there was something about his wild-eyed fascination with everything that called to something deep inside her. And almost immediately she did get him. By Christmas of her senior year, they had fallen in love, and he came to stay with us through part of the break, and then she went to New York to meet his family—and then suddenly, by summer they both had managed to get jobs at a magazine in the city.

"Next target: the Big Apple," I said. "Move over, Rhode Island. She's working her way west."

Grant pronounced it a disaster.

"God damn it. She can't go to New York with him. She barely knows him," he said, and he didn't even laugh at the irony of the thing when I reminded him that had been exactly our situation. Hadn't we—I—come from even farther away, from across an even greater cultural divide, to show up in New York back in the seventies?

He just pursed his thin lips and made a weird noise in the back of his throat.

"Hey, don't you think she can hold things together better than *we* did?" I said. "And look at us today—still here!" The only way I knew for sure that Grant had heard me was that he so studiously pretended that he had not. The little vein pulsing madly right at his temple was the only outward sign. I recognized that vein from previous encounters with unpleasant truths.

But then New York wasn't even the worst of what he was asked to accept. Whit wanted to do documentaries, and by the following fall, Sophie told me he had lined up a film crew and equipment and financing and was planning to do a film about an orphanage in Brazil. This was a place his roommate had told him about, a one-of-a-kind institute where volunteers could come and help the third world street children who find their way there, throwaway kids who otherwise would have died on the streets. Whit wanted to do a film about the way this orphanage had changed lives—both those of the kids and of the volunteers from high-income families in the United States who had had their eyes opened to poverty.

And Sophie was going with him. She told us she would write stories about the place and the people, and he would film the journeys of the volunteers and how the experience had changed them. They'd live on the property, writing and filming for at least six months; the directors were psyched about the publicity, and Whit had gotten backing from some real heavy hitters his father knew. Everything was happening fast, things were just falling into place, she said, and from the tone of her voice, I could tell that she was overexcited and scared out of her mind and also that nothing was going to stop this.

"There are way too many exclamation points in all our conversations about this," I told her calmly. "Can't we take it down a couple of notches and just talk about it realistically, problems and all?"

"The only *problem,* if you must know, is that Dad doesn't want me to do it. He's e-mailing me every day telling me that I shouldn't just go along on Whit's trip, that it's not really my project because I didn't think it up, and that I'm getting in way over my head, and I need to think smarter."

I sighed. That was always his mantra for the kids: *Think smarter.* I'd hear him shouting it at them out in the driveway the year he was coaching the basketball team, and then again when he'd review their history assignments with them, or test them on physics questions or algebra equations, or when they were ice-skating on the pond or downhill skiing. *Think smarter.* What the hell does that really mean, anyway? Why is *that* the thing to send children out into the world with? If I were summing up my worldly philosophy in a two-word command, it would most likely be, *Be real.*

Naturally Sophie wanted me to run interference for her and Whit with Grant. As if I could convince him of anything. He and I were already arguing about the trip and what it meant. I accused him of wanting everybody he ever loved to stay in New Hampshire, close by where he could keep an eye on them; he said I saw romance in even the most wrongheaded and dangerous schemes, and that I would think it was equally perfect if Sophie had insisted on signing up for the space program or joining the circus or—or taking a time machine back to the Stone Age. He said she'd never shown the slightest inclination to go make documentary films in Brazil until this guy came along, that it wasn't her project, and that she was just an appendage. Is that what I wished for our daughter's life, that she would become an afterthought or an appendage to some man? And how were we supposed to believe that Whit even knew what he was doing? He was a spoiled rich guy who'd never been told no, and this wasn't even his money he was using—and on and on and on.

And then suddenly one day, in the middle of the fight, he cleared his throat and announced he'd feel better if they at least got married first. It would prove Whit's commitment or something like that. I knew what he was doing: throwing down the gauntlet, putting everything he had on the roulette wheel, sure that Whit and Sophie weren't that serious. I did not approve.

But they said yes. I've often wondered why they listened to him; after all, they were already living together in New York, and they were both old enough to do as they pleased. Sophie told me on the phone one day that her father had been right to insist on this, and that they were going to do it.

"If this is just to get your father's blessing for the trip, you do not have to get married," I whispered into the phone, which was subversive of me, but I thought it needed to be said. "I hate to think of you tying yourself to this guy just because your father says you have to. That is not a good enough reason to start your life together."

I couldn't believe how much I sounded like my mother. Or how much Sophie sounded like me.

"No, no, of course that's not the *only* reason," she said. "God, Mom. It's the reason we're doing it now, but I know we would have eventually gotten married anyway. Besides, I *want* to get married! I think it's a great idea. I want to have a wedding in the backyard under the rose arbor and I want to invite everybody from high school and make it a big party, and I want to wear a dress that has lace and pearls on it and a big veil. Okay? I want a really, really big veil."

And so that's how it happened that we had a big wedding last June—backyard reception, everybody from high school, everybody from *elementary school* even, and a huge white dress with pearls and lace and a big, big veil, father giving her away, flower girls, ring bearer, the whole bit. And if Whit seemed a little less than excited over all the wedding details, if instead he concentrated exclusively on the details of their Brazilian venture and had to be reminded to go out and buy rings and rent a tuxedo and line up a best man—well, I figured it was just the way his personality worked. He was a documentary man and had a lot on his mind, was the way I saw it.

But then—in September, just when we were all used to the idea of the marriage and the trip and the prospect of doing without Sophie for months on end—there was another surprise.

"I don't want you to tell anybody, but I started a baby," she said to me on the phone one day.

"You what? Wait. *You* started it? Did you have Whit's help at least?"

"Well, you wouldn't think so, the way he's acting about it."

Then it hit me. I sometimes have a nine-second delay, like all your better talk shows. "Oh my God. Sophie! You're pregnant?"

"Apparently I am."

"So then this wasn't . . . planned?"

"No, of course it wasn't planned," she said, and laughed. I couldn't get over the laughter. "It was a complete and total failure-of-birth-control surprise."

"But I thought you were on the pill."

"Well, sure, I *was* on the pill, but I was having some side effects, so my doctor said she'd give me a different pill, and then she called the wrong pharmacy for me, only I didn't know, and when I went to my own pharmacy, they didn't know what had happened but they said they could get it, and then I had to work late every night because the magazine was shipping and so I missed, like, just the first week, but I thought it would be all right, but then she said—"

"Sophie. Sophie. It's okay. I get the idea. An administrative failure of birth control."

"And totally not my fault."

"Well . . ."

"Mom! It was not my fault."

Except, darling, that there are other forms of birth control besides the pill. There are condoms, you know. But really—what's the point in lecturing? Instead, I said, "So. What does this mean for the trip?"

"Well, I don't want to go to South America and have a baby there," she said. "At an orphanage? Are you kidding me?"

"And what about Whit? What does he think?"

"Well," she said. "I don't really know yet, because we haven't talked about it. I think maybe he'll want to postpone the trip until next year, and we can take the baby along, too. Then I think it would be fun— living in South America!"

"Are you going to propose that?"

"Propose what?"

"Waiting. For a year."

"I think it would be better if he came up with that idea. Don't you? Since he's the one who hired the crew, he's the one that's going to have to figure out what everybody is doing next year. Don't you think this is enough advance notice that they can change things? I mean, the trip isn't for three months." Then she got quiet for a few long moments. I could hear her sucking in her breath, the gravity of the situation hitting her. Then she said, "If he does have to go, that's perfectly fine, too. I'll be very mature and understanding."

So that's how it happened that she stayed in New York, turning down our offer to come home and wait in New Hampshire for the baby to be born. And that's how Whit took off for South America with his film crew and his father's friends' money, a married man determined to follow his plan despite all the obstacles that had been put in his path.

I don't say this to too many people—especially not the people in my family—but I feel some admiration for a person who can do that, who can be unwavering in the face of plans changing and people screaming and crying and threatening and acting as though everything has gone totally to hell.

And then I remember that it's my daughter he's disappointing, and I feel a little less sure.

SOPHIE AND I snuggle down under the covers and watch the last hour of *Sleepless in Seattle,* and then later we're hungry so I get up and make us some soup and more tea. I've no sooner gotten in bed than my cell phone rings, and it's Nicky with, "Hey, Mamalu. I just called home and Dad told me you're with Sophie. He said there's some kind of emergency. What's going on?"

I fill him in, and he says, "So why isn't Whit going to come back and take care of her?"

"He will when he can," I say, and Sophie looks at me.

"Dad's really pissed at him, you know." He's eating something crunchy while he talks, as usual. "I think he'd like to put a contract out on him."

"It's going to be fine," I say. "Nobody's going to put a contract out on anybody."

"Yeah, well, he's in some kind of sucky mood. I told him about the hiking I'm doing this weekend up in the White Mountains, and he said he doesn't want me to go—get this—because he can't have two children in mortal danger, especially when you're not even there to do half the worrying for him. So what's up with that? I can't live my life because Sophie's baby is giving her trouble?"

"Oh, Nicky. Just cut your father some slack. He's working on his book and he's crabby right now."

"Yeah, he's like, 'Why is it always about life and death with you?' He has no trust in me, Mom. He thinks I don't have any sense."

"He knows you have sense."

"That's what he *said*. I'm just going by what he told me. I'm supposed to sit in my dorm room until this baby gets born, apparently. Maybe I shouldn't even eat these pretzels, 'cause you know, what if I choke on them, and then Dad would have a tough time."

"Nicholas, let me just ask you something. Does everything have to be right on the edge for you? Could you maybe just do some winter hiking that doesn't involve ice and mountain peaks and going out all alone to prove you can do it? Just for a bit?"

"I wasn't going to be all alone anyway. Christ! What do you people take me for?"

"You forget that we've known you your whole life."

"I think this is displaced anger because Whit won't come home."

"Displaced anger?" I can't help but laugh. "Where did you get that from?"

"Psychology class. I *do* learn stuff here, you know."

"I know you do. Listen," I tell him. "I've gotta go help Sophie. You take care of yourself and try not to slip through the ice, okay?"

"You either," he says.

AT SOPHIE'S insistence, I sleep in her bed next to her that first night instead of going to the living room ten steps away, but truthfully, I'm glad because it turns out that once the lights are off, I discover that I need to watch her every second. I don't get much sleep at all; the radiators, controlled by some mysterious cold-blooded building superintendent who must think everybody is freezing, keep letting out blasts of suffocating heat and then making high-pitched clanging sounds, like Chinese gongs at the new year. The bed is small and hard and unfamiliar, and a slice of bright light from the street falls right across my face. But mainly I stay awake because I can't seem to stop my mind from racing, and besides that, I just need to stare at Sophie's face, which is as white as the moon, with dark smudges under her eyes. Even in sleep, she looks worn out. How can you be both tired *and* asleep? At one point I get so neurotic that I reach over and take her pulse while she sleeps, just for information's sake.

I wish I knew how much blood she really lost, and how exactly she's supposed to make more to replace it. And, even more important, if anyone is really doing anything to make sure that baby stays in its place. All those brave things I said to her: does she suspect that I don't know what I'm talking about? The doctor had sounded so confident—but of course, it isn't *her* daughter who might yet lose her baby.

Oh, this is not a good path to be going down, but I have no way of stopping myself once I'm on it. I feel like getting out of bed and going into the hallway and calling up Grant. This is just the kind of situation he's so good at identifying as nonsense. But I can't call Grant now. I'm mad at him, and besides that, I realize with a pang, there's nothing he could say that would make me feel better.

So it seems like I spend the whole night alternately half dozing and staring at Sophie, and I get startled and anxious whenever she turns over in bed. I'm almost relieved when the first gray light comes around the shades and it means I can unkink myself and get up and start the day. But naturally as soon as I realize I could get up, I fall into a deep, overheated sleep where there are bad dreams waiting for me. First I've run away from home, and there is blood and a car and a baby crying somewhere in the distance and a whole bunch of ominous things that I can't remember, bells ringing and alarms going off and a woman shouting. And when my eyes fly open, it's eight thirty and Sophie is the woman who's shouting. She's talking on her cell phone, pacing back and forth, and she's furious.

"No. It's not like that at all! . . . No, I have to stay *in the bed the whole time.* Yeah, like until May. . . . Yeah, *you* think it's easy. You just try it." She looks up at the ceiling and blinks rapidly and then she slumps down onto the floor and sits there leaning against the doorjamb, not facing me. When she speaks again, her voice is no longer angry, but it's sullen. "Yeah, it's great she's here. *Somebody* needed to come take care of me, that's for sure. . . . So how much longer do you think? . . . Good God, Whit. Not even if it's an emergency? Well, yeah, she's staying as long as she needs to. She's my mom! . . . Okay. No, I know. I know. I will. All right. Yeah, you, too. Bye."

She slams the phone shut, bursts into sobs, and comes over and throws herself on the bed. "I hate him! I hate him! I hate him!"

I scoot over and hand her a tissue, and she blows her nose and puts her head in her hands, still sniffling.

"Poor Sophie. It's very hard," I say.

"He's a fucking idiot. Dad called it right. Whit cares more about his stupid documentary and those stupid orphans than he cares about me and his own baby. Do you know what he said to me just now? Can you fucking believe this? He said I should keep my chin up. My chin up! Is that something that a sane man would say to his wife who is *bleeding* and might lose their baby? 'Keep your chin up'?"

"I know, I know. But, Sophie, so often men don't know what to say. Women have been complaining about this for years. It may now be a national epidemic."

"Well, *that's* the understatement of the year! He *never* knows what to say! He's a fucking spoiled rich guy who's always gotten what he wants, and he's never had to care about anybody else before! He's emotionally stunted, is what he is! And oh, lucky me! I married him!"

"Sophie, honey, you—"

"Look," she says, and turns on me then. "You are married to a saint, to somebody who knows what it means to love somebody. So nothing you can say right now is going to help me because you don't know what it's like to have to talk a man into caring about you. Daddy never would have left you when you were pregnant! He *never* would, and you know it."

"Sophie—"

"He stuck right there by you the whole time you were pregnant, didn't he? I bet when you had morning sickness, he would even hold your hair back for you when you barfed. You know what he told me? He said that when you were pregnant with me, you craved Hershey bars with almonds, and that he'd get up and go out every night and get you some because no matter how many he bought the night before, you'd find them and eat them all and then want more. And he didn't even mind doing it. He was laughing when he told me about it, like it was just the cutest thing about you. *He* wouldn't have taken any amount of money to go away and leave you then! He just wouldn't have."

He did do that, bought me Hershey bars with almonds and sat with me when I was sick. But he wouldn't do that now. The years Sophie remembers are from when he was all about the family, when we were the highest priority. It seems like a fairy tale now. I look over at her, see how angry and puffed up her face is. Maybe I should tell her that now I couldn't get her father's attention if I dyed my hair purple and streaked through the house naked, and that all he seems to want from me lately is precious silence so he can do his work. She wouldn't believe how many nights I take food up to his study and then go back downstairs and eat alone. Or how it's even worse when we sit in silence together at that big old dining room table.

"I will never, ever get over this," she says to me. "What he's doing to me."

"Well," I hear myself saying lightly, "you might be surprised at what you can forgive and get over. Marriage is a long road, and along the way there are lots of things—"

"No, Mom, *no*. You don't have any right to compare anything that has happened in your marriage with *this*. You just don't. So don't even try. You managed to marry the best, most committed guy in the universe." She starts to cry and laugh at the same time. "Dad is so committed, he's even boring. Maybe the most committed, boring person on the earth. But somehow even though you were so young, you knew that was going to be a good combination. How did you *know*? Just tell me that."

1977

I knew within four days of the wedding that I had made a terrible, awful, horrible mistake in marrying Grant.

It had seemed a good idea to have our trip across the country serve as our honeymoon. After all, he said, what could be more romantic than being alone together in the cab of a U-Haul truck, our wedding presents stacked in cardboard boxes behind us as we camped our way across America on our way to begin our new life? But here is what I learned the first week after the wedding: I'd married a control freak. A nose-drops-dependent, sniffling, geeky, *miserly* control freak.

First of all, there was the matter of the rental truck. *He* had to be the driver at all times; whenever I was at the wheel, he hissed and sucked in his breath. All these histrionics, despite the fact that I was an exemplary driver. And then the entertainment factor: he only listened to talk radio. All talk, all the time. Country music, the staple of the stations dotting the huge middle of the United States, made him ill. He couldn't tolerate any static whatsoever from the radio; he got headaches. And when we'd stop for breakfast or lunch, he didn't—or wouldn't—ever engage waitresses in conversation, even those super-friendly midwestern ones who called him "hon" and tried to flatter him into chatting. He would just sit there blinking uncomfortably, looking pained as I talked to people, trying to make it seem like we were just any ordinary, happily married pair of newlyweds trekking our way to New York City.

And then there were the accommodations. We'd decided to camp rather than waste our wedding money on hotels. We'd need all the money we could save once we got to New York before I found work. I was fine with this, picturing us pitching our tent by lakes and in forests, staring into the campfire at night before falling asleep in each other's arms. But apparently, Grant had some kind of safety fetish and could only consider staying at AAA-approved, concrete campgrounds—the non-woodsy kind with chain-link fences, on-site managers, and rec rooms (although naturally he wouldn't set foot in an actual rec room, not wanting to talk to or even see other people on this trip). Campfires were out. So was sleeping in the nude. And he was far more afraid of mosquitoes and gnats than he was of killing us with lethal doses of bug spray while we slept in our tent. I lay awake each night next to him, my skin slick with Deep Woods Off— necessary, he said, to discourage the bugs from biting *him*, even if I was willing to offer my own skin for their snack time.

Oh, I could go on and on. And in my own head, I *did* go on and on, compiling a long list of our differences. Each day—as we covered the required three hundred miles so that we could get the U-Haul truck to New York in the required ten days—looking out at the flat, corn-riddled landscape, and listening to the soporific droning voice of talk radio, I sat silently in the passenger seat, clenching and unclenching my fists and plotting divorce.

I wondered how it would happen. Would I simply get out at the next town while he was using the bathroom in some fast-food place (he wouldn't go to gas station restrooms, of course) and slip away across the highway, leap over the concrete barriers, and hitch my way back to LA? Perhaps I'd catch a ride with somebody driving a sports car, somebody who'd be thrilled to spend money on motels instead of saving every last goddamn penny by making us camp. Or maybe some kindly older couple would swerve over to the side and stop for me, and I'd go home with them and it would turn out they had a fascinating life story to tell me that would change everything. *I can see in your eyes that you've married the wrong man*, the woman would tell me. *Why, when*

I met Bert here, he was so good at talking to me that I knew my whole life was going to be one amazing conversation after another. I didn't care that we were poor. And you know why? We could really, really talk to each other.

As soon as I thought that, I opened my eyes and looked over at Grant. He was hunched over the steering wheel, frowning as he drove, and humming some tuneless thing, the same four notes over and over again under his breath. Here it was, the height of the summer, and we were driving through Kansas, through heat and humidity, yet he was wearing black pants and white crew socks, and the pants were too short for him, so his skinny little ankles in their pathetic little ribbed socks stuck out. He scratched his nose and ran his hands through his hair and then started humming again. He'd forgotten to shave on one side, and he was squinting hard over the top of his sunglasses. I had always thought that the whole Grant shtick was just so adorable, the way he couldn't be bothered to care about so many things because he was in his own little world, but now I felt nothing but despair.

"What are you thinking about?" I said.

"What?"

"What are you *thinking* about?"

"Oh." He shrugged and smiled, a little sheepishly. "I don't know. I guess I'm thinking about labor unions."

"Labor unions. You're really thinking about labor unions."

"Yeah."

"But what about them? Are you thinking about the people who belong to them, or their history? What is there to think about? Are you . . . counting them?"

He laughed. "Well. No. I'm thinking how great it is that they saved this country."

I folded a map that was crumpled up on the floor at my feet. "Do you ever think about us? About our marriage? Or about what it's going to be like when we get where we're going?" I said slowly. "You know, our *marriage.*"

"No," he said. "I figure that part will just take care of itself."

"No, no. You've got it backwards. It's *labor unions* that will take care of themselves. Us, you have to actually think about." I looked out the window and felt my eyes stinging. What, what had I done?

Grant reached over and put his husbandly I-have-a-right-to-be-here hand on my knee. "Do you know where you want to stay tonight? Did you look at the Triple-A book?"

"No," I said, looking out the window.

"Well, it's four thirty. We should look soon."

"I don't want to look."

"You don't want to— Wait. Are you . . . crying?"

"No. Yes."

"Holy shit. You *are* crying! What's the matter? Wait. Are you un-happy?" We were nearing an exit just then, and to my surprise, he pulled off and stopped the truck. There was wheat, wheat everywhere. Maybe even some corn, who knew? Clouds of dust came up around the windows, and we sat there, both of us looking through the wind-shield. The engine ticked slowly in the sunlight.

"Are you unhappy?" he said again.

I started to cry harder. "*Yes,* I'm unhappy. I'm miserable."

He pursed his lips and cleared his throat and started tapping on the steering wheel, playing imaginary drums.

Finally he said, "I guess this isn't something to do with your not wanting to look in the Triple-A book, is it?"

I stared at him.

"No," he said. "Is it because I said I was thinking about labor unions instead of marriage? Because if that's all it is, I just don't know yet how to *think* about marriage. I think I'll learn, if—"

"It's *everything,*" I said. "We didn't get a honeymoon, and we have to stay in the most ridiculous, sanitized, *stupid* campgrounds every single night—not even anywhere beautiful, not even places with lakes and flowers! And I'm sick of talk radio. I *hate* talk radio! And I don't like it that you won't ever let me drive, and I hate our tent!" I didn't know until that moment that I had any particularly negative feelings toward the tent, but I was throwing in everything I could think of. I even dragged up the fact that my thighs were so sweaty they were sticking to the plastic seat—he jumped in to say that's why he wore long pants—and I blew up and said we should just turn on the air conditioner, and he said that made the gas mileage too hideous to be believed, and I burst into fresh tears and said, "This is supposed to be our honeymoon! Who has a summer honeymoon in the middle of the country without goddamn air-conditioning?"

He was quiet for a long time, and then he said, "Okay. I know what we have to do. This is one of those times when you have to regroup, go back to square one. Call in the reinforcements. We're going to a motel. And then we'll go out to dinner, to a great restaurant—"

"Somewhere with tablecloths."

"Absolutely there will be tablecloths," he said. "And flowers, fresh ones—"

"And no red plastic ketchup bottles on the table."

"None! No ketchup even in the restaurant at all—that's how fancy. And you can order anything you want. We won't even think about money tonight. Okay? Tonight is all about us."

I put my head down and cried harder. I hadn't expected such kindness and understanding.

"And no more talk radio," he said. "Music, even if it's filled with static. *Country music,* even!"

That night, after a dinner of lasagna in an Italian bistro in the middle of a town we called Cow Fart, Kansas, we stayed in an air-conditioned motel, in a real bed with clean sheets. We took a shower together in the white-tiled bathroom and soaped each other up. He shampooed my hair and washed my ears with the tips of his fingers. I told him I loved him, and later, in the middle of the room, stark naked, he actually clicked his heels in the air, like a cartoon character expressing joy. We turned on the radio and learned that Elvis had died that day, and in honor of him, we turned down the lights and danced in the hotel room to the Elvis songs they were playing on the radio. I danced with my feet on top of Grant's.

"You see?" he whispered to me. "We can be happy. We'll be okay."

AND THEN—well, then my brother got shot in the head.

He didn't die. The bullet went through his skull, grazing a part of his brain, and then went out through the back of his head, knocking him unconscious. Some schoolchildren found him lying in a puddle of blood on the sidewalk.

I found out the day after it happened, when I called my mother from a pay phone outside the diner where we'd eaten breakfast. I called her just to say hello, to check in. It was the first time I could trust myself to call home without crying or begging her to send a posse out across the country after me. There, standing in the dusty phone booth in the parking lot, with little pebbles gathering underneath my toes in my pink striped flip-flops and gnats swarming around my newly shampooed hair, I learned that my brother was in intensive care.

"He's alive—for now," my mother said in a voice that sounded like it was packed in cotton batting. "They don't know much else."

I twisted the cord of the pay phone around and around my index finger until it cut off the circulation. The little white numbers on the phone were raised, like bumps. I'd had sun poisoning once; my fingers thought these bumps were like the itchy rash I'd gotten and had scratched, even though I'd been told over and over not to touch it. Bumps and bumps. There wasn't any air in the phone booth, not any that was suitable for breathing, so I kicked the door open and hurt my toe. Grant was standing far away with his hands in his pockets. He was staring across the street at a strip mall and grinding his toe in the dirt. For him, it was still just a regular day. He'd made his wife happy, and now he wanted to get back on the road.

David was in the intensive care unit, with round-the-clock care, my mother said again. It was as if she was simply programmed to go through a list of things to tell people who called, and sometimes there was a glitch and she repeated herself. She talked in a high, thin, urgent voice, like a little girl's, shaky and uncertain. She told me several things, and then repeated them: The bullet had missed all the really important, kill-you-outright places. He was on sedatives and pain medication now, so he just slept all the time and couldn't talk, but he'd been conscious right after it happened. He'd joked with the ambulance driver, someone said, so there was that. His speech was still intact. But the joke had been about how the world had gone black and he was going to have to learn to see with his ears.

"But who would shoot *David*?" I said.

It was just one of those senseless things, she told me. A stranger did it. Just came up to him when he was in his car, stopped at a red light in South LA, and shot him in the face point-blank. Crime wave, she said. Terrible things happened that we didn't even know about.

"South LA?" I cried. "Oh my God. He shouldn't have been there."

"You know David. He has friends from everywhere," she said.

But my heart sank. I knew that South LA meant it had been a drug deal. My brother had been buying drugs in South LA so that he could sell them to his friends in the Valley. He was such an idiot. Such a stupid idiot. But I had sat out there by the pool and smoked weed with him, so in a way I was a collaborator. And if you *really* want to know the truth, it had been me who had introduced him to marijuana in the first place, years before. I'd brought some home and for fun had put it in the spaghetti sauce, as though it was just any spice. Like oregano, I thought. I'd see what my family acted like when they were high. Wouldn't *that* be fun, seeing my father get stoned unknowingly? Then, as it happened, my parents had gone out that night, and David, who was fourteen, had eaten plates and plates of the spaghetti and then had been so overwhelmed with giggles he'd fallen on the floor in a heap. We'd played Twister, laughing so hard we could barely breathe and falling all over ourselves. I'd told him, before he went to bed that night, "This is weed you're experiencing—you're high," and watched as his eyes widened. A month later, he'd bought his own ounce of the stuff, and two months after that, he had a thriving dope business.

God, I was a horrible sister.

My mother said, in a low voice, "This happened to punish me. That's the only thing your father and I know for sure. It's karma, you know. For leaving like I did. I leave, and my son nearly gets killed."

"Oh, Mama, that's not the way the world works," I said. "Look around you at how many people do terrible, terrible things and nothing bad ever happens to them. Karma is either the most faulty system ever, or else it's just one big joke."

She started to cry. "Please, please don't say that. We can't ever argue with each other, not ever again. People should stand by each other, and that's what I'm going to do. I was wrong to leave your father and think only of myself. And if David lives I am going to stand by everyone for the rest of my life and just tell you all every day how much I love you."

I cried, too. I was the worst, most guilty person in the whole story. And yet I knew that when I told Grant everything, he would defend me. He would say, Don't be ridiculous. These things happen. Your brother would have discovered weed on his own, even if you hadn't given him that first clobber of it in the spaghetti.

That's what he would say, and his eyes would be placid and gray and his voice wouldn't go up or down in tone. He just accepted things, the good and the bad. I wanted to be back at home with my mother, to hold her hand and tell her that she didn't have to tell me she loved me every day. I already knew it.

I said that I would come back home, and she said, "But you're on your honeymoon," and I said, "That doesn't matter."

She started to cry in earnest then and put my dad on the phone— I heard him protesting in the background that he didn't see the point of talking, but she made him anyway. He was monosyllabic, like somebody who'd been awakened in the middle of the night. He didn't seem

even remotely well enough to have any opinions. I asked him if the two
of them were eating, and he didn't seem to know why I would ask a
question like that.

When I hung up, I went over to Grant, who was now in the truck,
looking at the maps and whistling. I told him what had happened. A
bead of sweat rolled down the inside of my tank top, tickling me all the
way down to the waistband of my shorts. "I'm so sorry, but I need to go
back home," I said. I shielded my eyes from the sun and looked up at
him in the truck. "I don't think I can go with you to New York anymore."

I watched the color leave his face. "I'll come with you," he said. "We
can turn around now and we'll stay there a couple of days, until things
settle down, and then we can set out again for New York."

"I don't think things are going to be all right in a couple of days,"
I said. I ran my hand along the inside of the truck's open door, won-
dering what it would be like if the door were to slam on my fingers.
Would that make the pain in my heart better or worse?

"Well, then, as long as it takes," he said. "Surely they'll know more
in a few days, at least. We can get things squared away there, and *then*
go to New York."

"No," I said. I knew I wasn't going to be ready to go to New York in
a few days. "Listen," I said. "You have a job waiting for you, and you're
supposed to turn in the truck in New York City, and we're already on
such a tight deadline. You go on ahead and get settled, and I'll go take
care of my brother—"

But didn't marriage count for anything? He said we were married,
damn it, and that's what married people did: stand by each other in
times of difficulty. Hadn't that been what I agreed to when we got married? This was our first test. Didn't I know what "for better or worse"
even meant? He and I had made *vows*. This is how his parents had
lasted so long. They stayed with each other. His father never would
have let his mother go off alone. This is what you *do*.

I told him I didn't think that applied here. It was too soon, for one
thing. And this was a situation that had nothing to do with our mar-

riage, or him, or anything about the future. I pointed out that he'd lose the job that was waiting for him—the one with the man he'd most wanted to work with in his whole adult life, the guy we had taken to calling The Great Man Himself. Plus, there was the deposit he'd put on the truck. If we went back to California now and then to New York at some later time, we'd have more trouble finding an apartment later on. I really believed all this stuff I was saying.

"Really," I said. "I need to do this."

The truth was—and I didn't know this until I got on the plane, until I'd clicked the seat belt closed and accepted a martini, my first ever, from the stewardess—the *truth* was, I didn't want him with me. I wanted to have this experience all to myself. This was *mine*. Grant had no place in the tiny hierarchy of people who could know about my brother's drug deals gone wrong, and my mother's crazy theories about karma and her foray into feminism and all the rest of it, and the way my father closed his eyes when the world demanded even the slightest thing of him.

These were *my* people—my flawed, crazy people—and they were in trouble and I needed to go back and stand with them. Grant would be fine. I had told him that: we'd be a married couple later on, I told him. I had some unfinished sister-and-daughter work to do. It was bad luck, is all.

"I'll call you," I'd said to him in the coffee shop at the airport.

"But will you ever really come to New York?" he asked. "I'm your husband, and I don't want to be away from you."

"Of course I will!" I said. But as the plane took off and I took the first sips of the martini, what I was feeling was something else altogether: as sad as my brother's trauma had been, there was something else flickering in the back of my mind, something I didn't even want to admit to. And that was that I had received a reprieve, a pardon, a free pass out of marriage and another chance at being back in my home again, with my mother and father—and yes, a sick, injured little brother, all of whom I needed so desperately. I never should have left.

I had gotten to run back into childhood just before the gate shut me out forever.

GRANT TRAVELED the rest of the country to New York in record time, staying in concrete campgrounds and listening to talk radio to his heart's content, I'm sure. And once he got there he discovered it was much harder than he'd imagined to find an apartment and set up housekeeping. It was one man against the whole unfathomable system of city landlords and rental agencies. Besides, he said on the phone, how could he possibly figure out what type of place I'd like? How could he be sure he'd pick just the right apartment? Perhaps I'd forgotten, in my absence, how inept he was at daily life. Instead, he told me in one of our late-night phone conversations, he'd accepted an invitation to live in the meantime with The Great Man Himself, of all people. What fantastic luck!

The Great Man Himself had a wife and twin toddlers, and an apartment they were willing to share. Yes, they'd invited him! In fact, Grant had been given the wife's study for his bedroom, which was just great because she was a dancer putting on a show and she needed to work at the studio now instead of at home. There was already a double bed in there anyway, along with a desk and boxes of family photos and Christmas decorations and all the paraphernalia of family life, boxes of old baby clothes and toys. It was sweet, he said. The toddlers came in and woke him up with kisses and pokes in the eye every morning. One of them insisted he wear the toilet plunger for a hat, which was apparently a great honor.

It was a perfect arrangement, he said, because—well, because it gave him a chance to get acclimated to living in New York and to working for the university without being quite on his own. Had I been there, he told me, he probably wouldn't have relied on others. And then he would have missed out on the greatest friendship of his life. He actually said that: the greatest friendship of his life. With good dinners and conversation and wine.

"And they can't wait to meet you," he said. "Please, please come soon, whenever your family can do without you."

I told him I would. David had awakened from his sleep, but he was paralyzed from the waist down and had lost the sight in one eye and some of his hearing. He was going to be staying in rehab for a long time, it looked like. There wasn't much more I would be able to do for him.

Grant said, "Well . . . he'll have people who can help him recover," and I could hear glasses clinking and laughter in the background. I heard a man's voice say, "Tell her we're turning you into a New Yorker, plying you with bagels and brioche. And tell her this—tell her we're already half in love with her just from her picture, although we suspect that's just a decoy photo you're trying to impress people with!"

"Wow, The Great Man Himself has a normal human voice," I said. "He doesn't boom like I thought God would sound when he talked."

Grant laughed. "I know! Did you hear him?" he said into the phone. "That was Jeremiah. I think he's beginning to believe you're not really real. So you see, you *have* to come and prove him wrong."

[nine]

2005

I love this, being back in New York. You know what it's like? It's like being young again. I feel anything is possible.

Sophie and I settle into a nice, easy rhythm with each other, as I knew we would. I'm enough like her to know what cheers her up, and so we do plenty of it, as much as we want. We loll about in bed watching movies and napping and eating off and on, whenever we please. I get to play the part of Lady Bountiful, making chicken soup and homemade wheat bread, roasted vegetables, stir-fries. I bring in *People* magazine, romantic comedies on DVD, fragrant moisturizers, lip glosses, nail polish in a variety of colors. It's as though we exist in a kind of bubble—an overheated, one-room, exclusively female bubble, surrounded by everything we could want. Outside, branches scrape against the windows of her apartment, the sun rises and sets, the wind blows, and car horns honk. Inside, we give each other manicures and pedicures, and I comb her hair into upswept hairdos with tendrils, and the radiator bathes us in plumes of warm air. We decide we should both wear bangs. I comb mine down and straight until I look like Chrissie Hynde, the lead singer of The Pretenders, which I have to explain to Sophie was a band from the years I lived here before. Sophie wears wispy bangs, combed to the side, that emphasize her wide gray eyes.

We both are working, too. I've set up a makeshift drawing table in the corner of the bedroom, and I'm finishing up the Bobo pictures, concentrating on getting the expressions just right. How's this for a distinction? My editor says I'm the queen of making animals look like they're brimming with goodwill and human feelings. "One millimeter speck of brown paint in the wrong place, and people suddenly remember that squirrels are just rats with tails," she said once, which made me laugh.

Sophie, who works as an assistant to the deputy editor for *La Belle*, a general-interest magazine for young women, has been assigned during her confinement to read unsolicited manuscripts—stories that ordinary people send from everywhere, hoping they will get printed in the magazine. Most of them don't have a chance, but Sophie's job is to read them and decide if they should get seen by an editor. It could be a discouraging job, having to dash so many people's hopes, but some of the stories are funny and touching, and she'll often read paragraphs aloud to me while I paint.

These manuscripts get brought to her each week by Christina, another assistant from the office, who will often stay and have tea with us. She's charming and quirky, and I love how she gets Sophie laughing about the office gossip and politics. Soon she becomes a regular for dinner, which is good because we get sick of ourselves sometimes and need new life to be brought in from the outside.

"You have to be careful around my mom," Sophie tells her, and slides her eyes over to me. "My mom has this talent—I guess you could call it a talent—for adopting people. You'll talk with her for five minutes and she'll get you to tell her all your secrets, and by the end of the night she'll know everything about you."

"Sophie, that is so untrue," I say, laughing.

"Nobody knows how she does it."

Christina laughs and says she has no secrets, which is of course not so, and pretty soon she and Sophie and I are talking about men and bosses and living in New York, and how you know when you're happy, and whether men experience happiness the same way women do—which are all fascinating subjects. Not long after that, Lori and her roommate, Tara, start coming up, too, and in the evenings we have something of a salon. We all gather on the bed and on pillows on the floor, knitting and talking and laughing and eating.

Everybody has man trouble of one sort or another—there are men who are noncommittal, and men who are too clingy, and men who leave wet towels on the floor and who are *also* too clingy, and then, of course, men who have chosen to go to Brazil—and I love how we sift through the layers of feeling, telling stories, trying to explain the mysteries that can't be explained. I feel as though I've been doing this all my life.

"How is it that you can know for sure that you don't love somebody anymore, but then when you hear he's getting married all of a sudden you want to throw yourself out the window?" asked Lori one night.

"It's just wanting what you can't have," Christina said. "Human nature."

"If you got him back, you wouldn't really want him," Sophie said. "Whatever was wrong before would come right back in no time. And you'd just throw him over again."

"But what if everything had changed? What if you were wrong before? What if you made the wrong decision?" asked Lori. "How do you know?"

"My mom's the one with the happy marriage," Sophie said. "Ask her how you know."

They all looked at me, expectantly, and my throat got clogged and I couldn't speak. I know less than anyone on this subject.

ONE DAY Sophie and I are sitting on the bed and I get out my paper and watercolors and start to paint her. I make her look hopeful and radiant. I have noticed that every day she's getting stronger and happier, except that she always seems to feel down after she and Whit have talked on the phone or after she's read his e-mails. I don't think he's saying things to upset her, but I know that sometimes a man can break your heart worse when he is far away but happy, and you realize how tangential you are to his real life.

Grant calls her several times a week but does not ever ask to speak to me. And one day he sends a box of Hershey bars with almonds with a note that says: "Just in case you have the same cravings your mom did."

"So, I guess you must talk to Dad when you go out to the market or something," she says once.

"Why do you say that?"

"Because I never hear you talking to him. I thought he'd be calling you every day."

"Well, he's pretty busy with his book."

"Oh," she says, and I can feel her looking at me even as I go back to my drawings. I've decided that Bobo's mother's sweat suit needs just a bit more shading.

One day while I'm out I call Ava Reiss and let her know that I wish to suspend our therapy sessions for the foreseeable future.

Making that phone call felt great. "Thank you for all that you've gotten me to think about," I told her voice mail cheerily. "But for now I'm looking forward to simply being with my daughter and living the unexamined life."

How lucky it had been not to get Ava Reiss herself on the phone. She does not believe in the virtues of the unexamined life. She would have said, "But Annabelle, we have to explore the fact that you said you don't want to be married anymore. What about that?"

Maybe she wouldn't have said that, I don't know. I am on vacation from my marriage to Grant; from his silences; from our dark, cold house; from missing my mother; from the way the wind blows against the siding on the north side of the house and makes a howling sound and the way the snowpack builds up on the shady part of the driveway; from feeling that I constantly need to lose ten pounds and make lunch dates with my friends so I can hear of the demise of their marriages and their fears for the future; and from that feeling of dread I have just under my breastbone each morning when I wake up.

Sophie and her friends are women who have been disappointed by men, but I can tell they are sure that this is only a temporary state; they believe that love will come and transform them. Men will start behaving correctly, or new men will come and carry them to a time when they won't be confused or disappointed again.

But then there is Lori's question: "What if he was the one, and I've missed him and can't get him back? Will I always have to live in uncertainty?"

That would be the worst thing, they all agree: living with uncertainty.

ONE DAY I'm working on my watercolor of Sophie, complete with pink cheeks and tendrilly hair, looking like the epitome of young, healthy impending motherhood, and she says, "Will you paint a picture of the lima bean?"

She means the baby. She's been calling it a lima bean, or a baked bean, or just Beanie. "You mean . . . from the ultrasound picture?" I am trying to think how this could possibly work. A portrait of someone curled up like a Cheeto?

"No, no." She waves her hand. "The way you imagine her to look. A portrait of our fantasy of her. When she gets born."

"Um, excuse me. Back up just a second. Did you say . . . her?"

She laughs and squeezes her knees. "Oh, did I?"

"Sophie! Is that true? Oh my God! Beanie is a girl?"

She nods, and her eyes fill with tears even though she's smiling. "She is. I'm having a girl. I just found out. That day . . ."

I put down my paintbrush and go over and hug her. "Oh, baby! Oh, my goodness! A daughter? This is so exciting! Wow, wow. What did Whit say when you told him?"

"Um, I haven't told him yet."

"No? Not yet? You're waiting for just the right moment."

"Yeah, and the right moment will be when he's here and the doctor is handing her to him."

I laugh. "Really? Wow, you have a lot of self-control. I'd probably not want to tell him, but then I'd be on the phone blurting it out."

"No," she says, still smiling, but it's furious, chin-thrust-out smiling. In a moment, she could cry again. "It's not self-control. I just don't want to tell him. This is knowledge that is just mine, all mine— and well, now yours, too."

I hug myself. "A *girl*! A little girl. I can't get over it." I sit on the bed next to her and hold her, and I can't help it, I think of my mother—this whole chain of women we're making, how far it stretches into the past and how much further it will go into the future. My mother would have loved to have been here for this moment. It's almost as though she knew it would arrive. One day not long before she died I was visiting her in the nursing home, and we sat together in the sunroom, talking. She'd been divorced from my father for years by then, and had had a decade-long happy marriage to a man she met at a singles dance, who died one day of a stroke when he was taking out the garbage. After a few years on her own, she'd moved to a retirement community in New Hampshire to be near us. We sat looking out through the huge floor-to-ceiling windows. There wasn't any sun, just snow heaped up on the pond outside, but it was beautiful just the same, we agreed. Not a California beachy kind of beautiful, but still, filled with the kind of scenic wonder you might see on a calendar on the January page. How in the world, I had asked her, had we California women been transplanted to a winter worthy of the January page?

And that's when she shook her head and said, "All because of Grant—a man we didn't even know for most of our lives. We couldn't have predicted it. You being here. Of course, looking back, it was the thing that had to happen, but you're so far away from what I thought your life would be." She adjusted the turban she'd taken to wearing since her hair had fallen out. "And it'll be that way for you and Sophie, too. You won't recognize who she becomes. You know that, right?"

I squeezed her hand, too choked up just then to speak. She said, "I just hope she has a little girl so she can know what it's like to be challenged every day of your life, the way we've been." And we both laughed.

See? says Ava Reiss in my head. *You think you can go on vacation from the unexamined life, but you really can't.*

I turn and tell Sophie, whom I still recognize just fine, "You know what I think we should do in view of this new knowledge? I think we should get ourselves on the computer and order us some pink outfits. And a white wicker bassinet with ruffles."

She looks uncertain, but then she says, "That'll be so much fun. I guess it's really real, isn't it, when you know this is a person who actually has a gender. You realize you're going to have to buy her stuff."

I pick up her laptop from the floor by the bed and together we sit and cruise all the cool baby sites. We buy little onesies and stretchy suits with farm animals on them, bath towels and some newborn pajamas, little knitted booties, blankets, and hats. It's a riot of fun. And then—*click*—we purchase a bassinet, the kind that comes with a canopy and gingham bumpers. Laughing, Sophie says she doesn't know where she'll put all this stuff when it arrives.

But you have to have things for the baby, I tell her. And besides that, there's always room. You make room, is what you do.

IN THE game of chicken that Grant and I are apparently playing, he is the one who gives in first and finally calls me. This is a major triumph, of course. He has never liked long, involved phone conversations, and now he sounds like somebody who has a list of talking points in front of him. He ticks them off. He has a cold. Chapter six is giving him fits. His knees are stiff. It's just snowed. The oil delivery guy came today. How am I? What is Sophie doing? How is the weather in New York? Do I get out much? What does the doctor say?

I answer him in a careful voice that is devoid of any anger or passion. I say I'm sorry about his cold, his chapter, and his knees, but then I don't rush to fill the silences, as I would have done before I took a vacation from dealing with him. While I'm talking, I take a notepad and sketch a picture of Sophie's bedroom, the bedside table with our cups of tea and a plate of brownies next to the lamp.

I tell him that Sophie is fine. She had an ultrasound last week, and everything seems to be going well. No more bleeding.

"Oh," he says. "So I suppose that's made her feel better."

"Yes, every day that goes by, she's getting stronger."

"Good, very good." Silence. "And is she feeling well?"

"Would you like to speak with her?"

"No, no, that's fine. I talked to her earlier today. I just wanted to see how things were going with you and see if you need anything."

"Not a thing. We're fine."

Long silence.

He says, "Well, then I'll hang up now and get back to work."

"Okay."

"Oh! Yeah. I was thinking, though . . . maybe for spring break, you know . . . maybe Nick and I could take a drive and come see you and Sophie."

"Oh. That would be good, I guess. If you're far enough along on your book."

He laughs a little. "Well, I won't be. But I should come and see her. And you. Before the baby comes, you know."

"When is that?"

He laughs. "Well, who knows when babies come? Don't they have their own timetable that nobody really knows?"

I stay silent.

He clears his throat. "Bad joke. You mean when is spring break? Don't worry. It's two weeks from now. This is just advance planning."

"Okay, then. Sounds nice."

"Okay. Well, we'll talk. So . . . good-bye, then."

"Bye."

"I do love you, Annabelle."

"Yes. Me, too, you. Good night." I click my phone closed and look up to see Sophie staring at me with wide eyes.

"What?" I say.

"Oh, nothing." She gets busy smoothing out the covers and yawns and stretches. Then, after a few minutes, she says, "Um, are you and Dad mad at each other?"

I smile at her. I am still trying to be a good example. "No. You know how he hates talking on the phone."

She laughs. "Well, that's true. He definitely is an in-person kind of guy," she says, but she looks uncertain. "Still, I thought he wouldn't be able to stand having you out of his sight. I thought he'd be calling you every night."

I can't help but laugh at that idea. "To tell you the truth, Sophie, I think he's a little relieved to be alone these days. He's really working hard on his book. And also, he knows you and I are having good bonding time. I think he doesn't want to interrupt us."

She rubs her mound of belly and yawns. "He's such a good guy. You know?"

"Mmmm."

"So what's this book of his about anyway? He hasn't even told me about it."

I tell her the short version, that it's the labor history of a factory, about a time when the factory shut down at the turn of the century, and how the workers all mounted a protest and took it over and kept it going so they wouldn't lose their jobs. He's doing the first comprehensive study of this shutdown and its results, interviewing the sons and daughters of some of the workers . . .

"Wow, that sounds fascinating," she says. "And this is the first study of it? And the book is going to get published and make him rich?"

"I don't know about rich, but it's certainly going to be published. And the thing is, it looks like he's going to be named acting chair of the department in the fall, so he wants to fin—"

She frowns. "Why? What happened to Mr. Winstanley?"

"Well, it's been the gossip of the whole year, actually. I can't believe

I didn't tell you. He left his wife and married a grad student, and they're—"

"*What?* He married a *student*? Jen's dad married a student?"

I had forgotten somehow that Jennifer Winstanley was in the same class as Sophie. That's the trouble with small towns; there are a million connections you have to keep track of. Everybody's in on everything in some way you aren't able to remember.

"Well, yes, a grad student, and they're—"

"Oh my God. Mr. Winstanley? That is the ickiest thing I have ever heard of. Ewww. He married one of his students?"

"Actually, she wasn't *his* student. He met her at a conference, I heard, and then she transferred to the college, and they fell in love, and then when he realized he had feelings for her, he got divorced."

"Poor Jen! And her mom is *so* nice! God, I can't believe he left Mrs. Winstanley after all those years because he got the hots for some student. That is so sickening I think I'm going to barf right here."

"Sophie, come on. You know this kind of thing happens. It's practically a cliché it's so common."

"Not to people like the Winstanleys! He was a strict, upstanding guy. I always thought he was nice when I'd go over their house."

"Over *to* their house. You didn't go over their house; you'd be in midair."

This old line does not distract her from her outrage; in this, she's exactly like all the faculty women. We all want to hear the details and then to express the mighty outrage. We all love the drama of the situation, and of course, the delicious opportunity to pity poor Mary Lou.

"God. You hear stuff like this and it's enough to make you hate men. You know? You don't hear of women doing this—deciding when they're middle-aged that they've just had enough of their husbands. What is *with* these guys?"

"It happens both ways," I say lamely. "People change, they get bored, they see that their lives are drifting away and they're not happy, they feel trapped . . . who knows what it is?"

She stares at me. "I can't believe you're defending him!" She throws a wadded-up Kleenex at me. "He's a jerk."

"Well, no, I'm not *defending* him. I'm just saying that it's simplistic to assume there's just that way of looking at the story. There are always more sides to these things than it looks like on the outside. And people change; their needs change . . ."

"Yeah, Clark Winstanley changed, all right. He changed into a letch. And you can defend him all you want, but you know that Dad would never, ever do this kind of thing. He just wouldn't. You must know that. I bet not many women can say they feel that sure of their husbands."

She says this accusingly, as though I've had it too easy. Unearned security or something. I want to say something more about complexity and about all the ways marriages fail, but she's a woman with a husband far away, and I can tell she can't hear it now. And God knows I don't want to upset her. When you're scared for your life, there is comfort in at least being on the right side of the moral divide.

"You know what Dad said?" she says. "When I was talking to him about getting married to Whit, he told me that when you go into marriage, you have to do it for only one reason—because you know that's the person you really are going to stay with forever, and it doesn't matter what they do or who else you meet or what kind of troubles the two of you find yourselves in. You're in it. You make this deal that you're going to always work things out. Period. You dig in and you make it work."

"Jesus," I say, laughing. "That must have scared you out of your mind. He makes marriage sound like a Siberian prison camp."

"But you're a prisoner of luuuvvv," she says. "That makes it all okay. Because you're perfectly safe. Someone has said he will love you no matter what."

• • •

IS IT bad to say that the best part of each day is when I go out to the market to stock up on groceries? There are glorious oranges, apples, asparagus tips, and dark green spinach leaves, all laid out in boxes and so fresh they're practically glowing. This is what I remember loving about New York: the little markets here, how even in the winter they have the feel of an abundant summer, with their array of bagels and multigrain breads, olives, crackers, smoked salmon, and cheese, all there, just beckoning. In my years of living in New Hampshire, I'd forgotten how the city in winter smells like buildings and pavement and car exhaust and wool coats, and not simply like the hard, cold, metallic air of snow and ice and pine trees. It feels wonderful just to walk down the sidewalk, passing people who are rushing by me and who don't know the first thing about who I am and couldn't care less.

Some days now, before I go back to Sophie, I permit myself this: to sit in the sunshine in the park, watching and remembering. It feels as though I could almost walk back to the past if I wanted to, find it all still waiting for me here. I have walked these streets with my heart cracked wide open, stood in these outdoor markets, handling tangerines and grapefruits, when all I wanted was impossible love instead of being content with the warm, round citrusy nourishment that was being offered to me.

One day, lying on the bed next to Sophie, I tell her that I've realized New Hampshire is all about settlement and barricading yourself—even its games involve hard pucks and face masks. But in New York, even in winter, the whole place is open and filled with possibility. It's the energy here, I say, the way it runs beneath the surface of everything.

She laughs. "That's not energy you hear. It's the rumbling from the subway, you nut."

"Yes, even that!" I say. "It's like there's a whole other world you can step right into. You could lose yourself here, blend into a crowd and never have to face up to your old life."

"Mom," she says. "When you talk like that, I can't help but get the unsettling idea that you don't like your old life."

"Sophie," I say very carefully. "Sophie, you *do* remember what your father is like, don't you?"

"What do you mean?" she says.

I laugh. "Now, I know that he's a very good man, and that you idealize him somewhat, but you do remember that he can be a very black-and-white thinker, don't you? Remember the time you had a big fight with your best friend in middle school, after she said all those mean things about you?"

She nods.

"And I thought you should wait a few days until things calmed down and then go over to her house and talk to her? But your father was certain that she'd crossed an unforgivable line and that you should never speak to her again."

"Oh, yeah. He said 'Think smart—why would you want somebody like that in your life at all?' and *then* he said it was even a good thing that it had happened, because now I could see the kind of person she was, so I would know never ever to trust her." She shakes her head.

"Yeah. I'm just saying. Good man, on the side of right, against all that's wrong, but sometimes . . ."

She laughs.

"And, well now that it's only him and me in the house, all that *rightful* thinking and goodness has nowhere to go but at me. It can be a bit much."

ONE DAY I go back home after a morning in the park and Google Jeremiah.

Not that Googling is a crime, but it is a ridiculous thing to do, and of course once I thought of it, I had to do it anyway. I type his name into Sophie's computer while she's in the bathroom, praying that I can find out something quickly and can slide back over to the Baby Gap site before she reappears.

The pages take a long time to load. Here is what I learn in the three minutes I have: He is no longer on the faculty at Columbia. He lived in Sweden for a while. His books are not doing particularly well on amazon.com. He might now be in New York.

He is a widower.

I take a deep breath.

Sophie comes back into the room, looking like a woman from the Renaissance with her pale skin and upswept hair. She is smiling when she gives me the thumbs-up sign; still no blood. The baby is staying in place.

I casually click over to a census report on the population of New York City. More than 8 million people live here, I tell her. Can you imagine the chances of running into any one person you know?

"It's infinitesimal," she says.

1977

And so here we are, at Jeremiah.

That part of things. The wonderful, awful, scary part.

Jeremiah was married, a married man with toddlers. Let me just get that out of the way first, because that was almost the main thing about him. It defined all else, just the same as his slightly curly, glossy dark hair and those magnetic blue eyes, his loutish smile, and the fact that he was in his early thirties and was already a college professor because of some brilliant study he'd done years before.

Carly, his wife, was tall and willowy and wore leotards and leggings with flowy diaphanous dancer's skirts, and yes, little ballet-type slippers, the kind that lace up the calves. Her naturally red hair was always in a careful, tight bun with tendrils, and she had a flat, almost concave stomach and a thin, nervous face that registered what she was thinking all the time. She was jittery and drank lots of coffee, and to me she was a glamorous older woman who had already had a successful career as a dancer. Now she, too, was in her thirties and the mother of adorable twins and married to a man whom people regarded as The Great One. She didn't need anything else to complete her, while at the end of that summer, just having turned twenty-one and now married, I was practically fresh from the primordial ooze, still made of jelly, unformed and undirected, with my wounded heart hanging back, in California.

I was hurting for David, who woke up in the hospital stunned to find himself so altered. At first he didn't want to talk to anyone, least of all my parents, who fought as though he could not possibly hear them, and as though, in this semiprivate hospital room, with both of their children in attendance, they could refight once and for all the battles that had consumed them their entire marriage. It would have taken a team of psychiatrists to sort it all out, I said to David when I got permission to take him outside one day. I pushed him in a wheelchair to a courtyard, where we sat and talked. We were hiding from the drone of the daytime television shows in the hallways of the hospital, the smell of the food service trays, the squeak of nurses' shoes on the tile floors, the chipper voices of the therapists who came bouncing into David's room only to retreat like wilted daisies upon exposure to our family drama.

We were so sad, but we couldn't say we were sad because my father was stone-faced and grim with anger and might blow up, and my mother was swollen with tears that would leak out if you so much as looked in her direction. Everything that happened between the four of us in that room felt as if it was because of an unstated agreement we'd signed on to without knowing it. We seethed and roiled and put on a good face for David, who was the most dejected of all but who was in the process of growing the hard shell he would need to keep living.

That is what I know now. Then all I knew was that I needed to go every day to the hospital and try to navigate my way through all these muddled feelings, which was a lot like weaving together blackened ropes along with strands of hope and togetherness and trying to come out with a nice tapestry that said our family would be all right.

The good parts—and there were some—were when I got David off alone and some of his hard tortoise self came off and there was the pink wound underneath that we could look at and actually even laugh about. We would go to our hidden courtyard, a jungly, overgrown place an orderly had shown us, where the staff went to smoke dope and hide from their supervisors when they were on breaks.

"I think it's symbolic that this is a jungle, since we're obviously under attack by family napalm," I said to him one evening there. "It's like Vietnam in there with Edie and Howard together."

He said, "*I* think it's symbolic that it's a jungle, because if I have to stay in this place much longer, I'm going to plant some seeds here and grow my own marijuana."

We both laughed. His eye was all bandaged up, and he had some idea that when they took the dressings off, the eyeball itself was going to roll onto the floor. But he thought that was funny, too, once we were outside. He had a deep, rumbly, wet laugh now, as though the accident had dislodged something in his respiratory system and he was filled with fluids. He said he wanted two things: for me to get the hell out of here and go to New York and start my life, and for me to arrange to get him some weed. Could I do that? Maybe go to the nurses' station and look around for an orderly who looked like he might be stoned? "Just stand there and watch until you find the one who's the most incompetent and who can't seem to stop laughing, even when he's emptying bedpans," he said. "He'll know how to get me some weed."

We laughed ourselves sick over that idea, and then he said, "But really. As soon as you can, you've got to go. Go. I mean it. Grant's waiting for you. You're *married,* for God's sake. But first, the weed. A lot of it."

I scored him two ounces of weed from one of his stoner friends and got to New York on a smoggy, humid Thursday afternoon, four weeks after Grant had arrived. I was an unholy mess. Grant met me at the airport, and I was so tense that he had to unbend my fingers to release them from my carry-on bag so he could hug me.

We had a beer at the airport bar, and Grant kept squeezing my arm and talking about The Great Man and Carly and how cool they were. They were so happily married and the twins were too cute for words, he said. He had bags under his eyes, and he only looked lively when he talked about them. When I asked him about himself and his classes, he couldn't think of anything to say. It was, you know, what you'd think, he said. The students were smart. The classes were hard.

The Great Man had told him it was always like that at first; you had to work twenty-hour days when you were new and try your damnedest to keep one step ahead of the work you had to do and convince everybody, the students and the university and the department, that you could make it. But then once you had it all under control, once you'd proven yourself, life would get better. He spread his hands wide and cleared his throat. The academic life was going to be harder than he ever thought, but he was ready for the challenge. He kept saying little cliché things about how you had to work 110 percent.

I'd been through so much, I couldn't even relate to him. My husband, I kept thinking. *Husband.* Hadn't that sudden wedding just been something of a joke? I realized I didn't know anything about him at all, not really.

The beer—it was his first beer since we'd been together in Kansas, but I insisted he drink it because I needed him loose—oiled him up only a little, and he said he was relieved that I had come back to him. His eyes were glassy behind those giant lenses. He said he hadn't been sure I would actually ever join him. His hands drummed on the tabletop, keeping up a nervous beat. *Oh,* I thought. *Look at that. He's been biting his fingernails.*

"So how's your family?" he asked, then looked past me at the television set on the wall, which was just then showing the Santa Ana winds in California, with palm trees whipping around and particles of ash raining down on the landscape like snow. "Bet you're glad you got out of that little weather pattern," he said, taking out his wallet to pay the bill.

I didn't even look at the screen. A wave of sadness hit me at the mention of California. "I wonder if David will ever walk again," I said. "He's lost so much."

"But he's better off than they thought at first. At least there's that."

"But he's so much worse off than he was before he got shot. That's the thing that makes me feel so sorry for him. I can't help thinking about everything he lost."

"I understand," he said. "But it seems to me you've got to stop that." He gave me a sad, kind smile. "You really can't do much about it. He's got his own life."

"Well," I said, and paused. "He doesn't have much of one left."

"No, no, no. I don't think that's the way to look at this," he said, and I felt like I was being given a peek into this part of his personality that was always going to be so hard for me to deal with: the part that says you can't look at bad stuff. Everything has to be turned to the good. "How does it help David if everybody is just wallowing in pity for him? He doesn't want people to feel sorry for him. We need to cheer him on, let him know that bad things happen but he can recover."

What if we just need to cry with him? I thought. But I didn't say anything. Grant took my hand and kissed every one of my fingers. "Do you know something? When I get up to talk in front of my classes, I feel like my whole face has turned bright red. And then I think about you, and I say to myself, 'Well, Annabelle loves me, so I can't be all bad.'" He dipped his head and smiled at me shyly in a way that stopped my heart.

"I'm sure you're great," I said. "You've always been a wonderful teacher."

We laughed uncomfortably because we both remembered then that I had no idea what kind of teacher he was. In fact, I'd never seen him teach anything, not one thing. He steered me out of the bar, through the airport, whispering that he was going to have his way with me as soon as we got to the apartment. We kissed for a long time in the car, and he ran his fingers along my cheeks and chin and gazed at me. "The thing is, when we have relations at home, we're going to have to be ultra, ultra quiet. I don't even think we can breathe hard without the twins waking up."

"Did you really just say 'relations'?" I said.

"Yes." He looked confused. "What's wrong with that?"

"Well, I don't know. I guess that for me, as somebody who's just come from hanging out with my *relations,* it doesn't exactly make me think sexy thoughts when I hear that word. Couldn't we call it something juicy, like . . . oh, I don't know . . . *fucking*?"

He grinned. "I'd forgotten how earthy you are."

"Will we get our own place soon?" I said. "Because, to tell you the truth, I don't think I can fuck without breathing hard."

"Sure," he said. "I'm at school all the time, but you can look for places for us. And, Annabelle?"

"What?"

He had a pained smile on his face, and he touched my nose. "Could we, you know, *not* call it fucking? Please? That word just has a bad connotation for me. If you don't want to say 'relations,' then what if we called it 'making love'? How would that be?"

"Making love sounds nice," I said, and I felt immediately shy around him. He was such an innocent, such a simple, good-hearted innocent who came from a planet where people were circumspect, didn't say bad words in public and thought that families were meant to stay together and that when you went to bed with someone, it was only out of love. And he loved me. Of course, that was probably only because he hadn't realized yet what he was in for. But still, I might be okay with him, if I tried really hard.

That night after we crept into the dark, sleeping apartment and made love, I lay awake for hours, listening to the sounds of sirens Dopplering down the street, people walking by outside laughing and talking all through the night, doors slamming elsewhere in the building. How did people live under these conditions? Did no one ever sleep? With the streetlights outside, it was almost as bright as day in the bedroom where we slept. The room was filled with books about feminism and dancing, and about feminist dancing. My head kept bumping into a box labeled "Jeremiah texts."

Before the sun was quite up, I woke to the sound of screaming and then a child saying, "Owie, owie, owie!" and a woman saying, "Stop it now, both of you!" Then there was a heated argument about whether this particular injury required a Band-Aid—the woman didn't appear to think so, but the child was adamant—and then, as I put the pillow over my head, I heard a détente of sorts: a flesh-colored Band-Aid could be applied, but this injury, whatever it was, did not merit one of the colored Band-Aids that were for real troubles. I fell back to sleep, but then, in what seemed like moments except that the sun was now shining in the window, there was the sound of walls and ceiling coming down, and the refrigerator opening and closing right at my head, it seemed, and the same woman insisting, "No, no, no. I told you that you can't put water on your granola. Granola is for *milk*. And you can't pour the milk. No, no, *no*! Put that down. I have to do it!" And then she cried out, "Jeremiah, God damn it, will you *do* something here? I've got to get out of here, and these kids are *killing* me!" The twins were apparently dismantling the kitchen, board by board from the sound of it, and I heard a man saying, "Can't you just speak in a regular voice? It only makes things worse when you get hysterical about every little thing. You should put the milk in a little pitcher and let him pour it out himself."

"Maybe you have time for that, but I don't have *time* to clean it up after he pours it all over the place!" the woman said. "And did you bring up the laundry? Brice smells like he has a poop, and I changed the last four poops, so it's your turn."

I heard Grant laughing into his pillow, next to my ear. "It's wake-up time," he whispered, and pulled me close. We kissed for a few minutes with pandemonium and discussions of poops raging two inches away from us on the other side of a flimsy piece of wallboard.

"So . . . what are you going to be doing today, do you think?" he whispered.

"Um . . . looking for an apartment?"

He laughed and swung his legs out of bed. "Excellent idea. I've got classes and meetings all day, but if you want, maybe we could meet for a late lunch on Broadway. I only have twenty minutes between my meeting with the dean this morning and my noon class, but we could grab a hot dog or something around 2:40. But then I really have to get back."

"Okay, sure," I said slowly. "How will I know how to get there?"

"Oh. Well . . ." He looked around uncertainly. "God, I don't know how to explain it. You can walk it if you want, just head down to the end of the street, and then turn right and go two more blocks . . . Wait. Actually, you should ask somebody. Contrary to what you think, New Yorkers are very friendly."

"Do you have classes every day?"

"Yeah. And I'm on a committee and I have students I'm advising. And then there are office hours . . ."

"I'm never going to see you, am I?"

He bit his lip and looked regretful. "Well, I come home at night. We'll have joyful reunions all the time, just like last night."

It was beginning to dawn on me what I had just done: flown across the country to be the houseguest of strangers. Grant was going to be gone all the time, and I couldn't even afford to spend the day doing what I might do if it was our own place: recover from jet lag by soaking in the tub while I ate a pint of chocolate mint ice cream and talked to Magda on the phone. I was going to have to get up, get dressed, be a lively and easygoing houseguest, grateful and interested in all things. And Magda was long-distance. I wouldn't be able to afford to call her.

"Listen, I gotta go get in the shower," he said. "I'm already late."

"Are you going to at least introduce me to . . . those maniacs out there?" I whispered.

He stopped and looked at me, dismayed. He was holding up his khaki pants and his blue button-down shirt, ready to bolt out of the room. "I . . . can't. I don't have time. And don't call them maniacs, okay? They're very nice. You'll see. And they know you're here. Just go out there and say hi. They know who you are. Tell them you want milk and not water on your granola. Trust me. It'll be fine."

"All right, all right. Go. Forget it." I turned back over in bed, faced the wall.

"Come on, you're not shy or anything," he said. "Just go out there."

Just then the door banged open, and the two-year-old hellions came dive-bombing onto the bed, kamikaze-style. I turned in time to catch a flash of two red-haired shrieking elves hurtling toward me, just as one landed right on my rib cage and nearly punctured a kidney with his elbow and the other started jumping up and down in the center of the bed, screeching, "Gwantie! I got a Band-Aid! Gwantie, wook at my Band-Aid! Gwantie, *wook*!" I tried to pull the comforter up over me while at the same time covering my head with my arms, hoping to save my eyeballs and some of my major organs from being punctured.

"Hey, hey, *hey*—wow, you do have a Band-Aid, Lindsay! Hey, Brice, be careful!" Grant was saying through the yelling and jumping, tugging on the comforter, but then there were footsteps and somebody else laughing. I peeked through my arms to see a man within inches of my head, a man with a shock of brown hair and blue eyes, bending, leaning across me, his arms outstretched, laughing as he managed to grab a flailing kid in each arm. It felt like nothing less than magic, as though he'd snatched spirits right out of the air. And then, very smoothly and competently, with both children twisting, screeching, and kicking in his arms, he backed his way out of the room. I was still struggling to hang on to the covers so that my naked body wasn't completely exposed, and when I looked up, I caught him giving me a slow, conspiratorial wink—me, this stranger he had never seen before—looking at me as though he'd known me always. As he closed the door, he said, "Hey, we'll just pretend this isn't the way we met, okay?"

WE MET properly in the kitchen later that morning, after everyone else had finally left. By then I'd already explored the apartment, which I adored. Sure, it was small by California standards, but it had impossibly high, elegant ceilings and lots of rooms and hallways, fascinating little nooks everywhere. I loved how everything was both polished and disorganized, which seemed to me a lovely balance somehow, just the way a house should be. There were Oriental carpets and light oak furniture in the living room, a fireplace, and tables, and everywhere were heaps of books and papers and stuffed animals. On the carved wood coffee table, there was a Brio train and a headless baby doll, and, astonishingly, a crystal bowl with peonies—risky with the two-year-olds, I thought, but there it was. A stereo system. Big windows with shutters and flowered chintz curtains, bookshelves filled with double-decker rows of books. The dining room had a formal table with striped up-holstered chairs, and there was also a desk overflowing with papers in the corner, and more bookshelves, and stacks of folders in a carton on the rug next to the desk. History stuff. No doubt this was the room where The Great Man worked. Down the hall toward the back of the apartment was the twins' room, sunny, with two cribs, brightly colored plastic crates filled with toys, and a rag rug. I peeked into the room next to that—the master bedroom, small and cluttered with orchid-colored walls and an unmade king-size bed that took up nearly the whole space piled with flung-off clothes and quilts.

I wandered back into the kitchen to look for something to eat. It was sunny in here, too, with big windows overlooking a tiny lawn next to the fire escape. There were butcher block countertops and a round oak table, which, judging from the crumbs and bowls and spilled milk, seemed to be where people actually ate. I was rummaging through the cabinet looking for the granola when I heard something behind me and spun around.

"Hi," he said. Then, seeing my face, he said, "Oh, sorry to startle you. Here I come barging in on you yet again, just when you thought you'd maybe have a moment's peace." He talked slowly and calmly, the way you'd talk to a wild animal, to soothe it. "Reduced schedule this year. I'm on sabbatical, actually—so I'm afraid I'm always popping in and out. Really quite annoying." He'd been to drop the children off at their day care, he explained, a woman in the neighborhood who watched six or seven kids in her apartment. This situation wasn't exactly ideal, he said, but what could you do with two-year-olds who weren't potty-trained yet?

"The kids are adorable," I said.

"Oh, adorable, sure," he said. "But that's just a safety net that nature provides so you won't abandon them on the side of the road with the rubbish one morning. Because, make no mistake, they are *trouble*." He looked at me and smiled, one of those knowing half smiles. "So did you find everything you were looking for?"

I blushed. "I was looking for granola," I said. "I thought . . ."

"Oh, quite right." He showed me the earthenware canister where it was kept, and then got out a bag of coffee from the refrigerator and some filters from a drawer, meanwhile talking in a matter-of-fact, self-deprecating way, until I could calm down. I hadn't unpacked yet, so I was wearing one of Grant's T-shirts, which said, "Historians do it longer," and the miniskirt I'd worn on the plane, and my hair was messed up, so I kept trying not to look at him, on the superstitious theory that if I didn't look directly at him, then he couldn't see me either. But out of the corner of my eye, I could see that he was thin and taut with energy and wearing jeans and a black T-shirt with some kind of Chinese writing on the front, and he kept smiling at me and flipping his longish brown hair out of his very blue eyes.

He showed me where the bowls were kept, and then he got out cups and pointed to a banana in the fruit bowl, apologizing for the morning wake-up and the chaos, and then the generalized state of disarray of everything, motioning around the room in a gesture that took in the whole house and possibly all of New York. When the coffee was done, he poured us each a cup. There was only skim milk to put in the coffee, no cream. Carly didn't allow cream in the house while she was trying to get herself back into shape, he said, laughing. "You'll get used to us, I hope," he said, and he sat down in the wooden chair across from me at the round oak table.

"So here's the rundown that Grant was probably too polite to give you: the children are loud and crazy and we haven't housebroken them or tamed them one bit," he said. "And Carly is a dancer and the main organizer around here, except that she's gone half the time these days trying to whip herself and some retired dancers back into shape so they can put on a show. Retired, in the dance world, means they're all of thirty. It's horrendous, really, what dancers have to go through, and I'm thought not to be truly supportive or sympathetic enough, though, in all fairness to myself, I do try. Still, I have crimes."

I blinked. "What are they? Your crimes?"

He looked at me and laughed. "Really? You want to know? You like the gory details, huh? Okay. My crimes." He drummed his fingers on the table. "One, I don't find one-eighth inch of extra flesh to be a major, life-changing disturbance. Two, it's been said that I'm not busy enough lately, due to my reduced schedule. And, let's see, I've also been accused of not having enough bad stuff happening in my life, so that I lack depth and understanding, which is true, but what can you do about that? Go out and look for bad times?" He shrugged, and we both laughed. "*And* I don't do the dinner dishes until the next morning. That may be my very worst crime."

"Really!" I said.

"Dreadful, I know," he said. "I've yet to meet a woman who can stand the sight of caked-on dinner dishes once fifteen minutes have passed after the meal." He laughed. "Carly says she *cannot* relax knowing that food is hardening on the plates. Just can't do it."

"She can't?" I said.

"Don't even *try* to tell me you aren't similarly afflicted."

"I never thought about it, I guess," I said. "I think if dishes eventually get done, then . . . well, who cares?"

"Exactly! Just my point. But I've discovered a peacemaking remedy for this problem, which—I don't know—might actually be considered yet another one of my crimes." He leaned forward and whispered, "Instead of doing the dishes after dinner, I just put them in the oven. Ingenious, right? Right?" He leaned back in his chair, grinning.

I laughed.

"You know," he said, "or maybe you don't know since you haven't been married so long yet—but let me tell you: the one with the most free time loses in all marital discussions. It's a given. So if you're the less busy person, take my advice and fake extreme busyness. I wish somebody had told me that back when it would have helped."

I laughed. "Well, that leaves me out, I'm afraid, because nobody on earth could be busier than Grant."

"I suppose you have a point. Well, then you'll have to go to Plan B, which is just to embrace the laziness and kick back and enjoy it. Luxuriate in it. Do your nails, brush your hair, yawn a lot. Take up lounging. It's a path that also has its benefits. Work at lowering people's expectations. That also can be quite effective."

He got up and started washing dishes then—both the ones from dinner, which had to be taken from the oven, and the breakfast bowls—and I stood beside him and dried them, which he teased me about. "If you're going to embrace laziness, this is not a good start," he said. "You should be tossing your hair or something." He let the stopper out of the sink, and the water bubbled out. "Oh, yeah, Grant said you're an artist," he said. "That may mean you can't lounge as much as you need to."

"Well, I don't know about being an artist. I was studying art in college."

"That sounds serious."

"Well, I should be serious about it, I guess. I mean, I dropped out of school. But now it's time to think of what I'm going to do, so I've got to go out and get some supplies, I guess, and decide what I'm going to try for." My head was pounding from jet lag. "Do you have any aspirin or anything?"

"Aspirin?"

"I have a headache. A jet lag headache, I think."

"If I may say so, I don't think this is jet lag. At least getting a headache is what always happens to me when the talk turns to work and dishes, which we've been irresponsible enough to let happen. But I do have aspirin, if you want."

"Thank you," I said.

"They're in the bathroom cabinet. Somewhere. Here, I'll show you. You might as well get used to our system of disorganization right away."

"We will get our own things," I said, following him to the bathroom. "You're so kind to let us live here, but you obviously don't have to buy our aspirin!"

He laughed. "No, don't worry. We're grateful you're here. You don't know it yet, but you're part of our plan to save our marriage. We should probably be paying you." He was smiling, and I couldn't imagine what he meant, so I just smiled back. We tramped into the bathroom together, which was all black and white tile and had a high window that looked out over a fire escape. He pulled towels and medications and heating pads and cosmetics out of the cabinet, until finally he triumphantly produced a bottle of aspirin and held it up like a trophy. Then he guessed correctly that I wouldn't want to use the smudged bathroom glass, so we tramped back to the kitchen, where he filled a glass with water and handed it to me.

He had to leave soon after that; there was someone else he was advising besides Grant, who was doing splendidly, he assured me, just splendidly, a hell of a teacher. He stopped himself at the door, patting himself down and checking his briefcase to make sure he had keys and subway tokens, all the required documents. He didn't; he sighed noisily and went back to his bedroom to get a file folder. I stood there in the entryway, admiring the artwork on the walls, the Indian prints and carvings.

There was an awkward but lovely moment when he came back. We stood there in silence for maybe four or five seconds. I felt him looking straight at me, like he was memorizing me. I squirmed. I wished I'd combed my hair. Then he smiled. "Are you going to be okay here? I can't believe all I've done is talk about myself. It was really just to get you acclimated, so you wouldn't think we're lunatics. I promise you I'm not like that, really. I do know that you've been through a terrible time with your brother and all, but I'm just so glad you're here—you *and* Grant." He smiled and leaned closer. "Will you promise me that you'll be lazy and indolent for the rest of the day? Go exploring, and tell anyone who asks that you're far too beautiful to work."

IT WAS the middle of September. The early-fall weather was cool and clear, the sky behind the buildings glowing a deep blue. This couldn't be the same country that contained California, with its parched, barren wideness, its freeways and long tracts of empty, wasted space, malls and parking lots, rows of apartment buildings surrounding pools. Everything here was compact, efficient, concrete. I loved how, walking along the sidewalks, you were aware from the rumble of the subways that you lived only in one layer of the city, while other people occupied the spaces around you that you couldn't see. And I couldn't get over the way people cultivated the minuscule inches of soil they had been given to plant. Marigolds and morning glories rose up from the tiniest patches. Some people actually grew grass—miniature lawns— in their window boxes.

Grant was hardly ever home that whole first semester. He took to being an assistant professor the way some people take vows in religious orders. It consumed him. The only time I could snap him out of it was when we were having sex, which we did all the time whenever he was home. I'd amble uptown to the university sometimes in my California sundresses, hoping to remind him of our shared roots. Remember Isla Vista? Remember the beach, and the way we'd once made love in my parents' swimming pool? Remember the day you asked me to marry you? Remember *why*? But always I'd find him distracted, tucked away in the tiny little office he shared, his own half neat and orderly and with files stacked perfectly on the desk while the other section, belonging to a woman who wore only brown and looked frightened to death if you so much as said hello to her, was filled with squirrel knickknacks, post-cards from the Grand Canyon, and mugs half full of old coffee, loaded with floating green stuff.

I teased him about her. "Don't you ever just look over and think, 'Well, what the hell? What would it hurt to go over and bend her backwards and have a passionate fuck right there on the desk?'"

He stared at me. "Please. Don't talk like that. You scare me sometimes."

"Do I?" We were standing in his office. His office mate—Bronwyn Lorimer—had just stepped out for something. I kept my eyes on his while I started slowly undoing the thirty pearl-size buttons down the front of my dress.

"Come on. Stop it." He looked around. "Why are you acting like this? Are you trying to get me fired?"

I went over to him and kissed him, and after a moment, he saw the futility of trying to push me away and kissed me back. But then when he pulled away he said in a low voice, "We shouldn't talk like that in here, that's all. Who knows when people will just barge right in?"

"Oh, yeah. God forbid people should see us making out. I'm sure that's never happened before on this campus." I sat down in his swivel chair and surveyed his office, with its four-inch window and metal shelves. "I'd go crazy if I had to be in this office all the time."

He cleared his throat. "Well, that's because you're an artist. You need light and landscapes. But I'm just grateful to have a desk and a quiet place to think."

At first I was dedicated to contacting real estate agents, but then I gave up. All the empty, available places tended to be in dangerous neighborhoods, the kind with drug addicts lying in the streets. The late 1970s was not a good time for the city. President Ford had refused to bail New York out, and it looked as if everything would just go under. Jeremiah and Carly said it would be ridiculous for us to leave, when we all got on so well together.

And we did. Carly was wonderful to me. She had a throaty, exciting voice and a way of confiding in me that made me feel as though we would someday be old friends. One day she told me that she and Jeremiah were better when they lived communally. "It makes us behave," she said. "I can't seem to do marriage in private. Over the years, I'd say our best years have been when we had spectators."

"What does she mean by that?" I asked Jeremiah, and he laughed his easy, intimate laugh and said it meant they didn't fight as much because they didn't want to argue in front of other people. "Perhaps you haven't noticed, but Carly is kind of, uh, a passionate person. She can scream and carry on, and when she's alone with me, I seem to bring out all her fury, for reasons I can't seem to help. So—and you'll love this—you know what we call you and Grant when you're not around? The 'marriage saviors.' If we make it to our golden anniversary, I promise you there'll be a special plaque with your names on it."

I LOVED living with children, even though they were exhausting and opinionated and not toilet trained and showed no signs of ever becoming civilized humans. Still, they made me laugh a hundred times a day. They were both cherubic, with Carly's red hair and Jeremiah's huge blue eyes, and deliciously fat, golden bellies, and when they were sleeping or cuddling with you while you read to them, you could almost forget that they could turn into rampaging maniacs with no warning whatsoever, fighting over toys and screeching and spilling milk and flinging food and being unwilling to put on their coats or get into their pajamas or finish their dinner. Lindsay was serious-minded and managed her brother (seven minutes her junior) with a hands-on-hips imperiousness that made all the adults laugh. Brice was clownish and clumsy and would do anything for a laugh. Carly once observed that when he walked into a room, the wallpaper started automatically peeling off the walls. But they called me Anniebelle and crawled in my lap sometimes just for fun, and the day I read *Goodnight Moon* thirteen times in a row, Lindsay said she loved me best of anybody.

As much as I was fascinated by the children, though, I was outright mesmerized by Jeremiah and Carly. I had never known people to be so cheerfully honest about the deficiencies and difficulties of marriage.

It was so *adult,* the way they were always throwing up their hands in exasperation with each other and having hissing fights in front of us, fights that seemed to me both comical and ironic. But not scary, not at all scary. Their disagreements were so unlike the arguments my parents would have indulged in, which always felt sort of dark and ominous. Carly could get furious with Jeremiah over his opinions about books and films and plays, just as often as she'd get mad about the fact that he had let Brice go without a diaper, or that he was hiding dishes in the oven and then forgetting and preheating them.

And whenever the four of us were together—at the dinner table, for instance—and they and Grant would get to talking, I felt as though I was a kid permitted to stay up late and sit at the adult table. I felt so young and incompetent around them, like I would never catch up, never understand how to live a cosmopolitan life. Jeremiah and Carly were older and they were physically beautiful, and they had furniture, wineglasses, dinner guests, daily planners, and a whole household that ran on something approaching chaos, but which still ran. It thrilled me to discover that running a family didn't have to be an all-consuming enterprise, the way my mother and her friends did it, but could just happen in an offhanded, casual fashion. Jeremiah and Carly and their friends were sophisticated and cool, and to my shock, Grant seemed right at home with them, able to hold his own talking about authors and playwrights and artists. It made me see him in a whole new way, as somebody who knew things. He could be a New Yorker, while I was just a baby. A California child.

Sometimes, though, they'd all be talking, and I'd be left out, and when I would look up, Jeremiah's eyes would be resting on mine. He'd have just the tiniest smile on his face, a lifted eyebrow, a smile that seemed to acknowledge that everything that was happening at the table was all just superficial bullshit, that he and I knew the real stuff.

I'd want to look away, but I couldn't. I'd been marked by his understanding of me. There was a little scorched place inside me where he had seen.

We, his eyes said—we, he and I—were the ones who truly understood.

I KNEW Grant and I shouldn't stay and yet we couldn't bring ourselves to leave, so we all four fell into a pattern of life that somehow
worked out. Grant and Carly were the industrious, busy ones, heading
out the door early in the mornings with their importance wrapped
around them like cloaks. Jeremiah called them the ants and said that
he and I were the grasshoppers, and they had to take care of us. I had
temp jobs sometimes, typing in banks and offices that required that I
put on panty hose and skirts and close-toed shoes, which Jeremiah
called my pitiful attempt to show myself to be a would-be ant. But
many more days I was at home, and there were those days when Jeremiah and I just hung out. One of us would take the children to day
care in the morning and then we were on our own. He showed me
around the city, took me on my first subway ride standing in the front
car, hurtling through the underground darkness. We went to parks
and museums. We'd go to the market together, plan dinner, walk
around the neighborhood, then settle down at home with our books
and our imagined work. I sketched things, he typed at his desk. We
met in the kitchen for heated-over morning coffee, padding around
in our socks, watching the late-afternoon sun slant in through the
windows while we drank wine and cooked dinner.

He told me he was supposed to be spending his sabbatical writing
a book about something having to do with the history of an uprising
in upstate New York, but he said he wanted to switch fields, to write a
book about the philosophy of creativity instead. He was sick of the
work that had once come so effortlessly to him. He wanted to find the
seams of people's stories, of the spirituality and mysticism they carried with them, and then he laughed his always self-deprecating
laugh. He was tentative and almost formal around me, put-upon and
beleaguered, but in a funny way, and always ready to laugh. He knew
such a wide variety of things: he could play the guitar, speak three

languages, cook gourmet meals, and talk to just about anybody on any topic at all. At the market, I'd go off to pick out fruit and come back to find him squatting down talking to some street person about redevelopment or the constellations or the best way to light a cigarette if you didn't have any matches.

I confessed to him that I didn't know what I was supposed to be doing. I should do art, I supposed. Or maybe I should go back to school, get my degree. Should I be painting? Working more? Getting a full-time corporate job? Who knew? One day he said, "Why the fuck does everybody have to *do* something? Why can't we just enjoy ourselves? I think that's what you should do. Resist, resist. Do as little as possible for as long as you can." He moved his arms in the air, like waves, when he said, "Resist, resist." His voice was like silk and velvet.

Grant, when pressed for an opinion, held the same one he'd always held, that I was vastly talented and should be doing art for my own self-fulfillment, for art's sake alone. And Carly thought I should be looking for studio space and galleries to show my work, and possibly lining up mentors, if not benefactors and backers. This was what she referred to as "support."

"I would like to support your art," she said to me one day, "but I notice you're not doing any. And I want to know why. Are you depressed, do you think?"

I stuttered through some explanation about not really having the time and space. The truth, which I was much too shy to ever admit, was that I was way too disorganized and confused. Art was the last thing I could think about in this new life. The most I could do was sketch pictures of the peonies in their glass bowl in the living room or portraits of the twins on the move, and I never intended to show anyone those.

"Perfect!" she crowed. "No time or space? That we can fix! Can't we, Jeremiah?" She and some friends had taken over some old factory space in SoHo, a giant, unused loft where once there had been machines and heavy shoe-making equipment. Other artists, too, were trying to set up studios there, and she told me that if I was truly seri-ous about doing my art, I could maybe join in a co-op, start claiming my own space. I didn't think I qualified as a "serious artist," the way Carly and her friends might define it.

"I like her, but she scares me," I said to Jeremiah one afternoon when we were trying to wrangle the children into playing with Play-Doh, and he laughed and said, "Yeah, she's fucking scary. Always has been. Really one of your more *intense* individuals."

I swallowed. "But very, very committed. A good person," I said.

"Oh, yeah. Goes without saying. A terrific person. Grant, too."

"Absolutely."

"You two are without a doubt the best marriage saviors going."

And for a moment our eyes met over the top of the children's heads. He brushed his hair out of his eyes, and I looked away.

ONE DAY I came home from a temp job working in a bank and there he was, pounding away on his typewriter at the kitchen table while the kids banged on pots and pans with wooden spoons. He held up one finger in the air, like somebody saying, "Wait!" and told me he'd had a flash of an idea for his book. This wasn't a treatise on creativity and labor unions after all; it was a novel! He could barely stop typing. He looked almost feverish. He'd been writing all day and the ideas were just pouring out of him, he said. He was trembling with energy.

Lindsay's diaper smelled to high heaven, so I whisked away the twins and changed both of them, and then I sat on the rag rug in their room with them and blew bubbles from a plastic wand while they tried to smash them. When Jeremiah came to join us, he was smiling.

"It's a novel! It's really a novel!" he said, and he grabbed Brice by the hands and started jumping up and down with him. "Oh, Bricey, your mama is going to be so mad when she finds out what Daddy is doing with his sabbatical. Who would have guessed that I'm writing a novel!"

"But why should she be mad?" I said. "Isn't she, like, all in favor of everybody being as creative as possible?"

"Ha! Have you observed *nothing* in your time here, my dear Annabelle? That's lip service. Girls—excuse me—*women* are allowed to be creative, but guys are supposed to be paying the bills. Being a Columbia professor of history and all that."

I had to admit he had a point. Carly had ambushed me one night early on, after the guys had gone to bed. "You can't let these years go by, you know. It's bad enough that you've displaced yourself, stopped going to college because of your *husband's* career, but luckily you landed in New York City instead of in South Podunk, North Dakota, like so many college wives. So now you need to take over your own life and make sure you get exactly what you need out of the deal. Get things the way you want them."

But how, when I didn't even know what I wanted? I had squirmed under her gaze. We needed money, I told her. That's why I'd signed up with the temp agency. Already I'd worked at a bank, a talent agency, a public relations firm, and a law office. That seemed fine for now.

Carly slammed her fist down on the counter and said all that was shit work. "You know what this is? It's depression!" she said. "When an artist is not doing her art, she starts to lose touch with her essential self."

"I don't really think it's depression. I might just not have any ambition," I said.

"Well, I'm not going to give up on you even if you're giving up on yourself," she said. "Just remember that when you're ready, there are plenty of opportunities. And sometimes you need to push yourself through the next door. For God's sake, just don't do what I did and have children."

I couldn't believe she'd just said that. It seemed to me permissible to be vocal about not wanting children in advance—nameless, faceless children that you would never know—but to speak so callously of existing children was surely wrong. She saw my expression and leaned forward suddenly and spoke through clenched teeth.

"Listen, I love my kids as much as anybody loves their children," she said. "I bow to *no one* when it comes to being a good mother! But I'm talking about something else now. A career! And not getting swallowed up by all the domestic concerns. Kids are great when you're ready for them, and I'm not going to sugarcoat it and say that it's just the most wonderful thing in the world, a woman's greatest crowning achievement, because it *isn't*. I lost my body when I had those twins. Having two at once was a piece of bad luck, really." She stared at me again, daring me to disapprove. "Annabelle. I'm talking from *the standpoint of my body*. That's all I'm saying. I gained fifty-three pounds that I've had to sweat off every inch of. But I'm doing it. I'm flourishing again, but I'll never make back that time. You—you have nothing constraining you, and yet you just go out to shit jobs every day. Let me tell you, because nobody else will: *you need these years*. I won't ever be great because of the time I took off. You don't know it, but the longer you just stand in place . . . You're losing time. I'm older than you are. Be careful, is all I'm telling you. Stop letting people take advantage of you."

"Who's tak—?"

She tucked a tendril of red hair behind her ear. Her nostrils flared. "Your *husband*," she said. "And mine, too, if you let him. I heard that last week you took the children to day care twice. I warn you: don't let him do that to you. He's the one with the free time. Men have all the cards. Don't let them take yours."

ACTUALLY, THOUGH, it ended up being Carly herself who took my free time. She had a fight with the day-care lady, Marjorie, a motherly woman I had come to like on my frequent trips with Jeremiah to pick up the kids. Marjorie was in her forties, an old hippie-type with one long gray braid down her back, harried but sweet, and she genuinely seemed to like the children in her care. Often she and I and Jeremiah sat outside on the stoop, drinking a glass of wine at five o'clock while the kids played in her tiny gated yard. But Carly had problems with her. Now that Brice and Lindsay were about to turn three, she only wanted books read to them that did not have sexist references. The moms in the books should *not* be shown as the only ones taking care of children. They should not wear aprons or cook. The dads should be shown grocery shopping and putting children to bed. It was, I thought, an excellent point—but what were we to do about it? Stop reading books altogether?

No. Apparently she had a plan to remedy the situation, and one night after the kids were in bed, she brought a bunch of the day-care books out of her bag, along with some Magic Markers. We were going to black out the offending passages and change some genders, she said with a big smile.

"Wow. How did you get these?" I asked her. Behind her, out of her line of vision, Jeremiah raised his eyebrows for my benefit and pantomimed somebody shoving books into a bag and tiptoeing away. I had to stifle a laugh.

"Well, today," she said, "I told Marjorie I wanted to join the twins for lunch, and she said okay. And then, while we were having a picnic in their little back area, I just slipped inside and put about ten of the books in my bag. And now tomorrow I'll give them to Jeremiah to take back. Next week I'll see if I can't get some more."

"Wow. You just *took* them?"

"Yep! Don't look at me like that. Marjorie should be happy about it. She's one of us, you know. She and her husband are both feminists. He marched against Vietnam and she hasn't shaved her legs in about a decade. So I think she probably would have done this herself if she'd had the time. I actually see doing this as a kind of present to her."

Marjorie, of course, didn't see it that way. When she caught me trying to slip the books back on the shelves the next day, she was horrified at what we'd done. I hastened to explain about women in positions of power and the importance of boys and girls growing up realizing women could be anything they wanted, but my mouth was dry while I was doing it.

"But . . . isn't this . . . like censorship?" she said. I explained again. I couldn't think of anything else to say. It had been a terrible idea.

"But Goldilocks was a *girl*!" she said, thumbing through the book and discovering that Goldilocks had become a boy named Locks, a change that Carly had thought was particularly brilliant. "She had curiosity, and stamina, and judgment, all good qualities . . ."

"Carly said it was sexist," I said, although I was suddenly sure that Goldilocks was not sexist at all.

"You know," said Marjorie. "I love Carly's children, but I'm just about sick to death of Carly Ferguson-Saxon herself. She came in here yesterday and asked me a million questions about the lunch I was serving—was the macaroni made from whole-wheat pasta, where did the apples come from, and wasn't it interesting that the little boys happened to get their food first before the little girls did? When really it was all because of where they happened to be sitting. And then she went into this whole big thing about nap times, and which songs I sing. I tell you, she's a pain in the ass."

"She's got a lot of opinions," I said.

"And you live with her! I don't know how you do it."

"I find her . . . refreshing," I said loyally.

Marjorie stared at me. "I don't know how you do it," she repeated. "But I don't need this hassle. I think I'm done with her."

She gave Jeremiah and me a note that evening when we went to pick up Brice and Lindsay. They had two weeks to find some other arrangement. Marjorie and her husband were cutting back, the note said. They were sad to say they could no longer offer day care.

As we walked home, Jeremiah and I couldn't stop laughing about it.

"Fucking Carly!" he said, shaking his head. He was pushing the twin stroller with Brice and Lindsay in it. "I can't believe how she gets us into such scrapes. Is she unbelievable? Now we can't have day care anymore because she's a book thief! And you know what this means, don't you?" he said. "For you and me. You know what this means."

"What?" I said. Just his saying the words "you and me" made me weak.

"We're going to have kids around all the time. She's going to ask you if you'll babysit them. Just watch."

She did, promising that she'd keep looking for other arrangements for them, but the time for her show—or *happening;* she didn't like it to be called a show because that put too much pressure on the dancers, she was quite firm about this—was drawing close, and she needed even more hours out of the house. "Since you're not doing art anyway . . ." was the way most of Carly's sentences now started.

"But do you want to do this?" Grant asked me. We were taking a walk that evening. It was late November, and at last it was truly cold outside. The leaves were mostly in piles, and I scuffed through them as we walked down the residential streets. I looped my arm around his so he would have to slow down.

"I guess so," I said. "I mean, I like the kids and all."

"Well, then, the way I see it, there are two good reasons for it," he said cheerfully. "It's a way to pay them back for letting us live with them. And maybe you'll get some experience taking care of kids so that when we have our own, you'll be all set."

Something about that made me mad. "I can't believe you just said that."

"What? What's wrong with that?"

"I think it's sexist. I mean, why is it up to me to pay them back for letting us live there? And also, why should I be the only one to get experience taking care of kids? What about *you*?"

"What are you talking about? I'm working a million hours a day. You know that. And what's wrong with saying you need experience? We all need experience in things."

"But what about my painting? Don't you care anymore that I'm not doing my art?"

We had stopped walking. He stood there looking confused. "Well, then why don't you paint if you want to paint? What's stopping you?"

I was as shocked as he was that I was having this fit, but I plowed onward. "What's stopping me?" I said. "Just where am I supposed to paint? *Where?* In the corner of our tiny little room, where I can't even keep bobby pins without them getting in somebody's way? Or maybe on the kitchen table, where the twins constantly knock everything over? Where would *you* suggest I paint?"

He looked stricken for a moment; his eyes were like holes in his face in the shadow of the streetlights. He held up his palms, the universal gesture of an innocent man being wrongly accused. "Hey, if you want to paint, then we can find a way to make that happen. You've never talked about this. Didn't Carly know some people you could rent from . . . somewhere . . . and paint, you know, all together? A kind of co-op deal?"

"I'm not going to paint with a bunch of artistic snobs." I burst into tears.

"What's going on here? How do you know they're snobs?"

"Because they are! Because I met them. And because Carly thinks I just let everybody take advantage of me, and she doesn't know that I'm not ready to paint with a bunch of people who think I'm just an amateur! I'm out of place here. I don't know what I want to do, and so I'm going to do this damn babysitting thing because there's nothing else for me to do, but I want *you* at least to know that I'm miserable."

"Great," he said. "And what am I supposed to do about it? What do you want from me?"

"What do I want from you? What do you think I want from you? I want you to be my *husband*, and be on my side and look out for me. I want you to bring out the best in who I am." I struggled to think of words Carly had used. "I want you to empower me and make me use all my best self."

He laughed. "Good God! What is all this talk? You know I'm on your side. I love you! I adore you. Look, if you don't want to do the babysitting thing, then say you can't, and don't. It's simple."

"I didn't say I didn't want to do it."

He sighed and stared off into the distance, squinting. He looked adorable, with the wind sort of ruffling his hair. But then he had to do that throat-clearing thing he did, and the spell was broken. "I don't get you. You want to do the babysitting, but you want to be miserable. Is that it?"

"Listen, what I really, really want is for us to move into our own place, and I want to have my own career, too. You're in way over your head, you're gone all the time, the only people I really know are Jeremiah and Carly, and now I feel like I *have* to take care of their kids so we can stay here, and I'm not doing my art—" I couldn't stop myself from crying and saying all these nonsensical things that I wasn't even sure I believed.

What I wanted was for him to keep holding me, to say I was beautiful, to say, *Don't be in love with Jeremiah. Love me instead.*

He shifted his weight to the other foot. "Annabelle," he said, "let's not fight. I've got a million papers to grade, and I'm writing a proposal, and I've got a student coming in at seven thirty tomorrow morning to talk about his grade. Just do what you want. I'll back you up. If you want to paint, if it's a real calling for you, then do it. If you want us to find another place to live, go back to checking with Realtors. If you don't want to watch Carly's kids, tell her you'll help her make other arrangements. Now let's go home. Can we?"

"Home, he says. Like we have a home."

"It's our home for now. And you can find us another place. Okay, baby?" He put his arm around my waist and leaned me against him, and we slowly started to walk back. We walked in silence for a long time. I couldn't believe how far we'd gotten from Carly and Jeremiah's apartment. The night air was crisping up. I leaned in closer, and he tucked me into his coat with him. I felt the anger draining away and was relieved. It had been like a small storm, nothing so serious after all.

"Anyway, aren't you a little bit happy here?" he said softly, crooningly, after a while. "I can tell that you like Jeremiah, at least. And he likes you. I see the happy way you two get when you talk to each other at dinner. Even if you don't really like Carly, you always seem to have a million things to talk about with *him,* right?"

My blood froze, and I felt my mind start racing backward, defensively. Was I going to be accused of something here? Did I need to start marshaling some arguments?

I didn't say anything, and after a moment, my blood settled back in its old familiar tracks, stopped beating in my ears. Grant was merely stating something lovely that he'd noticed. There wasn't any recrimination there at all. When we got to the front door of the apartment building, he took me in his arms and placed me on the bottom step, and then he stood on the sidewalk—so that we were almost eye to eye—and kissed me lightly on the lips, over and over again, a hundred little kisses.

And I just stood there and let his kisses rain over me, but what I was thinking was that maybe Jeremiah would still be awake when we went inside. Maybe he would smile at me again the way he had at dinner.

Part of me hoped he'd be there, but there was another part of me that just wanted to take Grant's hand and run away with him in the darkness. Maybe we could go back to California, live on the beach in a cave, and hide from this thing that was hunting me down just as surely as if I had a bull's-eye painted on my forehead.

[e l e v e n]

"*M*om. Mom, wake up. I have to ask you something."

I sit straight up in bed, on my ready-to-jump-in-a-taxi alert. The word *Mom* has always been able to do that to me—even uttered from five rooms away and in a hoarse whisper, it can jolt me out of the deepest sleep. I think of it like the special red phone in the White House.

"Oh, baby! Baby! Are you all right?" Before I'm even fully awake, I'm on my feet and turning on the light. Sophie is lying on her side, propped up on her pillow. Her eyes are dry, and she doesn't seem to be in pain. My heart rate settles back down to the normal range. "What's the matter?"

The clock on the bedside table says 2:47.

"I'm okay. I made up my mind not to wake you up, but I just keep thinking, and I can't sleep," she says in a perfectly wide-awake voice. "Then I was lying here, and I decided that some things are better when you talk about them in the middle of the night anyway. Have you ever noticed that? That in the middle of the night you talk about different things? Whit and I used to have some of our best discussions then. Maybe people are more real then. Do you think so? They don't have their defenses up."

She is obviously out of her mind and nowhere near sleep, so I rub my eyes and try to bring my mind into focus. "Okay. My defenses are certainly still asleep, so what kind of thing do you want to talk about? Are you feeling anxious?"

"I want to talk about open marriage."

"Open marriage? Really?"

"Yeah. That's where you're married, but you can have other part-ners and so can your husband—"

"Yes. I'm familiar with the term."

"Well, I want to know if you think it works. Because this woman I work with says she and her husband were going to split up, but then they decided instead to have an open marriage and sleep with other people, and she told us that saved their marriage because neither one of them gets jealous or anything. Like when her husband is with his other partner, then she just goes out with her friends and does what-ever she wants to do, like go to parties and maybe meet new people, and she says that when they get back together, they're both happier. What do you think about something like that?"

"Wow. It may be *too* much in the middle of the night for this dis-cussion," I say, "but my initial impression is that she's lying to you. I don't think it works. Not with most people."

"Yeah, that's kind of what I thought, too," she says slowly. She stares at the ceiling.

"It's one of those great ideas that turns out to be just not practical. It doesn't fit with human nature."

"But think about the Winstanleys," she says. "What if they could have had an open marriage? Don't you think it might have been better for them, really? I mean, if Mr. Winstanley got a little crush on someone else, then couldn't he just get it out of his system and still stay with his wife, and then the whole family wouldn't have had to suffer?"

"Maybe, but I'm not sure Mary Lou would have gone for that deal." I laugh a little, picturing practical, down-to-earth Mary Lou kissing Clark good-bye as he walks out the door, arm in arm, with Padgett.

"So what do you think? Could you have ever done it—forgiven Dad, I mean, if Dad was the type to get crushes? I mean, if you love somebody enough, won't you do anything to keep them?"

· · ·

THIS IS not what we're talking about.

Yesterday she spent a great deal of time at the computer, staring at the pictures Whit has sent her. At one point she called me over, and I stood next to her while we looked at the photos he's sent. They are mostly of adorable, dark-eyed children who regard the camera with shy smiles, and of construction workers building the new orphanage. There are vast, verdant fields with vegetables growing, and a shiny, stainless-steel kitchen where we see smiling people stirring and serving giant pots of food. There is the pleased but harried face of the director, and photos of the film crew, mugging for the camera, hoisting beers, walking around a town, playing Frisbee with the children.

And in one picture, just one picture, there is Whit, standing next to a woman who actually looks a lot like Sophie—a pert, ponytailed cutie in a green T-shirt and denim shorts—and for that second when the picture was taken, forever captured on camera, his arm is draped across her shoulders and he is looking down and smiling at her, a totally unself-conscious, beaming grin that could mean anything at all but of course means only one thing to Sophie.

Whit has fallen in love in Brazil.

When I saw it, I flinched just a little. And I wasn't surprised when Sophie flashed right past it, and then when we were all done, I saw her go back to that one and bring it up on the screen. I excused myself and went to make another pot of pregnancy tea and then I suggested we watch something fun on DVD. I grabbed *Sleepless in Seattle*, which has no scenes of marital infidelity in it. We didn't need any of that.

But now it's the middle of the night and the black dogs are howling in her head, and she is asking me if I ever would have forgiven Grant, and what can I say? I look at her and can't think of anything truthful that could help her. Am I to just pat my lonely, left-behind, pregnant daughter and offer some sweet assurance that she's married to a wonderful man, a man who would never, ever hurt her? Do I even believe that?

Who knows what to believe? What's clear is that it's three o'clock on a dark winter morning, and she is in her seventh month of pregnancy, and in Brazil her husband is either sleeping alone or he isn't, and either way, Beanie Bartholomew is coming into this world and will need love and sustenance and, more than anything else, a mother who believes herself to be loved.

I say slowly, "I guess I would try to understand. But it would depend on the circumstances, and if your father was really in love with someone else or just was lost and trying to make sense of things within himself."

She sighs a big, loud sigh and smiles at me. "You can't even relate, can you?" she says. "It's beyond belief for you, is what it is."

ONE DAY the phone rings, and it's Cindy Bartholomew, Whit's mother. She seems surprised to find me on the other end of the phone, so I have to explain about the sudden bleeding. She is suitably chagrined. We met at the wedding at our house, of course, and at the time I remember thinking she seemed charming and funny. She exclaimed that New England was just the most beautiful place ever, and she loved our house, our friends, the whole bit. We insisted that she and her husband stay in our guest room, and if after a few days I found her tendency to talk baby talk to her husband just the tiniest bit irritating, I enjoyed them overall. They told funny stories, especially when they'd been drinking. She and Clement are always jetting all over the country, monitoring their various investments, and whenever they're in New York, they try to come and check on Sophie and the progress of their grandchild. They'd like to come for a little visit. Would that be possible?

"Of course," I say. "We'd love to see you." Sophie, meanwhile, is shaking her head and diving under the covers even as I'm arranging the time.

"They're *family*," I tell her when I hang up. "Why don't you want to see them? And don't they, in fact, own this apartment you're living in?"

"Yes. *God.* They own everything. I feel like when they're here, they're making sure I haven't done some terrible thing to destroy the place. I always just want to get out of here."

"It'll be okay. It won't do us any harm to be nice to them. We can set up a party platter in the bedroom."

"Ugh. I suppose."

The Bartholomews arrive on a Sunday afternoon, and the four of us settle awkwardly in the bedroom, which is where Sophie and I have done all our entertaining. But this time it's unbearable. I immediately see what Sophie means: Clement, who is about twenty years older than Cindy, is a restless type, always looking as though he's just about to go to a meeting at which he expects to be told that he's been elected the king of the universe and that things on the home planet have gone terribly wrong. He paces around the apartment, huffing and sighing, opening cabinets, and tapping at the bricks on the fireplace. Cindy is obviously used to this kind of behavior; her well-made-up eyes follow him, and she keeps calling him Grandpa and telling him to go and do all the "Grandpa" things he needs to do, although I can't imagine what they are.

Finally he comes back into the bedroom doorway, where he looms like André the Giant, and makes a pronouncement. "Okay, I'm ready now to take three beautiful women to lunch."

Oh, but we can't. It is explained to him again. We can't leave the house. Sophie, in fact, can't leave her bed. To my surprise, Sophie stands up and declares that it won't hurt if we just go out for a little bit of lunch. It might even do her good.

"Wait," I say.

"No. Mom! How's this really going to hurt? I'll go downstairs, get right into a cab, and go to the restaurant and sit down immediately, eat, get into the cab again, and come right back." Her eyes are pleading, bright and intense. "I mean, I go to doctor's appointments—why not one lunch out?"

"I think they want you *lying* down," I say, but clearly I'm embarrassing her. Cindy Bartholomew is starting to make little henlike noises, trying to smooth things over, as if there's about to be a huge argument.

Clement is snorting. "I'll take responsibility for this," he says.

I'm aghast. There's no *taking responsibility*. An unborn baby could be in danger—how do you take responsibility for that? I wish I could tell Grant this story. The *old* Grant. We've always laughed about men like this, men who think they're so powerful they can intervene in matters of life and death.

Cindy twitters around us, worried. Clement assures us he will call the doctors, if necessary. He can get us a wheelchair if that would help . . . he'll have his cell phone and there will be three of us to watch her every second. It's not such a big deal.

Sophie is frantically signaling me with her eyes that this is something that must be done. She wants this.

So we go outside, blinking in the light and air. Clement hails a cab, and it parks obediently by the curb, like a trained puppy. The day is prematurely warm, filled with sunshine and promise. At home, there wouldn't be a day like this until late May. But here in New York, it seems like anything is possible. Sophie declares that it feels wonderful to be out in the air, and not on her way to the doctor. She is positive that the bleeding was just a onetime thing, an anomaly. It is important for her, in fact, to feel that her body is competent enough to hold on to a baby even when she's upright. This is great, great, great.

Cindy gives me a knowing look, one that I can't read. I take it to be a "we women know what we're doing" look. But not quite. We get to the restaurant—an elegant, dim place with lots of polished wood and thick, cream-colored napkins—and Clement proceeds to order mimosas all around. But then I really do fight him, and Sophie does, too: pregnant women aren't allowed to drink alcohol. No, not even one. Yes, times have certainly changed.

He sulks over this a bit, but then we manage to change the subject. Real estate, weather, the Bartholomews' recent trip to Italy.

It occurs to me suddenly, after a few sips of my mimosa, that we haven't mentioned Whit. So I do it. "Whit's project seems to be coming along well," I say. "Do you hear from him very often?"

The table gets quiet. Cindy nods and looks away. Clement orders another round, although we haven't finished the first one. Sophie gamely tells a story that Whit told her, about a child he met in a village, who thought that she could maybe come back to the United States with him if the right person won the election. That's what she thought an election was: a ticket. It's a lame story, and not totally believable, and after a moment's polite pause, Cindy asks me if it's been a rough winter in New Hampshire.

Later, when I excuse myself to go to the restroom, she follows me there. "Sorry that was so awkward when you mentioned Whit," she says. "It's kind of a sore spot now, this whole situation.... Well, I'm sure *you* know." She waves her hand in the direction of the dining room.

I am drying my hands on a paper towel. "Oh, yes. I know how *that* is. Sore spots," I say. I think she's come into the restroom to tell me something about her husband. I know the look of women who are about to report that their marriages are unsatisfactory in some way.

She is smiling at me. "Well, of course, right now you're the one most inconvenienced by this whole deal."

"Inconvenienced?"

"Yes, coming here. I mean, I'm sure we all agree that it was most unfortunate for Sophie to go and get pregnant at a time like this." She leans close to the mirror and examines her lipstick, which has kind of fanned out around the lines of her mouth. "I have been telling my son since he was sixteen years old that he has to take responsibility for birth control. And he didn't—and look."

"Well," I say, and I let out a tinny laugh. "I think couples sometimes make these decisions unconsciously. These kinds of things do happen."

"Yes, but sometimes one of them doesn't get informed." She straightens up and fluffs her hair and looks at me in the mirror. "I'm not saying that Sophie did anything wrong. It was his responsibility just as much as it was hers."

"Well, birth control has never been one hundred percent...," I begin.

"Yes," she says. "But my son has a promising career ahead of him, and now he's going to be a father at twenty-three. Do you know how much of a sacrifice that's going to require of him?"

"It's a sacrifice for both of them," I say quietly. "And right now, it seems that it's Sophie who's taken the brunt of it. He, after all, did go to Brazil just as he planned."

"His *career* was at stake. Do you have any idea of the hit he would have taken if he had canceled the film crew and backed out of the project? It was a ridiculous time for a pregnancy. And it could have ruined everything for him."

Okay, now I have had it. "Listen," I say, "I have been on your son's side, much to the chagrin of my family. I have truly and honestly believed that he is doing the right thing pursuing his dream and completing this documentary, even though he is—"

"Well, that goes without saying!"

"—*even though* he is abandoning my daughter, *his wife*, in her hour of greatest need. I have stuck up for him and defended his decision. She never once asked him not to take this trip! Not once. But that doesn't mean that she hasn't been suffering due to his abandonment. And this pregnancy has not gone smoothly, and yet, until she was put on bed rest, every day she managed to work and keep up the house, even though she was totally and completely alone—"

"It *was* her choice," she says. "I'm a mother of a son, Annabelle, and I see how women can be. Boys—*men*—are so easily manipulated. They're victims of their penises. They never see what hit them. A woman comes along and decides she's having a baby, and that's it. He's done for. Career plans: gone. And my son is only twenty-three years old! That's about fourteen in girl years."

It's then that I remember that Cindy Bartholomew is Clement's second wife, and that after a couple of drinks last summer, she laughingly admitted that Whit had been conceived slightly before Clement's previous marriage was terminated. So of course she would see the world this way—that women mastermind pregnancies as a way of forcing men into unpleasant decisions. I'm furious, of course, that she would lump my Sophie into this awful view of women . . . but while I'm mustering up all my anger, a funny thing happens.

So what, I think. So what if the worst is true and Sophie did manipulate her way into marrying Whit and then making a baby with him? It doesn't matter. That's how marriages start sometimes. That's how new people have always gotten here. Since the beginning of time, there have always been people standing on the sidelines criticizing, saying, "How could he want to be with *her*?" or "What does she see in him?" or "What were they thinking, getting pregnant now?" We don't understand love, that's the truth of it.

I turn and look at Cindy Bartholomew, all painted up and twenty years younger than a man who thinks he's going to always run the world, and it's as though I can see through to her essence somehow, how frightened she is behind all that puffery and makeup. I see it then—that this is just love she's expressing, love for Whit, and fear that his happiness might be in jeopardy. He is the child she conceived under questionable circumstances with an already married man, and now her heart aches for what might happen to him. It's love. That's all it is.

So I say to her what I'm always saying to Grant: "We have to let them make their own decisions. It's no longer our job to manage things for them. We have to let go and let them work it out."

It hits me that someday Sophie herself may be standing in just such a ladies' room, thinking about her firstborn, and fearing for that daughter's safe passage into love, and for some reason, that thought, all these mothers in restrooms marking out their territory, fretting for their children—well, it just makes me so happy that I take Cindy's arm and lead her back to the table, where Clement Bartholomew is right then hugging my daughter with tears in his eyes.

FOUR DAYS later Sophie has a doctor's appointment. The weather has turned gray and cold again, and we bundle up in our sweaters and coats for venturing out.

Her cheeks are bright and rosy. "I feel like I'm going to a movie— the movie starring Beanie," she says. Today they're going to want to do another ultrasound just to make sure everything's okay. We love ultrasounds; it's when we get to see little baby Beanie Bartholomew in all her tucked-in, radiant glory.

"Maybe she'll wave to us today," I say.

Also, today is March 5, which is only two months from the real due date, and that means that—well, this baby could actually be born. She would be okay. Oh, it would be scary; she'd probably have to spend some time in the newborn intensive care unit. There'd be drama and uproar and I'd have to suck in my breath and pace the corridor. But it could happen. I've been here for almost four weeks. Sophie and I have cooked this baby for an entire additional month, and no, I'm not claiming any credit, but I did do my share of making macaroni and cheese and keeping Sophie in her bed.

"If everything's okay," she says to me as we're getting dressed, "I think we should celebrate by going out afterward."

"We should celebrate by coming home and getting in bed and buying ourselves another month of being careful . . ."

"Mom. Everything was fine after the lunch the other day. And you said it yourself: if the baby was born now, we'd all survive. She has lungs."

"She may have lungs, but having a premature baby is no picnic, and it's you I worry about."

"Mom! Don't worry. It's fine."

"I have to worry. It's in my job description."

"But it would be best if you worried to yourself. That's what a really good mother should aspire to: silent worrying that she doesn't inflict on her child."

"Uh-huh. And we'll see how well *you* do at that in about two months."

She laughs. "I said *aspire*. I didn't say anybody could really do it."

The ultrasound is better than good. When the technician (Nina—we've had her before, and she has a calm, motherly presence) puts the wand on Sophie's abdomen, all three of us gasp. Because there, perfectly formed, is a little round face, eyes open, looking out at us. The head turns, and the baby brings her fist up to her mouth.

"Oh, my goodness!" says Sophie and starts to cry. "Look at her!"

I feel my eyes stinging, and I lean over and squeeze Sophie's arm. "She's beautiful. She looks like you. Look at that adorable little nose!"

I'm so moved that I get out my cell phone and call Grant and describe the baby's face to him. "She looks like your grandmother Petra."

"You never met my grandmother Petra," he says.

"Is there not a picture of her hanging in the hallway right at this very minute? A picture I have looked at nearly every day of my married life."

"Is there really?" he says.

"Grant, do you live in the same house I do?"

"Apparently not," he says drily. "I don't seem to run into you here."

I'm silent for a moment. And then I say, "You'll be here soon, though. Spring break, right?" And I'm surprised to feel this great warmth spreading through me—a great warmth that for once isn't a hot flash. I want to tell him about Cindy Bartholomew and something that I figured out about men and women and new people coming onto the planet, but I'm sitting there in the doctor's office and tears are running down my face and there's a baby's face looking placidly out at all of us.

Then, best of all, Sophie gets out her cell phone, too, and she calls Whit all the way in São Paolo, Brazil.

"Whit," she tells him. "Beanie is a *girl*. Yes, a girl! And you know what? She's smiling at me right now! Yes, on camera! An ultrasound! She has the cutest little nose, and my mom says she looks just like I did when I was a baby." She closes her eyes, listening, and then she starts to cry. "I love you, too. I know . . . not too much longer."

TO CELEBRATE, we go to lunch at a deli down the street from the doctor's office.

"Pastrami on rye with mustard," Sophie tells the waitress. She is elated, her face pink and glowing. "Piled high with cheese and onions. And coleslaw. Oh my God, coleslaw. Keep it coming. Ooh, and also I want a half-sour pickle. And a Coke."

I do not say, "What about heartburn?"

We sit in the booth and eat and look at the portrait that Nina snapped of the baby's face. Sophie says she will scan the picture and e-mail it to Whit, so he can see, too. I say we need vegetables for din- ner to make up for this salty, sinful, fat-filled meal, and that we are near the neighborhood where I used to live, and there was the most adorable little market. Does she feel like she can go with me to see if it's still there, or should we just go home?

"I can completely go!" she says. "I feel wonderful being out."

And so we go. I am possibly wrong to allow her this, but I do it any- way. We'll hurry right back afterward. We walk with our arms linked to- gether, and I'm telling her about how I used to love coming to this particular market in New York more than almost anything else about the city. It was such a shock to find in New Hampshire that a person needed to do the grocery shopping for a whole week . . .

I am still yammering on happily about sweet potatoes and rows of tangerines, rye breads, and half-sour pickles when we get to the mar- ket, and then suddenly the world tilts on its axis and slides out from underneath me. Everything goes so hazy that for a moment I think I am still in my bed, dreaming.

Jeremiah is there. Right there in the crowd.

Jeremiah. I see him. I could go over and talk to him. He is looking at apples. It's unmistakably him.

It can't be him. Look again.

It is him. How could I not know him? He has the same face, the same way of moving—everything's the same. His ear. His way of standing. He's wearing jeans and a jacket. His hair curls over the collar slightly. He picks up some apples and places them in a string bag. I stop talking; my mouth simply stops working, making sounds.

How—? But how could he be in this same space with me? So many millions of people, and now here he is, in the same market where we used to shop for food together? Who would believe this?

Believe it. Maybe I've gone through a wormhole in the universe— Nicky used to tell me about wormholes—and it's really 1977 again, and the twins will come bounding out from behind the cantaloupes, like that day we had to dismantle the whole display in order to find my house key, which Brice had dropped into the pyramid of fruit. It had worked its way all the way to the bottom, as if it were a living thing seeking darkness. I see Jeremiah's unshaven face from then, feel his sleeve brush against mine as he handed me pieces of fruit to hold. Even the hard times, I thought then, were so good, so funny and rich.

He's in New York. My mouth goes dry.

Jeremiah, hello. Yes, this is my daughter, Sophie. Why, yes, she does, doesn't she? She does look just like Grant. Of course.

Sophie's mouth is moving; she's talking, agreeing with me, I think, about the luxury of shopping every day. Or maybe she said this minutes ago, and the words are just now making their way through the cotton batting taking up space in my head. "It makes so much sense to buy what you need every day . . ." Her voice is fuzzy; I don't hear the rest of the sentence. I look down quickly. He'll go the other way. Gravity—or some benign force of the universe, centripetal force or something—will pull him away from me. We are not destined to meet again. Or . . . well, if he comes this way, he won't recognize me. I look completely different. We'll pass each other, and there'll be this blankness in his eyes when they fall on me. He won't have any idea. I'll pretend I'm looking at something on the shelf. I can't talk to him. I don't want him to see me.

He turns the other way and starts walking. I see his hair, thinner in back now and shot through with gray. His dark jacket is slightly too big for him. His posture never was good, but he always moved like somebody who was spring-loaded; now he's more slumpy than he used to be, stooped really, but it's a humble kind of stoop, as though he doesn't want to take up too much room in the aisle, as though it's out of consideration for the other customers who are rushing. A woman with two little children is near him, and I see him stop and reach over and pat one of them on the head, and then the other. He's in profile, and I see him smiling. He loved kids. He did. *Does.*

This is the present. This is happening, and Jeremiah is in this store with you.

Sophie is saying, "Should we get apples? I used to love Granny Smiths, but now they give me heartburn. I think Galas are better . . ." but her voice comes in and out, as if someone is playing with the volume control button.

Jeremiah suddenly stops, and I hold my breath, thinking that he'll turn and come toward me, but then he doesn't. After a moment, he keeps going, walking away from me, and then he turns the corner. I can't see him. I exhale. "What?" I say to Sophie, and we both hear the edge in my voice. She looks up sharply. I don't want to talk about apples. I can't.

"Are you all right? You look flushed," she says.

"I'm fine."

"Do you want Galas?"

"What? Sure. They're fine."

"But how many?"

"I don't know. Four, I guess."

"What? I can eat three myself!" She laughs. "Are you paying attention?"

"Then three." My hands, clutching the basket, are clammy. I feel like I might just faint.

She laughs. "No! Not three. You want some, too, don't you? How about we get six?"

"Whatever. That's fine."

"What's the matter with you?"

"The fluorescent lights are driving me crazy. Don't you hear that hum? I hate that."

"Okay," she says. "Do we need anything else? Besides ice cream. I have got to have ice cream. I want Chunky Monkey. That has health-ful bananas, at least. God, I hope I don't suffer from eating all that pastrami. Why did you let me eat all that when I'm seven months' pregnant? What kind of mother are you, anyway? They should take your license away."

"I just want to go. Let's go. I'll go to the other market later if we need anything else."

"One minute."

I stand rooted to the spot while she goes off to the freezer com-partment and comes back with a pint of Ben & Jerry's. We make our way to the checkout counter—Jeremiah is nowhere to be found, and I feel the most unexpectedly sharp pang of disappointment. This is ridiculous; it's like high school. Walking down the wrong hallway, see-ing the guy. The crush. Just like then, I don't know what to hope for. It's surely wrong to see him, but how can I not? I look at the magazines. Jennifer Aniston and Brad Pitt are now living in different houses. Will they file for divorce? I turn the pages quickly and put the magazine back, and then there he is. It is 2005. I haven't seen Jeremiah since 1980. I was still a child.

He's coming toward me, joining my line. Oh God. I could touch him. My hair over my face, I lean down and stare at the collection of gum and candy, and one of my hands flies up unbidden and cups itself around my eyes. He leans over to get some cough drops, my hand jerks downward, and our eyes meet.

Zap, and everything falls away, like in the dreams.

"Annabelle?" he says. His voice hasn't said my name in so many years, it's rusty with the sound of my name. "Oh my God. Annabelle! Is it really you?"

"Yes," I think I say. "Jeremiah."

"Wow," he says. He stands there with his hands at his sides, smiling, his eyes crinkled up. He needs a shave. His hair is too long. "I can't believe this." He is chuckling as he takes my hand and holds on to it.

We talk. He says things about the market still being here, and that he's back in New York after traveling in Europe, and something about how amazing this is. It's a perfect New York City coincidence. His voice is calm, like on that first day when he surprised me at his apartment, the day I was rummaging through the cabinets. He'd told me later that he'd watched me longer than I had known; my back was to him and my skirt had ridden up over my hips, and he couldn't stop staring. He'd gotten hard. That very first day. And now he's talking about apples, the ice cream he's holding and that Sophie is holding. Same kind. My ears are buzzing too loudly for me to completely hear him, and my toes swim up into focus. I must be looking down.

When I allow myself to look fully up at him, his eyes are shining with pleasure. His voice is the same. I take back my hand. I can't get over the fact that I'm touching him, and then that's ridiculous, so we hug, which requires some jostling of the groceries we're both holding. Sophie—oh yes, Sophie!—stands there smiling in polite bafflement, watching us, and after we hug in slow motion I introduce them, struggling to get my voice under control. "My daughter. Sophie, this is an old, old dear friend of your father's and mine. Jeremiah Saxon." There's a chalky taste in my mouth. I'm talking too loudly. He bows elegantly. I'd forgotten that about him: how courtly he could seem, with his old-world manners.

"So pleased to meet you," she says. It's surreal, watching them shake hands, his long slender fingers taking her small puffy white hand in his.

"Wow, she looks like you," he says. "Although now that I really look, I see such a combination of you . . . and Grant." His eyes meet mine in mischief at the hesitation there. *She is Grant's, right? Did you . . . stay together?*

I nod imperceptibly. *Yes. We made it. Although you don't deserve to know about this.*

His eyes are soft with happiness. With a mixture, really, of sadness and happiness. I can feel it washing over both of us. I'll have to soak this in and analyze it later. This must be what shock feels like, a haze of noises and impressions all at once. I hear the fluorescent lights while I notice that his face is looser somehow, less pointed, though I don't dare stare at him the way I want to. Sophie is hyper-alert to this sort of thing. She hasn't moved even one inch, and she's looking back and forth from one of us to the other and smiling. I have to get some control.

So we scale back, do the required rundown: Grant teaching at the community college. ("Still?" Jeremiah says, and his eyebrows lift, mildly surprised.) Two children. Nicky a freshman. And now a grandchild. Sophie's first baby.

When it's his turn, he says the twins are fine. Yes, they are nearly thirty now. Lindsay is a translator at the U.N. Brice works for the National Security Agency. How ironic is all that, huh? Neither married, no children. How lucky Grant and I are to have a grandchild on the way. He remembers how much we loved children. And he laughs. I see Sophie catch that, just as if an electrical signal has been passed between us with her in the middle as the interceptor.

"How long are you in the city?" he wants to know, and I explain that I don't really know. I'm here due to complications with the pregnancy, but everything is fine now. Sophie, on cue, whips out the ultrasound photo of the baby and Jeremiah rubs his eyes in astonishment that such things exist. It's all so remarkable, the modern age, technology that can photograph the unborn.

I tell him I understand that people can actually talk to each other on little pieces of plastic they hold up to their ears, and he laughs.

Then somehow we get to his wife and my husband, and he says mournfully that Carly died last year. Cancer. I already knew, but I feel something that was tight let go inside me, like a rubber band has just been broken. By then we've both somehow paid for our items, although I've barely been able to notice anything, and now we're mashed in the front of the store, in everybody's way. He asks in his polite, hesitant voice if we'd like to accompany him for a cup of coffee.

"No, no, we can't. We have ice cream we have to get home," I say quickly, too quickly.

"Well, then, another time?" His eyes are all over my face, boring into me.

"You two can go," says Sophie. "I'll go home and put the ice cream away. Really, go, Mom. You need some time off. It's fine."

"No!" I say, and my voice comes out too forcefully. I see Jeremiah smile shyly and look away. Sophie looks startled and laughs.

But I just can't go off with him. I can't have coffee. My knees are already practically buckled. It's too much already, his hand on my shoulder, the feel of his kiss brushing my cheek as we say good-bye. He gives me his phone number, folds a little piece of paper and tucks it into my hand, patting me, and Sophie tells him where she lives. I hear her saying, as though I'm her shy little kindergartner, that I don't get out much, that I'm deprived of real adult companionship. He smiles.

"I'll make sure she calls you," she says. "She could use an old friend."

She is flirting with him. I feel light-headed.

When he has gone and she and I are making our way home, I feel her eyes on me, and her step exactly matches mine on the pavement. "So what *was* that?" she says. "You look like you're about to have a heart attack."

I try to adjust my facial expression. "Oh, it's nothing. Just an old man who's going to bore me by telling me about his wife dying and how sad and pathetic his life is now, and he'll expect me to think of nice things to say to comfort him."

"Wow," she says and tucks her arm in mine. "I didn't know you had waifs and strays dating back thirty years."

"Twenty-eight," I say, staring down at the pavement while we walk.

"Whatever. But he seems like a nice old guy."

A nice old guy! As though he's just some harmless old man—is that truly how he seems to her? I'm stunned by feeling so disconnected, so confused.

"And God knows it'd do you good to get out of the apartment every now and then," she says.

The following Tuesday, against my better judgment and with my heart knocking about in my chest, I meet Jeremiah for coffee. Just to see. Because some things you simply have to know, as a person, married or not.

[t w e l v e]

~ 1978

*M*y first winter in New York was a cold, snowy one. No matter what I did—piling on clothes, drinking gallons of coffee—I couldn't seem to get warm and stay that way. On the days I wasn't working at some office for the temp agency, I walked around the apartment in bulky sweaters and huge bunny slippers. My nose ran a lot. I shivered.

I had hoped that Grant and I could go back to California for Christmas and the winter break, but he said he was too busy with things, and anyway, he didn't want to spend money. He needed to prepare for his second semester of teaching, he said. Instead, we took a few days off and went to upstate New York, to an inn that was near an old shut-down textile mill, a place where a utopian labor movement had been born and then failed. We trudged around the ruins of the place in the snow, looking at smokestacks and old bricks. Grant stood reverently on the wall of the foundation, gazing outward, while I shivered next to him. Outside, the snow was clumped in a stand of evergreens, and the watery sun was low in the sky. It was three o'clock in the afternoon, but it already seemed to be night.

"This is like church for you, isn't it?" I said. "An old factory."

He laughed and looked at me, blinking, as though he was only just remembering that I was there.

"Oh, Grant! You're so . . . so *you!*" I said.

"I'm obsessive, I know," he said mournfully. "I should have told you that before I made you marry me and dragged you across the country." But then we kissed, and his lips were the only warm thing in that whole place.

When we got back in the car, I said, "There's just one thing I don't really understand. Why was it Jeremiah that you wanted to work with? I mean, he doesn't seem to be at all interested in any of this stuff."

He'd been getting ready to back out of the clearing where we'd parked, but he put the car back in neutral and set both his hands on the steering wheel. "Oh, don't underestimate Jeremiah Saxon," he said. "It's true that he's bogged down with his family life right now, but he's done just some extraordinary research right in this mill, as a matter of fact. He's the preeminent guy when it comes to these utopian communities, to these social experiments where everybody was going to be equal. His writing on this, and his understanding of these movements, has been *superb*. Really elegant, amazing papers. And books. He's written several books on the subject."

"Really?" I said. I looked at the ruins of the place with new interest, felt my heart quicken.

"That's one reason I wanted to come to this mill," he said, and there was almost a flicker of hero worship in his voice. "Just to see, you know, what he's seen."

I looked around. Just some stones, a foundation, smokestacks, the trees. The river rushing past big chunks of ice, with the skeleton of an old water wheel. Just ghosts of whatever had once been there. Jeremiah had come here; he had stood on these rocks, written down notes about the ghosts. The place took on a different aura suddenly.

We ate dinner that night in a dim, candlelit old stone restaurant nestled against the hillside, and the proprietor came and sat down at our table and told us stories about the day the mill shut down, and how his parents had wept at the kitchen table. Grant was blinking and nodding, and his big, wide hands on the red-checkered tablecloth seemed almost to be twitching with the desire to write it all down.

"Do you want to take some notes?" I said to him later, when we got back to the inn.

"No," he said. "No. This is Jeremiah's mill. I'm just an interloper."

I looked over at him in time to see the awe just disappearing from his face. "If I could ever be as insightful as he is . . . His notes are meticulous. He understands everything."

"Don't say that!" I said, more forcefully than I meant to. "You have your own gifts. You have to respect what *you* have."

IN FEBRUARY there was a huge blizzard—they were calling it the Blizzard of 1978—and my brother called to see if I was truly able to stand life in the Northeast. He was living in a rehab center by then.

"And how are you finding the shackles of married life with the goofiest nerd on the planet?" he asked. "And you know I mean that in the best possible senses of those words. I have a lot of admiration for a guy who doesn't seem to know there's a world that exists outside of his own head."

"Yeah, well, maybe it would be better if I ever saw him," I said. "He works all the time."

"Teaching? I thought that was one of the cushy jobs—lots of vacations, classes only three hours a day."

"Not the way Grant does it."

He was huffing and puffing, and I knew he was wheeling his chair outside so he could smoke. His voice was muffled as he lit up a cigarette. Then he said, "Well. Cheer up. From my observations, it seems that married people who don't see each other can often maintain the illusion better."

"What illusion?"

"The illusion of happiness. You know. That marriage is somehow the magic answer. Tra-la-la and all that. When, really, all most people really want is to get themselves laid every now and then, and then be left the hell alone to die."

"No, they don't."

"Yes, they do. Trust me. That is life at its most minimal, bare-bones existence."

I leaned against the wall of the kitchen. In the next room, I could hear Jeremiah explaining to the children that they could only go out if they were willing to put on snowsuits, and that meant no more racing through the house naked and climbing up on the furniture. He always talked to the children as though he were a labor negotiator and they were warring factions. "Okay, now let's look at the risk/benefit ratio of climbing on the couch, when we could put on our snowsuits and head outside instead. Brice, you in?"

It had been six months since David's accident, and he had gotten just better enough, he said, to realize what he was going to miss for the rest of his life. He said he didn't believe in anything anymore, and why should he? His girlfriend had broken up with him—justifiably, he told me. Nobody really appreciated that paraplegic humor. She couldn't take all the jokes about how he wanted to commit suicide, the silly woman. Together since they were twelve goddamn years old, and now he can't stand the sight of her looking at him, the pity in her eyes.

"You're the only one who really gets me," he said. "You're not going to call the cops and report that I'm thinking of offing myself."

"Are you thinking of offing yourself?" I said.

"Oh, yeah. Hell, yeah. Wouldn't you, if you knew you were going to spend the rest of your life in some wheelchair, having aides know everything you do, and meanwhile people are coming in to tell you stories of other brave and upstanding folks who turned fucking lemons into lemonade and became amazing inspirations?" He changed his voice to a high falsetto when he said that last part. "I don't fucking *want* to be an inspiration to others. And why the hell should I be? I've gotta go do something on a grand scale just to make everybody else feel better about me not having the use of my legs anymore? Fuck that! It's a bunch of shit."

It made sense. "You certainly do not have to be anybody's inspiration," I said.

"Thank you," he said. "Tell that to Edie, will you? I think she wants me to be the first paraplegic to climb Mount Everest or something. Make a name for myself."

"So how *are* the parental units coping?" I asked him. Jeremiah tramped through the kitchen, carrying one navy blue snowsuit and one red mitten. He stopped and tilted his head at me, made a face. *Is everything okay?* I nodded. I mouthed back: "It's my brother," and he made a sad face, pointed his thumb up and then down, questioning. I waggled my hand in the air: so-so. Jeremiah gave me a sympathetic look and moved back to the living room.

David was saying, "Gah! Now there's a subject. There's a new separation in the offing. They don't want me to know, because, you know, I might not be able to stand the idea that *I'm* the cause of it. Poor fragile little David can't take the truth. They've got a crippled son, and they fight all the time—but oh God, let's protect him from thinking things aren't right."

"That's not how they feel. I know that's not how they feel. They separated before, and that wasn't because of you. Their marriage is stupid."

"Right. You know that and I know that, but everybody else is busy rewriting history. I was fake-sleeping one day so I wouldn't have to deal with them, and I heard Edie telling the social worker that things weren't working out with Howard, and that she's moving out. He's such a jerk. I tell you, be glad you're not actually interacting with that sweet clueless nerd you married, because you never know what you might find out. Best thing that ever happened to me was that Michelle knew she couldn't take care of a cripple for the rest of her life, and she didn't stick around to torture me about it."

I said, "Oh, David, you know Michelle doesn't feel that way. You made her break up with you, and I can't stand it when you talk like this!" There was an uncomfortable silence.

Then he said, "Yeah, riiiight. Well, I'm going to hang up now and go count my sleeping pills to see if I have enough yet to kill myself when the time is right. You take care."

"Wait." I licked my lips, which were suddenly dry. "Tell me. Are you really thinking of killing yourself?"

"Don't *you* start now," he said, and laughed. "Didn't I just explain to you that you're the only one who won't call the cops on me?"

"But I can't tell if you're joking!" I cried.

"Yeah, yeah. Of course I'm joking," he said in a serious voice. "What do you think? Now go back to your life. Waiting for Mr. Professor Nerd to come home and remember what your name is. I gotta go sweet-talk some nurse into giving me more pills than the doctor ordered."

And he hung up.

Jeremiah was in the living room still trying to entice both kids into their snowsuits when I got off the phone. Through the curtains, the sky was the color of lead, and a branch laden with snow was scraping against the window. I came and stood in the doorway, hugging myself, watching them. There was a lump in my throat the size of the coffee table.

"If we go to the park," he was saying to the children, "Annabelle and I will pull you on the sleds."

I realized I would have been furious if Grant had just signed me up for a task without asking first, but somehow I wasn't angry with Jeremiah at all. He looked over at me and raised an eyebrow, questioning, and I nodded.

Brice was riding the arm of the couch as if it were a bronco, and Lindsay was dancing and stomping on the carpet roses, a game she and I had invented on the days I used to pick her up from day care. For a moment, I felt like I was disconnected, floating somewhere up above them. My brother's life was in danger in California, and yet I was here in New York, in this crowded, cluttered apartment, and it was softly snowing outside, and there were these children who did not belong to me but whom I cared about, and also this man. This man! I looked at him, at Jeremiah, the way his hair curled down over the collar of his black turtleneck sweater, at his laughing eyes, his jeans with a pacifier sticking out of the pocket. He was sitting back on his knees, holding the snowsuit out toward Lindsay, as though he were beseeching her to come and let him put her in it, and he was laughing. My ears started pounding, as though the blood was coursing through them too fast and too hard. I wanted to sink down in front of him. His eyes crinkled at the corners, his lovely long fingers curled around the snowsuit, he called her name.

Somehow, working side by side, we wrestled the twins into submission and got them dressed for the outside. I'd lived my whole life unaware of the difficulties of snowsuits and hats that needed to be tied under the chin, and scarves wrapped around just so, and mittens that came on strings that had to be threaded through the sleeves. California parents have it so easy, I told him.

As soon as we were ready to walk out the front door, Jeremiah burst into laughter. "Oh, no! Do you smell that? We have a threshold poop situation."

"A threshold poop?"

"Well, that's the scientific term for it. Those are the poops that happen just as you are trying to leave home. Scientists still aren't sure of the precise cause, whether it comes from anxiety about leaving the house or if it's related somehow to the air currents of the front door opening, or the pressure of the outer garments. But whatever it is, we have to take care of this situation *immediately*."

The culprit was determined to be Brice, and Jeremiah swooped him up and laid him down on the living room floor and took off his boots, his socks, his snowsuit, then his sweater, his corduroy overalls, and his long underwear and his diaper while Brice squirmed and tried to escape. Then he changed the diaper while Lindsay and I danced around the room, mainly so I could prevent her from stripping down as well. He put Brice's things back on him, and we managed to get ourselves to the door once again.

He picked up Lindsay and I picked up Brice, and we headed for the door once again. I could see sweat glistening on Jeremiah's fore-head.

"Okay, do we have everything?" he said. "Everybody got boots and mittens and hats? Sleds? Okay, good."

As he turned the doorknob, there was a sudden explosion from Lindsay's diaper.

"Oh my God," said Jeremiah. "This is unprecedented. Quick! Man your stations! We are now officially under attack. Put the perpetrator into isolation!"

"How can this be?" I said.

He leaned against the wall, covering his nose and mouth with his arm. "I conjured these poops just by telling you about them," he said. "I will never speak of threshold poops again."

But then we had to catch Lindsay, who by this time had thundered off to the kitchen, pulling Brice along with her, shedding her boots and hat and mittens as she ran. "Come on, Bwicey! Let's go!" she was screaming. We were hysterically laughing. And when, after we had caught her and changed her diaper and reloaded her into all her clothes, we were once again nearing the doorway and Brice squatted down and started grunting, I slid down the wall, unable to hold myself upright anymore. It was all too funny. I was laughing so hard I couldn't breathe, but it was the kind of laughing that's bad; I was tottering dangerously on the brink of tears. I knew I would be crying soon. And Jeremiah slid down right next to me while the kids ran back to the kitchen, screeching.

"You know why this happened, don't you?" he said. "Because we mentioned the you-know-whats yet *again* just to say we weren't going to talk about them anymore. Apparently the universe is very strict today about this sort of thing." He reached over to pull some piece of fluff—hairs from a mitten—off my chin and then there we were, slumped against the wall, just looking at each other, locked in. Then, well, it was exactly like in the movies, that slow-motion staring into

each other's eyes and everything going all buzzy. I felt as though he
could see through to the place where my brother had just hurt me,
that he knew about the suicide scare and the guilt and the emptiness
of being so far from home. He saw all that; I could see it reflected back
in his eyes. I thought I would never be able to take another breath,
and he said my name, and, crying then, I said, *Oh, Jeremiah, my brother
is going to die* and then he leaned so close to me, in slow motion, until
his mouth was covering mine, and I couldn't breathe. He kissed me—
four long, soft kisses. First kisses, slow and questioning. I counted
them, weighed their intensity, and then I felt myself sliding underneath a current of air, which was just as scary as the time I had nearly
drowned when my family had first moved into the house with the pool
and I didn't know how to swim yet. There was the same sinking, airless
feeling, the panic in the lungs, my heart jackhammering on its way
down to this vast, soft nothingness at the center of me.

WHEN WE sat down to dinner with Carly and Grant that night, after
putting the children to bed, I was sure that all our spouses would have
to do was take a look at us and they'd know we'd been kissing. It was as
though our bodies were having a conversation all on their own, all
through dinner. I was aware of every single movement, each time Jeremiah lifted his glass to drink another sip of wine, every nuance of his
speech, the curve of his hand, the way his jaw pulsed when he spoke.
But fascinatingly, nobody seemed to notice. We ate spinach lasagna
that Jeremiah and I had made that afternoon after we got back from
the park. Grant, sitting next to me, bent low over his plate and ate
quickly, his eyes cloudy with thoughts left over from the day. Whenever anyone would speak directly to him, he'd look up and smile uncertainly, as though he'd had to pull himself back from a dreamworld
and hadn't quite dragged all his faculties with him. Jeremiah leaned
back in his chair, one elbow over the back of the chair, and gazed at
me, smiling. At one point, Carly, who was doing all the talking, got up
to pour us some more wine. For a moment, she stood there at the

head of the table and put her long, graceful arms up over her head and stretched, and I had to look away. How could he kiss me, how could he even look in my direction when she was so . . . so *everything*, so graceful and filled with sensuality?

Jeremiah smiled up at her. She refilled his glass, and he lifted it and clinked it against mine, and then everybody clinked their glasses, too, and she sat back down. I kept expecting her to say, "I can no longer have these people in my house. Obviously Annabelle has fallen madly in love with you, Jeremiah." I was waiting for this. Instead, she started talking about how tired she was, how difficult it was once you were over thirty to get your body to do what you wanted it to do. "Look at these arms," she commanded us. We looked at her long, thin, muscular arms. "And this abdomen." She stood up and lifted her shirt a little to show us flat, wonderful abs. "Hideous!" she said. She shook her fork at Jeremiah, and he grinned at her in his customary loutish way.

"You!" she said to him. "*You're* the one who wrecked this body of mine, using it long enough for your own lascivious, selfish purposes. You got it pregnant—and then you had to go and plant *two of them*, you sly, greedy bastard! But now it's mine, mine, *mine* again! I'm reclaiming it!" She fixed her look on me, and I felt my throat tighten. "Annabelle, watch it. That's all I can say. These men just take your body for their own selfish reproductive purposes, that whole procreate-the-species thing, and then *you're* the one with the lumps and the varicose veins and the bulges—and do they even care? They do not!"

She swatted Jeremiah on the head with a newspaper she picked up off the table, while he ducked out of her reach, laughing. I looked over at Grant, who was laughing, too, although the look in his eyes said he found this way more alarming than funny.

She got a phone call then, and went off to the living room to take it, and I got up and cleared the table and washed the dishes for once rather than loading them into the oven. Grant hemmed and sighed and finally asked if we minded if he went into our bedroom and worked on some papers he needed to grade. His eyes were tired and sunken.

My arms were in the dishwater up to my elbows. Jeremiah took up a dish towel. I could feel his body around me; it was like a force field. All I could think of was the way it had been when his lips had been on mine. Already tonight I had walked past that precise spot in the front hall over and over again, thinking of that liquid, flowing way he had reached for me, the way I had melted into him. That's what it had been like: melting! I wanted to tell him. Everything was so different now— touching these plates, his wineglass (and I knew exactly which one it was), the fork he had touched with his lips—it was all too much. We could hear Carly's voice in the living room, two whole rooms away from us. She was making some plan with one of the dancers, in her high, insistent voice.

"Well, *this* is certainly getting interesting," Jeremiah whispered, and then he laughed.

I nodded and looked down at the sudsy water, barely able to breathe.

"I am constitutionally unable to think of anything else," he whispered, laughing. "And may I say that you look wonderful tonight."

"I can't think of anything else either," I whispered.

He groaned and smiled at me. "Gives a certain spice to things, that's for sure."

"But it's not good," I said. "I mean, we're both *married*. Don't you think we should move out?"

"We?" he said, and his eyes bugged out and made me laugh.

"No, not *we* we. Me and Grant. We can't live here if this kind of secret stuff is going to go on. Can we?"

He laughed softly—how could we both keep laughing?—and he reached over and brushed a strand of hair off my face and tucked it behind my ear. "Move out? Don't you dare move out. I'm normally not a fan of drama, but . . ." He pulled me close to him and kissed me softly. I let him. I even kissed him back, as though I hadn't just said the thing about being married and moving out. *Look at me; I could forget everything,* I thought. *I could just go off with this man, rip off my clothes*

*and do it with him right here on the kitchen floor, and it has nothing whatso-
ever to do with what terrible things might follow. I can't even remember what
those terrible things are, not precisely.*

There was a noise just then from the living room, and we sprang
apart. I plunged my hands back into the dishwater; Jeremiah opened
the cabinet holding the glassware and stared into it. Carly came into
the kitchen, her bracelets jangling on her wrists as she opened the refrigerator. "You know something? We should keep a pitcher of cold
water in here, don't you think? I don't think I'm drinking enough
water these days, and I think the only reason is because it's not read-
ily available when I open the refrigerator."

"Good idea," I murmured, and Jeremiah said to her, "Actually,
you're never here."

She looked over at him. "I'm here now. And are you coming to bed,
sweetie? I've got an early call tomorrow."

"Sure," he said. "I'm just going to finish drying these—"

"No, no, no," she said. "No! I know you. You'll finish the dishes, and
then you'll go in the living room and put your headphones on, and
then you'll read, and next thing you know, it'll be the middle of the
night, and when you come into the bedroom, you'll wake me up. Come
on. It's selfish of you to want to stay up when I need my sleep."

He put the dish towel down very deliberately. "Okay," he said.
"Fine." And without a backward glance, he went off with her. She was
laughing and reminding him to be quiet when they passed the children's room. "And when you go in to pee, aim for the side of the bowl
and not the water," she was saying in a loud stage whisper.

I finished the dishes myself, turned off the lights, and turned down
the thermostat. Grant was working in our bedroom, and I could not
go in there. I couldn't. I wandered into the corner of the formal dining
room that had been turned into Jeremiah's study. It was dim in there,
lit only by the streetlight from the window. His bookshelves and
wooden desk were piled high with papers and books. A dictionary and
a thesaurus. A couple of textbooks about ancient Rome. I sat down in

his swivel chair and ran my hands across the spines of the books. There was a desk organizer with little wooden cubbies and piles of books and papers. I leaned over and turned on the green-shaded lamp. A grown-up lamp. His typewriter was on a little tray table next to the desk, and there was a bulletin board with a calendar. "Sabbatical" was written across the top in black Magic Marker, and on different days there were notations written in blue ink, in his expansive hand-writing. I stared at it; I'd had a handwriting analysis done once, and I knew that open, loopy letters meant a generous, open, loving person-ality. It seemed as if he was surrounding me here; his presence was all about. His pens were in a little cup, and I handled each and every one of them, picking them up tentatively and then putting them down. One—a fountain pen that I knew was his favorite—I picked up and then slowly, sensuously, ridiculously licked.

JEREMIAH WAS home the next week, and Grant had said we needed to make more money, so I took another temp job, working in a bank every day. It was exhausting, but I was glad for the time away. On Friday, it was snowing so hard that they let us leave early, and by the time I got home, it was really coming down. I took the subway, but even so I had to walk four blocks and I was soaking wet and freezing by the time I got to our street. As I fumbled with my key in the lock, Jeremiah flung open the door.

"Oh my God, look at you!" he said. He laughed. I must have looked a wreck. My hair was wet and filled with snow, and so was my cloth coat. And my pumps were ruined. He led me into the dining room and sat me down and knelt in front of me and took off my shoes and mas-saged my frozen toes. I kept trying to insist that I was all right and to squirm away from him, but he held up one finger and cocked his head, as though he were listening to something.

"Quiet, you; your feet have a message for me," he said. "Okay. Okay, I'll tell her. They're aghast that you would walk them around on ice cubes in nothing more than these—these ridiculous straps of leather.

They say they're from California, and they learned to walk around barefoot on hot pavement, but this is the *limit*. The ultimate limit. And, oh yeah, they say I'm to keep rubbing them until they can get some blood in there to warm them up."

I laughed. "Anything else?"

"Yeah, they want bunny slippers, and also they're requesting that you drink some hot tea. But first I have to bring them back to life."

He bent over my feet, rubbing away with his long, delicate fingers, and I looked down at the top of his head, all that brown tousled hair, and then suddenly, without warning, I was completely gone. As though there had been a signal between us, he looked up and smiled at me, and moved his hands farther up my leg, at first tentatively, over my panty hose, massaging as he went, smiling a serious, workmanlike smile, as though he were doing nothing more than kneading bread. I heard myself moan as his hands reached the hem of my skirt and then slipped underneath.

He took his hand away. "Come on," he whispered, pulling me to my feet. I leaned against him, and he kissed me until I went out of my mind, and then he started unbuttoning my shirt with his left hand while he held me with his right.

"Wait," I said, out of breath.

"What?" He stopped.

"Where are Brice and Lindsay?"

"At a playdate," he said.

"No one's coming home?"

"No. It's just us. All us." I didn't know where we would go, and I was a little surprised when he led me quietly into the bedroom he shared with Carly—a messy, large, dim room with clothes tossed everywhere, like costumes discarded after a play. We fell on the bed, into the tangle of sheets, and his body bent over mine while we kissed. We started unbuttoning and unzipping like we'd gone mad; clothes fell off or were thrown across the room. I unpeeled my panty hose and he gently removed them, and then we were naked and I heard him say, "Ooooh," from such a far-down place. I was aware of the sudden smoothness of his skin, the sweet, deep scent of him, the roughness of his cheek brushing against my breasts as he went lower to put his mouth all over me. With every place he touched on my body he unlocked something that until then I'd had no idea even existed. It was that amazing. I closed my eyes and buried my head in his shoulder, breathing him in.

When I came—a huge whoosh of feeling, an explosion I wasn't sure I'd recover from—he pressed me to him tightly and held me. And then, a moment later, he closed his eyes tightly and yelled out. He yelled! I had never made a man yell before. Afterward, we lay on our backs on the bed, side by side, panting, quiet. He reached over and stroked my stomach with his index finger and then circled both nipples and pressed his palm against my skin. I found that little hollow place between his shoulder and his chest and tucked my head there. Everything in my life was now different.

"You're amazing," he said. His penis, glistening, was flopped over onto his thigh, just within my reach. I touched it and he laughed a little and moaned.

"God. Are we awful?" I said.

"Reprehensible."

"We're no doubt going to hell for this."

"If we both go, though, we can do this in hell. It'll make the time go faster between the burnings from the hellfire."

"I have to ask you something."

He flicked his gaze over me, lazily, warily. "Shoot."

"Did you ever work as hard as Grant is working—I mean, when you were new? He told me you said everybody needs to work twenty-hour days at first."

"Oh God no."

"Then why did you tell him that?"

He bent over and kissed my nipple and ran his tongue around it five times. "Because," he said, "Grant needs to do that. It's the only way to make him feel truly safe."

"How many hours a day did you work?"

He laughed. "About three."

"Three? That's all?"

"I feel safest when I'm *not* working. My best ideas come when I'm not working."

I laughed. "I'm afraid I have a terrible crush on you," I said. I felt suddenly shy.

"Oh, yeah? Well, I'll match your crush and raise you one case of crazy mad love."

"You're teasing me."

"Am not."

"Well, then ... how long ... ?"

"Um, how long have you been here?"

"Six months, more or less."

"That's how long, then. To the minute."

"Really?" I laughed. "Isn't this kind of nuts?"

"If by nuts you mean the best thing in the world," he said, and sat on top of me, kissing me over and over, everywhere he could reach. Then he sat back and smiled happily. "You make me goofy with love," he said. "But now listen." His face suddenly looked so serious, my heart clutched. He reached down and started locating our clothes, handing them out. "What we won't do is get all worried about this, okay? Life has a way of taking good things and making them agonizing if you're not careful. This, baby, is a gift from the gods. I'm just going to live in it as long as I can. For this moment. Now."

"Now," I repeated.

He kissed all ten of my fingertips, and it was sealed.

JEREMIAH AND I had to scheme to make love; we were creative geniuses when it came to stealing moments and finagling our way to long, languid hours in the afternoon. I'd turn down jobs on days when he'd figured out a playdate for the children, pretend to leave the house with Grant and Carly, and then double back once they'd gotten on the subway. Once, on a workday, we met uptown in a movie theater during my lunch hour, and then we very nearly had sex in the dark back row before I had to get back to the doctor's office where I was working.

It was *so* good. It was religiously good. It was choruses of angels on high good. You want to know how good it was? It made me a better person, this falling in love business. I went around smiling at strangers, giving up my subway seat to anyone who looked even the slightest bit tired. It was as though my heart was beating a little faster all the time, my lungs took in more oxygen, my eyes took in more light. I moved through the world in a dreamlike state of grace. At work, in my temp job at the doctor's office, I was cheerful and energetic, willing to do all the hard jobs, even run the urinalyses and talk to difficult patients on the phone. And at home—well, at home, I was positively, preposterously magnanimous with everyone: with the twins, who were suddenly so dear to me because they came from him, they held parts of him in their DNA; and with the poor, benighted Grant and Carly, I was unfailingly kind and available.

I felt sorry for them, was the truth of it. Grant was nearly the best friend I had, and it pained me that I couldn't share this joyful news with him. I'd crawl into bed next to him at night, and see him burdened with his papers and his classes, see the furrow of his brow, feel his distracted hand reaching over to brush my hand away, and I'd just want to lay my cheek against his and say, "Grant! You have no idea how meaningless all this is, when you consider the grand scheme of things. Think of *love*, Grant! You really should fall in love. It's great!"

We even made love, he and I. It wasn't the same as what I had with Jeremiah, of course, but it had its merits. Although there wasn't any of the wild, screaming-banshee *wanting* that I was getting a little addicted to, there was a certain sweetness with him. You're not supposed to compare, I know, but it was all I could think about. For Grant and me, sex was friendly, conciliatory, thoughtful, companionable. We smiled at each other, touched each other's faces, settled afterward into a kind of lulling tiredness. Sex as tranquilizer. But with Jeremiah,

I was always finding myself out on the frontiers of the stratosphere, quaking and hoping eventually to be readmitted to my body.

There was, of course, the thrilling, scary part—trying to make sure we didn't get caught. There were close calls: a ringing phone and a spouse wanting to have a conversation about dinner when you were rocketing your way to a climax. A sudden change of plans, the necessity of streaking down the hall with your clothes under your arm, slamming the bathroom door just as the front door opened and the wrong person came home unexpectedly. An adventure any way you looked at it.

One rainy day in bed, Jeremiah asked me about my brother, and I had to bury my head in his chest for a very long time, because I was crying too hard to speak. I hadn't truly cried for David, and now everything poured out: the drugs, the danger, the sweetness, the things that might be my fault, the things that were clearly my parents' fault, the uselessness of blame in any case. All of it, running down my face. And Jeremiah holding me, taking it all in, asking me questions, comforting me. Not saying, as Grant would have, "There, now, let's look at the good part. At all the things David *can* do." Or: "There's really not much point in worrying for him—he wouldn't want you to."

Jeremiah knew how to hold all the grief, to balance it in one hand while holding me in the other—and that was the day that we got so much closer to each other that we very nearly missed the sound of the front door opening and closing, and he had to hide behind my bed while I hurried out to the kitchen in my bathrobe, sniffling and complaining to a harried Carly that I had somehow caught a terrible cold and had been in bed most of the day. While I talked to her in the back of the house Jeremiah sneaked out the front door and then made a big show of coming home.

After dinner, while he and I were washing the dishes, he said to me, "We need to come to some other solution for space. Someone's going to get hurt, and it might be us."

The next day, though, we were at it again.

We had just finished making love in the bed I shared with Grant; we were very democratic that way, using different spaces throughout the house, even the kitchen floor on one notable occasion, although I hadn't liked it as much as I had thought I would. The hard Italian tile floor was cold and made my head hurt. The living room couches were nicer, although more vulnerable—you might not hear the front door opening until someone was standing right there in front of you.

Anyway, we were in my bed—mine and Grant's—and we were lying together afterward, in the tangle of covers, and he said, "You know what I can't believe? That Grant is so oblivious to the woman he has in his own bed. To think that he could have been the one getting this instead of me. You're his *wife* and he's not even getting any. How completely screwed up is that?"

I had a moment of surprise, and guilt. Did he think—did he honestly believe that I wasn't sleeping with Grant? Worse, was I somehow supposed to be *not* sleeping with him, in Jeremiah's view of things? But the twins had awakened from their naps and were screaming outside the door. Jeremiah jumped up and pulled on his jeans, groaning. "Two things have to happen. I've got to find some day care for these kids, and you and I need to find a place to go," he said. "I can't be timing my love life to toddler naps," he said and blew me a kiss. "It's making me neurotic." He kissed me quickly and ran out of the room, and I could hear his cheerful, fatherly voice herding the twins off to the kitchen for a post-nap snack.

HOW WAS it, you ask, that our spouses never knew? Were we such good actors that we could conceal all this passion? Magda and I used to have endless whispered phone conversations about this. She thought I was crazy to think they didn't know, and while she was at it, she also thought I might have lost my mind. She just hoped the fever broke soon, before somebody murdered me.

"You have now exponentially increased the number of people who would like to see you done in," she pointed out as though this were really a reasonable concern. "That's why sleeping with married men is such a bad idea, safety-wise. And a married person sleeping with another married person? I just can't think how grim your statistics look."

I was laughing so hard in the closet that I had to put my hand over my mouth.

But really, Jeremiah and I were careful not to let our glances linger on each other, and not to let ourselves drift into one-on-one conversations during the evenings when our spouses were with us, not to show any emotion that might be construed as over the top.

Still, as Magda pointed out in her inimitable way, nobody can be *that* careful. Looking back, I have to think we got away with this only because both Carly and Grant were in such cocoons themselves with their careers that they truly weren't all that interested in us for a time. They had sent our hearts out to play, trusting us to come back when they needed us again. That had to be it. They sat daydreaming about their successes and missed somehow the little zaps of emotion that flew about the kitchen, the way it seemed Jeremiah and I were somehow alone together, even when we weren't.

It became excruciating just the same.

When spring ended, I blurted out the whole thing to a lady at work. Linnea Brown. She seemed like the kind of person who was accustomed to hearing people's secrets. She was older—probably nearly my mother's age, and calm and centered and wise. She wore long peasant skirts and hand-knit sweaters and her hair was naturally gray and curly, and she worked in the back office, typing insurance forms and doing the billing. One day, when I was sitting in the back during my lunch hour, helping her fold the bills and put them in the envelopes, she told me that she had been married to a wonderful man, but he'd had a stroke and died three years ago, and she said she'd never get over missing sex. "He was *brilliant* at sex," she said.

That's how she put it, just like that, as though sex were a subject you could major in at school.

"I've had a few affairs since then," she said, "but you know, when you have just the best sex ever with somebody, you don't want to give that up. It becomes everything. My husband was a *luminous* man. Do you know what I mean by that, dear? Have you ever been made love to by someone who lights up from the inside, and brings that light to you?"

So I told her the whole thing. I myself was having the best sex ever, I told her, except that the man wasn't my husband. She didn't look shocked at that, just drew the story out of me, and she seemed both saddened and thrilled with the details of it, at the way Jeremiah and I were sneaking around, the way we couldn't give each other up—not that we'd tried so hard. At times she clasped her hands in front of her, smiling and closing her eyes as if she was remembering and reliving this same kind of ecstasy.

"Of course we live in fear of getting caught," I said. "Dinnertime, when our spouses are both there, is *awful*. And whenever we're in bed, I'm always halfway listening for the key in the lock. We've had some close calls, but so far, we're in the clear."

I told her that he and I had agreed to avoid meeting each other's eyes whenever the four of us were together. It was like a game, really, ignoring him when Grant or Carly was there, pretending not to feel the electricity that just seemed to radiate from him, pretending indifference when his name came up in conversation with one of the others. It made us crazy for each other, was the truth of it. It was like the greatest aphrodisiac in the world, this not being able to touch, or to even acknowledge that we ever had touched.

Linnea studied my face, taking this very seriously. This kind of love, she said, was a grave and necessary business. When it was real, you had to guard it as though it were a helpless living thing. Because it was. It was your soul's expression of the divine when it was like that. She was convinced of this. "Do you really love him?" she said.

"Yes," I said. My eyes spontaneously filled with tears, much to my own surprise. "I'm in *agony* over this. My husband, his wife—I feel so sorry, so bad, that we might be hurting them, but what can we do? It's become everything."

"Listen," she said. "I'd like to make my apartment available to you and—what is his name, did you say? Jeremiah?"

"Oh, no, no, we couldn't possibly accept," I said.

"Yes, you could. You must, in fact. You can't keep making love in the place where you all live together, my dear. Dreadful things are going to happen. And if you don't have a quiet place to do this, then how are you ever going to figure out whether or not you really do love this man, or whether this is just your sex year?"

"My . . . what?"

"Your sex year." She laughed a little and smoothed out her skirt. "I have a theory that we all have a year in our life when we're meant for sex. It's the year you think of nothing else. We all have it. It's a marvelous time, really, although it can bring about a lot of agony, as you describe it. It's as though all of life is only about sex during that year." She cocked her head and smiled at me. "You're a bit young for it. I was thirty-three when mine hit. But you may just be precocious. Or who knows? Maybe you'll get multiple sex years. This one might just be your first. At any rate, you have the right to explore this, darling, and you need a safe, quiet place to do it."

So he and I started going to Linnea's apartment, a walk-up on the Upper West Side. It was a simple space, clean and orderly, with bookshelves, Turkish rugs, mismatched furniture, and a spacious queen-size bed that we carefully covered with towels before we made love there. We would turn on the stereo and fall on each other, rolling around on that bed, marveling at our good fortune—that the twins had been accepted to a nursery school, that there was no need to half-listen for a key turning unexpectedly in the lock, no need to suddenly leap in the air and throw on clothes. I brought baskets of food with us—chicken and olives, pita bread and hummus—and we would lie there, talking and eating. He would bring his novel, and read me the scenes he was writing. His voice was as naked and vulnerable as the rest of him as he read to me. I have always loved being read to, and long after that book was published, when years later I read it while hiding in the stacks at the public library, it seemed to me to be a book that could only be understood naked. I couldn't make any sense of it at all with my clothes on.

One Wednesday, in the late fall, he said, "Carly has no idea what a great debt she owes to you."

"Uh-huh. And what might that be?" I kissed him twenty times down his chest and abdomen. "For taking her husband off her hands?"

He gave me a long, sly look. "Well, in a manner of speaking, I suppose. And Grant, too. I guess you could say I'm doing him the service of taking care of his wife for him, so that he doesn't have to waste his precious academic mind on something as mundane as sex."

"But . . ."

"I shouldn't talk about them. We can't waste our time at Linnea's talking about this," he said. "This is a Grant-and-Carly-free zone. Sometimes I guess I just think of how we could have missed being together. That's all. I mean, it's such an accident, really, when you think of it."

"How did you and Carly meet?" I asked him.

He waved his hand dismissively. "It doesn't even matter. My life," he said, "is divided into two parts. The part that took place before I met you, and the part that is now. The Annabelle part of my life."

Such talk thrilled me. I had always been a rather disposable girl-friend, the one who was willing to have sex and go places but who was expendable. I had never affected anybody who was so sophisticated. Even though Grant loved me, and I knew that he did, I didn't imagine that I really *moved* him. He had given up his bed for me and slept on the floor, sure, in the apartment in Isla Vista, and he had possibly saved my life by giving me a reason to leave California, but would he have found a day care for his children specifically so that he could sleep with me? Would he have dared take a risk for me? Hell, he wouldn't even let me kiss him in his office.

"Grant," said Jeremiah, kissing me on both cheeks and then on my eyelids, "is a fool."

But things had to change. Linnea had warned me that something would happen; there were no thirty-year affairs, she said, especially when two couples lived together.

"Be ready," she said.

And one evening, after we'd been doing this from the summer through the winter and all the way until late spring, I found out what she meant. It started innocently enough. Grant, in an unusual display of public affection, grabbed me around the waist and kissed me while I was trying to get Lindsay to eat the rest of her yogurt. Across the room, I felt Jeremiah freeze. I knew him so well that it was as if my own blood froze in its tracks, too, along with his. I pulled away, awkwardly, from Grant, but Jeremiah swooped down out of nowhere and grabbed Lindsay and left the room with her.

"Owie! Stop, Daddy!" she yelled.

"Hey, I was just trying to get her to eat . . ." I said.

"She does not *ever* have to eat the rest of her yogurt!" he said to me as he went past me. He did not come back out. He spent the rest of the evening in his room with Carly, and the next morning when we got to Linnea's, we had the terrible fight I knew was coming. I had not been able to sleep for fear of it.

"I watch you with him, and I don't even recognize that person," he said. "You're not you when you're with him."

"Really? Who am I, then?"

"Yeah, *really*. Who are you? You're—I don't know—so passive and *submissive*. Submissive, that's it. Not the woman I know, the one who'll take chances. Who has a soul that needs expressing. You're *conventional*, is all."

It was, for him, the worst sort of insult. This is what set him apart, his unconventionality. Throwing away Columbia to write a novel. Throwing away his dancer wife to sleep with the wife of his friend. Even talking to street people, offering them cigarettes. Everything he did was for effect. He was just another kind of snob.

I could feel my face turn red. "Maybe I really am conventional," I said. "Did you ever think of that? That I'm a shallow California girl who was raised on the beach? That I'm somebody who doesn't see why life has to be so hard?"

"That's not what I'm talking about. I like the Californian in you." He ran his hands through his hair. "I don't know. It's not that. . . . It's just the way you are sometimes, with Grant. Like you have to look up to him, or something, be the little woman. You know? It's disturbing. It's actually a little bit sickening, the way you act." He stared off into space. I looked at his naked chest, and his big, graceful hands and tapering fingers resting there on Linnea's bedspread, and I got mad and scared all at once. This could end. He could drop me! He could see things in me that he didn't like anymore. He was operating under a moral code that I suddenly realized I'd never inquired about. It was okay to do this because we fell into *unconventionality*? It defied the power structure? But what if it didn't do that anymore? What if it became just another personal obligation? A relationship with requirements and assigned roles.

"What are we *doing*?" I cried. "Why is this all right?"

He looked at me with cold eyes. "Good question. Why is it all right with you?"

"It's all right because I love you. Because I have . . . a *soul* that finds expression in you . . . in *this*. Because when I'm here, I feel . . . I feel like I never want to be anywhere else. Like I'm in the right place."

"And you don't feel that with Grant." It was a statement.

"It's different with Grant."

He laughed. "It's *different* with Grant? Wait a minute." His eyes went opaque on me. "Wait. Are you—are you saying that you and Grant . . . do this? You sleep with him?"

"*Jeremiah*. Stop it." I swallowed.

"You *fuck* him."

"Yeah. Come on, Jeremiah. We just got married. I sleep in the same bed with him every night. It's going to happen. It's not like this. It's not anywhere near what this is, but it has to happen sometimes."

"No," he said, "it doesn't."

"What are you saying, that you and Carly never . . . ?"

"Never. Well. Once in a blue moon. Like, how old are the twins?"

"Come on. You did not sleep with her last when she got pregnant with the twins!"

He laughed bitterly. "No, of course not." He looked off into space again. "God damn!" His mouth was twitching. "I can't fucking believe this. You've got two guys loving you, and I'm just one of them. Who the hell do you think you are?" He let out a bitter, tight laugh.

Who, indeed, did I think I was? I sat there and thought that what I was supposed to do now was to tell him that he was the only one, and that sleeping with him meant more to me than anything that had ever happened with Grant or with anyone else, and it *would* be true, but I couldn't say it. I was furious now, furious and hurt.

I didn't say anything. I started putting my clothes back on.

He came over and silently started undoing my buttons as soon as I had fastened each one. He said, "So when you and he go into your room at night . . ."

"It's not all the time," I said. "Don't be ridiculous. It's not what you're thinking."

"I know. I'm being ridiculous. Come on back to bed. It doesn't matter anyway."

But things started to unravel after that. I could feel Jeremiah's eyes on me whenever I said anything to Grant. It was so unexpected, this jealousy, the way he would darken if there was even the slightest positive interaction between Grant and me. It came out in our lovemaking, too. He was more insistent, more emotional. He would hold on to my arms too hard; there would be moments when the look on his face actually frightened me.

One day we were in Linnea's bed, and we made love and it was intense and passionate and almost angry, and when we finished and were just lying there—a time I had once adored, with its easy, drowsy talk, his reading the novel to me—he said, "So. Did you and he . . . last night?"

As it happened, we had.

"No," I said. "No."

"Yes. You did."

I bit him playfully on the arm. "Then why are you asking me this if you don't believe my answer?"

He pulled his arm away. "Because I want to see if you're being honest with me."

"Look, why are you being this way?"

"Because I heard you. You were making love."

I stopped short. "We've been over this, haven't we? He's my husband. He expects that sometimes he's going to get laid. Do you want me to have to explain to him that I can't have sex with him because I'm sleeping with you? Is that what you want?"

He stared up at the ceiling for a long time. I held my breath and watched his eyes flicker. "That might be interesting. Interesting and inflammatory. Certainly unconventional."

"Jeremiah! What do you *want* from me? Huh? What am I supposed to do?"

He got up, all in one fluid motion, and started getting dressed, turned away from me.

"What?" I said. "Just tell me what you expect."

"If you don't know, then I can't possibly tell you," he said. He put on his jeans and buttoned his shirt, a soft blue flannel plaid one that I'd always liked. "I can't do this anymore. I can't trust you. And I don't have the stomach to just sit by and watch this play out."

"No. Stop. Tell me what you think I'm supposed to do. Tell me and I'll do it."

He smiled, a cold pitying smile that made me want to hit him. "I'm

not going to do any such thing, Annabelle." He picked up his backpack and walked to the door. I couldn't believe it.

"Fine!" I said. "Then I think the time has come for Grant and me to
move out." My mouth was dry. I waited for him to say that I shouldn't
do that, to beg me to stay the way he had the last time. But all he said
was, "Well, suit yourself."

"We'll start looking for a place immediately."

"Excellent idea," he told me coldly, and walked out and closed the
door.

I WAS so mad that I got dressed and went to the building next door
and, lo and behold, rented us an apartment. It was that easy. I was
shocked. Would it have been that easy all along? Were there apartments simply for the plucking?

We moved out of Carly and Jeremiah's place two weeks later, and I
made up my mind that I would not have any more to do with him.

Magda came to visit right after we moved. Grant was too busy, so
she helped me with the necessary settling-in stuff, buying a dish
drainer and a mop, bath towels and pots and pans—all the things
that I hadn't had to think about before now.

She tended to both Grant and me, in her vast, comforting way. She
was big and bosomy and knew how to talk as though she were spreading a healing balm over everything. She told Grant he needed to pay
more attention to me now that we were living by ourselves. When he
didn't care what couch we bought, she actually went and chucked him
under the chin and said, "Dahlink. You have to care! It's what you
signed up for, back there in California in that dust storm of a wedding
you guys had. One of the vows was caring about the couch. Don't you
remember that one?"

She made him laugh. He said okay, let's get the green couch with
the gold-flecked pillows.

When she and I were alone, her pronouncements were firm and
sure.

"Thank God you're through with Jeremiah," she said. "See? It's perfect. You had your affair, your minor scandal, and you got away with it. So now you can go back to your marriage and keep it your own little secret. And you even have a new green couch."

What a simple way to look at things! But, of course, I wasn't through with Jeremiah.

[thirteen]

He is sitting in Starbucks when I get there. Which is good. I couldn't possibly have sat there waiting and watching for him. There are some things I know about myself now, and I know I would have left.

As it is, I almost didn't come. I woke up with my heart pounding, realizing I'd dreamed about him all night long. Without even thinking, I rolled over and grabbed my cell phone and called Grant. I just wanted to hear his voice. Maybe I wanted him to reach through the telephone and stop me from going to see Jeremiah, to say something that would give me some kind of sign. I believe in signs, and the sign I got was not good. He said, "Is everything all right?" instead of hello. Who answers the phone, "Is everything all right?"

"Yeah. It's fine," I said to him. "I just wanted to say good morning to you."

"Good morning," he said and then fell silent.

"Did you get a lot of snow last night?"

More silence. Then, "Annabelle . . ."

"I know. The book. Sorry."

He let out a tight little laugh, annoyed as hell. "It's just that I'm trying to finish so I can come next week for spring break. And, as you know, this is my time to write."

After I hung up I lay there for a moment waiting to see if he would call me back, and when he didn't, I got up and went to take a shower.

Then there was the getting ready part. I put on and took off four different outfits, which was tricky in such a small apartment, with

Sophie in the next room drinking her morning orange juice and watching *Good Morning America*. I decided on my long black skirt and boots and a rust-colored sweater with flecks of brown and gold, because the outfit didn't make me look too frumpy and because the flecks bring out the colors in my hair, at least according to the mirror under the light in Sophie's bathroom. I had stood there staring at myself for the longest time trying to decide how I wanted him to see me. I put on powder and blush, eyeliner and eye shadow, but then I wiped everything off and just wore lipstick and a little mascara. I didn't want to look as if I was trying too hard. God forbid he should know what seeing him meant to me.

And now—well, here he is. When I step into Starbucks and see him, for a moment I can't even breathe. He's sitting forward in an armchair, talking on his cell phone, and when our eyes meet, he snaps his phone closed. We just stare at each other, and he smiles slowly, a smile that rises up out of 1980 just the way it shows up in my dreams—and I have no idea what my face is doing. Damn. All I had needed was a moment before he saw me, even just a second in which I could have pulled myself together. I feel weak when he starts coming toward me, threading his way among the tables, and then he's there, gathering me up in a hug that's tentative and guarded, but then tightens as he sees that he will be received and accepted. I am so scared. I hate and love this feeling all at once. Hate the way his eyes look right into mine as they always have. Hate that we are known to each other, that we fall together in what could be simply a friendly hug but isn't. And hate that I catch a glimpse of us in the window and see that I look much older, and eager and desperate. I shouldn't have worn this long skirt, I should have lost five pounds, I should have put on makeup, after all. His soft blue sweater is against my cheek, and it smells like the past.

I am so fucked.

"Come, sit. Sit down," he says in his courtly way as he releases me. "By some sort of miracle, I have actually managed to reserve a table over here by chasing people away whenever they looked in this direction. So tell me. What would you like to drink?"

"Just tea," I say. "Green tea."

He lifts his eyebrows and grins. "Really? No coffee? I seem to remember you always took it with—what? Extra cream and three sugars, wasn't it? It was more like candy than coffee."

"I've given that up," I say, but it throws me that he remembers. "Just tea now. I don't want to be jittery."

He laughs and holds out his hand and pretends it's shaking. "Then I guess I'll have to have the jitters for both of us. Tea it is. And do you take extra cream and three sugars with that?"

"No, no. Black is fine."

"But it's green," he teases.

"I meant—no, green is fine."

He laughs, and then he's gone, and I am grateful for a break from having to look right at him. I sit down and watch the back of him, the lazy way he walks. Loping, I used to call it. He still lopes, in that way that men who are confident move. He leans down and says something to a woman in line, and I see her turn toward him, smiling, caught by his charm. *Don't*, I telegraph to her, and then am surprised at myself.

When he comes back, he hands me my cup and sits down across from me, and we take sips simultaneously. He leans forward and says softly, "So I can't believe this, that one day I was there, on a routine errand, in my regular old market buying apples, and I look up and there *you* are. Queen of my past."

"Well. Yes. It's amazing."

"With a daughter yet! A *pregnant* daughter."

I smooth my skirt down and nod. Soon we'll be asking where the years have gone, like a couple of old people.

"Sophie, right? And how is she doing?" he says. "There's some ... complication. Or did I make that up?"

"No. Yes, there's a complication. Placenta previa. She had an incident of bleeding and had to be put on bed rest, so I came—"

"From New Hampshire. You're living in New Hampshire now?"

"Yes."

"With Grant, yes? Is he here with you?"

I shake my head. "No, he's still there. He's teaching and writing a book. It takes up all his time. The writing. You know."

We stop talking and take sips again. We're both being so polite it's putting my teeth on edge. It's because I know he doesn't care about any of this. It's just a script he has to get through. It's as though—and I remember this from before—our bodies are having quite another conversation running simultaneously. I have to put my cup down on the table because my hand is trembling. I feel him notice that, and when I look up, he's gazing at me. "Is this too weird?" he says.

"Well, it is weird, I know that, but how could it be any different? We haven't seen each other in twenty-something years—"

"Twenty-six years, eight months, two weeks, and four days," he says in almost a whisper.

"You did not figure that up."

"Shall I tell you the minutes, too?"

"No, please don't," I say. "We can't—I don't want to talk about all that."

"No?" he says. "Okay, well then, let's just be two old friends meeting at a Starbucks for a cup of coffee and a cup of tea." He sits up straighter and puts his knees together in a pantomime of propriety and grins at me and I see the old mischief. "And how *have* you been, Mrs. McKay? I trust that you and Mr. McKay have been well."

"Quite well, thank you," I say. "And you?"

"Shitty, actually." He's still smiling. He lowers his voice and reaches over and takes my hand, and the world tilts. "You, however, are like a vision. You look—may I say this? To hell with it if I can't. You are lovelier than ever, Annabelle."

See? I want to say something to that, but my throat sticks shut, and I have to lean forward to keep from coughing, and he's holding on to me, and—oh, this is so stupid! And there's no other place to look because every time I let myself glance at him, he is just gazing at me, looking more intense and antic than I ever remember. Like he's going to start laughing. I don't want to do this. This is not why I came to see him again. Or maybe it is. Isn't this what I really wanted—to know once again the way it feels when the world slips off its axis?

"Jeremiah," I say, and even saying his name aloud turns something loose inside me. I pull my hand back. "We have to be normal. I need this to be normal. Tell me—tell me what you're doing now. What your life is like. You can start with why things are shitty."

At last he talks, telling me about his writing and his consulting work; he does a little of this and that. He worked for a foundation for a while that tried to start a museum, but the funding has all but dried up. Nobody really cares, least of all him. He's lost interest in museums. He tells me that he writes a bit, he sees friends, he does some traveling.

Then he trails off and smiles at me. He is paying such *attention*. I have forgotten what it's like to have someone look at me this way.

I realize I'm shivering.

"Are you cold? Should we move to a table near the window where it's sunny?" he says.

"Oh, no. No, really, I'm fine." I talk about New Hampshire cold then. A safe topic. Everybody can relate to cold and ice. He listens, nodding and smiling, but I feel myself babbling. I tell him about Grant's grandparents' homestead with the orchards, and the pond with the ice-skating, and the apple-picking and the small-town celebrations and all the rest of it.

"I had no idea people actually lived this way," I say. "It—it's like something out of a novel."

"Certainly not *our* novel," he says and laughs.

"Hey, that novel was all yours, buddy. I barely recognized it by the time it came out."

His eyes light up. "Oh my God. Don't tell me you actually read it in print. I know for a fact you didn't buy a copy. I have the names of both the people who bought copies, and one of them was my mother."

I laugh. "No, I didn't buy it. As you can imagine, I couldn't very well have it in our house."

"Why? Don't tell me Grant considered me that much of a threat, even so much later."

"I think he'll always consider you a threat," I say quietly. And then because it feels as though I'm being unfair to Grant, I add, "I mean, it *was* quite a betrayal . . . he was understandably very hurt and angry."

"As hurt and angry as you were?" he says and bites his lip and looks right at me. I remember that—how he would bite his lip when he felt bad about something. Those times when we talked about what we might be doing to Carly and to Grant, when we would make up our minds that we should cool off a little. I would be nearly wild with hysteria, and he would simply bite his lip, speaking volumes.

I feel myself flush, and for a moment I can't speak. I take a sip of tea and then I look away and say, "Well. Yes. I was very angry for a long time."

"Well, but then you went back to him. And from the looks of things, you and he seem to have worked things through rather fabulously. The family homestead, kids and all. The whole nine yards, as they say."

"Yes," I say slowly. "We did. But it took a while."

He leans back and looks at me for a long time. "How could he not take you back? Come on. You're the best thing that ever happened to him. I turned out to be just a sad but ignorable footnote in the long and happy marriage of Grant and Annabelle McKay."

"Well," I say, "we didn't have it easy for a long time."

"Oh, who ever has it easy in marriage? Nobody. But you, Annabelle, at least got just what you wanted: all the safety and security and stability that somebody like Grant has to offer. And I say, congratulations to you for that." He lifts his paper cup. "Here—let's have a toast to the safety of Grant McKay. Angry or not, the man comes through."

His voice has taken on an edge I don't like. I can't help myself; I lean forward and say, "Do you want to know the honest-to-God truth? The real story? What actually happened is that I ended up falling in love with him. In the way I should have, probably, before I married him."

He lets those words hang in the air for a moment before he says, "Well, that's good to hear. It turned out perfectly for you, then."

"Yes. It did. It actually worked out. Who would've thunk?"

"Who, indeed?"

"And . . . what about you? How was it . . . for you and Carly?"

He rolls his eyes. "How was it for me and Carly? Now that is an interesting question, and one that would require a more serious, involved answer than I am prepared to give this afternoon when I have not been so good about going to my therapist lately. May I get back to you on that?"

"No," I say cheerfully. "Actually, it's now or never."

"Now or never, huh? And why is that?"

"Because I'm not going to see you again."

His eyes widen. "What?"

"Yeah. This is it. It's just a little break, a time out from our usual lives."

"Really."

"Yes. You didn't know that? You thought I was going to go and explain to Grant that you and I are going to strike up a friendship now, and maybe he'd like to join us? The three of us could have dinner sometime, perhaps. Talk about old times."

"What? You don't think that would be fun?" he says and makes his eyes go round and innocent. Then he grabs my hand again. "Oh my God, Annabelle, I've missed you so much. If you aren't a minx, I don't know what you are. I've gotta tell you something—since I now find out the shocking news that I'm not ever going to get another chance." He lowers his voice because a man has taken the table right next to ours and, inches away from us, is opening a paper bag with a muffin inside. "Do you know that I can't even read that book of mine anymore, because all I can see when I read certain parts of it is you and me, in bed, writing the damn thing?"

You and me in bed, he says. And something electric goes through me, which he notices, with some amusement. I see the satisfaction in his eyes. Nobody is going to tell *him* that I fell in love with Grant McKay.

"The love story part," he says. "Did it . . . well, did it make you remember?"

I'd read the book in the library, I tell him. I'd take the children for story hour, and then as soon as they were settled, I'd go upstairs to the place I'd hidden it in the stacks. Sometimes someone would have found it and taken it back to the New Fiction section, where just anyone could see it and check it out. I don't tell him that once I couldn't find it for three days, and I was worried that somebody had taken it out and I'd have to wait—and what if it was a person like me who keeps books for however long I want to? But then I found it again. Somebody had shelved it wrong. I remember the day I read the ending, when the couple broke up. It hadn't been that way when he'd read it to me before. I'd had to lean against the shelves because my heart was beating so hard.

He's smiling. "Us in bed. At—what was her name?—Lynn's house?"

Oh *yes*. "Linnea."

"Ah, Linnea. Saint among women. How many toasts have I drunk in my life to Linnea and her lovely bed. I still mention her nightly in my prayers of gratitude."

"But with the wrong name, apparently."

"In prayers of gratitude, it's the essence that counts. Don't you know that?" He takes a sip of his coffee and whispers, "I love the idea of you reading my book in the stacks while your children hear stories downstairs. I wish I could have known that was happening. I wish I could have reached you."

"Yes. Me, too, you."

I know it's all over my face how much I have held on to him, that he might even know about the dreams I've had of him at night, about the way his face would suddenly appear before me at any time at all through the years—while changing diapers, washing dishes, even making love to Grant.

He grins at me and pushes his hair back off his forehead and sighs. The novel embarrasses him now, he says, with all that sentimentality. He can't bear to read it. "It was, ah, a symptom of the times, shall we say?" he says. "All that bullshit trauma, the sabbatical, the difficulty in the marriage, the adjustment to having little kids rampaging through the house, dismantling the place brick by brick. You know, I was about as crazy as a person can be and still be at large. Those years . . . I mean, what was I thinking?" He holds up his hands, appealing to the heavens, and says, "I was stupid."

I sip my tea and feel a flush spreading across me. This is a dance we're doing. I've thrown down the gauntlet by saying I'm in love with Grant, and Jeremiah is setting out to show me that he can still get to me. Just watch, in a moment, he'll punish me by saying that I, too, was just a symptom of his stupidity, and then after a few more minutes of strained but otherwise polite and ambiguous conversation, we'll say good-bye and I won't see him again. But at least I'll know how to file away that whole period of my life. The good part will be that I won't need to hold on to those dreams that I realize I have always seen as a kind of message from my unconscious, from my soul, this guarded place that I have let Jeremiah be in charge of.

But the bad part will be that everything will have been diminished, made small.

Which, damn it, it was. It was small. I have been so idiotic, seeing those days writ so large, giving them such importance. Calling that affair *my soul*. Going to the library to read that book, even Googling his name—all that was making more of it than it really was, a ridiculous dalliance he took on when he was screwed up beyond belief and was rebelling. The truth was, I was a little shit of a wife, a cheating spoiled baby who luckily found herself forgiven by her husband. And I should get down on my knees and thank my lucky stars that I got out so unscathed. Run back now. *Now.*

I feel for my purse strap and am about to stand up and make some excuse when he leans forward and touches my arm. His eyes see down to the heart of me.

"Annabelle, I just want you to know that the loss of you was something I never got over. It was the worst mistake I ever made. I may not get another chance to tell you."

Don't look. Look away. Now.

"But you really are happy, aren't you?" he says. "I mean, happy in that overarching sense."

I nod and then shrug. Shake my head. Yes. No. I can't speak.

He's smiling, still leaning so close to me that it's all I can do not to reach over and run my hands along that stubbled jawline of his that used to make me so crazy. "It actually helps me, knowing that you didn't suffer so much after you spun away from me that last day." He shakes his head, puts down his coffee cup, and sighs. "For such a long time, I guess I wasn't sure we were going to survive all that love."

I put my hand up to shield my eyes as tears start to fall, and he says, "Oh, no! Oh, don't, please, please . . ."

I jump up and pull my hand away. "Stop. Let's not go into all that now! I can't talk about it," I say, more loudly than I realized, and I can't help it, I'm crying now for real. "I don't want to cry," I whisper hoarsely. Jeremiah stands up, too, and leans over and dabs at my face with the napkin he's holding, and I jerk away from him and say, "*No!*" Too loudly.

The man with the muffin looks up. His paper is practically touching my hip.

I put my hands over my face.

"No, talk about it. Tell me. If this is the only time we'll have, we need to talk about it," says Jeremiah in a low, urgent voice, standing next to me and pulling me toward him. "Let's get out of here, okay? Come to my place."

"I don't want—I can't leave with you," I say. "I need to go—to go back to Sophie's. I want to get away." I must look so foolish, with mascara going everywhere on my face, and my voice so shaky and ragged.

"But you're not okay. Stay with me a little longer. Let's talk this through. This is our only chance. Here. Why don't we walk?"

Outside, the sun is weak and watery, and there are puddles everywhere with little chips of ice still in them. "Let's just take one of those walks like we used to," he says. "Nothing heavy or sad. Remember that year we pushed the kids in their strollers for miles and miles while we tried to figure out your career and my book and why we didn't want to do the things that everybody thought we were supposed to do?"

"Yeah, I remember."

"Those walks maybe saved my life."

"Mine, too."

"Yeah. And look at us, here again. On a one-day-only free pass. Amazing, really, when you think about it."

So I go with him. We walk for blocks and blocks, and it's crazy how familiar and right it seems. Like we're outside of time. On vacation from real life. He takes my hand, and that's okay, too. We keep smiling at each other, without talking, and I can't get over it, that I'm here with him and how funny he makes everything. It's okay, really. He's the same, and we don't have to wade back through all that shit; it's enough to be here with him this minute, and that's what I want to tell him. That we really don't need anything more than this because it's enough to get me through the next twenty-six years and however many months and weeks and hours, and I'm wondering if he really did figure that up or was that something he just made up, but when I turn to him to say that, he stops walking and pulls me over next to the building, and then his mouth is covering mine and we are kissing like it's 1979 and not one second has passed.

He tastes of coffee and sweetness and something that is unmistakably familiar and known and *real*, more real than anything else I've been through since. He is in my blood; he has *always* been in my blood. And it's like all the times before when we kissed in public and everything went all hallelujah in my head, those times in the park when we took the kids on the swings, and the times when we raced home and jumped on each other in bed, or tore off to Linnea's house, laughing as we unlocked her door and, often as not, falling down on the floor in the entryway, kissing and rolling around on her Turkish rug and never making it to the bedroom. And maybe it's been only an hour since those days have passed, and these are the kisses that have lived on in those dreams—and maybe they *are* dreams; maybe I'll wake up and think, *Oh, I had one of those Jeremiah dreams, but this one was in a Starbucks!* And so when he says, "I live not far from here; will you come home with me?" I am helplessly ready to go with him, because I am no longer the sad Annabelle who has run away from home, I am the old Annabelle, and I need this. It is, in fact, rightfully *mine*.

I am about to say all the yeses that are in my head—but then my cell phone rings in the pocket of my coat, blaring out the first notes of "Thriller," which Sophie thought would be a funny trick, and I jump in midair as though I've been caught and am plunged right back in the present.

"Uh-oh, pregnancy alert? Could this be it?" says Jeremiah under his breath, close to me, but we pull apart as I take the phone out of my pocket. It's not Sophie, thank God. It's Nicky, and I shrug at Jeremiah and say, "*Other* kid," and answer it.

He's talking through a crackly connection; either that or he's eating something. His voice is maddeningly lazy and casual. It brings me back to reality. "Hey, Mom. I've got a question. Did Dad pay for next semester already?"

This is the kid—it's funny, really—who had an unerring sixth sense for knowing when Grant and I were making love. Let Grant so much as touch my breast in the middle of the night, and there would be Nicholas, materializing from out of nowhere in his fleecy sleeper, sucking his thumb and demanding to be put between us in bed. "He's returning to the scene of his origins," Grant used to say. "It's like the swallows returning to Capistrano."

And now here he is, driven by some blind instinct to preserve the sanctity of our marriage, perhaps. I can't think. "Why are you asking me this?" I say. "What's wrong?"

"I dunno. I'm just thinking maybe I'd like to take some time off, go traveling or something," he says. "If he didn't pay, I was thinking maybe I'll just take the money he was going to pay and go to Europe next semester. Backpacking. Doesn't that sound cool?"

"Wait. Backpacking? Instead of college?" I say. I roll my eyes at Jeremiah and he laughs. He's leaning against the wall with his arms folded, watching me be a mom. "Why don't you just go backpacking this summer and then go back to school in the fall like you're supposed to?"

"Because I'm not getting anything out of college. It's stupid. My classes are boring and I don't want to be here," Nicky says. "I thought you'd be the one who'd get that. You get me. Dad doesn't."

"Listen, sweetie, can we talk about this later? This isn't such a great time."

"Where are you? You sound like you're in the middle of a train station or something."

"Nope, I'm just outside on the street," I tell him. "Listen. Why don't I call you tonight?"

"But, Mom, I'm supposed to sign up for classes now, and I really, really do *not* want to come back to this place. I'm just wasting Dad's money here. Tell him that. He hates the idea of wasting money."

"Listen, just go sign up anyway. We'll talk about this on spring break. You are coming for break, aren't you?" Jeremiah detaches himself from the wall he's leaning on and wanders a few feet away, giving me some space. He stands and looks at a poster hanging on a little street kiosk as if it's the most fascinating thing in the world. It's such a luxury, getting to observe him without him looking at me. If I squint, he looks exactly the same as he did years ago—same weight, same way of walking, same *whatever* it was that used to drive me so mad for him. I'm grateful for the distance, I realize in surprise. This moment to think and breathe. I feel grounded again.

Nicky is whining about how his father is going to give him a hard time if he leaves school. He says Grant has never understood him, that I'm the only one who can help him.

"Well, he *is* a professor," I say. "He believes in education."

Jeremiah puts his hands in his pockets and rocks backward on his heels, not looking at me. He has a thoughtful, concerned look on his face as he watches a street person lurching down the street. I see him reach out and steady the man as he comes closer, see the way he reaches into his pocket and hands the man something.

The word *kryptonite* rises in my head. Jeremiah is my kryptonite. I am breathing better now that I'm even a few feet away from him. My strength is returning.

"Backpacking *is* an education!" Nicky says. "You gotta tell him that for me. You can make him see. *You* didn't finish college, and *you* did all right."

I should have postponed this conversation, but I didn't—because it hits me that I wanted this distance. I am actually prolonging this, hanging on to the phone as if for dear life. "First of all, honey," I say, "you and I are different people, and second of all, the times are different. And I've always wished I went back. It was a mistake."

I am not going to sleep with Jeremiah. I know that now.

"Get out of here," Nicky is saying. "You're like a *major* artist doing books! You got what you wanted without college!"

"It's not the way you think. I didn't do exactly what I wanted. Let's talk more about this later. This really is a terrible connection."

"All right," he says. "But if you talk to Dad . . ."

There's a cluster of static and we get disconnected. But for some reason, I don't take the phone away from my ear. I pretend that I'm still connected, and I walk over to Jeremiah in the sudden blankness of silence from the cell phone world, and I blow him a kiss and do one of those fluttery finger waves, point to the phone, make a sad face, blow another kiss, and mouth the words "I've got to go"—and then I walk away.

It's that easy to just ... walk away. Who knew you could do that?

The glow of holy light surrounds me as I go, nearly blinding me.

[f o u r t e e n]

1979

The apartment Grant and I moved to, when we moved out of Jeremiah and Carly's place, was small but acceptable. Its one drawback was that it was next to Linnea's building, which was unfortunate because I knew I would think of Jeremiah every single time I went in or out. It was a small walk-up above a market, with a tiny galley kitchen and a bedroom that would have been part of the living room but for the one step up that marked its boundary.

We settled in. Grant had a shorter commute, which made him happy. And he seemed to accept that I'd suddenly decided on the move. "It's time; we've lived with them for two years," I said, and that was the only explanation I gave. It was the same thing I said to Carly, who was a little more puzzled by what must have seemed a rash decision. Jeremiah stayed tight-lipped. I cried when I kissed the twins good-bye.

Carly said, "Wait a minute. Whoa. You can't disappear on us. You'll come back for dinners and celebrations. We'll still do holidays."

We did not go back for dinners and holidays. I made excuses each time. I ached to hold the children, to read *Goodnight Moon* again, for the smell of their hair and the way they snuggled up to me. But I didn't go back.

Jeremiah and I didn't see each other for a while. A long time, actually, weeks. I went into a depression. Maybe not a clinical depression, but a depression just the same. I wanted to sleep all the time; I lost my appetite. I would look for him on the street. On days when I didn't work, I would take the subway over to the old place, and then walk around the neighborhood, never quite allowing myself to approach his apartment building. Instead, I'd hang around at the end of the block and look down the street. Stupid, stupid. But all I wanted was to catch a glimpse of him—just to see him going into one of the markets, pushing the twins in their stroller, or loping down the street with his hands in his pockets. Grant was busy and distracted, and I yearned for Jeremiah, for the way he looked at me and *saw* me, for his long, tapered fingers tracing my features, for his face above mine in bed. Laughing. Reading me his secret book, which was so raw and beautiful, and which I loved because it came from some vulnerable place in him.

I replayed scenes in my head. It went from bad to worse, this feeling I had. It was as though I were physically ill. Grant noticed. "Could you be pregnant?" he said to me one morning when I was too tired to even get out of bed.

"No," I said.

"Well, then, what is it?"

"I don't know."

"Maybe you're depressed. Maybe you should talk to somebody."

"I don't need to talk to anybody."

"Why not? Maybe depression runs in your family. Your brother certainly—"

"I am not like my brother!"

He looked away. "Sorry. Forget I said anything."

Oh, I am still not getting to what happened next. You see how I delay? How I circle around the subject, and remember all the little stuff—that silly little argument with Grant, who was simply being a well-meaning, concerned husband? That's what I do, in my guilt. I make him the well-meaning one and don't talk about all the other times, the days he stayed so late at the university and then, when he came home, graded papers and listened to music on his headphones and didn't come to bed. How he forgot to bring home the milk and didn't notice that I'd changed the furniture around and never saw that I had a new haircut, and didn't take me by the hand or look into my eyes, not even once. How I was a piece of furniture to him. And then, when I was sad, he wanted to know if I was *pregnant*.

But I am getting to it.

I ran into Jeremiah in the park one day. It was not totally unexpected on my part. I knew he sometimes went there with Brice and Lindsay—and so I walked there one morning, rapidly, with my head down. It was winter by then, and the day was suddenly sharply colder, the kind of day that reminds you that nature holds all the power.

And there he was. Our eyes caught each other's. I lifted my hand to wave, but he strode right over to me. He left the kids in the fenced-in little play yard with the other children and nannies, and came to me and pulled me behind a tree, where no one would see, and we started kissing, just madly kissing. And groping, touching each other wherever we could reach. His fingertips were nearly digging into my arms. When we stopped and pulled apart, he said, as if he were in great pain, "I can't bear this. I have to see you."

"I miss you more than I've ever missed anything in my life," I said.

So we started up again. Throughout the rest of the winter, even though he was teaching again, we made time for each other. We went back to Linnea's, and when her place wasn't available, we used my apartment. Grant was never home; there was no chance of getting caught. Jeremiah said he didn't care anymore if we got caught anyway. It was different now, we were different now. For one thing, we didn't mention Grant or Carly. In the time we had together now, we undressed each other with less hurry and abandon, and although we'd sometimes spend hours just lying on the bed, holding each other and kissing and not even having real sex, the whole affair seemed more passionate and soul-stirring than it had when we were living in the same house. It was lit up differently, was the only way I could explain it to myself. It was now *on purpose*, not because we happened to meet near the broom closet when nobody else was around.

Spring came, and somehow still we managed. I couldn't go more than three days without seeing him. He was the sound track, the backdrop, the palette on which everything else was painted.

Then one day we were lying in bed and he said, "We are so fucked." It was late spring, a frustrating time. Change was in the air, but the weather kept forgetting it was supposed to be warm, and there would be cold, rainy, overcast days. As a Californian, I couldn't believe how long New York seemed determined to resist getting truly warm, to commit to good weather. Jeremiah and I spent our afternoon together in bed, reading his novel and then actually sleeping, my head on his shoulder, wrapped in each other's arms. He'd awakened first, and when he said that, his breath tickled my hair. It was almost an exhalation, that sentence.

I didn't have to ask what he meant. I took his fingers and kissed every one of them, and with each kiss I was thinking, *Don't*. I didn't think I could take it if he broke up with me just now when night was falling and summer was never going to come.

He said, "Annabelle. I don't think I can continue to live like this."

I closed my eyes and said, "Oh, please, not *now*. Can't we wait to have this conversation?"

"I don't think so," he said. He rolled over on top of me, and kissed my nose and cheekbones. "I think," he said, "that we have to come to some decisions we've been avoiding."

I swallowed and blinked. His eyes were boring into mine. He was going to break up with me again.

"The fact is," he said, kissing my eyelids and my nose, "I want you all the time."

I could scarcely breathe. "You do?"

"And." He took a deep inhalation. "I've been doing some thinking. I don't love Carly. I realize that I haven't for some time now."

I couldn't speak.

"She and I don't share our lives. We might as well be living apart. We don't even *kiss*. I went to kiss her the other day, and she flinched.

She actually drew back like I was going to bite her or something. What the hell?"

He was looking at me, so I nodded.

"There was never a whole lot," he said, and then he shook his head. "No. I made up my mind I'm not going to talk about that. Not going to complain about the marriage." He sighed. "The point is—the whole point is that she and I can't stay together when obviously the marriage is a sham and I'm in love with someone else." He rolled onto his back and lay there with his arm flung across his forehead.

"Oh," I said.

He turned and looked at me. His eyes were lit up in a way I'd never seen before. "That's what you say? Just 'oh'? You don't want this?"

"I do," I said. I scrambled up and sat cross-legged next to him. "I'm just . . . taken by surprise, is all. I mean, this is a lot to think about. And what about the children?"

"We'll work that out. I've been thinking about this for a long time. You are my life. You're the person I wake up thinking about and you're the last person I think about before I fall asleep. It's you that I tell things to, it's you that I want next to me."

"But Brice and Lindsay—"

"I won't have to give them up, Annabelle. People share custody. We can do that, too."

I pushed my hair behind my ears. "Will Car—"

"Of course she will. She's no monster. She realizes as much as I do that it's better for children when their parents are happy. You know that. We both come from families where the parents stayed together for the sake of kids. They did us no favors, did they? Listen to me. This will be hard. It'll be hard as hell. But it's the answer. It's the only way."

"Jeremiah, what *happened* to make you feel like this? I mean, are you *sure*? Have you thought this through?"

"What do *you* think? Have I thought this through? I've thought of *nothing* else. Come on, you feel the same way I do, I know you do. I see the way Grant lets you down. I shouldn't speak against him, I know. He's a great guy. A brilliant historian. A decent person. I wouldn't want to take anything away from him, but, Annabelle, hear me out. He doesn't love you the way I do. Or maybe—what the fuck?—maybe he does and I'm just blind here to whatever the two of you have. I shouldn't think about it, I know. It's none of my business what you have with him. But you need me. I'm your lover. I am falling at your feet. I will do whatever it takes to make you happy. You tell me what you want, and I want to be the one who provides that."

My heart was pounding. "But Carly and Grant will be so stunned. It hurts to think of their faces."

"Collateral damage," he said softly. "That's what they are: collateral damage. It's very sad, but there's nothing we can do."

I wanted to call a time-out, put him into suspended animation, and go to the phone right that minute and call Magda. Jeremiah wanted *me and only me*? I mean, I was thrilled, but I was doubled over with heartburn and something else. An adrenaline rush. A sick, horrible adrenaline rush. My hair was in my eyes; I had to keep pushing it aside. Dusk fell across the chest of drawers, where Grant's clothes were stacked, with mine, on the top. This room would have my husband in it soon. I suddenly saw it all in a kind of speeded-up, time-lapse photography, a comic sequence of a camera pointed at the bed: Grant and I waking up there this morning, stretching, getting out of bed, dressing, me making the bed. Then me lying there this morning after he'd left, watching a television show, reading a book. The bed is empty for a while, and then the camera shows Jeremiah arriving, us ripping our clothes off, getting under the sheets, making love, then sleeping. Then we get up, I make the bed again, and later Grant and I get in the bed. It could be a film: *A Day in the Life of a Bed*. The bed of a bad woman.

Jeremiah was now up and pacing. "How will we do it? That's the question," he said. "That's what we have to do next: work out the details." I turned on the lamp, hoping that would help me calm down.

His face was drawn as he put on layer after layer of clothing. I had always maintained that in California, people had much less suspenseful fucks. Clothes practically fell off. In New York, to undress you had to be determined. Every day a striptease.

Two days later, he called me on the phone and said, very fast, "Okay. I've worked it out. I want us to leave." He'd been talking to a guy he knew who had a cabin in the woods on his property in upstate New York. We'd go there now that the semester was over and stay for the summer, and he'd finish his novel. This would give everybody a chance to get used to the idea. Carly would be upset, but she wouldn't be surprised, not when she truly thought about it. They hadn't been really together for so long. She deserved more. In the fall, we'd come back to the city, and he'd resume his life at Columbia and see the kids twice a week like all the other divorced dads he knew.

By then I had talked to Magda and Linnea, and both had agreed that things had to come to a resolution. Certainly it seemed—especially the way I told the story—that Jeremiah was the person I had the most connection to. If I could only have one of them, and apparently that was the rule, then it would have to be Jeremiah. He was the one who made my heart sing, as Linnea put it. Magda had some lingering fondness for Grant and the way he'd saved me from my parents' crazy drama, and also for his commitment to my doing art. But Linnea knew that Jeremiah was the one for me. She'd seen me blossoming with his love, and tears came to her eyes when she heard that he wanted to make it official.

"He's a good man," she said. "He's like my Paolo."

I got more and more excited by the idea as he and I made the plan for our getaway. I loved him. And it was so clear that I couldn't live without him. Just the way he looked, making those plans, made me happier than I'd ever believed I could be. This face, this shoulder I tucked myself into, this wonderful sexy body—all of this was going to be mine.

. . .

WE DECIDED to leave the following Saturday. According to the plan, that afternoon he would tell Carly he was leaving her, while at the same time I would tell Grant, and then we would meet at Grand Central at six. We would catch the 6:37 train to New Haven, where we would spend the night with his college roommate, who had a car he wasn't using for the summer.

"It will be a hell of a bad day, but then we'll have each other," he said to me. "I'll meet you by the clock at six. No later than ten after, you hear? No matter what happens, no later than ten after. My heart won't be beating right until I see you."

I actually had to make an appointment with Grant so I could tell him. He had been planning to spend the whole day at the library, as usual. But he agreed to come home at three o'clock, which would be perfect. I spent the morning packing my things and putting the suitcases under the bed so they wouldn't be the first things he saw. Then I paced the tiny apartment while I waited for him to come home. I pictured Jeremiah at his house, doing the same thing: packing and waiting until it was time to tell Carly and the children good-bye.

My stomach hurt with shooting pains every time I thought about him. How was he going to be able to say good-bye to his babies? Even I had barely been able to tell them good-bye when Grant and I moved out, and I had only known them for a few months. But he was sure it would be fine.

"I tell them good-bye all the time," he said. "They won't know when I leave this time that it's any different. How could they know?"

What I thought was, *But you know. You know that you're not going to be there to put them to bed anymore and you're not going to smell how delicious they smell when they wake up in the morning, and how it feels when they laugh, and even what will happen to them when you go.*

"You worry too much," he said. He bent me back into a passionate kiss. "That's part of what I love about you: the way you feel everyone's troubles, almost more than your own."

So that's what I was thinking of as I packed everything into our wedding present luggage. The apartment felt echo-y when I had finished. I didn't even pack all that much, just my clothes and toiletries, and some things from the kitchen. Jeremiah had requested that I bring my garlic press and my Moosewood cookbook. I took a painting down off the wall, something that my art teacher had made for me—a watercolor of an oak tree near a lake.

At three fifteen, I heard Grant's key in the lock, and I sat down on the couch and wiped my palms on my jeans. My mouth was dry, and I wished I'd thought to have a glass of water near me, but I didn't feel able to get up and get one now. My knees were weak.

He came in and put down his backpack and then just stood there, looking at me in surprise. He looked like a rooster, with his hair sticking up in a million cowlicks. "Well, hi," he said and smiled. "Why are you sitting there . . . like that?"

"Like what?"

"On the edge of the couch. Like you're waiting for a train or something," he said. "You look weird. Did you just get off the phone?"

"Grant," I said. "I have something to tell you."

"Can I get a snack first? You want anything?"

"No," I said.

"Really? Have you eaten lunch? I had some peanuts from a vending machine at the library, but obviously peanuts can only take a person so far." He opened the refrigerator and stared inside. "Oh, there's this leftover takeout. Can I have this?"

"Sure," I said.

"Moo goo gai pan," he said. He said it a second time, in a singsong. "Moo *goo* gai *pan*." He came walking back into the couch area—you couldn't call it a living room—with the cardboard container and a fork. He would never even try to use the chopsticks they always put in the bag. "Hey, you know what? This is actually better than it was the other night. Of course, I was eating it at one in the morning, and I had heartburn all night, so maybe that's coloring my memory. But it's good. Sure you don't want a bite?" He held out a forkful in my direction.

"Grant," I said and swallowed. "I have the most difficult, horrible thing to tell you, and I don't know quite how to do it, so you have to sit down and let me say it."

He put down the container and stared at me with wide eyes. I could see his Adam's apple working up and down. "Something's wrong?" he said. "Is it your brother? Oh, no. Did he—?"

"No," I said. "It's not him; it's me."

He sank down beside me on the couch and took my hand. "Are you all right? Did something happen? Are you—wait! Are you pregnant?"

My eyes filled up with sudden tears, which made him reach over and take me in his arms. And this was so much worse than anything I'd pictured happening—worse, in fact, than the rampaging I had prepared for. It hit me that I hadn't really thought about the actual words to use.

"No," I said through tears. "No, I'm not pregnant."

"Then what? Oh, you poor baby," he said, and I had to pull away from him, stand up, and march across the room. I had to harden myself to this, to stop crying, but I couldn't stop. My eyes just kept making more and more tears, and Grant felt sorrier and sorrier for me. Finally I yelled at him, "Stop it!"

He sat back, blinking in surprise. "Well, then, tell me. What's going on?"

I started sobbing for real. "I-I'm leaving you," I said.

He didn't say anything, but the light went out of his eyes in stages. After a moment, he folded his arms like he was pulling them in for protection. Somehow this gave me courage. I had to go forward now. There wasn't any way of going back. Jeremiah had said, "When you're telling him, picture my face. Visualize what it will be like Saturday evening when we're together on the train. How happy we'll be."

"I'm not happy, and I want to leave," I said and took a deep breath. "I'm sorry, but that's the truth."

He looked down, rubbed his thumb on the toe of his shoe. "Okaaaay," he said. "I see. And when did you decide this?"

"I guess I've been deciding it for a while," I said.

"You've just been *deciding* it."

I nodded. "For a while. I've thought about it long and hard."

"Have you now?"

"You and I don't seem to have anything together anymore."

He took that in, filed it away, nodded. "Is this . . . is it your family?"

"No. Yes. Well, maybe a little."

"So you're going back to California, are you?"

"I don't think so. Not right away."

"But—what will you *do*? Why are you doing this now? I mean, it's crazy for us just to live apart. We can't afford it, and besides that, if you—if you don't like me and you need time away from me, you've pretty much got that." He stopped talking, and then he said, "Oh. Ohhh. How idiotic of me. There's someone else."

I licked my lips and looked up at the ceiling. *Jeremiah's face, Jeremiah's face.* "Yes," I said, and swallowed hard. "I'm in love with Jeremiah."

Some sentences just come out in capital letters and hang in the air, and this was one of them. I could feel the reverberations of it. I waited for him to stand up and come over and hit me. I thought he might throw the coffee table over. Actually, I couldn't imagine what he would do—anything but what he did do. He just sat there looking at me quietly, rubbing the toe of his shoe back and forth, and then he looked down at the floor and said in a flat voice, "Really. Imagine that."

"I know. It's the worst thing that could have happened. I'm sorry."

"Wow," he said. "Wow." He shook his head, like somebody shaking water out of his ears.

"I'm sorry," I said. "I really didn't mean for this to, you know, happen. I'm so, so sorry."

Suddenly he whipped his head down between his knees, moving so swiftly that I jumped. He was clasping his hands in front of him. I looked at his wedding ring and wished this would be over and that I would quit saying I was sorry.

"You're leaving me to be with him, then?" he said finally, from between his knees.

"Yes. When we finish talking."

He kept his head down, didn't look at me. "Does Carly know?"

I hesitated. "He's telling her."

"Now?" He sat back up.

"I think so."

He actually laughed at that. "Wow. What an orchestration this is, huh? Two people each getting told the unthinkable. Did you two rehearse what you'd say? Do—what do they call that?—*role play*?"

I stayed silent.

"Do you mind if I ask you how long this has been going on?" he said. Then he held up one hand. "Wait. Never mind. I don't need to know that. There's no reason on earth for me to know that, is there?"

I came over to the couch and sat down on the footstool in front of him. "I'll tell you whatever you need to know, whatever helps. We didn't want to hurt you."

He barked out a bitter little laugh. "Ha! Here's something you could do for me. A little thing. Just during this conversation if you wouldn't use the word *we* for you and . . . him. I mean, until just a second ago, if you said *we*, I would think you meant you and me."

"Of course," I said. "I don't want to be insensitive."

"Oh, no! It would be *bad* to be *insensitive* at a time like this, wouldn't it? It's one thing to just leave a guy without any frigging advance notice, but you wouldn't want to be *insensitive* in the bargain."

In the hall we heard a door opening and a woman's voice calling to a guy named Cal. It always sounded like she was saying, "Cow! Cow!" and Jeremiah and I had once laughed about that. He'd yelled, "Sheep! Sheep!" At the time I'd wondered if Grant would have ever made a joke like that, and then it had hit me that he wasn't ever home long enough to have heard her yelling for Cal. I'd added that silly thing to my justifications for leaving him. Now that he was here I felt so horrible I practically had chills.

He was silent for such a long time, leaning forward as though he was trying to keep himself from passing out, and then I saw that he was crying. Oh God, he was weeping. For *me*. He kept his head down, but his fists were covering his eyes. I didn't know what to do, so I sat there. The clock on the stove said 3:55. I still had plenty of time. I didn't know what to say or do. Should I try to comfort him? I was about to start crying again myself.

"Oh, Grant," I said, and touched his back. He didn't pull away.

When he spoke again, he said, "I can't believe this."

"I know. We—I mean *I*—I didn't mean for this to happen."

He looked up at me. "You know what the bad part is? The awful thing is that I have admired and loved the two of you *so* much. That's the thing. I don't think I'll be able to just stop so quickly."

"Oh my God, don't say that," I told him. This was so typical of Grant that it took all the air out of me. Couldn't he even do the expected thing, play the part of the wronged husband and get fucking furious? As bad as that would be, it was preferable to this. "You should hate us. I'm sorry. Not 'us.' You should hate me! Go ahead. Get mad at me if you want to. You can yell and scream. Get it all out. I don't want you to have to hold it in."

"I wish I could," he said. "I know it'll come to that. I'll get mad. I have the rest of my life to be mad, I guess. I'm going to have to go through all of it. But right now . . . right now I'm just so ridiculously . . . well, blindsided."

"You *were* blindsided," I said. I rubbed his back a little, like I could be his friend through this maybe.

"How long . . . ?"

"Do you want to know? Do you want to know the whole thing? Because I'll tell you, if you want. I will."

"Yes. Tell me that. Just that much, no more."

"It started the winter we got here."

He drew in a breath. "Really?"

"Yes."

"Wow."

"Yeah."

There was a long silence. "How did you do it?"

I was startled. "How did we ... what?" I said, and then after a moment, we both laughed.

"No. Not *that*. I mean, how did you get away with it? How did I not know?"

"Well," I said. I licked my lips, which were suddenly very dry. "You really weren't there very much, and—"

"Don't say anymore, okay? Be quiet now."

"Okay."

"Okay." He kept breathing, in, out, in, out, as though he had to concentrate to remember to do it right. "That's all I want to know. That's a long time. Longer than I would have thought."

We were silent. The sun made a parallelogram on the wooden floor. I watched its edges wobble and dull as clouds went by, and then I watched as it brightened and sharpened again. My whole self ached. I was one big toothache of a human being. I had hurt this person who was bent over with pain, pain that I had caused, and nothing I could do would make it even one iota better. I decided that I would watch as three more clouds went by, and then I would get up and leave. I couldn't imagine what that was going to be like—actually going in and getting my suitcases from under the bed and walking out the front door—but I had come this far, and I had to do it. There wasn't a way to turn back.

Then he was the one who got up. He rose in one sudden motion and went into the bathroom and closed the door, and I stood up, too, and got the suitcases from the bedroom and dragged them to the front door. When he came out of the bathroom, I was standing in the kitchen area. I didn't know what to do with my hands, so I folded my arms.

"There's something I want to leave you with," he said. "This is just between you and me now. Nothing to do with Jeremiah."

"Okay," I said. I licked my lips again. I felt as though I had no more moisture in my body. I wasn't precisely sure that he wasn't going to land a blow that would level me. I braced for it, but instead he took my hands and looked into my eyes, unflinching.

"You have a core of sadness in you," he said. "I've felt it. And I have some ideas about where it comes from—you know, the family stuff and all that. I thought you and I might, you know, be together enough so that we'd get rid of that. But we couldn't, and part of that is my fault, and timing, and my teaching and all that. Maybe you needed somebody who could be there for you full-time. You deserve that, I know. And if he makes you happy, if he can give you that, then I just want to say that this is what's probably supposed to happen. Maybe—I think this is possible—maybe you've found the love of your life."

"Oh, Grant."

"And so I'm glad for you. Really, really glad. Because you need to grab on to whatever you can in this life, whatever makes you—whatever makes you happy. There's so little of that in life. That's grace, you know. A concept that, by the way, I didn't know I believed in."

There was a lump in my throat. He saw me trying to swallow, and he put his forehead against mine and held it there. "It hurts like hell," he said. "That it's him—I mean, I've lost both of you, I know that. But I'm not so dumb that I don't think things happen for a reason. And maybe my place in all this was, you know, to *introduce* you to the person you'll always love. How's *that* for shitty irony, huh? Grant loves the girl but hands her over to the guy he admires." He shook his head and closed his eyes. Then he pulled his hands away from me and said in a different voice, a sterner voice, "Okay. So go. And don't call me, okay?" He opened his eyes and looked right at me again. "Don't, *do not,* come back, either. If for some reason this doesn't work out, I'm sorry, but you can't come back."

I tried to hug him, but he pushed me away, and then we said good-bye. I wasn't crying. I couldn't cry; I was dry as dust. And then, before I knew it, I was out in the hallway with the suitcases and hauling them down the stairs, thinking, in my shell-shocked, dramatic way, *Good-bye to all this!* and then I was down on the street. I hailed a cab, in slow motion, and went to Grand Central.

Jeremiah's face. Jeremiah's face. My new life was beginning. I walked away from the old, and I didn't let myself look back, even at the building. I was so afraid Grant might be at the window. I could practically feel his hand there on the glass waving good-bye, and I couldn't bear it.

It wasn't for another week that I realized that Grant hadn't even lifted a finger to try to make me stay. He had just released me the way you might whisk away a rogue feather that landed on your shoulder.

I GOT to Grand Central at a quarter 'til six, which gave me time to lug my two suitcases to the ladies' room. I went to the bathroom and splashed water on my face. I stood for a long time looking at myself in the mirror and tried to smile. My hair was in a bun but the ends were falling out, so I twisted it up again and shoved the bobby pins back into it. My eyes looked scared. Someday, I thought, I'll remember this moment just before my new life took shape. Maybe someday Jeremiah and I will tell our grandchildren about this day, the day we ran away, knowing that we were meant to be together. But for now I looked drained and sickly. I put on some lipstick, tried to pull myself together. I was going to be with the love of my life, and I didn't want to look so tragic.

When I finished, I took everything back upstairs to the clock. We'd agreed to meet at the clock, which is where everyone always meets at Grand Central, so all around me people were standing, waiting, or else flying into someone else's arms, kissing, hugging, laughing,

yelling, clapping each other on the back and then walking off together. I was so young and alone, standing there with that frozen
smile on my face, that look of expectancy, waiting to be chosen.

And he was late.

First he was only five minutes late, and then it was six minutes and
then seven. I told myself I couldn't look up at the clock until at least
fifteen whole minutes had passed. I concentrated on staring at the
floor, at all the trash that had been so carelessly tossed about: old
tickets, gum wrappers, gum. Then I stared at shoes. Men's shiny wing-
tips, children's sneakers, high heels clicking on the hard floor, loafers
scuffed from age, sandals. Even boots, some idiot wearing boots
though it was clearly and obviously springtime, a time for new
beginnings, time to put away all the stuff of winter. I felt sorry for the
boot-wearer.

Twelve after six.

Maybe I should buy our tickets.

No. It was better to wait.

I allowed myself to look up and search the crowd of faces coming
toward me—all blank, unknown faces, filled with hurry and pain and
thoughts I couldn't read. I shivered. I could not think of what would
happen if he didn't come, although once that thought had appeared,
it was difficult to chase it back to the corners. It bloomed then, pul-
sating and radiant in capital, bold-faced letters, with asterisks around
it. It was a headache of a thought.

What if he does not come?

But then—was it?—yes! Someone with Jeremiah's hair color was
coming from the area of the stairs, and thank God THANK GOD it *was*
Jeremiah; the relief that flowed through me was almost like oxygen. He
was loping, not running at all, even though we were late, and the
thought sprang into my head that maybe we wouldn't make the 6:37
after all, but who cared, *really*? We had the rest of our lives; we could
catch any damn train we wanted. We could just go somewhere dark and
cloistered and kiss and drink and tell each other about our getaways.

Mine was taking shape as something I'd probably be able to live with and talk about. I was not too disappointed with the way I'd handled things; I was already forgiving myself, filing away the grief of a broken marriage . . . and then through all that self-forgiving I was doing, it hit me that Jeremiah had no suitcase. And then when he was still far away, his eyes met mine, and he made the smallest of gestures, a slight, ironic raise of his eyebrows, a pursing of his lips, and on such flimsy evidence, I knew everything I needed to know—that I was alone, all alone in the world. He hadn't told her, he hadn't left, and it was me he was coming to say good-bye to.

I remember everything about that time, of course, everything from the texture of his shirt that I cried into, looking down at the scuff marks on the floor of Grand Central, the hum of noise all around us buffering what he kept saying over and over again: "I love you so much. I love you so much." The reeling inside my brain, my thoughts swinging around inside like a tetherball coming unhinged. Bright flashes of light.

He couldn't tell them. The children. The children's eyes and faces, their little hands . . . Brice was stuttering, Lindsay was bossy; they needed him so much. And today—his voice choked—today they were playing a loud game, loud but innocent, so innocent, and Carly was screaming at them, so how could he leave them to her? To her anger? And yes, he knew she wasn't *always* angry, but she was often angry enough, and because of that he had to make it work with her. And make no mistake, it would be work. He had to stay and be the buffer between her anger and those children. He loved me and he was sorry, but we couldn't run away. He kept biting his lip. We had to stop, we had to stop seeing each other, there was no hope for us, no hope for love in a world gone mad with regret.

He actually said those words, "a world gone mad with regret," as though he were the narrator of the coming attractions at the movies, *intoning* them, and after that I stopped listening and prayed that I would stop loving him, immediately. If I just paid attention to his body language, to the look on his face, I could see that he was relieved and proud of himself, and when he closed his eyes and said in a fake agonized tone of voice, "Oh, I'm so confused," I wanted to hit him, wanted to scratch his eyes out. I screamed, "You fucker! You *fucking* fucker! And *this* is the first time you've thought of all this? *Now?* You didn't know this before?"

He tried to say something. I could see his mouth moving, see his eyes wide and black and sorry, but I couldn't hear him through the pounding in my head. Blackness was starting to fill in all the white spaces around his head. I was about to fall down, I couldn't feel my legs anymore, and the next thing I knew I was running, and then I was somehow in the ladies' room, where I lost everything I hadn't already lost, and I could hear the floor shaking from the trains that were leaving the station.

Would it be too melodramatic for me to tell you that I never saw him again? But it's the truth. I did not. I was angry for such a long time—and that fury was good. I fed it breakfast, lunch, and dinner and rocked it at night and nurtured it along because I understood it was all I had.

[f i f t e e n]

🍃 2005

"What's the matter?" says Sophie when I get back to her apartment. "You look drained. Didn't you have a nice time?"

"I had a very nice time. I'm just tired," I tell her, draping my coat over the back of the chair in the bedroom. I *am* tired, now that I think of it, tired and shaky. I had caught a glimpse of myself in the tiny oval mirror in the downstairs hallway and was shocked at the two bright circles on my cheeks and how wild my eyes looked. *Holy God*, I think, *today I stood in public, kissing Jeremiah. I am now officially lying to my husband, and even worse, I don't know what is going to happen with me.*

I want to just get straight into the bathtub and sit there staring at the white tile until I can figure out how I feel about what I've just done. But Sophie is sitting up in bed with the light off, with the lavender comforter wrapped around her, sniffling and looking mournful. "So . . . was it depressing to talk to your old friend? It was, wasn't it?"

"Depressing?"

"Yeah. You know, with how run-down he seems." She blows her nose into a Kleenex. "Didn't he say his wife died? So I bet he's all depressed and pathetic and just wants you to cheer him up." She hiccups.

"Are you crying?"

"No . . . yes. A little bit." She pulls at a thread on the bedspread and puts on her little-girl voice. "Could you just come and get in bed with me? Pleeease." And now she really is crying.

"What's wrong?" I sigh and take off my shoes and climb in next to her. The room feels overheated and stuffy, and all I want is to leave again. But she throws her arms around my neck, and we lie there while she sniffles softly. "What is it, baby?" I say. "Should I not have left you alone?"

"No, that part was okay," she says into my neck, which I realize is getting wet. She pulls away and blows her nose on the tissue I hand her. "It's just that I now know the truth. I found out the real truth."

My heart stops. She *knows*?

"He—he's sleeping with Juliana. I know it for sure now."

"Wait," I say. "Did I miss something? First, who is Juliana?"

"She's that woman in the picture. The one Whit was practically making out with."

"Not making out with. Smiling in the general direction of."

"Whatever. You know the one, which is significant right there. Anyway, I found out her name today, and also that she's the daughter of the contractor at the orphanage. And she's *always* there with him."

Maybe there's something wrong with me, that faithfulness doesn't have the ring of golden reassurance that it seems to have for others. There are so many ways a marriage can implode, is what I think; sexual infidelity is just one of them, and actually, not even all that interesting. More often, I feel, being unfaithful happens when about five hundred other safeties have failed. But I know I'm alone in this assessment. Ask the faculty wives. No one agrees with me.

"He told me her name!" she says. "In fact, practically the whole e-mail is about her—how her father is building the place, and she's nineteen, and they've been playing double solitaire and so far she's beat him by about six hundred and forty-five games to two, and so now he's teaching some kids to play so he can brush up on his skills and *avenge his honor.*"

"So what?" I say. "He loves *you.*"

She reaches over and pulls her laptop off the bedside table. "Just *look* at this, will you? Read this and tell me you still think that!"

Nearly every day now I am required to read and decipher things in Whit's e-mails, all of which seem to me to be deeply personal, loving e-mails that he would *die* if he knew I was seeing. I have to say, he writes great, sexy notes to her, each one like a big, wet, erotic kiss. He can't wait, he writes, to be with her again, rolling around in their bed, to feel her nakedness underneath him . . . he goes on and on. Fascinating though these are, I should not be seeing them.

"Juliana!" she says. "If he's telling me her name, that means she's important to him. And look! Just look at her big eyes," she says.

"So she has nice eyes. So what? And his mentioning her doesn't mean she's important to him. I think if he were cheating on you with her, he'd be less likely to tell you the woman's name, wouldn't he? He'd keep it a secret."

"He's playing *double solitaire* with her, Mom."

"Sophie, honey, double solitaire is just a card game."

"*I freaking know it's a card game!* That's not the point! The *point* is, why can't he just wrap up the filming and come home, if he's got so much free time he can play double solitaire with another woman?"

I look at her and purse my lips. "Don't do this to yourself, sweetie. Why do you want to torture yourself with this?" I say. "I think you're the luckiest woman in the world. You have a monogamous man, and you and he are having a child, but for some reason, you're letting yourself turn into a paranoid maniac. You mustn't let your imaginings get the best of you. You're just tired. Have you drunk enough water today?"

She gives me a pitying look. Yes, *pitying.* "You probably don't realize this, I know, but Whit is actually a very sexy man," she says. "*You* think of him as a kid, but trust me: women look at him and they want him."

I laugh. "You think I don't know that about him? I can recognize a sexy man, even at my advanced age."

"I didn't mean that," she says. "It's just that you and Dad . . . Well, he's not exactly . . . *on fire.*"

I look at the ceiling and the thought comes to me that I have somehow turned out to be just the opposite of my mother. My mother brought her sexual opinions and needs and wants freely into the daily conversations we'd have, even at the breakfast table. Maybe it's because I was so allergic to these conversations that I have never once strayed into that territory with Sophie. I don't think I have ever said the word *orgasm* around her. I've never alluded to any sexual thoughts whatsoever. What was wrong with me? I probably should have. And now, in her mind, it's clear I have no sexuality whatsoever.

So I say very carefully and evenly, feeling as if I'm venturing into delicate territory, "You know, I think every generation thinks it invented sex. Your father and I—"

"Oh, don't tell me he was ever wild!" she says, and laughs.

"He was . . . is . . . amorous," I say.

"I mean, you and Dad seem like . . ."

"What do we seem like?" I say when she trails off. "Tell me what it was like being our daughter. What did you see?"

"I saw . . . lots of consideration, and good manners, and . . . fun, and, I don't know, a traditional division of duties, I think," she says slowly. "You were very much the head of the house, making sure everything ran smoothly, and he came home to play games and do things with us, but—well, he was distracted, too. And strict, always wanting us to do exactly the right thing. You were always the one paying attention, but it was like you had to keep reeling him back in. He did the peripherals, I guess. But he was the one we had to please. You were the easy one, the pushover."

"Really," I say. "So you're saying then that I was the *mom*."

She laughs. "Yeah, you were the mom, and he was the rock, I guess. The one who loved you and held you up, and you were the softhearted person who ran around trying to make sure everybody was happy."

"And"—I pause, try to phrase this just right—"I take it we didn't exactly radiate a kind of, I don't know, *married passion* for each other. Like people who couldn't keep their hands off each other."

"I remember coming into the kitchen once and you were kissing," she says. "I mean, really kissing, not just one of those peck-on-the-cheek things. But when you heard me, I remember, Dad sprang back and did this whole pantomime like he'd been caught at something. It made us all laugh. Do you remember that?"

I don't. I have no memory of that at all.

"Know something? Whit told me that about a year or so ago, he walked in his parents' den and they were—I shouldn't tell you this. I'm awful."

"Oh, no, go ahead. I insist."

"Well, they were, you know, actually *doing* it. Like, ewwww. And it was such a weird thing, he said, really the last thing he was expecting to see, that he couldn't even register it at first. He said he just stood there staring at them, kind of in shock, like his eyeballs had gotten burned or something, and finally his dad turned around and said, 'Do you *mind*?' and so Whit backed out of the room and closed the door and that was that." She wrinkles her nose and giggles. "You've got to admit, it's a disturbing image, the Bartholomews *doing it*. The other day when we were with them out for lunch, it was all I could think about."

"Thanks a lot," I say, laughing. "Now when I see them next, it's all I'm going to be able to think about, too."

"And his dad with that saggy belly—ugh!" She shudders.

I'm about to say something like, "Sex is not just for the young and beautiful, you know," when she looks down and starts picking at the tufts on the bedspread and says, "You know what I wonder? I just wonder if Whit can be a father like Dad, when he didn't get to experience, you know, the whole pregnancy thing with me. I'm going to be a *mom* when he gets back, and . . . Well, is he still going to love me?" Her eyes well up with tears.

"It's an adjustment, that's for sure. It is for everyone. But you just do it. You'll both figure it out as you go along. That's what marriage is."

"But . . ."

"But what?"

"He's such a *passionate* guy, Mom—more like a boyfriend than a husband, you know? There's this way that he's not domesticated yet, and now he's been free and when he comes back . . . Oh, I don't know what I'm trying to say."

I know what she's trying to say. I tell her the thing I truly believe—that sex and love and parenthood and complications can coexist, that you can be happy even when sex is something you steal away for once you've gotten the last of the dishes washed and the kid with the fever to finally go to sleep. But then my throat is suddenly clogged up with so much sadness and longing and regret that I think I will choke. It's because of today, because of all the jumbled stuff Jeremiah stirred up in me—memories of that raw, yearning sexuality that Sophie is talking about, that youth and passion that she has no idea I even know about.

I won't have that again.

That's the truth of it. It will not come again, not in this lifetime. I was standing there on the street just hours ago, and I was laughing and free, kissing Jeremiah on the street like we were a couple of teenagers—and why did I feel the need to run away? When maybe what I was being offered was a chance to feel something again. To feel something that has to do with me, just *me*—not in relation to Grant or Sophie or Nicky. Just me, Annabelle Bennett McKay. Don't I deserve to feel that again?

I had this, I lost it, and what I got instead was . . . what? The right to be in this room listening to my daughter. And that's *good*. But why can't I have it all—passion and motherhood and family?

After a while, the shadows lengthen in her bedroom, and I get up, stretch, and go in the kitchen to cook some spaghetti for our dinner, and she comes into the kitchen, too, wearing the bedspread like a giant cape that trails on the floor, and she sits on the stool wedged in by the brick wall, and when I look over at her, she smiles.

I'M IN the market a few days later, holding a cardboard container of blueberries—Sophie's latest craving—and trying to make up my mind about whether I'm really willing to spend five dollars on a half-pint of them, when my cell phone vibrates in my pocket.

I see that it's Jeremiah. For one difficult moment, I consider not answering it. But by the time I make up my mind to press the button, my heart is beating faster.

"Oh!" he says. "You answered. I was just getting ready to leave a voice mail."

"I can hang up and you can call the voice mail back if you want," I say, and he laughs.

"No, no. This is better. I'm actually calling to see if I can tempt you to come see me. I have something I think might be of interest to you."

I laugh. "I'm sure you do, but I thought we made it clear that we're not doing that anymore."

"Ah, yes. So you claim," he says. "But I notice that you're still taking my calls, so that gives me hope."

"Well, a sane person probably wouldn't take your calls, it's true."

"Most sane people don't," he says. "Um, where are you right now?"

"I'm out buying blueberries."

"Is this a pregnancy craving, by chance?"

"It is. But they're outrageously expensive, so I'm standing here debating whether they're worth it."

"Unless they're four thousand dollars, they're definitely worth it. Pregnancy cravings have to be indulged. Don't you remember?"

I love this, the way he has always been able to make me laugh, the sly manner he uses to bring me back to myself. So when he says, a moment later, "Of course I never knew you pregnant, but as I recall, even as a non-pregnant person, you had some pretty strong, awesome cravings," I am almost light-headed.

"I want to see you," he says. "Please tell me you'll pack up your blueberries and come to my apartment."

I try to protest. I *do* protest. I tell him I can't come to his apartment, I don't think this is a good idea, it can't come to anything, blah blah blah, but I'm laughing because he keeps groaning as I talk, and anyway, we both know I don't mean it the way you have to really mean something like this, and when I finally run down and stop talking, he says, "I'll come to meet you, then."

"But—"

"No, no. This needs to happen. Now where are you? Tell me your exact whereabouts."

"Union Square."

"Great—Union Square. Meet me at the northwest corner. I'll be there in ten minutes, eleven at the most."

"Jer—"

"No, no. You are to wait, motionless, until you see me. Think no bad thoughts while I'm on my way to you. Then, once I'm there, we'll figure out what we're going to do with this newfound insanity of yours."

I can't stop myself from laughing.

"Promise me. No bad thoughts until you see the whites of my eyes."

"But I really don't think it's a good idea for me to go to your apartment," I say.

"And is this because, for the first time ever, you're frightened of my overpowering animal magnetism? Or are you just worried that I'm going to force you to live there with me and be my love slave?"

"I—"

"Look," he says, and his voice takes on an edge. "What *is* this? I'm not trying to lure you away from your life. We can't sit down in a quiet apartment and talk about our lives? We're adults, Annabelle. We have a past. We care for each other, but that doesn't mean you're in any danger. This can't be *you* talking."

"Okay, listen to me. I promised Grant I'd never talk to you again. That was part of the deal for getting back together with him. All right? Now do you understand?"

There's a silence, and then he explodes in laughter. "You had to give me up? For all time? Wow. I've never been a bargaining chip before."

"Yeah, well—"

"I'm not sure how I feel about this. I'm seeing myself in a whole new way here."

"Could you just please—"

"Also, Annabelle, honey, I hate to point out the obvious, but surely you've noticed that you've already broken that promise, ah, *twice* now. Is it going to be that much more awful for him if you see me a third time?"

"I don't know. I guess not. Maybe you're right." He *is* right. Of course he's right. I'm being ridiculous. I'm a grown woman; I have my own life, apart from my life with Grant. And—well, I deserve to be able to look back at my past. This feeling, these longings, are not going to go away without my truly examining them. Even Ava Reiss would agree that you can't truly move forward until you've been brave enough to know who you really are.

"You and I both know that people shouldn't make those kinds of promises—or worse, even *ask* somebody to do that. Jesus. That's like promising not to feel anything for the rest of your life, and the woman I knew twenty-six years ago would have never made that kind of promise."

"Okay," I say.

"I'm coming to meet you. We'll take it from there," he says and hangs up.

I call up Sophie and tell her about the blueberries I've bought and that I'll bring to her soon. "Are you doing all right? Because I just got a call from Jeremiah, that old friend of mine we saw the other day . . ."

"Yeah, Mom. I remember Jeremiah," she says and laughs. "That just happened, you know."

"Well, he's in the neighborhood and wants to meet me for another quick cup of coffee. So if you don't need anything, I thought I'd do that. If you don't mind."

"Of course I don't mind," she says. "I'd be shocked if you didn't go."

"You would?"

"Mom. Come on. You take care of everyone. It's what you do."

· · ·

HIS APARTMENT turns out to be a smaller Upper East Side version of the one we all had together, up three flights of stairs, with high windows, wood floors, and lots of light. He even has most of the same furniture as before: his desk, the bookcases, and the kitchen table are all the same. All around are stacks of books and magazines, papers, open file cabinets with manila folders spilling out of them. There are big, splashy, messy paintings on the walls, a wine bottle and one lone glass out on the counter. Stacks of mail. His laptop is on the couch next to a blue knit throw that I remember. I used to play with the fringe on that thing when I read to Brice and Lindsay.

He says, "So this is it—the palace," and smiles. He takes off his black leather coat and waits while I remove my coat and hand it to him, and then he hangs them both in the closet and turns back to me, and there's one of those awkward silences as if there isn't a thing in the world that we can talk about. Which is weird because all the way here, he'd been telling me about his trips abroad, the lectures he's been giving at universities, and the way that the world of museums has changed—all reassuringly dull topics that had allowed me to calm down, even to the point of feeling a little bored.

"So how long have you lived here?" I say. It's such a Jeremiah space—the cooking smells, the casual disorder, the artwork—all of it exactly like it once was. Minus Grant and Carly, of course. And the twins. It strikes me that this might be like the home we would have made together.

"Oh—what is it now? Ten years, I guess. We lived in Germany for a bit after the twins graduated from high school, and when we came back to New York, we moved here." His eyes twinkle at me and he takes my arm. "You should look around. I bet you'll recognize most of the furniture. I have a tough time throwing anything away, you know."

Except me, I want to say. *That you did rather brilliantly.*

He walks down the hall toward the kitchen, calling over his shoulder, "Would you like some tea?" and when I say yes, he says, "Really. Make yourself at home." I walk around, peeking into the tiny, black-

and-white tile bathroom and then into the bedroom, which is right next to the kitchen, and is large and dim and with a disheveled bed right in the center of the room. His bed was always a mess, now that I think of it; we'd be practically in cardiac arrest we were so frantic for each other, and yet we always had to stop and remove clothing and books and papers from his bed before we could fall down on it and make love. And—well, here we are. This room is so much like the old room, it even smells the same. Here are his clothes, dropped everywhere, and I could go over to the bed and pick up his pillow and hold it close to me. I could stretch out here and close my eyes, and no time at all would have passed.

He's talking to me from the kitchen—patter that I know is meant to put me at ease, but I'm barely listening because suddenly I have to sit down. I'm sitting on his bedroom floor with my head in my arms, flattened by emotion. Everything hits me at once: his voice, this place, the way he looks at me, how he can make me laugh, and yes, the awful way he left me. And then there's sheer *wanting*. I want him. I look up at that bed with its covers all in a wreck, and I'm so scared that we two will soon be in it, rolling around just as if twenty-six years didn't even matter.

And then I'm scared that we won't.

There are pictures on the walls of the children—as bright-eyed toddlers, middle-sized kids, and then lovely young adults. I stare up at them from the floor, remembering Lindsay's fat little hands circling my own and Brice's crazy, maniacal laugh. And then I see it: a framed black-and-white photograph of Carly on the bedside table. I pull myself up and go over and pick it up. She's wearing a French cloche-type hat, with little wisps of her hair sticking out, and she's looking into the camera with her eyes brimming and huge with feeling and her mouth drawn up in a little knot.

Collateral damage.

That's what Jeremiah called her back then. Her and Grant. They were to be our collateral damage.

He calls from the kitchen. "Do you want Earl Grey or some of this herbal crap? Let's see—I think there's chamomile and, oh, here's something called Sleepytime. *That* probably isn't a good idea . . ."

"Earl Grey is fine." Carly's eyes in the photo look sad. I clear my throat and then call to him, "So, Jeremiah. Did Carly ever know . . . you know . . . about us?"

There's a beat of silence. The refrigerator motor turns on. "God no," he says. "At least I don't think so."

I take the photo and go stand in the doorway of the kitchen and watch him taking down two mugs from the cabinet and setting them on the counter. "What do you mean, you don't *think* so? How can you not know something like that?"

I'd forgotten how he domesticated he is, the way he moves around so confidently in the kitchen, how he looks when he concentrates, and the way his square hands become so limber as he arranges things just so on a black wooden tray: the spoons, the cream, the sugar bowl.

He sees me watching and smiles. "Ahhh, Annabelle, perhaps you've forgotten the kind of relationship Carly and I had. We made it a point never to talk about anything except how terrible it was that I didn't work as hard as she did. Surely you remember that."

"So, you told me that day at the train station that you weren't going to leave her, and then you went back home, but . . . then what? Did you just sit down and eat dinner together and act like nothing had happened?"

"Nothing *had* happened, in Carly's world."

"But I mean *you.* Were you sad? Were you angry? Didn't she look across the table and even suspect a little bit how close she'd come that night to losing you?"

He pours the hot water from the kettle into a green teapot, and for a moment the steam obscures his expression. When he answers me at last, his voice is weary. "Oh, who freaking knows what she knew, Annabelle? Why does it even matter? I came back home, and the twins probably needed a bath, and Carly no doubt wanted to go off by herself. We probably ate dinner. Went to sleep, got up the next day. Time passed. What can I tell you? Why do females always love to muck around in this stuff?" He's smiling. "What's the point? Here. Let's have our tea, and then I want you to come with me. I want to show you something."

"No," I say, and we're both caught short by my tone. "*No*. How can you just say that? This stuff is *important*."

He bites his lip. "No, it isn't," he says. "Not really, not in the grand scheme of things." He comes over and hands me a mug of tea and stands close to me and tilts his head, in his charming way, and says softly, "What *was* important—and what will always be important—is that you and I almost made a life for ourselves. Together. And when that didn't happen, when I decided to do the so-called *right thing*, it didn't really matter whether Carly knew or didn't know, because the bottom line was that you and I weren't going to be together. And that hurt both of us for a very long time, and now we're here with apparently one afternoon to spend together out of the rest of our lives. And I, for one, don't think we should spend it beating ourselves up. Okay?"

"So then there was nothing at all? No repercussions?"

"What *is* it with you?" he says. He looks amused. "You want some reassurance that you weren't the only one who had to suffer? Is that it? Well, if it's any consolation to you, I did suffer. I had to live with this woman for the rest of her life, knowing I wouldn't have *you* anymore. Isn't that enough suffering for one man?" He's teasing me as he takes the photograph out of my hands and puts it facedown on the table. "Now come on, Annabelle baby, let's drop this. Let me show you this thing I saved for you." He wraps his arm around my shoulder and gently propels me into the living room. "You'll get a kick out of this, I promise."

And so, reluctantly, I allow myself to be led into the hushed, overstuffed living room and over to the desk that had once held so much fascination for me, simply because it was his. I remember being awed by the pens in the pottery bowl—oh, and the night I licked one of them. God, I was so young then!

"I was cleaning out some old boxes the other night, and I came across this," he says. "Do you remember?" His eyes are dancing as he reaches into a drawer and pulls out a copy of *Goldilocks and the Three Bears* and presents it to me with a flourish. *Goldi* had been crossed off with Magic Marker, so it just said *Locks and the Three Bears.*

"Oh my God yes. I remember doing this," I say. The cover has three cartoon bears with a blond child sitting up in a bed, wide-eyed. Carly had insisted that I not only change the name, but also that I draw a cap on Goldilocks's hair so she would seem to be a boy. Locks. How is it that this one book didn't get returned? We must have forgotten to take it back with the others. I look up at him.

"Carly's foray into feminist lit," he says, and grins. "Remember how she defaced all those books, and then it was you and I who had to go and tell the day-care lady what she'd done?"

"Well, but that's not exactly—"

"What a raw deal *we* got, huh? But you know what I realized? Without this one single act of hers, you and I probably wouldn't have gotten together. *This* was the beginning of you and me. Ta-da! *Locks and the Three Bears.*" He does a little flourish.

"No, no. Wait," I say. "Jeremiah, that's not what got us started. Don't you remember? Carly made me sit up with her one night and cross out all the sexist things with her, and then *I* had to sneak them back in the next morning before the day-care lady noticed—only then she caught me, and she was so mad. It was awful. And remember? She told us she wouldn't watch Brice and Lindsay anymore after that, and then you and I walked home together, trying to figure out what we were going to do with the kids." I open the book and look at all the black marks I'd made, at my handwriting changing the wording, and everything about that uncomfortable night floods back—Carly lecturing me on how men will always try to take my power away, and me feeling so young and uncertain but going along with her just to be nice. Why was I always trying to be nice back then?

"Well," he says, "you may have had to make the marks, but I think I finally know *why* she had you do it. And trust me, it wasn't in the interest of feminism." He ambles across the room and sits down on the couch and sprawls his legs out in front of him and smiles at me. I know this tactic of his: get farther away from me, make me come to him. It's cat and mouse. But I am too upset.

"She said we had to do it because children's books were too sexist," I say. "She gave me a long speech about that. And about power. Men taking away my power."

"No. That wasn't the real reason. The real reason was that she didn't want me to finish my novel, and she knew I was close to finishing it. So she *wanted* the kids to get kicked out of day care. Because if they couldn't go to day care, then *I* would have to watch them, and I wouldn't have the time to write my novel while I was on sabbatical. It was very Machiavellian of her. Very Carly-esque, you might say."

"But, Jeremiah, she didn't even know about your novel then. Don't you remember? You kept it a secret. It was *our* secret."

"She was quite a piece of work," he says. "She made sure she got things just the way she wanted them."

Damn it! Doesn't he remember? He doesn't even remember the day he started the novel and we sat on the floor together and talked about it, the day he realized that writing a novel was what he most wanted to do. And Carly didn't know anything about it! It was me. He and I were the ones who figured out that that was what he should be doing. I am suddenly struck by how he seems to admire this view of Carly he's conjured up. Have we really told ourselves such different stories? We're now a love story that got started because Carly didn't want him to write? No, no, no.

I should let it go, but I can't. "Let me remind you," I say patiently. I sit down on the edge of the ottoman across the room from him, putting the *Three Bears* book on the coffee table between us. "*I* was the one that Carly asked to watch the twins. Remember that? Since I wasn't doing art anymore, she thought I should be willing to pay you guys back by taking care of the children. She seemed so angry with me that I wasn't doing art."

He smiles and says in a soft, silky voice, leaning forward so close he could reach over and touch me, "Yes! That was Carly for you. She always had opinions about what everybody was supposed to be doing with their lives. But we outsmarted her, didn't we? She didn't figure on the fact that there *you* were, not only beautiful and willing to go to bed with me, but also *quite* willing to listen to my stupid-ass prose and even tell me it was wonderful." His eyes are shining, and he bites his lip and cocks his head. "Annabelle, please just come over here and sit next to me. I can't get over seeing you here. I never thought this could happen. Us. Together again. Even if it's only for a short time, I just need to have you near me."

I shake my head and stay where I am.

"Aw, come on, don't be mad," he says. "Okay, let's just say you're right. It was *you* she wanted to watch the children. She didn't know a thing about the novel. Okay? I've got it all wrong."

"No. Forget it. I'm sorry."

We sit there in silence, and then he says, "Well, I *do* remember the important stuff: you and me chasing each other around the apartment when the kids were napping. And all the close calls we had." He smiles down at the book, touching it as though it's a sacred talisman from the past or something. The fucking Holy Grail. I hear the heat come on and a radiator clangs somewhere down the hall, the noises of domestic life. I'm feeling almost faint with such a mixture of feelings—disappointment and lust and also as though something is draining all the hope I've been carrying for so many years. I look at him and wonder if I was just one in a series of lovers he might have had during his marriage to Carly, a marriage I now think was always unstoppable. Why hadn't I seen that at the time?

"I've often wondered just what we really meant to each other," I say slowly.

He looks up and smiles at me, and I think it is a practiced smile, something you might see an actor doing in rehearsal. "You know what I think?" he says softly. "You saved me. I think adrenaline, especially sexual adrenaline, is really a drug that can actually keep people from going off the deep end. You and me—that sex with you might have saved my life."

"So we're going to think of it as simply sex?" I say. "I think what you're really saying is that it was the adrenaline that saved you. It wasn't really me at all."

"No, no, no! It *was* you. Why are you taking everything the wrong way? You, Annabelle, *caused* the adrenaline. I'm trying to tell you that you saved me. I mean, I'm still not sure we could have kept it going for a whole *lifetime*, but it was great while it lasted." He smiles sadly, and he suddenly looks tired, and for the first time since I ran into him, I'm aware of how much older he is now, how really changed he is. He falls silent and then he rubs his hands hard over his face and sighs.

The silence that falls between us seems to demarcate something. I am shocked at how hollow I feel. He gets up and walks to the kitchen, and I watch him leave. He is moving slowly, wearily. I am probably more trouble than he bargained for. *He doesn't remember how it was.*

This is such a mistake, being here. There's a noise from the kitchen; he's rinsing his cup. I remember how he used to put the dirty dishes in the oven, his act of rebellion against Carly's rules. I suddenly want to get air, to go back outside, to get away from this view of things. When he comes back into the living room, he's carrying the picture of Carly, holding it out to me, saying something like, *This was taken two days after we found out the cancer had gone into remission. We renewed our vows. She said we had to. I didn't want to do it, but it was actually quite . . . moving. I was there for her for the end, the way I should have been all along.*

My blood is beating so loudly in my ears that I can barely take in what he's saying. What then does he see on my face that makes him come over and touch my cheek? He says, "I've made you mad. I'm so sorry, Annabelle. I didn't mean to hurt you again."

"It's okay. It's just that I thought—I thought that we saw it the same way, and we didn't," I say. I look up into his face, which now seems naked with pain. "I just can't have you calling it adrenaline, when it was love. It *was* love. Big love. And I've held on to it all these years, even though I wasn't ever going to see you again; I thought of you and dreamed of you, and when things were hard for me, I remembered that *you* had loved me, really loved me, and it got me through so much. And now—now you bring me here, you insist that I come, and you're just trying to act as though we had some toxic chemicals in our blood or something. What you're saying to me is that it would have been a horrible mistake for us to end up together."

He smiles at me. His eyes are watering. "No, it wouldn't have been a mistake," he says. "We would have worked it out, but it would have hurt so many people. But I missed you, too. I *still* miss you, Annabelle."

"But not the way I missed you," I say. "There was such a long time when I wasn't always so sure I could live without you." I'm light-headed.

"But you did," he says. And I have to agree.

He laughs and touches my nose with his index finger, and then we're staring into each other's eyes, and I think we'll probably kiss again, and that maybe we'll fall together after all and go into his bedroom and throw all his stuff off the bed and take our clothes off and make love one last time. It won't be the way it was once; hell, it won't even be what I had hoped for earlier today. But it could still happen, as a piece of theater. I feel myself tip and fall into his eyes, those swimming eyes. And then the electricity just fizzles, and *he's* the one who manages to resist. The kiss he plants on my nose is one of closure.

"Well," he says. "We both lived, didn't we? We have this great past together to look back on. That's more than most people have. And if I was unkind to you, I'm sorry. I was so fucked up back then. I probably should have been quarantined as a danger to society."

I detach myself from him. My body temperature seems to have

dropped about fifteen degrees. I'm almost shivering. "I'm glad they didn't quarantine you," I say. "I've loved you so much, throughout everything."

"But not anymore," he says.

He's wrong about that. I have it for him still. It's over in the corner of my brain now, diminished a bit by time and reality. It's lost some of its shiny promise. But it's there.

I let myself kiss him, but I leave without sleeping with him. I have to walk for blocks and blocks before I can admit that I went there hungry for the drama of him, that I had craved that heightened sense of loving and being loved once again. I am so lonely for love. I have to stop walking for a moment and lean up against the warm brick facade of a building, where the sun is beaming down. I watch a homeless man who is calmly waiting, approaching each person who comes by, asking for coins for his little paper cup, and then somehow out of all that—the homeless guy and the people shaking their heads at him and moving on and leaving him there, the warmth of the bricks, the sun shining down—I know that restraint was actually the best thing that could have happened, and that I am going to be all right, and that it's okay to still love Jeremiah just a little, or even a lot, and yet not do anything about it.

[s i x t e e n]

🍃 1980

*H*ere's a crazy thing. When I left the train station that day, I actually thought that Jeremiah might run and catch me, that any moment I'd feel his hand on my shoulder and turn to see him smiling at me. "I've changed my mind!" he'd say. "How could I possibly throw all this away?" Or maybe he would say that this had all been just a test—a test of my love.

When it started to get dark, and my arms and legs were aching, I went into a little run-down restaurant in a neighborhood I'd never been to before, and sat at a booth in the back all by myself. This was the first time I had ever been in a restaurant alone, and I sat there in the dimness for a long time, running my fingers along the carved initials in the wooden table. When the waitress came by for the third time, I ordered French fries and tapioca pudding and was surprised a little while later when that was exactly what was brought to me, glistening and gross. My brother had called tapioca "fish-eye pudding" when we were little, just so he could get both my portion and his.

I listened to the conversations of normal people and stared through the faraway windows as the lights flared and faded, red and green blinking on and off, headlights sweeping past. The door opened and closed; clumps of people arrived and departed, in groups, like schools of fish. After a while I noticed they were wet. It was raining. I saw the water rolling down the pane of glass, distorting the neon signs outside, the headlights of the cars. There was a loud clap of thunder, and the lights flickered but stayed on.

Maybe, I thought, I should call Grant. If I called him . . . if I told him I'd been hallucinating and begged him for forgiveness, would he come and meet me and take me back home? He was probably in such terrible pain right now. We could be in pain together, climb our way out of it by holding on to each other.

But he had said not to come back. There was no way he'd let me get near him again, and who could blame him? I had done an awful thing to him.

After the rain stopped, I dragged my suitcases outside and went to a hotel down the street. I had a bit of money with me; it was almost a surprise to realize that I didn't need to call anybody I knew and try to explain that I needed a place to sleep. I could stay in a hotel until I figured out what my next move would be.

I slept on starchy white sheets in a drab brown room with the sound of traffic bleating in my ears. The next day, I called my mother from a pay phone in the lobby to tell her what had happened, fully expecting that she'd insist I come back home. She didn't. She and my father were in the midst of their real divorce by then, and she was falling in love with a new man—"A keeper this time," she said.

"Oh, baby. You're going to be just fine," she said. "Really. I know you are."

"But I miss Grant," I said. "I hurt the person who really loved me, and I want you to give me some motherly sympathy."

She laughed. "People who get married when they're twenty don't know what love even is," she said. "Believe me, this is just part of the growing up you have to do, and I hate to say it, but it's better you're doing it now while you're young than when you get old like me. I married your father at twenty, and it's taken me twenty-three years to fight my way out of that marriage."

"Nobody's mother would say that but you," I said.

She seemed to consider that. "That's because I tell you the truth," she said. "Listen. Here's what I think you should do: take the summer to find a job you like and have some fun. And if in the fall you want to come back to California, then you should."

Just before I ran out of money, I got a job as a waitress in a little restaurant downtown, the kind of place where tourists gathered. I made friends with two girls there, Mona and Brianna, and the three of us lived together in Hell's Kitchen. For a while I felt as though I were actually on an odd vacation, a vacation with a job. We lived on restaurant food and ramen noodles and Diet Coke and Pop-Tarts, and the apartment was filled day and night with music and clutter and drama. We had lots and lots of satisfying drama. Somebody was always having company, and somebody else was having a crisis or a breakup of some sort. I had never seen such an overflow of emotion, or felt so in touch with everything I was feeling.

Nights after our shifts ended we would go to a club they knew, a place with loud, thumping music and a big disco ball that sent light spinning around the walls and floor. We smoked and drank and danced and shared clothes and makeup and food and laughter.

Once—I've never admitted this to anyone, not even Magda—I went back to the old apartment, the one I had lived in with Grant, and let myself in with the spare key I'd kept. He was at work, of course. I just wanted to be reminded of him, to touch his things. I looked in the refrigerator at the foods he would eat, I ran my hand over the coffeemaker we'd gotten for a wedding present, and then I went into the bedroom and looked at his shirts hanging in the closet, all neatly in a row. The last thing I did was lie down on his pillow on the bed, the bed of a bad woman. I took my shoes off and lay there with my head smushed into his pillow, smelling him around me.

Before I left, I did the dishes and then I cleaned the bathroom sink and the shower and left the can of cleanser on the countertop. I wanted him to wonder, to try to remember if he'd cleaned it himself. Would he think, *Annabelle was here*? No, certainly not. I thought of writing "I miss you" on the mirror in lipstick, but he would hate that. And he hated me anyway. Why make it worse?

I slipped out and went back home.

After that, I changed my look, started teasing my hair and dressing in sequins and tight pants. I learned to dance. I could carry an armload of hot plates and pour coffee into cups without spilling a drop—and every day my life as Grant's wife and Jeremiah's lover seemed to recede farther into the background. The only thing I didn't seem to be able to master was caring about anybody—not in *that way*, as Grant had once so charmingly put it. Although there were men all over the place, I didn't have sex. I didn't want to. The one time I tried to sleep with a guy, I burst into tears as soon as we'd both gotten our clothes off, and he practically made skid marks getting out of the apartment.

And then one day, just as I was beginning to get tired of living that way, Magda called me to say she was coming to New York for an interview with a small publisher who was looking for a graphic designer. She'd graduated—I realized that I, too, would have been done with college by then—and she wanted to get out of California and live on the East Coast.

We had a hysterical reunion after her interview. She was wearing her blond hair in a pageboy and she had on a string of pearls and high heels. She did not look like the person in the dorm who could smoke the most dope without falling over, or who had once stood on my bed in the middle of an acid high and yelled that she was the long-lost love child of Jimi Hendrix and Janis Joplin.

"Look at you!" I said. "You look like the picture of young womanhood meeting corporate America."

"And look at *you*," she said. I was wearing leggings, a bright pink blazer with shoulder pads, and a string of lime green beads, and I had my hair all frizzed up in a side ponytail tied with a man's tie. I could tell she was making some mental adjustments about me. "You look like an artist, girl!"

"Waitress," I corrected her. "And perhaps disco queen."

I showed her around the city and took her to my apartment, where she met Brianna and Mona, who were just getting out of bed. The place smelled like stale cigarettes and old beer. Brianna was heating up some cold pizza, and Mona was searching for the aspirin bottle in a pile of laundry. Magda proclaimed it was just like our old dorm room. We gave her some comfortable clothes to put on and showed her how to use blue eye shadow to greater effect, and she acted like she was cool with everything—but I could see the surprise in her eyes when she looked at me.

When I took her on the subway to get her back to the airport, she nudged me and said, "So which guy are you suffering from the most, Jeremiah or Grant?"

"Neither one," I said. "And I'm not suffering, either. I'm having fun."

"No, you're not. I've seen you when you were having fun, and this ain't the look."

I stared at the overhead posters on the subway and pretended I hadn't heard her.

"I don't think Jeremiah is ever going to come through, but I'm pretty sure you could get Grant back if you really wanted to. I think it's a good sign that he hasn't filed for divorce yet."

"It's probably just that he's too busy to find a lawyer."

"But maybe that's not the reason. Maybe he's waiting to see if you come back. You could check it out, you know. What's the harm in that?"

"The *harm* is that I don't want to. I'm doing fine without him."

"All right, I wasn't going to say anything, but I can't believe how you're living! You're not seriously thinking of keeping this up, are you? You're just, like, slumming for now, right? Right?"

"Actually, I keep thinking I'm going to go back to California in the fall," I told her.

"No, no, don't go back. Stay here with me. We'll do the city up right," she said. She patted my leg. "Once I get hired at this place, I'll get you a job, too, and you can go back to being an artist."

"But I might not even be an artist anymore. What have I ever really accomplished when it comes to art? Nothing."

"So what? Do you really think your calling is being a waitress? Is this what you actually want?"

"The other day, I'll have you know, I carried seven plates at one time."

"I'm not even going to dignify that with a comment," she said. She looked around appraisingly. I notice she wasn't wearing the pearls anymore, but her hair was straight and shiny and she hadn't taken up our suggestions for the blue eye shadow either. "You know, I like this city a lot. I think I'm meant to be here for a while. And who knows? Maybe I was sent here by the universe—or maybe by your mother—to help you get back on the right track."

"Well, it must be the universe, because I know it wasn't my mother," I said. "She thinks I've pulled off a brilliant escape act."

A MONTH later, Magda and I had an apartment together, and I was working at the publishing house as an assistant to the art director, a wonderful man who let me do sketches and who encouraged me, even though what I was supposed to be doing was mostly typing and filing. Magda was a graphic designer who was obviously going places, and she pushed me forward so that I kept getting more illustrating work until finally they promoted me. We were both doing well. Magda had always been more daring than I, alert to opportunities that I never noticed, and even here in New York, she seemed to have an instinct for navigating the system. She made us dress up for work every day and act professional, and she befriended the up-and-coming publishing types, people I would have written off as out of my league, because they were. We went to parties and book launches. We had our nails done. She dated lots of guys and seemed to like it that way. For a while I listlessly went out with a guy named Henry, who Magda said was a dead ringer for Grant but not quite as cute and without the advanced degree. I told her I liked him because he was too shy to do more than kiss me. Once he'd hovered his hand in midair over my breast, perhaps waiting for me to wriggle it into his waiting palm, but when I didn't, he politely withdrew it. I'd later told Magda that that was what made Henry a perfect companion for me, and she said that was the saddest thing she'd ever heard anybody say.

She had her own problems. She'd gotten involved with a man who wanted to get married, and she and I spent all our free time discussing what was wrong with her that she didn't want to marry him.

"Why don't I feel it?" she said one evening. "I mean, he's nice, he treats me well. He's going to be rich, his mother likes me, and he wants to go to Paris for our honeymoon. But I just keep thinking—how do I *know* I'll be able to stand him for the rest of my life?"

"Don't look at *me*," I said. "I'm the last person who can advise somebody on this. But I will say that if you're already thinking you won't be able to stand him, chances are that's accurate and you should pay attention."

"But I *always* think that. In fact, I don't think there's anybody in the world I could stand to be with if somebody told me I had to do it for the rest of my life."

"I kind of liked marriage," I said. "There's something really cool that happens . . . I don't know . . . when you have a partner."

"Really?" she said. "So then, what *did* happen with you and Grant, do you think? I mean, we've talked all around this, but we've never gotten down to absolute bedrock here. What happened to your marriage? Did you just stop loving him, or did you never really love him in the first place?"

We were cleaning up after dinner—take-out Chinese food, our favorite Sunday-night splurge. It was the night we stayed in and got organized for the week. It was funny: now that she asked me, I could remember so clearly that feeling of being bowled over by Grant. Of thinking that everything he did was funny and dorky but lovable. I thought of his large, capable hands, the way his whole serious face could light up when he was excited, even the way I felt when he'd been gone for a while and I saw him again. The way he fumbled so charmingly when he asked me to marry him. How I felt seeing him at the airport when I came to join him in New York. The safety of being with him and being completely myself, not having to fake it. How he fit with me.

"Yeah," I said slowly. "I really loved Grant."

"Until you fell in love with somebody else."

"Well, no, actually, you want the truth? I loved both of them, through the whole thing," I said. "I kind of still do."

She laughed. "You love both of them."

"Yeah," I said. "They each brought out different parts of me, but I could have been happy with either of them. It wasn't really my idea to leave Grant, even. I left him because Jeremiah was so miserable. But my choice would have been that we just kept going the way we were, with me loving both."

"You're something, you know that?" she said, and she was smiling at me in amazement. "As my grandmother would say, if you don't beat all. You can't have two!"

"Apparently not. But why not? They're both such amazing—"

"No, no, no," she said. "This way lies madness. I think you need to decide what you really want in your life and then stop flailing around and make it happen. What is it that *you*, Annabelle McKay, really want?"

"I want to go back to Grant," I said, and I realized as I was saying it that it was true. I missed having somebody who cared about me, who wasn't all flashing lights and craziness, a guy who came from steadiness and realness.

"Well, that's what you need to work toward, then," she said.

"No, he won't ever take me back. The one thing he said was that I couldn't ever come back. He might even be seeing somebody new by now."

"Yeah, well, until you're divorced, everything's negotiable," she said.

AFTER THAT, I decided that I would run into him on the street one day, sort of accidentally on purpose. It wouldn't be that hard. He had habits I remembered. He liked cinnamon raisin bagels from a bagel shop around the corner from our apartment, and so for three consecutive Saturday mornings, I planted myself in the shop, hoping he would happen by. He didn't. Then I got bolder and started loitering near his subway stop—and one rainy Friday night, bingo. There he came, holding a briefcase and an umbrella, and hurrying with his head down. He was wearing khaki pants and a rumpled blue shirt and sweater, and his hair was shining in the drippy glow of the streetlight. He walked right past me, without even looking up.

I slunk home and told Magda that he obviously hated me.

"I can't believe he didn't see me standing there," I said.

"Well, of course he hates you," she said cheerfully. "You took the guy's heart and stomped on it and then threw it up in the air and let it crash on the pavement, where you stomped on it again." She took me by the shoulders and shook me. "Girl, you betrayed him with his best friend in the world. Would you even *want* a guy who would take you back right away? He's going to ignore you as long as possible. You have to fight for him."

Then one day she came home and said, "Okay, I called him up today, and he's agreed to see you."

"You did what?" I dropped my purse on the couch and sank down next to it.

"I called him," she said. "And I told him that you and he should talk again. At first he said no, but then he sighed and said okay. He wants to meet in Donovan's Coffee Shop on Saturday morning."

I was sweating by the time I got there, and my hair was all wildly frizzy and curly, but he looked—I have to say—even more terrible. Like he hadn't been sleeping or ironing his shirts. I was overdressed, but I had worn a skirt since he had always liked my legs.

I watched how his hands shook when he tore open the little containers of cream to put into his coffee. He wouldn't meet my eyes, but when I looked somewhere else, I could feel him studying me.

"How's your work?" I said.

"Why are you still wearing your wedding ring?" He pointed at my hand.

"I . . . don't know." I put my left hand in my lap. "How's your work?"

"The labor historian business has never been better."

"Excellent," I said. I told him that I was "doing my art" now—a thing he'd always nagged me about.

"And you're living with Magda? That wasn't the way I remembered the original plan."

"Yes. I guess you already knew it didn't work out for me and Jeremiah."

"I figured as much."

"He didn't—well, that day . . . he didn't tell Carly. He—"

"Please." He held up his hand. "I don't think I can stomach the details of this."

"Of course not. Sorry. So how are things with you? Are you seeing anyone?"

He stared at me for a long time before he answered, like this was an impertinent question that I had no right to ask him. Then he cleared his throat and said yes, he was seeing someone.

"Oh, and is she living with you?"

He shrugged. "You know I don't really believe in that."

"Okay, so where did you meet her?" I stirred my coffee.

He let a long moment go by and then he said in a low voice, "At a conference."

"Interesting! And now she's in New York? Did she move here for you, the way I did?"

"Annabelle." He shook his head in exasperation and laughed. "She lived here all along. She's a historian, too."

"So you and she . . . you talk labor statistics all the time? That must be fun."

"Why are you doing this?" he said. "For what possible reason are you doing this?"

"Maybe I want to apologize."

"Totally unnecessary. You did what you needed to do. But I think the time has come that we might want to think about the future. Decide what we're doing here."

"In what sense?"

"You know. In the legal sense that we're not exactly husband and wife, so why not make it official?"

I took a long sip of my tea, mostly so I'd have time to think what to say. "Do your parents hate me? I'll bet your mother told you just to go ahead and divorce me and write me out of your life," I said. "She did, didn't she?"

He hesitated a moment and then nodded.

"But your father was probably more on the side of caution. He said to give things some time."

"My, my. It's as if you were in the room."

"Well, I'm with your father. I think we should give it more time," I said. "I think we should go out to dinner next week and see how we feel after that."

"Why would we do that?"

"Because—because we are open-minded, curious people."

He looked at me steadily then, his eyes traveling all over my face, and I could see that he was wavering, that deep inside somewhere he was building up walls and fences as fast as he could, but that they were being torn down at the same time by my smile and my eyes. But then, when he was about to say yes, something happened. His mother showed up in his eyes. I saw her clear as day, saw him go cold on me.

"It'll never happen," he said. "I have to get going." And then he called for the check, laid a five-dollar bill on the table, and slid out of the booth and out the front door, leaving me.

IT WAS stupid. I called Grant a few more times, but he always said he was busy. Four months later I started dating a guy named Luther, who was a sales rep at the publishing house. He was impossibly cute, but there was something kind of dangerous about him. He reminded me a little bit of Jay—he had that same sense of entitlement and expectation. They call that optimism, said Magda. She said I'd gotten so used to gloominess that I didn't recognize it when I saw it.

"And you might as well have fun while you're waiting for Grant," she said. "You can practice your moves on this guy."

She had broken up with the would-be fiancé and was now declaring herself on a lifetime plan of devotion to career, and possibly celibacy. I had pointed out to her that even though she might be correct that I was some kind of unformed chameleon who could adapt to anything, she was a *mule* who would adapt to nothing. Nobody's agenda suited her. She was determined to do everything her own way. This pleased her no end. I couldn't have paid her a higher compliment.

The next step—when it came—was entirely surprising and amazing and not choreographed by anything but fate. I was near Columbia on a drizzly, warm September evening and I hailed a cab, and when I went to get into it, Grant was somehow right there, too, having just come from his office and obviously thinking the cab was stopping for him. We both laughed when we recognized each other, and then I said magnanimously, "You take it," and he did a little bow and said, "Well, why don't we share it?"

I had just come from a meeting with a woman who had hired me to do illustrations for a children's book about outer space, and my head was full of planets and galaxies and the glass of wine she and her husband had served me while we talked over the details. I was still *on*. I'd been complimented and praised for my initial sketches, and I was on my way home to get dressed for a dinner out with Luther—but seeing Grant there, looking so professorial and manly, made my heart stop in its tracks and decide to reverse course.

It was five o'clock; the cab inched along, and during the whole ride, I could feel Grant's eyes on me. Everything felt perfect. It was as if I were imbued with a gigantic, supernatural energy. When we got to my apartment, I said, "Why don't you come up, and I'll cook us something."

The timing could not have been better. Magda was away for the weekend; she'd gone to visit her sister, who was giving birth to her third child. And our apartment was spotlessly clean because we'd both felt industrious right before she'd left and had scrubbed the whole place down. Grant and I stopped at a little market and bought some cheese and bread and wine and grapes, and when we got to the apartment, I made pasta with the late-summer fresh tomatoes and basil. While he was in the bathroom, I sneaked the phone out onto the balcony and called Luther and told him I was sick.

Everything felt right: the jazz I put on the stereo, the way the light caught the gleaming copper pots, the fresh daisies on the table. I observed Grant walking around the apartment, pacing with his glass of wine, blinking behind his glasses. He stopped at the bookcase and I heard him suck in his breath. I knew what he was looking at: for a wedding present Magda had given us *The Joy of Sex* and *The Joy of Cooking*. "The joys," we had called them. I still had them both, side by side on the shelf. He reached over and touched them, and I watched him from the kitchen and took another sip of wine. When he turned around, our eyes met and then he looked away.

He kept clearing his throat out of nervousness. While we ate dinner, we talked about his parents and his teaching load this semester, and then he asked about my brother.

"He's not good," I said. "I think he's in a lot of pain, and he's kind of hard to reach. I think he's taking lots of drugs."

"I always liked him," he said. "The last time I talked to him he was saying that there was some surgery they might do, but he didn't—"

"Really? You talk to him?" I said. "I didn't know that. He never mentions it."

"Yeah, well, it doesn't really have anything to do with you," he said. "I've always been fond of him. And it's horrifying what he's had to go through."

"He told me once that he's not going to be everybody's favorite paraplegic, working to be a hero for the rest of us."

"Yeah, he said that to me, too. He's tried as hard as he can to push everybody away. You have to be pretty strong to stay David's friend these days," he said. "He's a very sad, lonely, lost guy trying to fight his way back, and instead he's fighting himself."

This was another thing I'd missed—Grant's sensitivity.

"I miss you," I told him. "I miss you so much!"

He laughed a little bit. "No, you don't. Not really."

"I do. It's been devastating how much."

"Hey, could we skip the next reel of this movie? I've seen this one, and I really can't go there again."

"But I want to tell you. I know what I did was unforgivable, but—"

"Wait, Annabelle. Don't say anything more. I need to tell you that I'm filing for divorce. I was going to write you a letter."

"Wait. Do you mean to tell me that you decided to divorce me just while we've been here tonight? When I thought we were having such a nice time. Come on. Isn't this nice, being together?"

"It's very nice. But there's nothing left, so I don't see the point of drawing this out anymore. I've been thinking about it for a long time, and I think we should get our status ironed out, make it official, that's all."

"But don't you see that I still love you? I don't make pasta with tomatoes and basil for anyone else, you know."

He was watching me warily.

I gestured in the air. "I mean, look at us here! Isn't this what we always really needed? Time to be together and by ourselves? I've been so happy here tonight with you, and you can't tell me you don't feel the same. I saw the way you looked at 'the joys.' Remember that? How we laughed when we opened that present, and when—"

"Do you have to make everything so hard?" he said. "What's left between us, anyway? We had a very, very short courtship and marriage, and now it's ended."

"But I love you!" I said.

He looked away. "No, you don't. You only think you do because Jeremiah wouldn't leave his wife after all. Otherwise, you and I both know that you'd be off with him right now making babies with him and helping him write his novel. That was what you wanted and you didn't get it, and so I'm a handy substitute now that you're lonely."

"That's not it, that's truly not it. I made a big mistake. It was a horrible time for me, and I've done a lot of thinking about why I did what I did. I think I loved you *a lot*, but I was so young and stupid when we got married, and then that accident happened that made me go back home, and when I came to New York, I was still traumatized and didn't even know it. And you were never there, Grant—you completely abandoned me, and I didn't know anyone, and I just . . . I just . . . lost my judgment. I wasn't in my usual right mind."

He laughed. "I'm not sure you have a regular right mind." He looked longingly at the door. "I've gotta go, Annabelle. I have to get out of here."

"Grant, please don't laugh at me. I mean this, what I'm saying. It's our lives we're talking about here. I've been trying for months now to tell you how sorry I am and how I want another chance. I made a terrible, terrible mistake. Ask Magda. She listens to me talk all the time about how much I love you and miss you."

He kept looking at me, working his mouth around and around. It was in that silence that I knew I had him. A wide spaciousness opened up in me. I went across the room and took his hand, and he was helpless. He didn't even try to move away.

"And," I said, holding on to his hand and talking too fast, "you know you still love me, too. You're like one of those swans that mates for life. And I'm your mate. Face it."

"I can't," he said. "I really, really can't let you do this to me again."

I was so close to him that I could see myself in his eyes. He had a slight twitch in his lower lid. I whispered, "I will never hurt you again.

I will never, ever hurt you again," and brought my arms up to circle his neck.

"No," he said. "No. Annabelle, *no.*" He kept shaking his head, and then he walked to the front door and let himself out without another word. I was stunned. I stood there for a little while, wanting to cry and not being able to find any tears to cry with. And then I cleared the table and washed the dishes and put them away. My mouth was dry and my head was stuffy from the wine. I was drained and exhausted. I put on my nightgown and went and got in bed, turned on *The Tonight Show* for a while. Then I couldn't sleep, so I sat at my desk and started drawing.

At two o'clock, the door buzzed. Without even thinking, I leaned over and pushed the button, knowing already it was Grant. I met him at the door, pulling my wrap around me. And sure enough, he came charging into the apartment, his hair flying everywhere. He looked drunk. He pushed me up against the wall, and when he kissed me, his mouth was so hard against mine that I could feel his teeth. When we pulled apart his eyes were tightly shut, and he was grimacing as if he was in the very worst pain.

"God damn it, Annabelle, I can't let you do this to me again."

"I won't," I said. "I won't. I swear I won't. This time it will be different. You'll see."

He gripped my shoulders. "All right," he said. His voice was different from anything I'd ever heard out of him. "I've been walking ever since I left here. And I've been thinking about whether people can love each other even in the face of . . . of mistrust. And here's what I figured out. If I take you back, here's the deal. This is the only way I can accept it. I know something about obsession, and I know you'll never really get over . . . *him.* So—"

"No, I *am* over him—"

"This isn't really negotiable, Annabelle. I know you're always going to love him. But the deal has to be that you agree not to see him again or talk to him—"

"I haven't!"

"You can't tell me later that you've decided you're going to be friends with him. I can't be friends with that bastard."

"No. Not friends."

He gave me a level look, pushed me harder against the wall. "And we have to leave New York and get a fresh start."

"Back to California?" This was a surprise.

"That, or we can go to New Hampshire and live in the house I grew up in. My parents are talking about retiring and going to Florida, and it'll be our house. They're leaving it to me. And I-I'll get a job teaching in the community college. We can raise a family there."

"Community college? But you don't really want to leave Columbia—"

He put his finger up to my lips. "Sssh. I do want that. It's the thing I have to do to save this marriage. It's just the way things have to be. It's important enough to me to do this. But, if I leave all this, you have to do your part."

I nodded. "I will."

"No. Don't say that until you hear all the terms." He was speaking in a low, dramatic voice I'd never heard from him. "There's one more thing that is the most important thing to me. We have to make a pact to be completely and utterly faithful to each other. I'm not going to discuss it to death. And I'm not going to worry about whether I trust you anymore or not. I can't live that way, suspicious and thinking that the next guy you meet is the one you decide to run away with. I can't live that way, and I *won't*."

I shook my head. "No one should have to."

"I will be completely true to you, Annabelle. And you will be true to me. As simple as that. It's a fresh start. The beginning of our real marriage."

I nodded.

"It's our pact. A sacred pact. All that stuff from before never happened. Can you do that?"

"Never—?"

"A new marriage. I just want us to put the past behind us and get the hell out of the city and go and start our real life. Can you do that?"

"Yes." I lifted my chin.

"Really?"

"Yes, really."

"And we won't talk about it."

I nodded. "Okay."

He searched my face. "I mean it. I'm not going to mistrust you. I'm not going to look for evidence and read your mail and always think the worst, because I'm taking you at your word, Annabelle. This means everything. I won't have my heart broken again."

"No, no," I said. "Stop looking at me like that. I'm not going to break your heart again. This is what I want."

"Okay," he said. He didn't smile. "So. No cheating. No talking about *past* cheating. And we quit our jobs and move to New Hampshire."

"New Hampshire," I said.

"Yes. It's beautiful there. And we'll go skiing in the winter, and ice-skating on the pond, and in the fall we'll pick apples and in the summer we'll swim and have barbecues and our kids will grow up knowing how to fish and play baseball, and they'll be on teams, and maybe I'll be the basketball coach, and you'll paint and make our house look beautiful, and you'll make friends, and the house will be filled up with everything that's good—"

"Wait. There's something I want, too," I said. "If we're making a pact."

"Okay, what?" He tried to make his face neutral, but I could see there was still some fear in it.

"A baby," I said. "I want us to have a baby soon. There's no better fresh start than that."

He kissed me gloriously and truly and with emotion. It was the happiest I'd seen him. "Okay! Okay, yes, we'll have a baby soon. To seal the deal."

It was three thirty in the morning by then, and we went to bed and made love until the sun came up, when we got up and took a walk out on the streets, curled into each other. The diner opened at six and we ate doughnuts and drank coffee that was as strong and bitter as mud, and we talked to the cops and construction guys who were there getting breakfast, and I was the luckiest woman in New York.

Magda was right: I'd had my scandal, my freedom, plenty of blue eye shadow, and the chance to learn to carry seven plates at once. I'd had apartments and temp jobs, and now I'd met a woman who wanted me to draw pictures for children's books. Not only that, I had my marriage back and my husband trusted me again—and although I loved this crazy city dearly, I knew I was getting out of it in the nick of time and heading to the life I was meant for.

Our journey to New Hampshire, this time with a U-Haul filled with the detritus of our separate lives—two couches, two toasters, two television sets—was a very different sort of trip. We held hands in the cab and listened to cassette tapes instead of the radio.

And we didn't look back.

2005

*G*rant and Nicky arrive for spring break, and Sophie and I make room for them. I clean the place in anticipation of their arrival, put away all our cosmetics and hair appliances, and lay in plenty of food; and then they come stamping in with their boots and their huge jackets and their smells and their loud-voiced complications, and the place suddenly feels unprepared. She and I just have to slide over, content ourselves with the little bits of oxygen they leave us to breathe.

They are having a fight, for one thing—or what passes for one in Grant's world, which is little more than a tight-lipped silence on his part while Nicky rails against him, trying to make Grant concede a point. It's the problem of whether Nicky should be allowed to take a semester off, or whether that will mean the end of his ambition and his college career and lead him down the path toward ruination and disgrace. Apparently this discussion has been going on throughout their drive down, and from what I can tell, it doesn't seem to be moving beyond the same loop of exasperation. Every time I glance over at Sophie, she gives me a mock-panicky look, like Edvard Munch's *The Scream*, which makes me laugh.

Grant has that firm set to his jaw that I remember from our fights, the way he has of clenching his mouth closed while some little spasm in his jaw lets you know just how furious he is. When he comes in and kisses me, he whispers, "I may have to take that boy out and lose him in the subway."

"Don't you dare," I say. "He's my sweet patootie."

"Yeah, you say that now. No nineteen-year-old boy is a sweet patootie after you've been in a car with him for six hours straight. Trust me on this."

Nicky has a stubbly beard now and he looks both wilder and more muscular than when I saw him last, which was really only weeks ago, at Christmas break. Still, peeking out from that masculine puffery, he has that same little-boy way of ducking his head and grinning shyly. He's also in constant motion, pantomiming a boxing match, suddenly leaping in midair on the quest to touch a light fixture, or collapsing to the ground and doing a few push-ups. This makes Sophie nearly crazy.

"Can you *stop* moving for one instant?" she cries out. "You're making me so nervous I'm going to give birth right this second. And it is not going to be pretty!"

"Cool," says Nicky, now running in place. "I think the sooner you pop out that kid, the better you're going to feel."

"Not if the placenta comes first," she says. "Just in case you didn't know, I have to have *surgery* to have this baby. There'll be no *popping* it out."

He stares at her, and then I see him getting interested. He walks carefully over to the bed and leans down. "Wow, look at that thing. It's big. Can I touch it? Does it move? I mean, I know it moves. But can you make it move for me?"

"It's not an *it,* it's a *she.* And, yeah, she moves when she wants to. Here, touch right here. Feel that? I think that's the knee. She has very bony knees."

He reaches a tentative hand over to her abdomen.

"Press hard," she tells him. "She's deep down in there, you know. She doesn't just hang out on top all the time." I can see how pleased she is at his interest. "Here. Feel that? Ooh, she just kicked. Did you feel it?"

He sits back on his heels and looks at her with shining eyes. "That is so bizarre," he says. "Is it the weirdest feeling ever, having somebody kicking you from the inside? Wow. Like, she *lives* there. She thinks you're her whole house!"

"I *know*," says Sophie. "Believe me, she thinks she owns the place."

Grant, standing over by the door with his arms folded, looks at me and smiles. I know what he's thinking—he's remembering the time when I was pregnant with Sophie and lying against the couch cushions with a plate propped on my belly while I ate a sandwich and read a book, and Sophie suddenly gave a huge kick and the plate went spinning across the glass coffee table, landing so hard it cracked it. After that, he had called her Killer, and after she was born, I said he had to stop with the mean nickname. Of course, he couldn't; eventually I had had to fine him a dollar every time he referred to her that way.

Then—is he remembering this, too?—years later, when we were watching her streak victoriously down the field, kicking a soccer ball toward a goal while both her own teammates and the members of the opposing team stood stunned and immobile in her wake, he had leaned over and whispered to me, "My God, she honed that kick in the womb. She really is Killer."

We smile at each other now. He mouths the word "Killer," and I laugh. It's a nice moment. We're all together in this tiny apartment, and none of us is fighting. Nicky, in fact, has stretched out on the bed next to Sophie and he's taken over the television remote while keeping one hand resting respectfully on Sophie's abdomen, which he's calling "Beanie's house." He clicks over to a Nickelodeon special, something they both remember from childhood, and for a brief minute, they are laughing together. Grant and I step over the duffel bags and the jackets and hats and boots and paraphernalia, and go to the living room/kitchen-on-one-wall area, where he pours us glasses of wine and talks to me while I make pizza for dinner.

THEY STAY for five days, and really we do just fine, the four of us. Okay, we do pretty well. It's a little bit like old times, the good and the bad all mixed up together. We sit up in Sophie's bed with her and play Scrabble and Monopoly and scooch in all together and watch movies at night. I cook all their old favorites, even in this one-horse kitchen: pot roast and lasagna and an apple crumb pie. We make picnics and eat in the bed with a tablecloth flung over the bedspread.

Bad things: Nicky gets restless and we send him out on errands and to explore the city, and he stays gone too long and doesn't answer his cell phone. We're up half the night worrying about him before he returns, and then Grant says this is exactly why he has to go back to college next semester, so we can be sure where he is.

There's another bad moment one afternoon when Sophie talks to Whit on the phone, and she's obviously getting emotional and trying not to cry, and Grant gets so exasperated listening to her side of the conversation that he has to leave the room.

Good things: Grant, always a sucker for pregnant women, takes care of Sophie, bringing her whatever little thing she wants, and some things she didn't even know that she wanted, like a photography book about gestation, with gorgeous pictures of fetuses. He also assembles the mail-order bassinet we bought, whistling lullabies while he works. He even likes looking at all the baby outfits and teases Sophie about names he'd like her to consider: Grantina, Grantette, and Grantaluna are his top choices.

The best thing: The night before he and Nicky are to go back, Grant and I go out to a restaurant together, just the two of us. Nicky agrees to stay home with Sophie, and when we leave, the two of them are in the bed, watching television and eating take-out Chinese food.

Grant and I walk down to Seventeenth Street to a restaurant I have passed many times and always wanted to go into. It's cozy and warm in there, with a jazz quartet in the back, and we sit knee to knee in our little booth, and we talk. We're wary at first, but then the warmth, the wine, and just the fact that we've been apart for so long soften the edges of the conversation. He says the book is going fine, ahead of schedule actually, and that Clark has now announced to everyone that Grant is going to be the department chair. He's lonely, though, he says. The winter has dragged on, and he's run out of nearly everything in the house at least four times, including clean underwear. He's had to start washing underwear every day in the shower and hanging it to dry for the following day.

"You do remember where we keep the washing machine? You've lived in that house since you were a baby," I say, and he laughs. He can't remember all the stuff he needs to buy. He's been out of laundry detergent since week three.

"So let's change this horrible subject. Tell me this: what have you been doing since you've been here?" he wants to know. "Do you just hang out in the apartment all the time?"

"Mostly," I say. "I mean, I go to the market every day, and sometimes I go and sit in the park."

"It's scaring me a little, how much you like it here," he says, but he's smiling.

"I do like it. I always did like living in New York. I mean, I like New Hampshire, too, but sometimes I think . . ."

"What?" he says. He leans closer.

"Just that New Hampshire was best for me when we had kids at home. We had the whole community around us then. I felt as though we were part of something. Now—without them, I guess I've just lost my footing lately."

"Huh! And I thought it was my book that was making you so miserable."

"Well, yes. God, yes. The way it sucks you up. But, you know, I think it's more than that. I was telling my therapist that I feel as though I got fired from my job."

He smiles and looks right at me. "You didn't get fired. You did it right, and got promoted."

"That's what she said. I just have to figure something else out, that's all. Being here has shown me that I need more contact with the outside world, and not just with the other faculty wives. I mean, I like them fine, but the other day when I handed in my book, I took the subway and went to the publisher's office, and that's when I realized what I've been missing. Colleagues."

"Colleagues," he says.

"Yes. I haven't got it all figured out yet, but I'm thinking that Sophie is going to need some help with the baby, and maybe I can go back and forth—you know, spend some time here each month. I could talk to my editor about taking on a series . . ."

"Will I be included in this new life of yours?" he says.

"Play your cards right, mister, and you could be," I say.

We walk back to Sophie's, hand in hand, in the spring night. When we get to the door, he pulls me over and kisses me. "How many Wednesdays do you figure we've missed out on by now?"

"Grant, honey, don't take this the wrong way, but I think when I get back we need to suspend the Wednesday program."

He makes his eyes go round with mock alarm. "What are you *saying*? No more sex?"

"No more scheduled sex. I want spontaneous sex. When it doesn't feel like part of a to-do list. 'Clean gutters. Recaulk bathtub. Have sex with Annabelle.' "

He thinks about this, stroking my face and smiling. "I only did it for you, so at least you'd know that no matter how busy I got, we'd have that time."

"Well, thanks but no thanks. You know what I mean? I might want it three times a week sometimes. I may want it three times in one day!"

"Now that could be a problem," he says, and laughs.

He's standing close and pressing against me, smiling. He's looser than I remember. And he smells good.

"You know what?" I say. "I like you this way."

"What way?"

"When you miss me. When you're not looking at me like I'm just some impediment to keep you from writing your book."

He laughs. "I do miss you. Even all your crazy conversations about people's sex lives. Speaking of which, do you suppose there's any way of maybe celebrating the demise of our Wednesday morning sex program . . . now? Before I leave?"

But of course there isn't, short of the radical act of going to a hotel. Hard to do with grown children paying attention to your every move. The fact is, with the way this apartment is configured, I have had to sleep in the bed with Sophie, and Grant and Nicky have had to take the sofa bed in the living room. So instead, we kiss long and hard in the lobby, and for once he doesn't even seem to mind that people rushing by on the sidewalk can look in and see everything.

LATER, I wish we'd taken the radical step of going to a hotel. I wish we'd gone to a hotel, and then Grant had just vaporized himself back to New Hampshire.

The next morning, before they leave for the drive back, I wake up early and make a breakfast of scrambled eggs with spinach and feta cheese, tomatoes, and toast.

I'm so preoccupied with cooking and bringing things into the bedroom for our last picnic breakfast that I almost don't realize as I'm going back and forth that Sophie is smiling and talking about me. Why hadn't it occurred to me that this might happen? That this would come up?

"Poor Mom," she's saying when I come in with the pot of coffee. "She's been so lonely here with just me to manage, after she's been accustomed to all her waifs and strays."

"Please," I say. "Don't feel sorry for me. I've been fine. More than fine."

"I'm shocked she hasn't been able to find any waifs and strays in New York," says Grant, smiling. "Are you telling me nobody in this building needs her services? Nobody on the subway, even?"

"Well, actually," Sophie says. "Some of my girlfriends came by at first to get counseled about their bad boyfriends. And oh, wait. She did find herself one waif on her own—actually an old friend of yours! Boy, is he

a sad sack if there ever was one! He should be nominated the quintes-
sential waif and stray for all times."

I can hear little noises coming from deep in my throat. No, I am
thinking. *Nooooo.*

But everything seems to go in slow motion, like the seconds before
the car crashes, the windshield cracks, the high chair with the baby in
it drops to the floor, the 95 mph baseball meets skull. I have opened
my mouth to say something, *anything*, but she's already talking.

"Jeremiah," she is saying. "His name is Jeremiah. She's seen him a
few times."

Right?

Jeremiah? Your old friend?

Isn't that right, Mom?

[e i g h t e e n]

1981

I am so sorry. I don't really have the heart to go back to the past right now, given what has happened. What is there to be said, anyway, about our old life? We went to New Hampshire. We had a couple of kids. The years passed. I got old. I loved my husband but sometimes I dreamed about my former lover. Is that enough?

Okay, I will try.

AFTER NEW YORK, life in New Hampshire was a complete shock to my system. For a while we lived in the farmhouse alongside Grant's very polite but practically silent parents. I didn't think I would ever be able to adjust to a small town, to the idea of a milkman who didn't knock but simply came inside and put bottles of milk directly into the refrigerator—and who, if he noticed you were out of eggs, might just leave a dozen there as well without even asking you. And how neighbors here assumed you would always be in the mood for a visit. One day Penelope Granger, who lived on the farm next to ours, stunned me by explaining that everybody in town had the same recipe for pie crust, and nobody could remember where they'd gotten it.

I was asked to call Grant's parents Father and Mother McKay. I tried to be on better behavior than I had ever been on in my whole life. I shared cooking responsibilities with his mom, who had a life-long belief that men deserved three square meals a day just by virtue of being men, and that they shouldn't be expected to help out at all.

Worse, she knew I had broken her son's heart before, so she was wary around me. She was reserved, and I was "from away."

Then one night, I woke in the middle of the night to a shrieking sound, and found her outside trying to chase a fox that had gotten into the chicken coop. Together, in the moonlight in our nightgowns, we scared away the fox and then searched in the shadows for the frightened chicken, which was hiding under the boards of the shed, and brought it back to safety. The next day she and I were chopping onions together for dinner and she said, "Dear, do you think you could ever just call me Mother?"

When winter came, they left for a condo in Florida, and it felt very much as though the mantle of history had passed down to our generation and that the world was a weaker place for it.

But then Sophie was born, and life filled up with all that lovely, confusing chaos—crib and stroller and baby powder, breast-feeding and pacifiers and diapers, sleep deprivation and late-night drives in the car to get her to stop crying. She had colic and trouble getting teeth, and for months I wore her on the front of me in a corduroy pack. Women—all ages of them, young and old, from the college and from the farms and from the shops in town—came by to bring dinners and to sweep the floors, to point out that peppermint drops could ease colic and that a baby rocked to sleep near the clothes dryer would sleep longer and more deeply.

We made friends with other couples, and for a while we were all just entranced with ourselves for this incredible discovery we'd all made: it was possible to create new humans! Along came playdates and couples nights, when we got together at friends' houses and cooked dinners together. Theme nights: taco night, beef Wellington night, Indian curry night. There were backyard barbecues in the summer. Birthday parties. Trips to the lake. Faculty parties. Apple-picking. Caroling in winter. Ice-fishing.

I fell in love with my husband. I'd loved him up until then, sure, but now it was in a whole new way, as though a new room had opened up in my brain—I was swamped with love. It was rather like a second-stage rocket booster kicking in just when the first rocket had lost all its power. I was still overwhelmed most of the time, but suddenly alongside me was this sensitive, able, sexy guy I'd had the good sense to marry. He was in his element, was what it was, and he was happy. He made me laugh. Plus, he knew how to do so many things I'd never even thought about: he could ice-skate and fix the toilet when it ran and keep the pipes from freezing and bursting. He stoked the woodstove and taught me how to ski downhill. He shoveled snow, he complimented my cooking, he didn't mind playing king to Sophie's princess. He could play Candy Land all Saturday afternoon without once screaming, or cheating, and then kiss me ardently once we'd finally gotten Sophie to sleep.

Nicky was born in the flush of our love. We got a dog, a cocker spaniel, and later that year a picnic table and a swing set. We planted a vegetable garden and grew Swiss chard and tomatoes and marigolds, bachelor's buttons, and roses. Over the years, we acquired goldfish, guinea pigs, a tabby cat, and for one memorable year, a pair of guinea hens. A litter of kittens was born in the laundry basket. The children needed tubes in their ears one winter after eight ear infections. The boiler gave out one Christmas Eve, and we had to keep the fireplace going for days until we could get a guy out from New London to replace it.

At the center of everything were the children with their plump little arms, their dirty faces, their need for us in the middle of the night. Life was tactile, messy, earthy, inseparable from love. The children said funny things, and we kept a book in which we wrote down their memorable quotes. Even their ear infections, the time we all had the flu at once, the nights they were afraid of the dark, the nights we were all tucked in while the storms raged outside and shook the foundation of the house—all of it was rich and throbbing with life. I slept spooned up against Grant, and so what if we ended up getting up most nights two or three times, tending to children or the dog or stoking the fire in the woodstove? And what if sometimes there were cold silences that fell between us? There were fights and arguments and tears, times when I sat in the mudroom with the phone blubbering to Magda that he was insensitive and could be harsh, that he didn't listen. And then there was make-up sex, us falling on each other while cleaning up the kitchen, or else my awakening in the night to feel his questioning hand coming over to ask forgiveness and acceptance.

And there were all those nights I would look across the pillow at him and wonder who was this stranger that I shared so much with, how remarkable it was that we were together when we had such differences. Times when I was overwhelmed in the world and would run home to find him there, ready to listen and understand—the time my friend Jennie accused me of not working as hard as everyone else on the middle school auction committee. It sounds silly now. Of course it is. But it was real.

Then there were times I'd be washing dishes or throwing in a load of laundry and Jeremiah's face would inexplicably show up, flickering there in the outskirts of my mind. But that wasn't wrong, was it?

Or maybe it was just life.

Once my brother came to visit. It was a big deal, getting the place ready for someone who was paralyzed. I coached the children to be nice and welcoming to him. Grant built a ramp for his wheelchair so he could come in the back door. We were glad to have him there, but it was awful to see David so limited, so unhappy. You could see it in his eyes. He talked to the kids in almost a formal, stilted way, like he didn't want to get to know them, and Nicky especially was scared of him.

And two months after he flew back home, he died of a drug overdose. Grant was resolute in claiming it was accidental, that it had to be, but I was sure it was suicide, and could not be comforted. I had seen the shadow fall across him.

That was the beginning of things starting to fall away. I should have seen it coming: first there was David, but then, one by one, our parents, the cocker spaniel, and the barn, which burned down in a fire. Our best friends moved away and didn't write or call, another dear friend got sick with cancer and became famous, briefly, by writing about it, and then died . . . and finally the children moved out.

And now perhaps our marriage is another casualty.

I have lost so much, and I will lose this, too.

Oh, I am so tired. I want to lie down on Sophie's couch and stare out the window at the sky, at the birds that occasionally fly past in groups—and what do they call that, a group of birds? I've lost that word, too. A school of birds? A gaggle? A flock. Yes, that's it. A flock. A flock of birds.

I want to try not to think anymore. If only I could just not think for a little while, things would be so good.

2005

*A*fter Sophie said the sacred, unsayable word *Jeremiah*, after Grant's eyes had gone opaque and after he had said in his cold, final voice, with all of us staring at him, "Well, that is *that*, then, isn't it? That's the end of anything else that needs to be said," and had gone off to pack his stuff, Nicky comes and wraps his arms around me, his wild-man arms, and whispers, "Don't let the turkeys get you down."

"What?" I say.

He laughs. He'd heard that one of the presidents had written that note to his successor and left it in his desk in the White House—and he'd always wanted to say it, too. "It sounded good," he says. "I don't know what this is about, but one thing I do know is that you've got it going on where the wife stuff is concerned. Ten to one Dad's being an asshole."

"No," I say and disentangle myself from him. "That's not the way this is."

I go into the living room and say to my husband's back, "Grant, please. It's not what you think."

"And just how is that?" he says.

"Listen, I ran into him—Sophie and I ran into him one day while we were at a market buying stuff for dinner. We had just come from a doctor's appointment, so we were in a different neighborhood, and there he was. Buying ice cream."

He does not turn, just keeps folding things and putting them into his suitcase, his shoulders moving methodically, unemotionally, back and forth.

"Grant, I can't stand it if you don't listen to me about this." I can't see his face, so I go around to the other side of the couch. "The statute of limitations is up on this," I tell him. "You have nothing to fear from him."

He stops for a moment and looks right at me. His eyes are hard. "Well, now, Annabelle, that just isn't precisely true, is it?"

"Come on, this is ridiculous! Okay, fair enough. I saw Jeremiah Saxon. Twenty-six years have passed, and big deal! I run into him in a market, against all odds. And then, *yes*, I go for coffee with him. I sit in Starbucks with the man and hear about his boring, trite, dull life."

"And then apparently you went for *more* renditions of his boring, trite, dull life."

"One more time, Grant. I went one more time, but that isn't the point. That isn't what matters here. The point is—*the point is*—that after all this freaking time, you should know what I'm like. You should be giving me the benefit of the doubt. Even if I had seen him *ten* more times, a hundred more times, even if I'd invited him to come to New Hampshire to visit us, you should know me by now. *That* is the point."

He zips closed his suitcase and stands it upright. "Annabelle, there are so many things operating in my head right now that I cannot possibly sort them all out. But first and foremost is that you have lied to me before about this man, and you are not above lying again. Interesting that it was Sophie and not you who told me about your seeing Jeremiah—"

"And why do you think that was, Grant? Why in the world would I ever tell you something like that, knowing this was the kind of response it would get?"

"—and interesting that you didn't see fit to mention it, not even when we were alone last night and you were exclaiming how much you *love* New York City and telling me how you basically *never* go anywhere except to go to the market or to sit in the park. You don't bring up the one man, *the one man*, Annabelle, that we have an agreement about."

"Did it ever occur to you that we shouldn't have ever made such an agreement as that in the first place? That that so-called agreement is what is at the root of all our problems?"

"The root of all our problems," he says quietly, "is that you are in love with someone outside our marriage. And you haven't gotten over him."

"That is not true, Grant."

"Nicky!" he calls. "Get your stuff and take it to the car. Sophie, come give your old dad a kiss. We're heading out."

There's a flurry of activity then, the kids showing up and doing what he says. We all go through the motions of good-bye, just as though everything might be normal. His perfunctory kiss glides right off my cheek. And then, like that, he is gone.

ONCE THEY have left, Sophie goes into her room and closes the door against me. I take the sheets off the sofa bed and fold everything up. I stare out the window at the street for a long time, and then do some therapeutic dish-washing. Later, I make spaghetti for dinner. My mother used to say that red food is good when you are desolate.

I miss my mother. I wonder what she would say to me now, what possible good spin she would put on this. I try to summon her and the way she would always say something comforting about whatever love trouble I'd gotten myself into, but now that she's been dead for so long, she does not come.

When the fragrance of spaghetti sauce has filled up the house with comfort and warmth, I knock on Sophie's door and ask her if she wants to eat by herself or if she'd like some company.

She takes a long time before she says, "I guess I don't want to be by myself."

I bring in our food on trays, and we sit on the bed and eat, watching a rerun of *Friends*.

"This laugh track is giving me a headache. I hate phony laughter," she says and turns off the set, and then we push the food around on our plates in silence, not looking at each other.

"So you cheated on Dad with Jeremiah, is that it?" she finally says.

"It's more complicated than that, Sophie." I sigh. "This is stuff that happened between us a long time ago—long before you were even born."

"You know what gets me the worst? All this time, all these conversations we've been having about marriage and about being faithful, and I kept asking you about what you would do if Dad ever cheated, and you were just so blasé. And then all along it was you! *You* were the one cheating. I can't believe it. I mean, I can't wrap my head around the fact that *my mother* was out with somebody else, and my *dad* was the one trying to—trying to—"

"Sophie—"

"How *could* you? That's what I want to know. How could you do it?" She is crying now. "You have the sweetest, most faithful guy in the whole world. Remember when we were talking the other day and I said that about him? And you stood there *agreeing* with me and yet the whole time you *had* to be thinking that you were the one who had cheated! How does a person—"

"Sophie. Stop it. Listen to me."

"What?" she says. "Say it. Give me your excuses."

"Baby, there aren't any excuses. Every marriage has its problems. Everybody goes through different things and we all make horrendous mistakes at times. We hurt each other, we do things we regret, and we come to our senses if we're lucky—"

"*Mom!* Did you see his face? He was *devastated*. You didn't come to your senses, Mom! Dad thinks you're still cheating on him! And I don't blame him! You are, aren't you? You went out with Jeremiah again and again! I don't believe it. I can't believe this." She is rocking back and forth, her voice getting more and more shrill. "I can't even trust you anymore! How can I believe anything you say?"

"Sophie, stop this," I say. "You have to stop. If you want to have a sane, rational discussion about marriage and about my life, then I have to insist that you tone it down. I am not going to have you speak to me like this. We are talking about something that happened *twenty-six* years ago."

She stops talking and puts her hands over her face, a pitiable, forlorn child who will not look at me.

I get up and go to the bathroom, splash water on my face, and stare at myself in the mirror. When I go back into her bedroom, I sit down softly on her bed and reach over and touch her foot.

"Do you want to talk about it?"

She nods and blows her nose.

"First, let me just tell you that this happened long before I ever really felt *married*, if that makes any sense to you. And it was wrong—I'm not denying that it was wrong—but it just happened. I fell in love with two men. That's what happened. I didn't mean to. I wasn't trying to hurt your father. But, you know, Sophie, what I have learned is that sometimes love happens to you when you *don't* expect it. Love just comes for you. It was like—it was like some primitive force . . ."

She looks at me, and then her face crumples. "This can't be happening! I don't want to hear about this *primitive force* of yours. I can't listen to this!"

I stand up. "It's okay. You don't have to hear about it." I start putting on my shoes.

She's still crying. "You and Daddy had the per—the perfect marriage, and he's been wonderful to you, and now *nothing* is what it seems like, and how am I supposed to feel? You want me to feel sorry for you because you fell in love with two men? Look at what you've done to all of us!"

I turn and leave the room, and then, because that's not far enough away from her, I leave the apartment and go down the elevator and out onto the dark street.

ONCE I get outside, I can't think of anything else to do, so I call Magda on my cell phone. My hands are shaking. It's chillier outside than I had reckoned, and I forgot to put on my jacket. I have so much to tell her. The last time I talked to her I told her about what had seemed like the astonishing coincidence of running into Jeremiah. During that call, I was still giddily deciding whether to go for coffee with him or not.

She'd been very funny about the whole thing. "I think before I can hear any more about Jeremiah, I need you to tell me that you're *not* in some train station reenacting your runaway plan with him," she'd said. "Because I would need to lose a few pounds and grow my hair longer before I could even consider coming to collect Grant. He wouldn't even *look* at me the way I look today."

It's always been our joke—ever since she masterminded my getting back with him—that if I blew it again, she would no longer help me but would take him for herself. Even at the most difficult times of my marriage—times that I now know were just mud puddles compared to the ocean of trouble I find myself in—even when I was complaining loud and long about some slight of his, coming home too late, being thoughtless about Valentine's Day or Mother's Day, she was resolutely in his corner.

So I walk blocks and blocks and tell her about my two visits with Jeremiah, which would have been worth a whole phone call just on their own but I didn't have time—and then I have to tell her that Grant found out and is furious with me, and that Sophie is now up in her bed with her fingers in her ears saying, "LALALALA" when I try to talk.

There's just the long-distance cell phone hum when I get finished. "Hello?" I say. "Did we get disconnected? Can you hear me now?"

"I'm actually speechless, Annabelle," Magda says. "I don't know what the hell you should do. Walking the streets sounds like the sanest idea of all." And she laughs. "Jesus. You know what I actually think? I think this is one of the best reasons I can think of never to have children—so they don't find out that you're just a regular human being and then hate you for it."

"Now that you mention it, that is a good reason," I say. "I remember hating my mother for everything she did. I hated her finding feminism and leaving my father, then being with that jerk she was with, and *then* going *back* to my father. I was the most unforgiving about that. I saw that as her forsaking her feminist ideals, when I'd hated that she ever had any in the first place."

"Yeah. God. Mothers and daughters," Magda says. "Hard ride. But, geez, it seems particularly unfair that you're being hated for something you did before Sophie was even born. Doesn't the statute of limitations ever expire on something like this?"

"Well, that's what I want to know," I say.

"And I was just sitting here feeling sorry for myself because I forgot to get married and have kids."

"Yeah, well, if you ask me, you lived your life perfectly."

"Who knew?"

"If I could turn back time—isn't there a song that says that?"

"So what are you going to do, besides walking the streets of New York until your cell phone battery gives out?" she wants to know.

"I can't actually imagine."

"Well," she says, "if I could just make one suggestion, baby?"

"Please. I insist. Give me anything you got. I got nothing here."

"Well, I think you should stand strong and firm. Remember that you have nothing to be ashamed of. You're a wonderful, open, loving person, and you've given your life to raising these kids and being Grant's wife. Your long-ago affair with Jeremiah was the result of factors that have nothing to do with who you are now. You've done it all splendidly, Annabelle—much better than any of the role models you had growing up, that's for sure. And whatever happens—well, you have that."

"Thank you," I say when I can speak again. "But you're being way too generous. I have hurt so many people. I've ended up hurting everybody that I really love."

"Oh, tell them all to grow a pair," she says. "You and I both know the truth." Then she says, "Not that it matters, Annabelle, but . . . is Jeremiah still hot?"

I try to answer her, to say yes, yes he is, but all that comes out is a tiny noise from my throat.

"Hello?" she says.

"I'm sorry," I say after a moment. "But I can't—I think I have to go."

"Oh, baby," she says. "Oh, baby. This is so hard. But, you know, it's okay to always be a little bit in love with Jeremiah, isn't it? You can have that for yourself. It doesn't mean you're going to change anything."

I AM waiting for something—good sense to set in, most likely—and finally April comes, and the apartment becomes too small and too stuffy to bear. Spring is in full swing now, but the building management doesn't seem to have gotten the message. The heat blasts through the radiators the same as ever. I have hot flashes and wake in the night feeling baked, and I seem to be moving through life harboring a headache that won't shake itself loose. I am going through the motions: cooking food for Sophie, cleaning up afterward, eating, trying to sleep, watching television, drawing pictures, and waiting. I try to be available to her, but we decide that it's best if I start sleeping on the living room couch now that she is so large and I am so restless in the night, needing to kick off the covers and then pull them back on at least a dozen times. Even during the day I try to give her space by staying in the living room reading or painting. My editor has called and told me about a series of picture books involving children traveling around the world, and she'd like to see some sketches.

Sophie and I seem to be tiptoeing around each other. I hear her sometimes talking to Grant on the phone, giving her daily health update. *My legs are aching, and yesterday I had a headache, but the baby isn't kicking me so much today*. This is way more information than she gives to me.

On Friday, we go for the weekly ultrasound, and when it's over, Dr. Levine turns off the machine and turns on the overhead light, and then she says the time has come to put the C-section on the schedule. Sophie is at about thirty-four weeks now, and it should be done in her thirty-seventh week. How about Monday, April 25?

So Beanie Bartholomew will be a little Taurus, just like her mom. Stubborn and opinionated and earthbound, but also good and real and true.

When the nurse writes the date down on the calendar, I look over at Sophie, who lies there on the ultrasound table, twisting a Kleenex in her hand.

"Is this really the only way to get the baby out?" she asks in a surprisingly young, little-girl voice. "I always thought there was a chance I could do this, you know, normally."

Dr. Levine, who is my favorite of the obstetricians we see, smiles at her. "Well, the placenta has definitely stayed put over the cervix, so this becomes the normal way this time," she says. "And, Sophie, I know your mother would agree with me here—it's not going to serve you to think of this as *abnormal*. What's great about this is that we can deliver you a nice, normal baby, and that's better than a normal pregnancy or what you would call a normal delivery. I go for a normal baby every time."

"Do you think everything is really, really going to be all right?" Sophie says, and her lower lip trembles.

Dr. Levine pats her on the shoulder and says, "I think it's going to be just fine. You've done beautifully, Sophie, and you're almost at the end. You should be very proud," but then she sends me a quizzical look. At her signal, I follow her into the hallway while Sophie is getting dressed.

"How are things going at home?" she says. "Anything I should know?"

"No," I say. "Not really." Do I really have to explain to the obstetrician that I had an affair before Sophie was born?

Dr. Levine smiles at me. "Well," she says, and pats my arm. "She's just an emotional person, isn't she? I'm guessing it can't be easy for you living with her during this time. It would be great if this husband of hers could get home for the birth, wouldn't it?"

"Believe me, I'm ready to fly down there and frog-march him back here," I say, and she laughs.

This is the first person I've made laugh in weeks. I almost want to invite Dr. Levine out for drinks.

"SO WHAT exactly happened back then?" Sophie says to me in the cab on the way home. "Did Dad catch you two having sex and break up with you?"

I look out the window and don't say anything.

"Never mind. I don't really want to know anyway."

NICKY HAS a completely different take on things, one that doesn't automatically conclude that I'm a horrible person. He calls me to say that he thinks Grant is having some kind of midlife crisis or perhaps a psychotic break with reality.

"Mom, I swear, the drive up with him was like something out of a horror movie," he says. "He was like Darth Vader, just breathing and seething. Meanwhile he's driving like thirty-five miles an hour *on the highway*, and all these trucks are passing us and honking, but he doesn't care. He just *breathes*."

"I know, Nick. He was upset."

"So wait. What's going on? He found out about some guy you had a thing for in the past? Is that it?"

I hesitate. "It's complicated, Nicky. There was a man I loved, and—well, your father didn't ever want me to see the man again, and then I ran into him in New York and had coffee with him."

"You had coffee with him, and Dad freaked out?"

"Yes, basically."

"Okay, Mom. You gotta tell me. I can take it. Is my father insane?" I laugh.

"So when is Sophie going to have this kid?" he says.

I tell him the C-section is scheduled for the twenty-fifth.

"I'll be there," he says.

"But you can't. It's the end of your semester—"

"Mom, I have to be. It's so cool. I still can't believe how that thing kicked and tried to get me to move my hand off, like I was trespassing on her house or something. It was so amazing. Do you just sit in there all the time and stare at Sophie's belly and watch the knees and elbows go by?"

"Not so much," I say.

"Well, you should," he tells me. "That's what I'd be doing."

"Nicky, are you studying?"

"Uh, Mom, you're breaking up! I can't hear you anymore! Hello? Hello?"

"Nicholas David McKay, you are not fooling anybody. I hope you know that."

He makes the sound of a dial tone and then bursts into laughter.

I GET back from the store one day and before I can even turn my key in the lock, I hear Sophie on the cell phone in her room. She's shouting at Whit.

"But she's in four of the pictures you just sent!" she's saying. There's a silence. Then she says, "Well, what it *means* is that she's always around you. And that you obviously like the way she looks if you're going to keep taking her picture. . . . No! I am *not* crazy! I *know* that. I know you don't think—*no!* No, I don't think I can trust you!"

Her voice drops, and I put away the groceries in the kitchen, wishing that I didn't have that free-fall feeling in the pit of my stomach.

Then she says, "How can I know for sure? Everybody wants to sleep with you, and I'm here all alone and I'm as big as a house, and I don't know if I can keep this baby inside me for as long as it takes! No, no, no! You *shouldn't* have left me here! And—"

Then I hear her crying and she says, "I just found out that my mom cheated on my dad right after they got married. And now I don't know who I can trust anymore. *Nobody's* really faithful. And now my father isn't speaking to her." Silence. "No, he didn't just find out, Whit. She *saw the guy again!* At least twice. She's awful."

I don't hear anything more for a while and then she says, "Well, you can try to convince me all you want, but I just want to tell you one thing: this baby is going to be born on April twenty-fifth, and I want you to be there! . . . All right, then. Promise me! You promise? Okay."

I fix us vegetable burritos for dinner and take hers into her bedroom an hour later. She's lying on her side on the bed, staring out the window.

"Sophie," I say. "Sophie, you have simply got to let this go. You're making yourself miserable over something that has nothing to do with you. Really. Did you know that when I was twenty, my mother left my father so that she could go and sleep with another man, a scruffy artist who drove around in a van with drawings on it? My mother was the most conventional, straight person ever in the world, and she just went and had this affair, and went to feminist meetings and did all this wacky stuff, and do you think I stopped loving her or trusting her? I didn't. I just tried to make room for it somehow, and then it all passed. Sophie, people aren't put on this earth to meet every one of our expectations. That's what makes life so *interesting*, honey. Can't you see that?"

She turns and stares at me. "Is this supposed to make me feel better? Now you're telling me that my *grandmother* cheated, too? How is that supposed to help?"

I have to admit, she has a point. What was I thinking?

ONE NIGHT I wake up with a start and find Sophie sitting on the edge of my bed picking at a loose thread of my quilt. I have no idea how long she's been there, or how long I've known she was there. Her breathing seems to fill the room, so loud it had finally entered my dreams.

I sit up quickly and rub my eyes. "Are you okay? Is everything all right? Did anything happen?"

"I'm fine," she says. "I guess."

The clock says 2:34. When Sophie was a kid, she used to say we could make wishes when the time on the clock was consecutive numbers like that. She'd come running in to find me from wherever she happened to be just so we could make our wishes. At first I think that's what she wants to do now.

"Wait. Are you crying?" I say.

"No. I was, but I'm not anymore," she says.

"Well, what is it? Do you want to talk?"

"I just want to know one thing. Was it worth it?"

I let a beat of silence go by. "Seeing Jeremiah again, you mean?" I say.

"No. The *affair*. What you got out of it. Was it worth it, really?"

"Sometimes," I say, "sometimes you don't do things because of whether they're going to turn out to be worth it. You—you're just compelled by something that feels almost *other*. It's hard to explain to somebody else, but . . . well, do you really want to know?"

"Yes."

"Okay." I take a deep breath. "Well, I guess I would have to say that one thing that was happening was that the times were so different then. I almost can't explain how back then it didn't seem exactly like cheating. It almost seemed right, in those days, to reach out and grab what you needed for your life. You almost owed it to yourself. And, Sophie, I don't know if you can understand this, but I was barely married. I didn't even know myself as a married person. You're ten times more married than I was then. I'd met your father at school, and he did this kind thing of letting me stay at his apartment when my father stopped paying my rent, and then I went back to take care of my family and never expected that anything would come of your father and me—and then one day he just showed up and asked me to marry him because he was moving to New York. And I said yes."

She narrows her eyes. "You said yes? But why? Did you love him?"

"I did," I say slowly. "I really did. But now I know that there were pieces missing in myself, pieces I didn't even know I was supposed to have."

She's looking at me calmly. "I'm not going to be falling in love with somebody else."

"No," I say. "No, I don't think you will. The times aren't the same, for one thing. And you're way more grounded than I ever was. But, sweetie, other things will happen. You and Whit are going to face pressure, and you'll fight about money and sex and who does the dishes and who should change Beanie's diaper and a whole bunch of stupid things that you can't even imagine right now. But when that happens to you, don't let it freak you out and get you blaming yourself or Whit or boredom or the government or God or whatever. It's just life. And you'll get over it."

She's picking at the blankets again. "Mom, do you think Whit is cheating on me in Brazil? Because I really, really don't know if he can be away for—"

"Sophie, this is going to sound weird, but I think you're just going to have to get comfortable with the idea of living with some uncertainty in your relationship with your husband. You can't ever completely know or completely control another person. And when you make your whole life about trying to figure out what he's doing at any given point—well, then I think you're going to rob yourself of some of the joy of simply being together. Because ultimately that's all that matters."

"But what if love, as you say, 'just comes' for him?" she asks. "What if he ends up loving somebody else and wanting to leave me?"

"And what if he does? Anything can happen, darling. That's what life is—uncertain and crazy," I say to her. "You'll survive it if it happens. But remember that you have a shot of *keeping* it from happening if you let yourself truly love him instead of just trying to control him. Let him know how valued he is instead of how suspicious you are of his every waking moment."

She's quiet for a moment and then she says, "Whit is coming home on the twenty-third. And he says there's nothing between him and Juliana, except that he now loves to play double solitaire all the time."

"Well, that'll give you something to do while you nurse the baby," I say lightly.

We both laugh, and then we lie there in the darkness. After a while, her breathing becomes deep and even, and I know she's asleep. I lie there until the sun comes up, thinking about Jeremiah and how I can't summon anymore that lighter-than-air feeling I used to get when I'd think of him. The fantasy Jeremiah who wanted me so much and who was somewhere in the world missing me and pining for what he had thrown away doesn't exist for me anymore. Maybe I don't need that.

I look over at Sophie sleeping next to me, her face catching the gray early light coming through the window. She is no more ready to be a mother than I was, and it will take all the courage and strength she has to pull this marriage together and embrace the uncertainty. Did I fail this child somehow, give her the mistaken impression when she was growing up that life is serene and easy? Did everything come too easily for her—friendships and love and success, so that when troubles come, she has no idea how to cope?

Maybe. But lying there, I realize that I know something else now that I didn't know before: here I've been championing Whit and thinking he had to go to Brazil and that it was so important for his career, but now I know he shouldn't have gone. His place was here, and he's going to have to work hard to earn her trust again.

And there's another thing I know now, in the gathering dawn. Sophie has seemed so weak and emotional throughout this time, and I've often felt as though she was playing a passive, victim role in her own life. But it's not really been like that at all. She has never closed off her emotions, the way I would have done or her father would have done. No. The tough times came, and let it be noted that Sophie yelled and shouted, screamed and fought for her marriage.

That's something that neither her father nor I did.

We just walked away. And that's what I have to live with.

[twenty]

I try to call Grant because I badly want to tell him this thing I've figured out about walking away, but he doesn't answer his phone. Not through the whole morning nor in the afternoon. I picture him looking at the caller ID and seeing that it's me and deciding he doesn't have the energy.

He is still walking away.

That's okay. I know now that we're all in a waiting mode. There is nothing to be done when the time isn't right yet.

Right now it is enough that Sophie and I lie on her bed together in the evenings, Sophie knitting a blanket and me doing sketches of a baby in a café in Paris.

This is a call to my granddaughter to come and save us. I've seen babies do this trick before, so I know it is possible. Maybe it is the only thing that will work.

AND THEN, less than a week later, Sophie gets up predawn to go to the bathroom, and through the cotton batting of sleep, I hear a calm voice saying, "Mom. Mom, can you come in here, please?"

I disentangle myself from the covers and go to her, and then everything starts unfolding just the way it did in the heartbreaking scenario I had been imagining and fearing the most. In the harsh fluorescent light shining down on the white tile, in the white, white bathroom, there is bright red blood, alarming amounts of red, lots more than I would have thought possible. It is flowing and flowing, and Sophie stands in the middle of the bathroom, her face white, but she is not screaming, and she is not falling down, so we have that going for us. She lets me wrap her up in her bathrobe, and then I ease her over to the closed toilet seat, and I get my cell phone and call 911.

"My daughter is thirty-six weeks pregnant, and she has placenta previa, and she is bleeding—a lot," I say into the phone, and I give the address to the dispatcher, who promises an ambulance will be right there, as though we've all rehearsed our parts.

May I just say that it scares me how serene Sophie is? In a way I'd be happier if she were doing her usual yelling and screaming and railing against nature and Whit and even me. If she were screaming about how unfair this is, how she's scared or hurting or anything, but instead, she's closed her eyes and is breathing softly and deeply. They start an IV right there in the ambulance, and we ride through the glistening wet streets in a rainstorm, with the headlights falling away to let us through on our path.

This must be really serious, I think, *if even New York traffic is willing to let us take the street without argument.*

At the hospital, things are a bright, fluorescent blur, as if the whole thing has been filmed with a handheld camera. Nurses and doctors gather around, and they're all doing things to Sophie, who is still the worst kind of calm, like she might be leaving, is what I think. Maybe she's not even really here with me, not even now.

No, no, no! Don't think this way.

"Sophie," I say. I squeeze her hand and lean down and brush the little tendrils of hair off her temples. "You're doing fine. Everything's okay now. You know that, right?"

She smiles with her grayish lips.

Don't think this way. If my eyes even fill up with tears, they will send me out of here. I'm permitted to stay because I sit right there beside Sophie with my hand loosely holding hers, because I'm the person she can count on, the *support person.*

The medical people have apparently come to a decision, and then they scatter, hurrying off to get equipment and more people. I hear some of the words—"bleeding under control . . . clamped . . . take her upstairs . . . get this taken care of!"

"What is happening, please?" I say to a curly-haired nurse who is pulling the chart out of the holder on the door.

"Oh!" she says. "They didn't tell you? They're going to do the C-section now."

"But—is this wise? Is it time?" I say.

"She's thirty-six and a half weeks," she says cheerfully. "The baby's lungs are fine. No sense waiting for another bleeding episode."

"Can I be there?"

"Of course you can, Grandma. You're going to sit right up by Mom's head and keep her company. You've got the most important job of all, didn't you know that? They're bringing the stretcher for her now."

"Oh," I say, and sit back down. "Sophie, open your eyes, honey. Sophie, you're going to have the baby now. Did you hear?"

"I heard," she says softly. She looks at me with her wide gray eyes. "It's okay, right?"

"What?"

"It's okay? Are you fine?"

This is a joke from way back when she was two years old, scared of going into the swimming pool, scared of the dark, scared of feathers and dust. For weeks she went around muttering to herself, "Are you fine? Are you fine?"

I laugh. "We're all fine, honey. And Beanie's coming! This is her birthday, your baby's birthday," I say, and squeeze her hand.

And then the stretcher comes, and we take off for the birth room—all us chatty, smiling, emergency-competent people, bearing Sophie along with us, as though she's a queen and we're escorting her to the sacred temple.

A C-SECTION doesn't take long, and you don't see much, so even if you're squeamish, it's okay, I tell Grant. There's a screen blocking your view, and so I just sat with Sophie telling her how exciting this was, and then there was a cry, and the doctor—not Dr. Levine—said, "She's here!"

"Wow," he says.

She is six pounds and four ounces and she has a fringe of brown hair and blue eyes. But I guess they all have blue eyes at first—isn't that what we've heard? So who knows what color they will turn out to be. The important thing is that she's healthy, and they stopped the bleeding for Sophie, and she's fine now. Everything went as well as could be expected, no damage to the uterus. All's well that ends well, et cetera, et cetera.

I tell him about the blood and the ambulance ride, the way the emergency-room people made the decision and somehow didn't tell us. My words are tumbling all over each other. It's not the way he likes to hear stories. We haven't really spoken in detail since the day he left New York, nearly a month ago, and so when the story runs down, there is a moment of awkwardness.

"Well," he says. "This is all good news. How's Sophie's mental state?"

"Good," I say. "You would have been very proud of her, Grant. She was calm and in control, never once panicked, never cried."

"Good, good," he says.

A silence falls hard between us.

"So have you told Nicky?" he asks.

"No! I wanted to tell you first. I knew you'd want to be first—"

"Well," he says. "Well, thank you for that. Thank you. And I'm glad that things went well and that you got to be there. I'll get things squared away here and be on my way."

"You will? You're coming?" I don't know why this surprises me.

"Annabelle. Sophie's my kid. Of course I'm going to be there. What do you think?"

"Okay. Well—I didn't know, is all. I'll call Nicky to let him know, too. He may want to get a ride with you."

"What?" I can hear the impatience in his voice. "No, Nicky can't come. He's got his last week of classes before finals. He can visit when his classes are finished and he's taken his exams."

"I think he wants—"

"Well, I'll *explain* to him that he *cannot*. There will be plenty of time for him to see the baby once he's gotten through freshman year. He can even spend the entire summer being a devoted uncle if he wishes."

"Grant—"

"What, Annabelle?"

"Please, let's not make a federal case of Nicky's schooling, okay? You know, right when things are so happy and all—"

"They're going to be happy no matter what," he says. "But he *is* going to stay in school."

NICKY, OF course, doesn't see it that way. My phone call wakes him up, but as soon as I tell him about the baby, he starts asking a million questions about "the way the whole thing went down," as he puts it. It's sort of the antithesis of Grant, I realize; Nicky loves hearing about the ambulance ride and the huddle of medical people in the emergency room, and the way it felt when we first saw the baby.

"Did they have to spank her like they do in the movies?"

"I don't think they've spanked babies in this country for a hundred years, if they ever did."

"Good. You'd hate to think the first thing a kid goes through is physical abuse. They didn't spank me, then?"

"No, no," I say.

"Okay, great. Whew. So listen. I'll call Dad and get him to pick me up and bring me down with him."

"Nicky, you can call him if you want, but he told me that you've got your last week of classes and he wants you to wait until final exams are over."

"What?"

"Yeah. He feels pretty strongly about this. I'll e-mail you some pictures, and then you can come right after exams—"

"But, Mom, listen to me. I don't have any exams."

"What do you mean?"

He lets out a big sigh. "I'm leaving school."

"What? You dropped out of your classes?"

"Well, I didn't exactly drop out of them yet. But I haven't been to them in about three weeks. Since I came back from break."

"Nicky! What in the world—?"

"I know, Mom. I shoulda told you and Dad. But he just made me so mad, and I was taking these stupid classes that don't have anything to do with anything. And then I had the flu when the main paper was due in my history class, and the guy wouldn't take it late, so that's like half my grade is an F right there. So what's the point? And then I wanted to snowboard because the end-of-the-season powder has been totally, awesomely perfect, and then my friend Jason needed me to help out with this job he got on the slopes, and so I had to work be-cause I needed the money, and—"

"Oh, Nicky. Why didn't you tell us?"

"It was just a sucky semester."

"I know, but still . . ."

"Anyway, Mom, so I want to come see the baby. I've got to be there."

"Oh, Nick—I don't know what to tell you."

He gets quiet.

"Can't you just try to take your finals? You know how mad your father's going to be."

"Is that all you care about? Really? I'm an uncle, Mom. And I want to come and be with you guys—I want to be there when you're all to-gether, because this is a family event, you know, and I'm part of the family! Stupid Whit can't be bothered to come, and now you're trying to keep *me* away, too?"

I can't think. Then I say, "No. No, of course you should be here. I'll send you the money to come."

"No, that's okay," he says. "I'll call Dad, and I'm sure he'd love to Darth Vader me for another six-hour car ride."

"Nicky, I'm not sure 'Darth Vader' is a verb. And I think you might—"

"Might what?"

"Well, I just think you might have some trouble convincing your father that you should be here, is all. Promise me that if he says he's not going to come and get you that you'll just ease up and do what he says. Okay? We've got enough tension going on in this family right now without all this, and the baby will still be a new baby next week when you get here, you know."

"I freaking cannot believe you're saying this, Mom!" he says.

"Nick."

"I am coming, one way or another. I am not staying away just because of 'tension in the family.' I have to be there!" And he hangs up.

[t w e n t y - o n e]

🍃   2005

G rant gets to the hospital just as evening is falling. He ducks into Sophie's room as they're wheeling away her dinner tray. I'm sitting in the armchair by the bed, holding the baby, who is sleeping peacefully. Sophie and I are both so tired we can barely talk. We've spent the day cuddling Beanie—she's still Beanie even now that she's achieved non-fetal status—and cooing and cheering as she'd nurse and open her eyes and hold on to our index fingers. We're besotted with love.

All in all, a wonderful, satisfying day, but exhausting. Sophie, in addition, has spent nearly an hour on the telephone with Whit, reliving for him in exact detail every moment, and then trying to arrange an earlier flight home for him.

And now there's Grant coming in, rumpled and smelling of the outside world and carrying a bouquet of flowers and a giant lollipop.

"Hey, so is this the room where the cutest baby in the world is staying tonight?" he says, and Sophie says, "Oh, Daddy! Hi! I'm so glad to see you—come look at her!" He smiles and goes over and kisses Sophie first, but she says, "No, go see the baby. Mom has her. I think she has your nose!"

He comes over to me then, and I tilt the baby and move her blanket so he can see her face.

"The news reports I heard were correct," he says. "She is the cutest baby in the world, like they were saying on all three networks. Little Grantina Bartholomew, is that her name? That was the report on NBC, but CBS couldn't confirm it."

"Ha-ha," says Sophie. "Nice try. So far she's still Beanie."

He hands her the flowers and the lollipop, and she buries her head in the flowers. "Ooh, roses and lilies. They smell so wonderful. Thank you."

"So how'd it go?" he says. "I heard you got to ride in the ambulance with the siren going and everything. You really like to do it up in style, don't you?"

So she tells him the whole story, and he smiles and nods as she's telling it. At one point he's looking so longingly at the baby that I get up and motion to him to sit down and take her for himself. He gives me a grateful smile and sits down with her and makes cooing noises. She opens her eyes and stretches a little and then goes right back to sleep. We all watch this amazing performance.

"So no Nicky?" I say.

He doesn't look at me. "Nope. He's got work to do."

"When I talked to him, he didn't have any work. He was planning to call you and see if you'd bring him along with you."

"I talked to him," he says. "I told him no."

"But why?"

"Annabelle. He is driving me crazy with his irresponsibility—he's got to get his studying done."

"He dropped out of school! He doesn't have any studying."

"He hasn't officially dropped out. He's missed a lot of classes, yes, but I told him that he can talk to the professors and try to make up his work. I'm sorry, but I do not see why he thought he could get away with this—"

"He just wants to be with the family," I say. "He was concerned about Sophie and the baby, that's all. He wanted to feel a part of things."

Sophie says, "Hello? I'm a postpartum person here? And I don't want to listen to any bad things. Why don't I call Nicky and talk to him and see if he can come after his exams?"

"All right," I say quickly before Grant can object to even that. Her cell phone battery is dead, and so I go to my purse and get mine for her, and for a long moment she's punching his number and then waiting. Then she says, "Hi, Nicky. This is your sister, who happens to be a brand-new mama. Call me when you get this message. I'm sorry you're not here! Love you! Bye."

I give Grant a steely look. "You should have gone and picked him up."

He sighs. "I just don't want him to drop out of school. Why is that wrong?"

"Oh, Grant. It's wrong because you can't stop it. It's already happened. You should have at least gone and gotten him. We can't just leave him behind . . . he obviously wasn't ready for college, but that doesn't mean we just leave him out of things."

The baby jerks awake and starts to cry right then—perhaps realizing the family she's been born into—and Sophie says, "Will you please bring her over to me so I can nurse her? And maybe . . . could the two of you, sort of you know, maybe . . . leave for a bit? Like, maybe until tomorrow?"

"HAVE YOU eaten?" he says when we get down to the lobby.

"No. I had a candy bar last Tuesday, I think. Do you want to get something in the hospital cafeteria?"

"God no," he says. "There's a Greek place across the street. Let's go there."

It's pouring rain outside, but he takes off his jacket and puts it over both our heads and we run across the street into a diner that's way too dimly lit. We find a table in the back and he orders us glasses of red wine and then sits there, staring at the forty-page menu as though it's a thesis and he's going to be tested on it. Finally he puts it down and rubs his eyes and says, "I should have gone and gotten him."

The waiter brings the wine and stands there with his order pad, looking at us.

"Grant. What do you want to eat?"

"I don't even know. I'm going to try to call him."

"Two spanokopita," I tell the waiter. "And salads with oil and vinegar, please."

"There's no answer, just voice mail. Do you think I should leave a message?"

"Wait. I think I have his roommate's number saved in my phone," I say. "I'll call Matt and see if he knows where Nicky might be."

"Okay." Grant puts his head in his hands.

Matt answers and says he last saw Nicky at about two o'clock, and he told Matt that he was going to hitch a ride to New York. He thought he knew some people who might be going to New Jersey for a basketball game, and if they couldn't take him, then he said he was just going to use his thumb.

"He's going to hitchhike? To New York?" I say, and glare at Grant, who moans and rubs his temples.

When I hang up, the salads have arrived, but I'm not even hungry. I push my plate away. "He's out there in the rain on the turnpike somewhere trying to get to New York," I say.

"I should have gotten him."

"Of course you should have gotten him! Why didn't you?"

"Why couldn't he just stay in school? What is happening to this family?"

"This *family*? What is happening to you? Why do you have to act like we're all a bunch of ne'er-do-wells who are constantly falling short of your expectations?"

He looks up at me. "Is that what you see?"

"Yes! God, yes, Grant. You—" I start to say something and then just clamp my mouth shut.

"No, go on," he says. He pushes his salad plate away, too. "Tell me. Please. For God's sake, let's just get it all out in the open."

"I don't want to talk about it. We're in enough of a crisis right now."

"No, we're not. This doesn't even approach crisis level. Not really.

Chances are Nicky'll be popping up here just as soon as one of us has our first heart attack. You'll see. In the meantime, you have to talk to me."

"I *can't* talk about it," I say, but then of course I talk anyway. I'm furious with him. "You know what makes me the maddest? This is supposed to be a happy day. This is the day our granddaughter was born, Grant! Here it's a big wonderful day, and instead of celebrating, we're sitting here in this diner unable to eat even a bite because we're so upset! And why? Let me count the reasons, Grant. The first is that you are livid with me over something that happened twenty-six years ago and which has utterly no consequence to our current life, but which you have decided is of complete—"

"I know you think I'm mad at you. But I'm not mad."

"Yes, you are."

"No, I'm really not. I was. I was so shocked that you'd seen Jeremiah, and everything came out badly. I'm mostly mad at myself, if you want to know the truth. I haven't gotten anything done on my book, Annabelle. I'm no good by myself, but I'm no good with all the rest of you either." He sits there for a moment, leaning on his elbow and holding the bridge of his nose. Then he looks at me again. "You know what? I realized that I've spent my entire adult life trying to figure out what could potentially go wrong for this family in every potential situation, and I've run around like a wild man, trying to come up with a game plan for protecting all of you in every single situation. I feel like a basketball guard that has to guard every person on my team on the court. And *then* it turns out that that was a screwy plan in the first place because bad stuff *still* happened to all of you! Just look at what's happened. *You're* flailing around. You go running to a man who broke your heart before. Sophie gets married to a guy who somehow thinks it's not his job to be there when his daughter is born. And meanwhile my own son has decided he'd rather smoke dope and work at a ski lift like a bum than keep going to school to make something of himself." He holds out his hands. "And you know what? So what, right? Big deal. The main thing I've figured out is that I can't do it anymore. I can't. I can't keep you safe, Annabelle. None of you."

"I'm safe," I say. "We are safe."

He sighs. "I know that. I guess I know it. But whether you are or not, I can't protect you from everything anymore. And"—he takes a deep breath—"apparently I can't live without you. I'm just going to have to accept that, too, I guess. You're telling me now that you want a life where you spend part of the time in New York helping with the baby and doing illustrations . . ."

"I think that will be good for us. I need to have my own things to do."

"And what about . . . Jeremiah? God, it's still hard for me to say his name."

"This isn't about Jeremiah," I say. "I'm not going to see him. But it was wrong to make a deal where we wouldn't ever mention even his name or that it ever even happened."

"No kidding."

"It gave it too much . . . well, power. That I had once made that mistake. You can't just claim that stuff just didn't ever happen. It did happen! And just so you know, I never talked to him again after that day he left me. All those years, and I never talked to him."

"Yeah, well, I did," he says.

"Did what?"

"Talked to him. He didn't tell you about that, did he?"

"You talked to him?"

"I punched him out."

I put my hands over my mouth. "You did *not* punch him out."

"Oh, I did. When he left you at the train station—"

"But you didn't know about that. How did you know?"

"Annabelle. Think about it. We both still worked at Columbia. So one day I just went into his office and I asked him what the fuck had happened between you and him, and he told me."

"What did he say?"

"He said he couldn't do it. He gave some mealymouthed excuse about how he had to stay with his family, and how he'd never meant it to get to that point with you, and oh, he was so full of himself, so egotistical— I'm sorry, but he did not deserve you, Annabelle. He did not deserve even one minute of your love, and I just went over and punched him in the face. As hard as I could. And I told him he had hurt a person who had loved him enough to be willing to leave somebody who loved her *for real*."

"Why didn't you ever tell me this?"

"I didn't want to. I wasn't proud of it. I'm still not proud of it."

"You fought for me," I say. "When I thought you didn't care."

"Oh, stop it. If there was anything you knew, it was that I was an idiot for you. I was almost a quivering little puppy dog around you."

"No, you weren't. Now don't take this the wrong way, Grant, but you never really showed any true passion for me." He looks shocked, so I go on: "I mean, in bed, sure, but that's just sex. When it came to—"

"Just sex? *Just sex?* I have been madly in love with you for decades! And you took my heart and stomped on it and I took you back, and I have made love to you thousands of times, in every circumstance known to humankind—and you're saying I was never passionate about you?"

"You—you were always so mild-mannered."

"Well, woman, now that you know that I punched a man out in your honor, I hope you'll see my ardor differently."

"Wow," I say. "I wish I'd known. Also, Grant, you were gone so much of the time. I didn't even know you, and when you were home, you were just bound up with work."

"Well, yeah, that part *was* unfortunate. It was an unlucky way to start a marriage, when I had more work than I'd ever had in my whole life. Whether you know it or not, the university system demands that, which is why I figured we'd better leave Columbia and go back to New Hampshire. I figured if I gave all that up and taught at the community college, then at least I'd be able to be home. I wouldn't ever get famous, or do the research I wanted, but at least I'd have you and I'd be a halfway decent husband who could maybe keep you happy."

I study his face, the tired look in his eyes. Carefully, I say, "And . . . well, are you sorry?"

"Am I *sorry*?" He lets out a laugh. "I've been sorry as hell, Annabelle! Where have you been? This whole past year has been about me being sorry! It was one thing when the kids were little, not to mind everything I was missing out on. I *loved* what we were doing, I loved raising the kids—but there were times when I'd wake up and see you sleeping and I'd wonder if you were dreaming of *him*. And days when I'd be at work and I'd wonder if you were home calling him up. Or you'd get that dreamy, tragic look on your face sometimes and I'd want to know if you still wished he'd picked you over his wife and kids. Because a person never gets over thinking that sort of thing, you know, whether it gets talked about or not."

"You have been so pissed at me, Grant. And I've known it and I couldn't do anything about it. Why couldn't we talk about it? Why did you have to make that rule and then stick to it, like it was handed down by God or something?"

"I made that pact with you for a good reason. Because I figured he was a resourceful son of a bitch, and if he came around again, I didn't want to see him break your heart one more time." He runs his hand through his hair and exhales loudly. "But now . . . well, now I can't be the guardian of you. I never should've taken that on."

"It was a stupid pact."

"Yeah, well, it was my misguided idea of protecting you."

"Quite misguided."

"Okay, that's enough about how bad it was. Okay? Let's just say that mistakes were made. Twenty-eight years and plenty of mistakes were made. But here we still are, which is more than we can say for some people."

"Like the Winstanleys."

"That poor bastard. That woman—what's her name? Pigeon?"

I laugh. "Padgett."

"She's leading him around by the ear. It's pathetic. And she was telling the secretary of the department that when they get back from their trip, she's going to get pregnant."

"Are you . . . gossiping, Grant?"

"Well, I notice things," he says. "I notice a lot more than I say."

"When I come back home," I say, "you may need to talk to me about the things you notice. Is that a deal you could make?"

"You mean, *talk?*" He grabs his chest, pretending a heart attack.

"I mean talk. And—what else? There ought to be some more things I'd like to get written in, as long as we're reviewing the rules."

"We're reviewing the rules enough to know that there are no rules," he says. "That's just it. I have some things I'd like to get written in, too, if we were doing that sort of thing anymore. But we're not."

"What sort of things would you want?"

"Oh, that I get to coach the high school basketball team even though we don't have a kid on it, and that you come to watch the games. And that if we're not going to have sex on Wednesday mornings, that you help me make sure it happens, no matter how busy I get. And maybe that we don't have to talk about *every* single thing the kids do. Or the neighbors, either, for that matter."

"Okay. I could do that. But we have to talk, though."

"I said we'd talk, didn't I?"

"You have to think up topics. And you have to pay attention, as if you find me interesting."

"I *do* find you interesting," he says. "In fact, interesting is way too dull a word for how I find you. You fascinate me."

"Well," I say.

"I love you so much, Annabelle." He looks at me for a long moment. "Let's go to Sophie's apartment," he says, "and make love with every drop of energy we have left. Could we do that?"

"We do have the place to ourselves," I say.

"Since we misbehaved and got kicked out of the hospital room.

That was a stroke of genius on our part. Why didn't we think of that technique years ago? Annoy the kids and then when they get sick of us, we run off and have sex."

I laugh. "I think I've really missed you."

"You think?"

"Well, I've been mad."

"That could cloud your judgment, I suppose," he says. He pushes his plate away. "How far away is it, do you think?"

"Sophie's apartment? I think four blocks."

"Okay, maybe I can just about make it. Five blocks, I'm not so sure. But four I can do."

He calls for the check, and the waiter tries to engage us in a conversation about why we didn't finish all our food, and what the weather's been like, and how business is tough—but we don't take the bait on any of it. Instead we stand at the front door, hanging on to each other, smiling and rolling our eyes, until we can manage to break free. And then, once we're outside in the night, Manhattan puts on its best face: tall, lit-up buildings, cars moving steadily through the streets, people laughing and talking as they pass us on the sidewalk. The rain has stopped, and it's beautiful outside—everything clean and wet.

"I'm so happy," I tell Grant.

"Me, too. Can you believe we're grandparents? You're the most beautiful grandma ever."

I kiss him, and we walk through the fragrant spring night, leaning against each other. I tell him again about the wild ride in the ambulance and the wild long talks in the middle of the night, and then I am talking too much, and I just want to close my eyes and take in this moment.

"Oh, God," he says when we turn onto Sophie's street. "Is that—?"

And it is. A man is coming toward us, loping along on the sidewalk, all arms and legs and bouncing steps.

"Hi, Mom! Hi, Dad!" he says. "I didn't think you'd ever get here! My phone's out of battery, so I couldn't call you, but I got a ride down

with a guy from the college. He's in a band. How's the baby? How's
Sophie? Dad, listen. I know you're pissed at me, and I'm so sorry. I'm
really so sorry about school this semester, but I just couldn't—there
were a bunch of factors . . ."

Grant shakes his head and laughs, pulling the two of us toward him
in a huge three-person hug. We stand on the sidewalk, all of us swaying for a moment. Nicky is still talking, and I peek and see that Grant
has his eyes closed, and that he looks like a man who is going to have
to wait just a bit longer for sex, but who can probably live with that.
He squeezes my hand, and I squeeze his back in reply.

And then Nicky breaks the spell. "So this is great and all, but God,
I'm starving." He looks from one of us to the other. "Am I interrupting
anything?"

Acknowledgments

FIRST, I want to offer my sincere gratitude (and apologies) to the people I trapped in my car and forced into listening to plot points and character attributes while I drove them around: Diane Cyr, Leslie Connor, Deb Hare, and Kim Steffen, as well as my kids, Benjamin, Allison, and Stephanie. Then there are those who patiently read drafts and offered valuable suggestions and encouragement that kept me going: Alice Mattison, Nancy Hall, Lily Hamrick, Nancy Antle, and Helen Myers. Lynn Thompson and Dr. Josh Copel told me what I needed to know about obstetrical problems.

The Starbucks Corporation provided soft armchairs, heat, and wonderful music while I wrote, as well as plenty of people to distract me with clever conversations when the going got rough. And when I needed a respite from all the clever conversations so I could, you know, *really get some work done,* the public library in my town reopened with their own armchairs, coffee and tea machines, and lots and lots of books to look at. I want to thank Judy Haggarty and Sandy Ruoff in particular for making the library such a restful, creative place to be.

Shaye Areheart and all her staff have been unfailingly helpful, but particularly Sarah Knight, my wonderful editor. Sarah Breivogel, Kira Walton, and Christine Kopprasch have all been splendid helpers, steering me through the ups and downs of publishing. Nancy Yost, my agent, watches out for me and holds my hand.

Mostly, I need to thank my husband, Jim—who cheers me on and lets me act out and doesn't seem to mind too much that some days I'm living in the world of my novel instead of the real world.

About the Author

MADDIE DAWSON lives in Connecticut. She is happily married.